ONE HAND IN MY POCKET

Joyce Davis
Mikel Husband
Kendra Lee

BET Publications, LLC

SEPIA BOOKS are published by

BET Publications, LLC
c/o BET BOOKS
One BET Plaza
1900 W Place NE
Washington, DC 20018-1211

ISBN 0-7394-2187-5

Printed in the United States of America

CONTENTS

DECISIONS, DECISIONS, DECISIONS

Joyce Davis

ACKNOWLEDGMENTS

Writing "Decisions, Decisions, Decisions" was a labor of love, and I received a great deal of encouragement during the process. I'd like to thank my parents, James and Mary Lee Davis, and my brother, Rayford Davis, for their love, understanding, and constant support; my best friend, Danielle Dillard, for never tiring of listening to my drama; my mentors, Yanick Rice Lamb, Ingrid Sturgis, and Todd Beamon, for their guidance and confidence in me; and all of my friends, especially Karen R. Good, Mikel Husband, and Sonya Beard, who gave me honest and helpful feedback. And I'd like to dedicate "Decisions, Decisions, Decisions" to my grandfather, Detroit Lee, a trailblazer who, through his actions, taught me to use my God-given talents to help better the lives of my people, to fight for what I believe in, and to accept nothing less than what I deserve.

Gloria's bedroom was an utter mess. She had four outfits laid out on her bed. Not just the outfits, but the undergarments, shoes, jewelry, and makeup that would go with each. *This is ridiculous. I am not a child. This is not the first day of school. I'm a grown-ass woman, laying her clothes out to go to art school. Nobody is probably going to pay me any attention anyway. I just need to decide. Now.*

Her attempt to talk herself into a quick choice did not work. She spent another hour trying on clothes. She'd been nervous all week, unable to concentrate on her day job in the marketing department of the Department of Health and Human Services.

She remembered when she'd first become interested in sculpting. She and her ex-husband, Stewart, had been spending the day with Stewart's niece Mercedes, his sister Jean's daughter. Actually, Jean had finally guilted Stewart into spending time with Mercedes after he hadn't seen her in a few months. Gloria had tagged along for Mercedes's sake.

She'd known that Stewart still thought of his niece as a six-year-old girl who'd be satisfied with roller-skating and ice cream. He didn't see her as the thirteen-year-old young lady she had become, one who had just started her period, was a peer counselor at her junior high school, and even had a little manly sixteen-year-old boyfriend.

Gloria had looked in the Washington, D.C., weekly alternative tabloid, the *City Paper,* to see what was going on that Mercedes might be interested in doing. She'd found a beginner's sculpting session that adults and their teenage children could participate in together at the Anacostia Museum. So when Stewart had pulled up to Baskin-Robbins and Mercedes had let out an exasperated sigh, Gloria'd winked at her in the rearview mirror. The grin that had spread across Mercedes's face had made Gloria's day.

"Why don't we go by the Anacostia Museum?" Gloria suggested. "There is an exhibition there that I've been wanting to see, and Mercedes might like it, too."

"Aw, Mercedes doesn't want to go to a museum. She wants to go to the circus, don't you, sweet pea?" Stewart had asked.

"I'm a little old for the big top, Uncle Stew," Mercedes had replied. "What is the exhibit about?"

"Whatever it is, it's probably boring," Stewart had commented through pursed lips.

"Well, actually, it's an exhibition of sculptures done by high-school children who were under the guidance of professional artists," Gloria'd explained. "You do know that Mercedes is about to be in high school, don't you, Stewart? Just how many thirteen-year-olds do you know that are begging to go to the circus?"

"Whatever, Gloria."

Gloria had neglected to mention that there were a few beginner's art classes being offered at the museum that day, because she'd known that Stewart would suspect that she'd wanted to take one. She had learned that Stewart thought very little of art. He just couldn't see the purpose of it, besides something to hang on a wall or beautify a room. And he had very little respect for artists, most often referring to them as freeloaders who needed to get real jobs. Creativity was just not his thing.

When they had started dating, Gloria'd thought that her interest in the arts was one of the things that had attracted Stewart to her. But she realized later that he was just trying to complete his own package. He urged her not to pursue her passion to be creative, but to get a "real" job. So as a compromise, she had gone into marketing. She tried every so often to do something creative, taking African dance classes, keeping a journal, or occasionally splurging at an art store on paint supplies. She'd set up all of her materials in the garage and be happily creating for about a week before Stewart would start in on her.

"How long are you going to be out here playing?" he'd ask sarcastically.

"This is therapeutic for me, Stew."

"Well, if you have all of this free time on your hands, you could be doing a little overtime at work. Didn't you tell me that there was a new marketing guy they brought in? You'd better watch out, he could be there right now, working on getting that promotion that you should be getting."

"Well, if he gets it, he gets it."

"What the hell do you mean? Don't you want to move up? You've been in the same position for three years. It's time for you to move up. I think all of this artsy-fartsy stuff is keeping you from concentrating on your real job."

"Look, I got a real job like you wanted me to. And in my free time, I'm going to do something I enjoy. This painting is making me happy right now. It's relaxing."

"Well, don't relax too much or you may find yourself with lots of time on your hands to kick back."

"What do you mean, Stewart?"

"You know, if they promote that guy, he might try to get you fired, or your supervisors may not think that you are productive enough."

Gloria would try to put out of her mind what Stewart said, but eventually she'd allow him to get to her. *He gets on my last nerve. He never supports any of the fun stuff that I like doing. All he wants me to do is help him put on this front of being the perfect upwardly mobile couple. My job has to complement his. So what, he's just been promoted to district manager for Crestar Bank? I guess it won't do to have a wife on his arm who is not in a management position.* She started thinking about all of his coworkers' wives who were either stay-at-home trophies or high-powered business-women who had positions comparable to or just lower than their husbands'. And since Stewart did not believe in lazi-ness, the stay-at-home trophy wife was not an option for Gloria.

He wanted them to be a power couple so badly, Gloria felt as if he was continuously trying to manipulate her into being a workaholic businesswoman. But she fought it, unconsciously for most of her marriage. It wasn't until she knew that her marriage was not going to make it that she realized she was going against her nature trying to be the person that Stewart wanted her to be. She needed to be who she wanted to be and have someone to love her for being herself.

After a little more back and forth, it had been decided that they would go the museum. Gloria remembered that when she'd sprung her plan to stay for one of the beginner's classes in sculpting, Mercedes had been thrilled. Stewart had not. He had not wanted to be at the four-hour session. He'd wanted to take Mercedes to get some ice cream, espouse a few words of what he'd thought was his invaluable advice, and take her back to Trinidad before it got dark and someone in her neighborhood could steal his hubcaps or worse.

He had actually left the session early. And Gloria'd been happy to see him go. She and Mercedes had had a blast. Neither of them had ever sculpted before, so it had been a fun learning experience. When Gloria'd taken Mercedes home that evening, she'd run into Stewart's mother, Mrs. Johnston, whom everybody called Dear. Dear made melt-in-your-mouth pound cake and always had a Baby Ruth for her favorite grandchild.

Gloria had a great relationship with her mother-in-law. Her own mother had died when she was sixteen. Her father, Jim, was her heart, but he lived in Chicago. So Dear was really all the parental-type family she had around, and she loved the motherly attention Dear showed her. It was on this night that Dear had given her the greatest advice she'd ever received.

"Hey, baby. How are you feeling?" Dear had asked that night she and Mercedes returned from their day of creativity.

"Oh, things are okay."

"Where's Stewart?"

"I guess he's at home."

"Didn't he go with you all?"

"Yeah, but he left early. You know how he is about art."

"Oh, where did you guys go today?"

"I found out about this interesting sculpting program at the Anacostia Museum and Mercedes and I convinced him to go. He lasted about forty-five minutes."

"Well, at least he was there for that long."

"Dear, I just don't know. I know I shouldn't talk to you like this about your son, but I need to talk to someone. I'm suffocating."

"Yes, I knew this was coming. Let me tell you something."

Dear had proceeded to launch into this story about a man she'd had a short affair with while her husband had been alive.

"You had an affair, Dear?" Gloria'd asked incredulously.

"Yes. It's not something I am proud of. But that James was one of the most caring and intuitive men I've ever known. *Pffft*, I would do it again if I had the chance."

"Really?"

"*Umm-hmm*. I was still working at the hospital at the time, and he was a patient. Both of his legs had been broken in a construction accident, and I was helping to rehabilitate him. He was in my care four times a week for a year. To this day I still feel that that was the best year of my life."

"What was so special about him?"

"James understood me. He listened to me. He respected my opinions and wasn't threatened when they differed from his. He let me be myself and didn't try to force me into some mold for his friends. See, you think I don't know how my son is, don't you, Gloria? You forget I was married to his father, Stewart, Sr. Baby, you don't even know what suffocation is."

"Was it bad being married to Stewart's father?"

"He wouldn't even let me go to a concert, a play, nothing. He loved the fact that I liked to go out when we were courting. But when we got married, he wanted me to stay home and have children. He did let me go to church. But when I became the treasurer of the choir, he made me quit. No positions of authority. Nothing too fun.

"I think the only reason he allowed me to work is because we needed the money to pay the mortgage on this house and his job as a postman wasn't getting it. Then, when I started making more money than him, he started putting me down in front of our friends—talking about how I looked, the weight I was gaining, anything to bring me down. By the time he passed, he was a jealous, bitter man.

"But you could never tell Stewart or Jean anything about their daddy. Their daddy provided for his family. He was the breadwinner. The man of the house. Stewart doesn't even know that his father was once fired from the post office for stealing checks out of the mail. It was eating him alive that I was making more money than him."

"Wow, Dear. I never knew any of this. So this man who was your patient, did your husband know about him?"

"Never. Girl, he would have gone out and shot a big ol' hole in James. Stewart's father had a temper on him. Where do you think Stewart gets it from?"

"Well, why didn't you leave your husband, if you were so in love with James?"

"I had two children to finish raising. I was going to make sure they were brought up in a loving two-parent household. And they never knew about their father. I just kept up the charade. James wanted me to leave Stewart, but I told him I couldn't break up my family. My own momma ran out on us when I was little, and I just wasn't going to have my children being raised by some other woman who might abuse them. Plus it was a different time, baby."

"I guess. Why are you telling me all of this? Do you think I should leave Stewart?"

"I think you should do what is best for you. If I hadn't had children, I think I would have left my husband and gone with the man I knew in my heart I was meant to be with. You're young, baby. You have your whole life ahead of you. And you can't change a man. I see Stewart. He is just like his daddy. Don't get me wrong. He is a good man. He's not going to stop you from moving forward, but he has that same preoccupation with being worried about what other people think."

"Yeah, and I feel like I can't take it anymore. I've talked

to him about it for years. So much so that I don't even bother anymore. And you are right. He does put me down if I don't do what he thinks his friends will respect. Maybe I should leave him.''

"Baby, all I can say is do what is best for you.''

When Gloria had left Dear's house that night, she'd known she was going to leave Stewart. She had been in denial for a few years about the direction of their marriage. She hadn't even known if Stewart found her attractive anymore. He never complimented her. They never made love. He was forever working late and he didn't support any of the creative activities she wanted to pursue. She'd compromised her career goals and allowed herself to linger for years in an unsatisfying job that made Stewart happy. And the worst thing was that he disrespected her all the time. He'd belittle her in front of friends and coworkers. She didn't know why she'd allowed him to treat her so badly for so long. And until now, she hadn't even realized that it was from his own insecurities. He had her thinking she was insecure. She didn't think that Stewart was going to get any better.

It wasn't that she did not understand him, especially after she'd had that unbelievably enlightening talk with Dear. Stewart had always taken care of the family, ever since his father had died when he was twelve. She remembered him once telling her that he couldn't even remember a time when he didn't have two jobs. Even when he got nearly a full scholarship to go to Howard University, he still worked at a bank and did students' tax returns to supplement his family's income.

And he didn't mind helping to support his family, until Jean lost her job three years ago and never went back to work. He refused to support someone who could work. But he loved Mercedes, so he took on some of the financial responsibility of caring for her and his mother, who had retired early on a disability from her job as a nurse practitioner.

Stewart loved his sister. But Jean, who was six years younger than Stewart, just couldn't ever get it together. She tried, but she was very gullible and fell for any slickster with a good line. She would swear she was in love and spend every penny she might earn from her few and far between temp jobs to make sure her man had everything he needed or wanted. In retrospect, Gloria understood Jean better, too. She had to be looking for her father, who'd died when she was six, in all of these men. Jean idolized her father, talking about him like he was her knight in shining armor. Every time she'd meet a new man, she'd say, "Maybe he'll be just like my daddy—a stand-up type of guy, who'll take care of me and my child."

But what would usually happen was the guy would realize that Jean was tapped out or he would just lose interest and leave Jean, who was always completely surprised and totally devastated. She would get severely depressed and not want to do anything (take care of her child, go to work, bathe, etc.). She wasn't normally neglectful of Mercedes. She just wasn't very responsible and therefore had never moved away from home.

Gloria had actually helped Jean get an interview for an administrative assistant's job at the Department of Health and Human Services. She also tried to be friends with her, but Jean had a huge chip on her shoulder and was always trying to throw the help she was receiving from Gloria back in her face. More than anything, Jean was embarrassed about her state of affairs and envious of Gloria's independence. She tried to keep her feelings in check, but all too often that green-eyed monster reared its head, and Jean just let loose on Gloria with a barrage of guilt-inducing insults.

Gloria tried not to let Jean's mistreatment of her bother her, because she loved hanging out with Mercedes. Mercedes and Gloria had always gotten along. As a matter of fact, Gloria seemed to get along better with Mercedes than she ever did with Stewart. Maybe that was because she recognized a streak of creativity in Mercedes that she wanted to encourage. Before the divorce, Gloria made a vow to herself that no matter what happened between Stewart and her, she would not let her relationship lapse with Mercedes, or Dear for that matter. Those women had become an integral part of her life, sort of like a surrogate mother and daughter— something she desperately needed and would not lose.

It had been five months since Gloria's divorce had been finalized, and she was thoroughly enjoying her sculpting classes at the Corcoran College of Art and Design. She felt free and happy because she was creating like the famous black women sculptors she'd admired for years. She wanted Lois Mailou Jones, Elizabeth Catlett, and Augusta Savage coming out of her fingertips. She'd read numerous books and watched a few documentaries on these women. They inspired her.

When her fingers were kneading the clay, she was comforted. As she shaped and molded and worked the material, she relished the fact that she could do the same with her life now. Her life was a big pile of unmolded clay, and for the first time since she was nineteen, she would be the only one making the decisions about her life.

One of the first decisions she made, even before she decided to attend art school, was to change her hairstyle. Gloria had had a perm ever since she could remember. When she watched *Waiting to Exhale,* she immediately identified with Angela Bassett's character, who had spent eleven years growing out her perm to fit in with her husband's affinity for long, straight hair. That's what she had done for Stewart. And her hair was pretty—long and flowing, just like he'd wanted it. But she wanted to see what her hair was like without a perm. And in her quest to get to know herself again, she wanted to start from her roots, literally.

The last time she remembered not having a perm, she was twelve years old. Her mother had gotten fed up with her complaining about the combing of her naps and let her get a perm. But she couldn't even remember what it felt like to have bushy, kinky hair, except when her roots were growing out, and she rarely let that happen.

Well, things were about to change. She was going back to her roots. And she wasn't even waiting for them to grow out a few inches. She lit some candles, put on Quincy Jones's "Beautiful Black Girl," and got the scissors from her kitchen drawer. She started slow, cutting off chunk after chunk until she looked like a plucked chicken. Alarmed when she saw herself in the mirror, she threw on a baseball cap and drove straight to the nearest barbershop.

The Georgia rap duo Outkast was playing when Gloria walked into the male-dominated shop. She just loved being around a bunch of black men—although that day she looked a damned fool. She walked up to the first barber, who was dusting the neck of a customer with powder, took off her hat, and said, "Can you finish this for me?"

He just looked at her, quite unsurprised, and said, "Yeah, have a seat in the back. I'll call you in a minute. What's your name, queen?"

"Gloria," she threw over her shoulder as she made her way to the back.

She loved the respect she was already getting. No one ever called her sister or queen with her permed hair. She knew that being called these names were assumptions that people made because they thought that those with natural hair had a certain level of self-respect. She knew people also assumed that naturally coifed women were righteous sisters who always smelled like incense and never ate pork.

But that wasn't her. She'd eat a pig's ass if it was cooked right, as her grandmama used to say. Slightly ashamed of her own thoughts, she made a mental note to herself to try to make better eating decisions.

And I already respect myself, she thought as she flipped through a hair magazine. *I've just been taking pride in the wrong accomplishments. Granted, they were great accomplishments, but they were not benefiting me. Stewart got all the benefit. Yeah, a natural is only a hairstyle. But it's such a drastic change,* she thought as she caught a glimpse of herself in the mirror. The little bit of hair she had left was sticking straight up on her head.

An hour later, Gloria walked out of the shop with a Caesar. She could see her scalp. She'd left the front kind of natural, but had the edges and the back shaped. She looked so different. And she felt different, too. Every time she passed a window or a mirror, she wanted simultaneously to laugh and cry. She drove straight to her best friend's house.

"Damn, girl. What the hell did you do?" Danielle said to her when she saw Gloria's shorn head.

"I don't know, girl. I just woke up and realized that I wanted to be myself today. And that hair wasn't really me."

"Oh. Well, it's going to take some getting used to."

"Who are you telling?"

Gloria sat down on the couch, rubbing her newly shaved head. "Let's go shopping, okay? I need to get some girly things."

"I'll bet you do. Let me get my coat."

When Gloria finally got home five hours later and had laid out all of her new clothes on the bed, she sat in front of her vanity, just looking at herself, experimenting with makeup and earrings. She looked at every aspect of her face—which was now exposed. She loved her eyes, which she thought twinkled (although no one but her father ever noticed). She let her fingers trace her freshly shaped eyebrows that she had just tweezed, her wide nose, and her thick, well-formed lips, which she knew were one of her best features. "I'm beautiful," she said out loud. And although she had said that to herself before, right at that moment she truly believed it.

Everything about the sculpture classes Gloria was taking had been freeing and wonderful except for one thing. For the past week or so she'd been noticing a guy looking rather strangely at her from time to time. Not strangely like he wanted to attack her, but curiously, like he couldn't figure out where he knew her from. He was attractive—tall, thin (but muscular), and chestnut-colored, with a wide smile and deep-set eyes.

One day, Gloria was rushing to get to a class and inadvertently walked into a nearby utility closet, mistaking it for her classroom. By the time she realized she was not in her classroom, the door had closed and locked behind her. "Great," she said aloud as she felt around for a light switch. The next thing she felt was the crack of the wood door against her skull. She looked up from the floor to see the strange guy looming over her.

"Oh my God, I am so sorry," the guy said urgently, trying to help her off of the floor.

"Catch the door," Gloria said, recovering quickly and trying to reach around him.

"What?" he said, looking around in a confused manner.

The door clicked and he understood. "That didn't lock, did it?" he asked hopefully.

"Tight as a drum," Gloria answered.

"Oh, man. Is your head okay? I'm really sorry," he said, helping her to her feet and turning on the light.

"Oh, yeah, I think I'm going to be fine, except for what

I'm sure will be a baseball-size lump on my forehead," Gloria said, gathering up her smock and materials.

She almost jumped out of her skin when she looked up to see that it was her handsome stalker who was locked with her in the closet.

"I'm really going to be late for class this time," she said, trying to play off her high level of discomfort.

"Oh, what are you taking?" the stranger asked.

"Beginning sculpture. I love the class, but I'm late a good bit because I am always rushing to get here from work."

"I told them they should push that class back."

"Oh, you teach here?" Gloria half asked, backing away from him.

"Yes," he said, seemingly unconcerned about their plight. "Have you ever done sculpting before?"

"No, well, only one time before enrolling in this class," Gloria responded carefully, eyeing him. "Don't you think we should be trying to get out of here?"

"Oh, yeah, sorry. I'm sure if we knock on the door someone will open it. What made you want to take sculpting?" he asked while knocking loudly on the door.

"I went to this exhibit at the Anacostia Museum about a year ago, where I got to try all of these different types of artistic expressions, and I really enjoyed the sculpting. I thought the whole idea for the series was great. There was painting, weaving, quilting, and a couple of others. I was trying to get into the class of the guy who put the whole thing together. He teaches here. Maybe you know him—a Reginald something?"

Just then the door swung open, the custodian looked at the two of them, and snickered. "What are y'all doing in here?"

"Nothing," said Gloria, grabbing her head, which she realized was throbbing. "Thanks for letting us out," she told the custodian. "Okay, nice talking to you," she said with an awkward wave to her captor as she rushed out.

As soon as she'd left the closet, it hit Reginald like a ton of bricks. *That was the woman from the video. And she liked my series. She liked it so much that she enrolled in art school.*

His mystery woman was halfway down the hall before Reginald could get himself together enough to call after her, "Hey, that's me. I'm Reginald Waters."

He sat there, in the door of the closet, dazed for a moment. Something was different about her. The hair. In the video she had shoulder-length, permed hair. But now she had a neat little Afro pulled off her face by a headband. He thought it looked lovely on her, because he was able to see her eyes, which, he noticed, sparkled.

Reginald remembered the day he missed the sculpting session. It was one of the worst days of his life—the day that Jenelle had left him. He'd disclosed to her that he was HIV positive and they'd had a wicked fight. Lots of cursing and crying. He was so distraught that he couldn't get it together enough to make it to the sculpting session.

He had made it to all of the sessions in the Discover Your Inner Artist series that he'd created and curated at the Anacostia Museum. Every week for five weeks, he and a couple of his assistants would introduce an artistic expression (painting, quilting, basket weaving, woodcarving, and sculpting). There would be a short lecture to give some of the basic pointers, and then those attending could try their hand at that day's expression. There were also exhibits of locally, nationally, and internationally known artists as examples of each type of expression. He'd received such positive response for the series that he'd been asked to replicate the program at a number of different museums across the tristate area.

Luckily, he'd had all the sessions taped to study his teaching techniques. And he had just recently gotten a chance to view the tape of the sculpting session, because the museum handlers had misplaced it and couldn't find it for six months. Then it sat beside his VCR for another couple of months before he got around to looking at it when he was caught at home on a stormy night.

Watching the tape, he noticed that the camera continued to revisit a certain family. The father figure seemed quite uninvolved, running back and forth from the lobby every time his cellular phone rang. The girl and the mother (he guessed, although she looked a little young to be the mother of a teenager) seemed in sync with each other, really enjoying the class. And whatever it was the mother was creating, he really liked it. He'd been infatuated with that woman for weeks, watching the tape at least once every few days. He was starting to think something was wrong with him.

And here she was. Right in the school where he taught. He couldn't believe his fortune. He just knew he was going to see her all of the time because she was enrolled in the Corcoran. After doing some investigating, he found out her name and the sculpting class she was enrolled in. But his plans were foiled when he realized that his teaching schedule would have him tied up every time her class was meeting. He tried for a week or so to take water and bathroom breaks when he thought she might be arriving to or leaving her class. But he could never catch her, and his students weren't too impressed by his neglect of them.

That weekend, Gloria weaseled herself into an "uptown" benefit auction of artworks by local artists held at the

Museum of African Art. It had been easy enough to get an entrance, she told herself, trying not to be embarrassed about volunteering to hand out programs for the event.

As she applied lipstick in the bathroom, she thought about her mission to locate Reginald Waters, the teacher of the class she wanted to take, who happened to be on the board of the museum and was scheduled to make a few remarks. *I have absolutely no idea what he looks like, but I am going to find him and talk him into letting me into his class.* She adjusted her Miracle Bra, just in case she needed to pull out her big guns—her feminine wiles—to convince him.

Instead of going back to her post, Gloria got someone to take over her duties at the door for a few minutes, while she slipped into the back of the room right at the end of Reginald's speech.

Craning her neck to see what Reginald looked like so she could recognize him later, Gloria was surprised to see that Reginald was the guy with whom she'd been stuck in the utility closet earlier in the week. Why hadn't he introduced himself then? *Maybe because he thought I was an idiot who'd locked herself in a closet? But he'd be just as much of a fool because he locked us both in there. Not to mention the fact that he almost killed me with that door.* This new turn of events made Gloria a little unsure about approaching him. He was kind of creepy, she thought as she made her way back to her post at the door.

Gloria tried to keep an eye out for Reginald, but he disappeared during the auction. When one of the museum assistants asked her to deliver a message to him, she was relieved and nervous at the same time. After a fifteen-minute search, she finally tracked him down in a side room with all of the museum bigwigs and had to interrupt their conversation to give him the message. Gloria took a deep breath and tapped him on his shoulder. When Reginald turned around, she wondered why he looked startled.

"Hi," he said, surprised.

"Hello, Mr. Waters. I have this message for you," she said, giving him the note. As he took the paper, a statuesque woman with flawless mahogany skin, a brick-house body, and waist-length dreadlocks began tugging at his arm. All he had time to say to Gloria was "Please don't leave, I really want to talk to you," and he squeezed her hand for emphasis.

The warmth and strength of his hand and his urgent plea left Gloria a little flustered. She wanted to walk away, but she couldn't. She just stood there, watching the arresting amazon pull him across the room.

Gloria went back to her post by the door and waited for Reginald. After an hour went by, people started drifting out. But still she waited. And waited. After another hour and a couple of glasses of chardonnay, she got so disgusted with herself for seeming so desperate that she gave up and went to retrieve her wrap from the coat check. She was putting on her shawl when she felt someone helping her slide it over her shoulders. "Thank you," she said, not knowing to whom she was talking.

She turned around to see Reginald standing directly in front of her. "Oh . . . hi," she said, trying to hide her surprise.

"Hi. I'm sorry I took so long. Are you leaving?"

"Yes, it's a little late," she said, cursing to herself silently that she had already put her wrap on.

"Can I walk you to your car?"

"Sure," she replied, happy that she had parked her car a couple of blocks away.

"I've seen you around the Corcoran."

"Yes, I've been taking sculpting classes. I'm a beginner. I didn't realize it was as hard as it is, but I love it," Gloria said rapidly, wondering why she was rambling all of a sudden. "Wait a minute. Weren't we stuck in a utility closet together earlier this week?"

"Yes, I believe so. That was me," said Reginald, grimacing in embarrassment. "How is your head? I see the swelling is not as bad as you thought it was going to be."

"Earlier this week I was mistaken for a unicorn, but now I think I look more like I overdid it in a soccer match."

"I'm so sorry. I was hoping that you would forget that unfortunate incident."

"I did, and everything else for three whole days," teased Gloria. "A cop found me wandering around down by the monuments, muttering something about a clumsy art teacher."

"Okay, okay, okay. What can I do to make it up to you? Can we get coffee sometime?"

"You mean can you buy me dinner?" said Gloria, milking the situation and marveling at her self-confidence. "And you haven't even properly introduced yourself to me."

"Oh, yes. I'm Reginald. Reginald Waters."

"I know. I'm Gloria John . . . Rainier. Gloria Rainier," said Gloria, nearly forgetting that she had gone back to her maiden name.

"I know. And you take the sculpting class way on the other side of the school from the painting class that I teach on Mondays."

"How do you know my name? And why do you know what class I take?"

"I have a confession."

"Should I get the police?"

"No, no, no. It's nothing like that. When we got locked in the closet, I recognized you from a videotape I have."

"Oh, my God. What are you, some kind of freak?"

"No, no, no," repeated Reginald, chuckling at her wide-eyed concern. "I had this sculpting session taped at the Anacostia Museum, and you and your daughter were in it."

"Right. That's where I know your name from. Wait a minute . . . my daughter? What are you talking about?"

"Well, you were sculpting with some young lady."

"Oh, Mercedes . . . that is my ex-husband's niece."

"So you're divorced?"

"You certainly are direct."

"Look who is talking."

"Hey, why didn't you tell me who you were when we were in the closet?" asked Gloria, choosing not to elaborate about her marital status.

"I'm sorry. Gosh, I'm saying that a lot tonight. You were talking so fast and we were out so quick. And then you left so rapidly that I just didn't have time to get out who I was," said Reginald, realizing he was locked in a permanent state of apology.

Gloria had been told often that she talked entirely too fast and too much—never letting anyone get in a word edgewise. All of her friends just learned to talk over her or told her to shut up. And she didn't mind. She knew she was a chatterbox.

"Yeah, all of my friends say I have the fastest mouth in the South. Anyway, so how did you come up with the idea for the art series?"

"Well, I'd been teaching and studying art for years, and I just thought that it would be good to link all of these different types of art together. Sort of like a taste test. People could get a sampling of five different types of art. And it worked out great. I've had offers come in from other museums in this region to replicate the series."

"I can imagine. You've sure got me interested," said Gloria, adding, "in more ways than one," to herself. "Oh, I guess this is my car," she said with a bit too much regret in her voice. "It was a nice night huh? And you guys made a lot of money for a great cause."

"Yes, the children's hospital will really benefit from tonight's proceeds."

"Okay, well . . . thanks for walking me to my car."

"No problem. I enjoyed our chat."

"I hope I wasn't too hard on you," said Gloria, trying to leave on a positive note.

"Not at all."

As she got into her car, Gloria tried to hide her disappointment that Reginald was not asking for her telephone number.

"Take care," he said to her as he closed the door to her car.

Gloria cursed herself all the way home. *One day I'll learn not to be so freakin' sarcastic.*

As Reginald walked back to the museum, he wondered why he hadn't asked Gloria for her telephone number. *She seemed intelligent and witty and she is very attractive. It has been almost seven months since I've seen Jenelle. And that relationship is clearly over. Am I not ready to start dating again?*

What if I start seeing Gloria and I really like her? What if we fall in love, just like Jenelle and I did? And then I have to tell her about my HIV. What if she leaves me, just like Jenelle did?

Snap out of it, Reggie, he told himself. *Good Lord, I'm already obsessing and I don't even know Gloria. How can I map out how our relationship will end, when it hasn't even begun? If I decide to ask Gloria out, I won't let this one end up the way the last one did. I'll come clean early on— a couple of dates in. I never want to hurt a woman the way that I hurt Jenelle again. And I never want a woman to look at me with the kind of disgust that Jenelle had when I told her about my HIV. No, that is never going to happen again.*

Gloria had spent all day Saturday preparing for her first date with Reginald on Sunday afternoon. She collapsed on her futon after a full day of beautifying activities. She'd gotten her hair twisted, her nails manicured, and had bought a new outfit, with shoes and a bag to match. She hated when she did this for a first date, wasting a whole day preparing for something that was probably going to be a bust.

And she just hated Stewart for putting her back in the dating game again. *Forget him,* she thought, resting her legs on her coffee table. She was probably blaming the wrong person. *I* did *leave him.* And she surely didn't regret that decision, even if the consequences were sometimes unpleasant.

The other day, she and Danielle had gone to a happy hour, and a man had struck up a conversation with her by patting his lap and saying, "Girl, you sure got a lot of junk in your trunk. You can rest that lovely load right here, baby." Gloria had been so stunned that she hadn't known what to say. But Danielle had: "Don't make me have to unload my .45 in your tired ass." Gloria didn't know why Danielle had to go there. She was always trying to scare somebody with her lying self. The fool had backed off though, so she didn't have too much to say to her girl.

But those situations hadn't popped up that often. *And besides,* Gloria thought to herself as she sprayed oil sheen on her small twists, *I've got a date with a fine, intelligent, artistic man.* She was ecstatic that Reginald had asked her for her phone number when she'd bumped into him at the Corcoran a few days after the benefit. Although she'd really wanted to give him her home number, she'd still felt that she didn't know him quite well enough yet. So she'd given him her work number. After one lunchtime conversation, he'd asked her out. She was glad that they were going to a book signing so she didn't have to get dressed up. Checking herself in the full-length mirror before walking out the door, she couldn't believe that looking effortlessly beautiful took so much time.

Gloria could see Reginald leaning against the window of Sisterspace as she walked up to her favorite black-owned bookstore. He was so engrossed in a book that he didn't even see her come in.

"What are you reading?"

"Oh, hey. Um, *Race Matters* by Cornel West."

"That's been out awhile, hasn't it?"

"Yeah, but I can't find my copy, so I was going to buy this one. Cornel is a wild brother. I like his style."

"Yeah, he is kind of out there sometimes. I saw him at Howard a few months ago. Have you ever heard him speak?"

"Yeah, I caught him at American once. He was on this panel about the role of the black church in the AIDS crisis. A lot of folks weren't digging what he had to say, but I was."

"That sounds interesting. You'll have to tell me about it sometime. So, I hope I'm not too late for Nikki."

"No, they just came out and said that Ms. Giovanni would be out in a few minutes to read, and then she'd sign some books. Do you have it already?"

"No, I was going to buy it tonight. Let me go get it."

"Here you go," Reginald said, handing her a copy of Giovanni's *Love Poems.*

"Thanks, I'll be right back."

"Where are you going?"

"To pay for the book."

"Don't worry about it. It's already taken care of."

"Oh, thank you. You didn't have to do that," Gloria said, pleasantly surprised. No man had ever bought her a book on a date before, much less a first date. As a matter of fact, she didn't think that any man, besides her father, had ever bought her a book, period. Stewart hadn't even noticed that she loved to read until they were moving in together and he complained about carrying her eight boxes of books.

"I like to see you smile, and I hoped a book would do the trick. I guess I was right, because you are beaming, beautiful," said Reginald, touching her arm.

The date was perfect. They clicked immediately, and had a great rapport. After the book signing, they went for coffee and talked for hours about everything from local politics and art history to Jerry Springer and Stevie Wonder. They discovered they both had appreciation for anything artistic and they both liked to talk, listen, and learn.

When she got home, she opened *Love Poems* to read Nikki Giovanni's inscription again, which read BE BLESSED AND HAPPY. YOU DESERVE IT. NIKKI G. She flipped through the first couple of poems and noticed there was some writing on the page above a poem entitled "A Happy Reason." THIS ONE REMINDED ME OF YOU. I HOPE I GET A CHANCE TO READ IT TO YOU ONE DAY. REGGIE.

After reading the poem, Gloria just sat on her bed, happy. She let herself enjoy the feeling of being the object of Reginald's affection. She had been debating calling him. Although she really wanted to, she was trying to follow some dating rules she had set for herself so that she would not seem desperate. One rule was never to give out her home telephone number until after the second date. This way she could avoid men she decided she didn't want to date anymore having her home number.

But looking at Reginald's note, she didn't care about any of that. She picked up the phone, dialed his number, and held her breath as it rang. *Damn,* she thought to herself as his answering machine came on. *I can't hang up. He might have caller ID and I don't have the block yet.*

"Oh, hi, Reginald. I just wanted to tell you thanks again for the book. I just read your note and it was sweet. I guess I'll talk to you soon. Give me a call if you get a chance." Gloria had hung up the telephone before she realized that she'd forgotten to leave her telephone number. She could have kicked herself. *I hate dating,* she thought as she slid the book under her pillow for sweet dreams.

* * *

Gloria was ecstatic to get a message from Reginald on her work voice mail on Monday. Reginald had gotten her message and had tried to *69 her because she hadn't left her number. But his cousin had called him after she had, and he wasn't able to reach her. The best part of the message was that he wanted to see her the next night if she was free. After listening to the message three times, she called him back and they made a date to go to the movies. He held her hand all night, even in the theater throughout the entire movie. And when he dropped her off at home, he walked her to the door and gave her a warm hug and a sweet peck on the cheek. She couldn't wait for the next date, which she hoped would be the next day.

She was a little disappointed when Reginald didn't ask her out for the next night, but he'd told her he definitely wanted to see her on Thursday. That made her so happy that she started to get a little concerned that she liked him so much after having only been out with him twice. *I need to slow my roll. But I like this type of attention. And it's from the kind of guy I want it from. He's intelligent. There's no ostentatious show of wealth. He's got great manners. Somebody raised him right. And he's not a work in progress. I'm not going to sweat this. I'm just going to enjoy it.*

"So, did y'all go out again last night? Is that why I couldn't get your hot behind on the phone?" demanded Danielle of Gloria during their daily afternoon chat on Friday.

"Yeah, girl. This one is nice. I mean really nice. I mean walk-down-the-aisle nice."

"Hold on, Miss Always-and-Forever. Don't buy the farm before you've tested the soil."

"You're right. You're right. I've been trying to calm myself down. I really have been thinking about him a lot."

"I don't know when you have time to think about him. 'Cause you're always with him."

"Don't hate."

"Don't be ridiculous. You know I've got more men than you can shake a stick at. What did y'all do last night, anyway?"

"We met for happy hour at the Zanzibar and, don't you know, this boy can get his dance on. I mean, he really wore me out. But he was cool, not buck wild like M.C. Hammer or somebody. Don't get me wrong, though. He wasn't too reserved to get his Bankhead Bounce on a bit when Outkast came on."

"It seems like you guys had a really good time."

"Yeah, we did, but, girl, you will never guess who we bumped into—Up. In. The. Club."

"Uh-uh. You better not say that tight-ass ex-husband of yours!"

"Reggie was spinning me around and I ended up facing the bar for a minute. I was having such a good time that I had my eyes closed. And when I opened them, that fool was staring me right in my face."

"I know you were geeked."

"Actually, for a split second I forgot that I've been divorced for almost a year. But when I remembered a heartbeat later, I gave that sucker a big ol' cheesy grin before I turned around and really got into Reggie."

"Did you tell him that your ex-husband was there? And what the hell was he doing at the Zanzibar? I didn't even know tightwad got down like that. A club? He's never even been in a club, has he?"

"Not as far as I know. But I didn't care. Yeah, I pointed him out to Reggie later."

"And how was that? Was Reggie jealous or anything?"

"Well, he asked a few questions."

"Like whether you were still letting Stewart have some?"

"Not like that," said Gloria defensively. "He asked if we were really finished, and weren't still indulging in any aspects of our former relationship."

"Like I said, 'Were y'all still having sex?' "

"Well, the answer was a definite 'no.' He asked about Stewart's background, what he did, where he worked—that type of thing. I guess it was a little strange for a moment."

"Did you tell him all of that?"

"Yeah. I don't have anything to hide. And I really didn't mind after he told me that he just wanted to see what type of man would mess up a good thing with me. He's a sweet talker, girl."

"Um-hmm."

"After that, he didn't give Stewart another thought except to ask me if I was uncomfortable and did I want to leave."

"Sounds like he was really taking care of you. Hey, you didn't get drunk, did you? You know how you get in the club."

"Ha ha ha. It's funny. He doesn't drink, and when I'm with him, I don't really, either. I may have one glass of wine or something, but he has me more intoxicated than any liquor ever could."

Danielle made a gagging noise. "You are starting to sound like one of those ridiculous romance novels."

"Like the ones you have on your bookshelves?"

"Whatever. Anyway, so he didn't mind that Stew was there?"

"I told you. He didn't care. He was cool with it and so was I. We stayed until about ten or so and then we left— drenched to our drawers."

"Well, did y'all do a little slow draggin'?"

"Slow draggin'? Fool, I haven't heard that word since the ninth grade. You are so country."

"You did understand what I was asking you, didn't you?"

"Look, we did not slow *dance*. I do not need to be rubbing all up on this brother too soon. I could really get myself into some trouble."

"Well, a little trouble ain't necessarily a bad thing. And besides, how long has it been since you've gotten yourself into a little sweet trouble?"

"Not long enough," said Gloria, lying to herself to try to keep the lid on her pent-up sexual frustration. It had been a long time since she'd been with a man. She did have a one-night stand a couple of months after her divorce was final, but just thinking about that moment of weakness filled her with shame.

"Girl, I got to go," Gloria said abruptly.

"Um-hmm. That boy got you all hot and bothered, don't he?"

"Shut up. I'm going."

"Bye, hot pants."

"Bye, big mouth."

As Reginald sat next to Gloria on the deep couch of a quiet coffee bar Friday night, he could not stop thinking about touching her. They'd been out on three dates, and he was literally burning up with the anticipation of their first kiss. Last night he'd given her a hug and had to take two cold showers when he got home, just to go to sleep. It wasn't just that she was beautiful; it was the way she paid attention to everything he said. He even liked the way she interrupted him, like an eager student who couldn't wait to please the teacher.

He loved that she was down for anything. He told her that he was kind of an outdoorsy guy and liked to go camping every once in a while. And she was open to that. He just knew she would cringe when he told her that he liked to go fishing and would love to take her with him. But—surprise, surprise—she and her father had been going fishing nearly all of her life, and she knew where to get the best bait in the tristate area. Reginald could not believe that he had stumbled upon a woman with whom he really wanted to start a relationship.

He'd sensed that she was particularly headstrong and fiercely independent. He guessed that she was so protective of her independence because it was newly acquired. It took him a while just to get her to give him her home number. She was trusting him now, and he knew it was past time to tell her about his HIV. He just didn't want to break their flow. Things were going so well, and they were feeling so good about each other. He didn't want to ruin the excitement of being in a new relationship.

But he had to tell her soon. As he hugged her good night on her doorstep that evening, he told himself that he would tell her the next time they went out. He was afraid to tell her, but he felt like he was falling for her, and he wanted to be honest. He wanted her to love him for him—all of him, including his HIV.

Saturday night, Reginald had a surprise for Gloria.

"Where are we?" Gloria asked as Reginald pulled up in front of a small redbrick building with two long windows in the front. The name THE RENAISSANCE was painted on a plaque above the door.

"My place. Come on," he said, opening her car door.

"Your place. Is this where you live?"

"And work."

"Oh my God, it's beautiful," Gloria said as she walked into the most exquisitely-designed art gallery she'd ever been in.

"What's up there?" Gloria asked, pointing to the spiral staircase in the corner.

"Oh, that's my living quarters. There are a couple of bedrooms and a kitchen up there. In the back here is an office and a couple of bathrooms," said Reginald, pointing down a short hallway.

"This is a really great space," said Gloria. "I love it. Do you have shows here?"

"Yes. I've only had a couple here so far—mostly of local artists' work or my own. But this isn't what I wanted to show you. Come here," he said, grabbing her hand and leading her into an elevator.

"You have your own works. Like what? Paintings?" asked Gloria, as the elevator descended one level.

Her questions were answered as soon as the doors of the elevator opened. She was speechless at all of the paintings in his workspace. There were at least forty or fifty works of all kinds (oils, watercolors, charcoal drawings, and even collages) on all different sizes of canvas.

"Are all of these your works?" Gloria asked once she regained her speech.

"Most of them. A couple belong to some of my friends."

"You are so talented. These are amazing," Gloria said, her eyes not able to remain on one work for too long because of the draw of the others.

"This isn't what I wanted to show you, either," Reginald said, walking away from her.

"1 don't think I can take much more tonight, Reggie."

Gloria watched Reginald as he retreated into a dark corner, moving canvas after canvas. "Come over here," he called to her as he turned on a soft light.

Gloria was astounded by the series of six oil paintings and charcoal drawings that were lined against the wall in the corner. The paintings were of two curiously familiar women interacting with each other. It only took her a minute to realize that these likenesses were of her and Mercedes. But their hair and bodies where changed.

In one painting they were depicted as angels with huge afros and billowing wings. In another they were mermaids with long fishtails and dreadlocks. On one canvas that was nearly as tall as the ceiling, she and Mercedes were sitting in a field of crimson poppies with their hands thrown in the air and their hair—thousands of yellow and orange butter-flies—fading into a fuchsia horizon. There was only one charcoal drawing where she and Mercedes appeared as they may have once looked in real life—crouched over a table, molding a blob of something.

"Clay," Gloria said out loud, as she turned to Reginald.

"You're my latest and my greatest inspiration," said Reginald, quoting Teddy Pendergrass.

Gloria couldn't say anything else. She just hugged Reginald. She hugged the man whose muse she had become. She was so overcome with emotion that she did not notice she was crying until Reginald began wiping the tears from her cheeks.

"It has been a really long time since anyone has inspired me to paint like this, Gloria. I just kept watching that tape and I could not get you and your niece out of my mind. I realized that what I was looking at was two women really enjoying themselves, letting their minds go, allowing them-selves to create whatever they wanted to. And I wanted to do that, too," said Reginald, kissing Gloria's damp cheeks.

"I can't believe you did this. These are beautiful. Just unbelievably beautiful."

As they pulled away from each other, their lips brushed and Reginald's whole body tensed up.

"Are you okay?" asked Gloria, noticing a strange look on Reginald's face.

"Oh, yes. I'll be right back," he said, disappearing into a room off to the side.

Gloria studied the paintings while he was gone. She felt a sense of euphoria she'd never felt before. She didn't know what she'd done to deserve Reginald, but she promised herself that she would not mess this one up.

"Hey, baby, I'm not feeling so well," said Reginald, coming back into the room.

"Oh, what is it?"

"I don't know. I just need to get something to eat or something. You wanna get a bite?"

"Sure," said Gloria, wondering why Reginald was acting so nervous all of a sudden.

"Okay. We can come back another day and I'll show you the rest of the place."

"I'd love that. And thank you, Reggie."

"For what, baby?"

"For letting me help you without my even knowing it."

"I needed you and I didn't even know it."

"I guess we were both caught off guard," admitted Gloria, walking toward the elevator.

"Yeah, I'll take that kind of surprise any day," said Reginald.

"Amen," said Gloria, seeing her likeness staring back at her as the elevator doors shut.

Gloria had seen Reginald every night for the past six nights and she wanted to see him again tonight. They were supposed to go back to his place so that she could see more of his artwork. She still hadn't gotten over being his muse. Danielle told her that she thought Reginald's painting of Gloria without her knowledge was weird, and suggested that he could be a nutjob. But she had a sneaking suspicion that her best friend was just a little jealous of her.

She could understand. If Danielle had told her that a man she had been dating had secretly been painting pictures of her for weeks and she didn't know it, she'd be a little envious herself.

What is it about this Reginald anyway? Gloria wondered to herself. He was nothing like Stewart, for one thing. He appreciated her for her.

But there was something about him that she could not put her finger on. A sadness? No. But there was something reserved about him. Was he keeping something from her? Why couldn't they see each other tonight? This was the second Wednesday that he'd begged off. But he'd been the one urging her to see him every night since they met—except Wednesdays. When she inquired, he just said he had a previous engagement, but did want to see her Thursday night.

She'd asked him all of the right questions. Was he married? Did he have any children? She'd even slipped in a question about mental disability running in his family. And they'd both talked about their past relationships.

She did think he had an unusual zest for life. He lived every day to its fullest and he appreciated the smallest things. For example the other day she'd been extremely frustrated at work, and he'd convinced her to get up from her desk and go look out the nearest window for five minutes. She was suprised at how much better she felt after such a short break. She loved that about him. He made her want, as cliché as it was, to stop and smell the roses.

But why hadn't he tried to get close to her? She knew that he was attracted to her. When he held her hand, he could not stop caressing it. He was always touching her face for one reason or another. But whenever she tried to initiate a deeper kiss, he avoided it. Intitially she thought she had bad breath or body odor, but she did a thorough check (including asking Danielle, who assured her that she was funk free).

Sometimes she felt like she was going to burst from being

so near him. When he put his hand on the small of her back or his leg brushed hers as they sat together in a movie theater, she fell ripples of excitement running through her body. She didn't know how long she could hold out. And she was beginning to wonder why she had to.

"Girl, I don't know what to do," complained Gloria to Danielle. "We've been seeing each other for three weeks now and I've tried all the little tricks that I know. He still won't . . . you know."

"Get down with the get down."

"Yes, as you so eloquently put it."

"I don't know how you do it, girl. I have never been out with a man who wasn't trying to go deep-sea diving by the third date, and here you are three weeks in and you can't even get him to test the waters."

"Well, do you have some suggestions, hot mama?"

"Are you sure you want to open Pandora's box? I don't think he is that type of man, girl. You might scare him away with my artillery."

"You're right, Danni. Stewart wanted to have me committed when I dressed up for him in that licorice bikini you bought me."

"Oh, . . . that was harmless. It didn't even need batteries. He's just so uptight."

"Okay, back to my current problem, 'cause I've gotten rid of that other fool forever."

"Riiiight. Riiiight. Well, my suggestion to you, dear heart, is to take matters into your own hands. The next time an opportunity presents itself, just get on him."

"Get on him? You mean attack him?"

"Well, don't swallow his head. But don't let him get away with a peck and a pat. Show him you want more, girl. Be a woman."

"What if he rejects me?"

"He ain't no real fool. He just needs a little encouraging. He probably just respects you and doesn't want to offend you."

"You don't think that I should say something to him first? Try to talk to him about it?"

"I don't even know why you said that. You know that you are not going to go up to him and say, "Reggie, why don't you want to tongue me down?"

"No. You're right. I would never say it that way."

"Go ahead. Ask him why he doesn't want to get close to you and see how uncomfortable you both feel. It'll be weird."

"All right, all right. I'll try it your way. But if he rejects me, you'll have to deal with my mouth."

"And when don't I have to?"

"Whatever. I'm going to be a woman. I can make the first real move. I can do this."

"You sure as hell can."

"And I sure as hell will."

Gloria had her new attitude with her the next time she saw Reginald. It was Saturday evening, and they really hadn't made any plans. They ended up at the Corcoran to pick up some work he'd left there. As they passed the class-room where Gloria took her sculpture class, she decided she wanted to show him what she'd been working on.

"It's coming along," said Reginald as he walked around her work-in-progress.

"Can you tell what it will be?" she asked, putting her arms around his waist from behind.

"Let me get a look at it from over here," said Reginald, disentangling himself from her embrace and backing all the way across the room to near the pottery wheel.

"How can you tell what it is from way over there?" asked Gloria, trying to disguise the hurt in her voice.

"I can see how beautiful you are from waaaaay over here."

"Reginald, I . . . ," said Gloria, stumbling for words. She really wanted to ask him why he did not want to get close to her, but she was terrified of what his answer might be.

"What is it, baby? Come over here. I want to see you create something," he said, dipping some clay in water and placing it on the pottery wheel.

"Right now?"

"Yep. Come on. Please."

Taking off her coat, Gloria silently walked over to the wheel, sat on the mat and started kneading the clay. She began pounding the clay, taking out her frustration on it. For a few minutes, she nearly forgot Reginald was in the room until she felt his body behind hers. His arms were around hers and his hands were covering hers, helping her to shape the clay. Gloria couldn't help letting her head rest against his chest. She felt it rise and fall against her. As she felt his breath against her temple, she let go, unafraid.

Reginald wasn't even looking at the clay. He kept his eyes on her, letting them wander down the length of her neck. He wanted very much to place his lips where his eyes were burning a path. Realizing that they were no longer molding the clay, Reginald let his hands move up the length of her arms to her shoulders. As he kneaded the tenseness out of her shoulders, she let her head fall forward, giving in to his impromptu massage.

Wanting to see her face, Reginald turned Gloria around. He saw that her eyes were closed, her lips were parted, and her head was tilted upward. *She's expecting to be kissed,* he thought. She looked incredibly inviting to him. Her hands were caressing his chest. He wanted so badly to feel his lips against hers, but he knew where a kiss would lead, and he just couldn't. Instead he bent to kiss her collarbone. Then her jawline. When he got to her ear, he knew that he was in trouble.

Gloria and Reginald were cheek to cheek. His leg was thrust between hers. Her fingers were in his hair. But Reginald still wasn't making that move. Sensing his hesitance, Gloria took control of the situation, pulling his head down to hers. Reginald gave up, closing his eyes and letting their lips meet. He couldn't even comprehend the passion that he was feeling. He'd never felt like this about a kiss before. All the nerves in his body were suddenly concentrated in his tongue and his lips. He put an arm around her waist and the other behind her head as the kiss deepened. He wanted more. He wanted to be in her. And at that thought, he remembered what had happened the last time he'd kissed a woman so deeply. He remembered how far it had gone before he'd stopped. He remembered her reaction when he'd told her his secret.

He abruptly pushed Gloria away from him. It took a few seconds for her to realize that they were not kissing anymore. She looked up at him. He saw the trust in her eyes. He couldn't hurt her. "I can't. I'm sorry," he mumbled and then turned, picked up his coat, and walked out the door.

Gloria sat on the mat, paralyzed. Her lips and body were still burning from Reginald's touch. *What the hell just happened? One minute he was here giving me the type of loving attention I've never gotten from anyone, not even Stewart. And the next minute he was gone. No excuses, no apologies, no nothing.*

She didn't know what to think. She didn't even know what to do. She was too stunned to cry and too confused to be mad. She just sat there, shocked.

What happened? Did I do something wrong? she wondered, quickly replaying the evening's events in her mind. Everything had seemed perfect. It was an unplanned but perfect night. All of a sudden, her heart dropped. Maybe he was married. Maybe he wasn't as attracted to her as she was to him. No, that could not be it. She'd felt him against her, hard as a rock. What was wrong? What had happened?

She decided that before she let herself get all upset, before she let her own insecurities make her crazy, she would get an answer from him. Grabbing her coat, she walked distractedly to her car. She stopped by Negril, his favorite Caribbean food spot, to get some sustenance for the conversation she wanted to have with him. Whatever Reginald's reason was for leaving, she knew she needed to be prepared for it.

She dialed Danielle on her cell phone to get her opinion on the situation. When Danielle didn't answer, she was relieved. She'd dialed her best friend from force of habit, but she really felt like this was something that she and Reggie should keep between themselves. She wanted a grown-up relationship with Reggie, because she already knew she wanted a future with him. He was what she wanted, and she was going to respect their relationship by not telling Danielle about everything that happened between them. That had been one of the problems between her and Stewart. She had told Danielle everything, and that is not how a serious relationship, much less a marriage, is supposed to work.

Gloria was happy to see Reginald's car when she pulled into the parking lot of the Renaissance. "Now, just be calm," she said out loud to herself. "There is bound to be a good explanation for why he walked out. Just be understanding, because you want to know the truth."

As she rounded the walkway, she heard loud arguing coming from the house. She heard Reggie's voice. "I loved you, helped you take care of Shawn, and what did you do? You left me."

And then she heard a woman's voice. "Well, I just couldn't deal with it. I couldn't handle it."

"Then what the hell are you doing here now? You are no longer a part of my life. And I sure don't need your pity."

"That's fine. I just wanted to see how you were—see if you were okay. I'm out."

"And leave the key. Don't you ever let yourself into my house again."

All of a sudden, the glass door flung open and a woman came rushing out. Because she was walking so fast and not paying attention to where she was going, she nearly knocked Gloria over. "You can have his crazy, sick ass," the woman threw over her shoulder as she walked off down the street.

Stunned, Gloria picked up her keys, which the woman had knocked out of her hand. When she looked up, Reginald was standing in the doorway with a pained look on his face.

"Who was that?" Gloria demanded, a little too angrily. She immediately regretted the question and the way that she'd asked it.

"I . . . it . . . Glo, baby, I just can't talk to you right now," Reggie said.

"You can't talk to me. What the hell do you mean?" said Gloria, beginning to let her temper spin out of control. Here she had kept herself calm. She had come over to his house with the express plan to be understanding and willing to listen to whatever he had to say. And what did she find? Him fighting with a woman with whom he'd apparently been seriously involved. This was too much. Too many new things in one day.

"Look, I just want to know what happened tonight. Why did you—"

"Jenelle is none of your business . . . I mean, she's nothing," he added, trying to clean it up. "Glo, I've just got to be by myself right now. I just . . . please. I'll call you . . . okay?''

''You'll call me?!?!'' Gloria said incredulously. *Is he crazy,* she thought, trying to process everything that had happened between her and Reginald in the past few hours.

''I gotta go,'' Reginald said as he closed the door.

She stood in the parking lot, staring at the door. For the second time that day, Reginald had left her confused and bewildered. And now she was mad. She couldn't get any resolution, any explanation, nothing. She didn't know who this Jenelle was. She didn't know why he'd pulled away from the best kiss she'd ever had in her life. She didn't know anything. And it appeared that she wasn't going to find out anything from him today, or anytime soon.

Reginald lay on his bed, fully clothed. He was so traumatized by his day that he couldn't do anything, not even take off his shoes. He just lay on his bed, wishing he could go to sleep. But his mind wouldn't let him. It was running like O.J. Simpson through an airport. *Of all the people to be sitting up in my house,* he thought. *I did not need to see Jenelle. What did she want anyway? After she kicked me to the curb, now she was going to show some concern? Please.*

And, oh my God, Glo. She looked so confused. So shocked and so hurt. I hate to hurt her like this, but I need some time to think. I cannot take another woman leaving me. Even though I think I love Gloria. I want her. But will she want me after she knows the truth? No, I can't tell her. I just can't. Maybe it would be best if I just did not date anymore. I'm tired of getting my heart all involved, only to have it crushed.

With all of the drama, Reginald realized that he was a couple of hours late taking his medication. He rushed to the kitchen to take his pills. Reginald hated the nausea that came with taking his medication late. *See what happens when I let women get involved in my life? I forget about what is important. I just need to concentrate on my art and the Renaissance. Maybe I'll paint. That's what I'll do. I'll just paint and think about it. I won't make any rash decisions. I'll take some time to think this through. The answer will come to me. I hope.*

Driving home, Gloria really wanted to call Danielle. She had to talk to somebody. She was trying to be mature, but she needed some consoling. She needed to talk through this with someone. What was going on with Reggie? Why was he trippin' so hard?

Between dialing Danielle and being consumed with her thoughts of Reginald, Gloria didn't even notice the car slowing in front of her. By the time she saw that the car had stopped, it was too late.

Stewart couldn't believe his latest quandary. His supervisor's secretary was hot for him. He was working late and she'd shown up with Thai food and red wine. He was trying to decide whether to risk his career for a little office romance when his phone rang. He couldn't imagine who would be calling him at work this late at night. He started not to answer, but something made him pick up the telephone.

"Is this Mr. Stewart Johnston?"

"Yes, this is Stewart Johnston. Who is this?"

"Mr. Johnston, this is Beneatha Jenkins from D.C. General. Your wife has been involved in an accident."

"My wife?" asked Stewart, a little confused.

"Yes, Gloria Johnston. That is your wife, isn't it, sir?"

Stewart answered yes because he wanted to know if Gloria was all right.

"Oh my God, how is she?"

"She has a mild concussion, but she is going to be all right. She will need to stay in the hospital for a few days, just for observation purposes. Mr. Johnston, can you come down to take care of a few matters? It would probably be nice if you were here when she wakes up."

"She's unconscious?!" Stewart asked, alarmed.

"Yes, she also dislocated her shoulder. We had to do minor surgery, but she is going to be fine."

"What else happened to her? Is she hurt in any other way?"

"Just a few cuts and bruises and a small gash on her chin. But really, sir, she is going to be fine. Please come down. Do you know where we are located?"

"I know where D.C. General is, good grief. I'm on my way."

Gloria heard somebody calling her name. It was Stewart. Thank God her husband was there for her. "Stew, I am so glad you are here," Gloria said groggily. "Can we go home now?"

Stewart looked at the doctor, who nodded his head. "Yes, sweetheart, I'll take you home soon."

Gloria smiled and drifted back to sleep.

When she awoke the next day, she saw her father standing in the corner talking in hushed tones with a man in a white coat. "Daddy?" Gloria said.

"Yes, baby," Jim said, moving to her bedside. "How are you feeling?"

"What happened?" she barely got out.

"You had a little accident, angel. But everything is okay and you're going to be fine."

"But what happened?"

"You rear-ended someone. Don't worry. That's what you have insurance for. And no one was seriously hurt."

"I had the strangest dream. Stewart was in this room and we were still married. It was weird."

"Well, Stewart was the first one here. He called me and he's right outside. Do you want to see him?"

"Um . . . yes," said Gloria as she tried to move her arm. "Ow. Oh, ow. What is wrong with my arm?"

"You dislocated your shoulder, but that's about it, except for a few cuts and bruises. You're going to be fine. Let me get Stewart. I'll be right outside, okay?"

As the doctor explained her condition to her, Gloria decided the best course of action was to try to do as little moving as possible. She was happy to hear that she would be released the next day.

"Hello, Gloria. How are you?" said Stewart as he walked in the door.

"I'm still here, thank goodness. Thanks for coming down. I hope I didn't put you out."

"We were together for ten years, woman. I'm always going to care about what happens to you," said Stewart. "You are going to be staying with Dear for a while until you get a little stronger. I'll come by to check on you sometimes. Is that okay?"

Gloria couldn't believe Stewart was being so caring. "You want to come check on me? Wow. Is this the Stewart that I was once married to, who missed his niece's elementary-school graduation for a business meeting?" Gloria asked.

"I'm human sometimes, Gloria."

"So I nearly had to get taken out for you to start caring, huh? Just joking. Of course you can come by. I'd really like that."

"All right then, see you soon," said Stewart. He strode out of the room after planting a kiss on her forehead. That surprised Gloria, too. At that moment, she remembered why she'd fallen in love with Stewart. He could be sweet and caring—when he wasn't being a self-centered, manipulating jackass.

Reginald had called Gloria a number of times in the past few weeks and gotten the answering machine. He rarely left a message, and most of the time was relieved when she wasn't there. He was a little concerned that he had not seen her around the Corcoran for the past few weeks. When he inquired in the business offices and they told him that she had withdrawn from the classes, he assumed that it was because of him.

He missed her, but he didn't know what to do. He missed the way she looked at him, like he was the most important person in the world to her. He missed the undivided attention that she gave him when he talked to her. He longed for her conversation and her inspiration.

He wanted to see her, but he had no idea what her reaction would be. He'd stopped calling after he left several messages. He drove by her apartment complex a couple of times, but never saw her car. He stopped that, too, because it made him feel like a stalker. But he had to see her because he was worried about her, or so he told himself.

Who would know where she was? he wondered. Her best friend would, but there was no way he could call Danielle. First of all, Danielle was undoubtedly on her side, and might curse him out if he even attempted to contact her. His only other choice was Stewart. He remembered that her ex-husband was a vice president at the main Crestar bank downtown. He debated calling Stewart for a few days and then decided he'd throw his pride aside. He just had to see if Gloria was all right. And he knew that Stewart would know where she was. Those alimony checks had to be going somewhere.

He stopped by the bank on a whim one day while he was downtown. And just as he was walking in the door, he saw Stewart in the lobby.

"Stewart," he called to catch him before he got in an elevator.

When Stewart turned around, he was truly suprised to see that it was his ex-wife's boyfriend calling his name. "What can I do for you, Reginald?" he asked as if he were talking to a peasant.

Sensing the awkwardness of the situation, Reginald made his case quick. "Man, I was hoping you could tell me if Glo was okay. I haven't seen her in a few weeks. She hasn't been at school. I'm a little worried about her."

"What do you mean you haven't seen her in a few weeks?" said Stewart, hating the way that Reginald referred to Gloria as Glo—as if she were one of those Pink Ladies from the seventies movie *Grease.*

"Well, we sort of had a falling out. And she hasn't returned any of my calls. I guess she dropped out of school because she didn't want to see me. I don't know what is going on with her. I don't even know where she is. Can you put me in touch with her?"

"Um . . . Gloria was in a car accident," said Stewart, disgusted that Reginald would think Gloria would quit something she loved to avoid him. "She's been recuperating at my mother's."

"Oh, Lord. Is she okay?" asked Reginald, extremely concerned.

Stewart could see that Reginald was really upset, and he started to walk off and leave the artsy fool in the dark. Something had been stirring in him since he'd been dropping by his mother's house every few days to check on Gloria. He was still trying to decide if he wanted to explore what he was feeling about his ex-wife.

"Yes, she's going to be just fine. She dislocated her

shoulder, but that is about it. I don't know what is going on with you guys. The best I can do is give her a message,'' Stewart said impatiently.

"Okay. I'll take anything. Please tell her that I really didn't mean to leave her like that and wish that I had done things differently and that everything is over with Jenelle. No, don't tell her that. Just please tell her that I am sorry and to please call me. I really need to explain some things to her,'' said Reginald, a bit shaken. "Thanks, man,'' he added, touching Stewart's shoulder. "I really appreciate it.''

As Stewart stood watching Reginald walk slowly out of the building, he felt a little sorry for him. But that feeling quickly faded when he realized that he was going to be passing messages between his ex-wife and her seemingly unfaithful boyfriend.

Gloria couldn't believe that Reggie had gone to talk to Stewart at his job. Reggie had no respect for Stewart. He thought that any man who would try to force his wife into a career she did not want to make himself look good was insecure and not a real man. Of course, Reginald's dislike for Stewart might also have something to do with the fact that she'd complained to Reggie all the time about how Stewart had mistreated her while they were married. But that was neither here nor there right now. When Stewart told her that Reggie had apologized and wanted her to call him, she immediately got a warm feeling all over her body. And then she got mad at herself for feeling that way.

She knew she wanted to see him. She even knew that she was going to see him. She'd already planned out in her mind what she was going to wear. She wished she was stronger. But she cared for this man and was happy that he wanted to see her.

She still didn't understand why he'd left that night. She'd

replayed the whole scenario over in her head so many times she could probably write it into a play.

Even though she'd been back at home for a few weeks, she decided that she would still make him wait another week before she called him. She figured she could afford to now that she knew he was sorry. She hated when she played games, but she didn't want to seem too anxious to see him. Plus she needed some time to prepare. She wanted to straighten up her house, get her hair twisted and her nails done. She had to be perfect when he came by.

Reginald couldn't wait anymore. He hoped Stewart had given Gloria the message. He thought he saw her coming out of Sisterspace one day and almost caused an accident making a U-turn in the middle of the street, only to find out that he was mistaken. He had to see her.

On his way back from the cleaners Saturday morning, he decided he'd just stop by her place. When he drove up, she was taking out the trash with one hand because her arm was still in a sling.

"Let me help you with that," he called to her as he got out of his car.

"I got it. Thanks," said Gloria, not even looking up, thinking it was her pesky younger neighbor, who was always trying to get into her pants.

"Glo, let me help," said Reginald as he took the bag from her hands.

Gloria looked up in complete surprise to see her man standing before her. She was so happy to see him that she completely forgot her plan to remain calm, cool, and collected when she saw him.

"Reginald," she said, smiling widely.

"Hey, girl," he said with a broad grin. "You look good."

"Oh, please," Gloria said, slightly embarrassed, looking

down at her ashy knees and half-painted toe nails poking out of her bunny slippers. "What are you doing here?"

"Your hair is beautiful," said Reginald, reaching out to touch her twists, which were just beginning to dread.

For some reason that gesture made Gloria angry. *How dare he just show up after weeks of not seeing me and think he has license to feel my locks.* "Don't touch my hair," she said gruffly as she moved out of his reach.

"Oh," Reginald said, a little startled. "I'm sorry."

"Well, you might as well come on in. It's cold out here."

Reginald could smell the Egyptian musk oil on her as she carefully passed by him, making sure they didn't touch. He couldn't help looking at her ample behind in a pair of gym shorts he'd given her one day when they'd played a game of one-on-one at his gym. "I always love the way you look in my shorts."

"What do you want, Reggie?" asked Gloria once they were inside, becoming more annoyed by the minute. She really wanted just to be happy to see him. But he was acting like nothing had happened and it had. He'd better become apologetic really quickly, or she was going to be forced to do something she really didn't want to do—ask him to leave.

Gloria's down-to-business attitude snapped Reginald out of his momentary memory lapse. For a minute, he was thinking they were still together, things were great, and he didn't have this huge secret to lay on her. They were standing in her livingroom, where she'd once served up a nice home-cooked meal for him, and he realized he was right back where he was before he and Jenelle broke up. He didn't want to hurt Gloria, but he had to be honest with her.

"How are you feeling?" he asked, trying to stall. "I didn't even know you'd been in an accident, until Stewart told me. Are you all right?"

"I'm so sick of people asking me that quesiton. I'm fine. And how dare you go down to my ex-husband's job. Who do you think you are?'' said Gloria, hoping she was not saying it so harshly that he would get mad, but wanting to get her point across about him invading her private life without her permission.

"You weren't returning my calls. They said you withdrew from school. And your car was never here, baby,'' said Reginald. "I didn't know what to do. I had no way to get in touch with you.''

"Don't call me baby. And what are you? A stalker? You've been riding by my house?''

Gloria couldn't believe what she was hearing. He was tracking her down. That was great, a bit weird, but great. "You could have called Danielle. I gave you her number one time,'' she added.

"Oh, yeah, me calling Danielle,'' said Reginald, sarcastically. "That would have gone over real well. If I want someone to call me names, I'll sit in the front row at Def Comedy Jam.''

"Okay, maybe you couldn't have called her, but you didn't have to go to the bank. You could have called Stewart.''

"I was already downtown.''

"So what, were you just in the neighborhood today, too?''

"Well, yes. I was dropping off clothes at the cleaners.''

"You use the cleaners by the Corcoran. Since when do you use the cleaners over here?''

"Well, one time when I was driving by to see if you were here, I noticed a special they were advertising in the window at this cleaners up the block and—''

"Okay, look, I could give two shits about your cleaning habits. What do you want?''

"I want to talk about that night.''

"Oh, now you want to talk about it,'' said Gloria as she sat down on her futon.

When Reginald sat down beside her, they were so close

that their legs almost touched. Gloria could see his chest rising and falling beneath his sweater. She suddenly felt the urge to rip open his sweater and kiss him all over his chest.

Shaking that image out of her head, she jumped up and started rearranging the knickknacks on her bookcases.

"I want to explain about what happened that night," said Reginald quietly.

Gloria turned to look at him. The tone of his voice scared her. She had no idea what he was going to say. She'd waited so long for this explanation, and now she wasn't sure if she wanted to hear it. She sat back down beside him, giving him her undivided attention.

"Gloria, I wanted to make love to you so badly that night. I just couldn't."

"Why not?"

"Well, because I wanted to protect you."

"Protect me? From what?"

"From me."

"From you? You're not making any sense, Reggie. Just tell me. Are you married?"

"No. I wish that was it."

"Well, what is it?"

Reginald took Gloria's free hand in both of his, looked in her eyes, and told her.

"I'm HIV positive, Glo."

To Gloria, everything went blue in the room. She felt like she'd been sitting on a bomb, it had exploded beneath her, and now she was floating above the two of them.

"What?" she whispered, pulling her hand away.

"I have the HIV virus. And I didn't want to infect you. I didn't know how to tell you. I loved you. I mean, I love you."

"Wait a minute. Wait a minute. You have AIDS?"

"Well, no. I have the virus that causes AIDS."

"Oh."

Gloria didn't know what to say or how to feel. She just collapsed back onto the futon, staring at the man she thought she was falling in love with, who'd just told her that he had a life-threatening disease.

They sat in silence for a few minutes that seemed like an eternity to Reginald. He hesitated to break the silence. Gloria was no longer looking at him. She was staring straight ahead, blankly.

"I wanted to tell you so many times. I just didn't know how. I missed you, baby. I want to be with you. We can still make this work."

Gloria snapped out of her trance at his last remark. She turned to him, just staring and not saying anything. Then she slowly rose from the futon and made her way toward the kitchen.

"I know this is a terrible shock. But it's not as bad as it sounds. Let's talk about this," said Reginald, following her to the kitchen. "My doctor says that every problem can be talked through. I don't have AIDS. My T cell count is high. I'm healthy as a horse. I may live for another forty years. Glo, please say something."

Gloria had walked to the back door and was now holding it open. All she could manage to get out was a whisper of "please leave."

"Oh, no, baby, please. Let's talk about this," pleaded Reginald, his voice cracking. "Let me tell you all about how it's going to be okay. And then I'll leave. Let me tell you how I got it. I'm not gay. I've never been with a man. I don't use intravenous drugs. I got it from a woman I was dating. See, she wasn't honest with me like I'm trying to be honest with you. . . ."

Reginald was following her to the kitchen, trying to explain as fast as he could but also trying not to overwhelm her with information. "Look, I know this is something you need to think about. But we can still be together. I'm on

the cocktail. We can use condoms, spermicides, whatever
you need to feel safe.''

Gloria's face was contorting. She wasn't even really hearing Reggie, who sounded distant and muffled like he was
talking to her through a cloud. She was becoming blinded
by the tears that were welling up in her eyes. She opened
the back door wider and, without looking at Reginald, told
him to get out in a voice she did not recognize.

"I've never felt like this about anybody before. I love
you. I know you love me. Please, Glo.''

Gloria raised her one good arm, put her hand on Reginald's
chest, and pushed him out the door. And they both just stood
there, him looking down at her and her looking at her hand
on his chest. When she looked up into his tear-stained face,
he saw how much he'd just hurt her. He just turned and
walked away.

Gloria slowly closed her kitchen door. She sat down at
her kitchen table and cried. She cried like she hadn't since
her mother died.

Gloria sat on her futon, thinking. She didn't know anybody
who had AIDS. Or at least she thought she didn't. She
thought about all the people she knew, at work, at school,
her friends, her family. Nope. Nobody. Did she miss some
telltale signs that would have told her that Reginald was
sick? He wasn't sickly looking. He was fine as hell. His
body was tight. There were no lesions on his face, hands,
or any parts of his body that she had seen. He was athletic.
She just didn't understand.

And she considered herself a pretty open-minded and
intelligent person. She knew that AIDS was a sexually transmitted disease. She and Reggie hadn't even gotten to second
base yet. So why was this bothering her so much? Why
hadn't he told her sooner? If he had, would she have contin-

ued to date him? She shuddered to think of how she would have been trying to get out of seeing him.

Gloria hated having to ask herself these questions. She was such a do-right type of person, but now she was in a situation where she had to hold herself to the same high standards that she expected everyone else to hold themselves to. Her morals were being tested, and she didn't like the uncomfortable feeling it was giving her.

With AIDS as much in the news as it was, she felt like she had read hundreds of stories about the disease. But being honest with herself, she realized that she didn't really know many details about HIV or AIDS. She didn't even know the difference between the two. She knew people lived with AIDS for a long time. She'd read about people falling in love with people with AIDS. And when she read those stories she always felt a strange mixture of warmth, self-righteousness, and pity. *Isn't that nice? See, there is someone for everyone. Even people with AIDS can be in loving, committed, happy relationships.*

She remembered seeing a woman with AIDS on the cover of *Essence* magazine a few years back. After reading the story, she'd been not only proud of the woman, but also proud of the man who loved her enough to marry her, despite her condition. Gloria had even been a little envious of their relationship, thinking if a woman with a communicable terminal condition could get a good man to commit to her, why was she having so much trouble with her marriage? She'd known at the time that that was not the type of love she and Stewart had.

She'd even said to herself a couple of times that if she fell in love with a man who had AIDS, she'd give it a shot. But that was a hypothetical and she never expected it to come true. She didn't know what to do. She cried for three days, speaking to no one, not even going to work. This was a man she wanted a future with, and for all she knew he could die tomorrow. His news had hurt her so badly that she wanted to hurt him, too—just as much as he had hurt her.

But at the same time, some part of her wanted to be there for him, to help him, to do whatever she could for him to make his life easier. And she couldn't imagine her life without him.

But what would her friends say? What would her daddy say? Even though he'd never met Reginald, she'd told him about her new man. And if there was one thing that her father could not stand, it was a liar. She remembered when she was fourteen and she'd gotten caught with a boy in the house and tried to lie her way out of it. She'd been grounded for a whole summer—no phone, no television, no friends. All she could do was read and listen to music. Her daddy didn't play, and he was certainly not going to be feeling Reginald's secret.

All Reginald could think about was Gloria's reaction to finding out about his condition. Why did he keep inflicting himself on women this way? He knew his situation. He knew what a shock it was for a woman to hear that the man she loved was HIV positive. This was the second time he'd looked into the eyes of a woman he knew was falling for him and told her he had HIV. After Jenelle, he vowed that he would never do it again. But Gloria had snuck up on him. She was his muse, and he'd hurt her terribly. It had been hard enough to tell his family. His relationship with his brother, Stanley, was still shaky and he'd been HIV positive for four years.

"Why don't you just find a good HIV-positive woman? Then you guys don't have to worry about infecting one another," Stanley had told him when he was going through the breakup with Jenelle.

"How ignorant is that?" he'd replied. "You can't pick who you fall in love with. Plus you don't even understand how the virus works. We'd still have to be just as careful. We could have different strains. We could make each other sicker."

"I'd never bone a chick with AIDS," Stanley'd said.

"How do you know you haven't already? Do you even know how many women you've slept with? Did you ask any of them if they'd been tested? Have you even gotten tested? I've been positive for four years and you've never even been tested, have you?"

"I don't need to be because I'm a man. I don't get down like that. I don't mess around with no freaks like you do."

"Don't act like I contracted the virus from 'hoing around. You know what happened. You know when I got it I was in what I thought was a committed relationship."

"Whatever, man."

"You'd better get tested, Stanley. Just to be on the safe side."

"Why? So I can live with the fact that I'm going to die?"

"You are going to die. Everybody is going to die."

"But not as soon as you."

"You don't know that, man. You could walk out that door and a bus might hit you. You don't know when your time will come."

"You know what I do know? I know I ain't got no AIDS!"

"All right, man, all right."

Reginald knew that Gloria was not like his brother—an ostrich with his head stuck in the sand. But he also knew what people's reactions were to learning that someone they cared about had the virus. He knew that all Gloria could think about was AIDS. He had the dreaded AIDS virus. He was going to die. And not just die, but die a painful, horrific death. He'd seen tons of stories in newspapers and on television detailing the end of the lives of AIDS patients. Why didn't they ever show people living with AIDS, enjoying life and contributing positively to their community?

He rarely saw or read those types of stories—his story. Here he was, having been HIV positive for four years, and his life was the best it had ever been, except that he was HIV positive. He was teaching at the Corcoran. He was painting again, proving wrong yet another one of his brother's ignorant pronouncements—that those who can't do, teach. And best of all, he had found a way to use his talents to help others by starting Artists Against AIDS, a program that helps youths who have just learned of their HIV or AIDS cope with their new diagnoses. He hadn't even had the chance to tell Gloria about this program.

But would any of those things that made him happy and proud of himself mean anything to Gloria? Reginald was sure she had seen plenty of stories about how daunting and fatal AIDS was. He knew she was educated about the virus because they had talked about it a number of times, but he had always steered the conversation away from the subject. Even though he thought she knew the basics, it wasn't like she had it or knew anyone who did. It was different when you knew someone who was HIV positive or you had the virus yourself. He should know.

When Gloria arrived at Dear's house, she didn't even know how she had gotten there. She jumped when Jean knocked on her car window.

"Hey, girl. What are you doing sitting out here in the cold?"

Gloria got out of the car, not saying anything.

"What's wrong with you?" asked Jean, noticing that something was just not right with Gloria.

"Is Dear here?" Gloria asked.

"Yeah, she's in there watching *Guiding Light*. How come you ain't at work?"

"I didn't feel like going today."

"Oh . . . well, I called up to the Department of Health yesterday. I'm supposed to be going down for an interview next week."

"That's nice."

"I'm running to the store. You want something?"

"Nah," said Gloria, making her way up the steps, not even wondering why Jean was being so nice to her.

"Hey, Dear," Gloria called as she entered the house.

"Gloria. Girl, what are you doing here in the middle of the day?" Dear asked. "Come on in the back."

"What's going on with Reva and Josh?" Gloria asked, inquiring about Dear's favorite soap characters.

"Reva done messed up again. She lied to Josh about Alan and he dumped her without even giving her a chance to explain."

"Sometimes explanations don't do any good," said Gloria as she entered the room to see Dear reclining in her favorite chair.

"How are you doing, baby? You sound like you have something on your mind."

"Oh, I'm all right. I just thought I'd stop by and check on you."

"In the middle of the day?"

"I'm on my lunch hour."

"Oh," said Dear, noticing that the clock over the televsion said 3:49. "It's a little late for lunch, isn't it? Never mind. Go in there and cut yourself a piece of cake before you sit down.

"And cut me a little slice, too, while you are at it," she added as Gloria followed her instructions.

"How is your diabetes, Dear? Are you taking your insulin and everything?"

"I'm just fine. Dr. Griffin said a little sweet now and then ain't gonna kill me. And I'm seventy-one years old. I know how to take care of myself. So bring me my cake."

"Okay, okay, okay," said Gloria, who had already cut Dear a slice. She loved the way coming over to Dear's house made everything okay for just a little while.

"So what's going on, baby?" asked Dear, taking her piece of cake from Gloria.

"I have a friend that has a problem. Dear, would you have stayed with James no matter what happened to him?"

"What? Well, do you love him?"

"Who?"

"Whoever this man is that you're talking about."

"Oh, Dear," Gloria sighed. "I just don't know what to do."

"Well, I'm not going to ask you your business, but if you really love each other and you know in the innermost depths of your heart that he is your soul mate, then you should at least give it a chance."

"Well, we've only been seeing each other for a couple of months, and we've been going through a rough patch for the last couple of weeks. But I really believe that he could be the one. We just haven't had ample time to explore it because of this huge complication that stopped us from seeing each other."

"You mean that you stopped seeing him because of something that he can't help, right?"

"How did you know that?"

"I've been on this earth a few more years than you, sweetie. I've seen a lot. So, what are you going to do?"

"I don't know, Dear. I just don't know."

"All I can tell you is to go with your heart, baby."

* * *

Stewart could not believe that Gloria was seeing a man who was HIV positive. *Was she sleeping with him? Was she seeing him before we were divorced? Have I been exposed to the virus?* he wondered. He knew that Gloria was supposed to hang out with Mercedes today, so he decided to meet her at his mom's house.

Jean was in the living room when he entered Dear's house.

"Hey, boy. What are you doing here?" asked Jean.

"Oh, I just stopped by because I need to talk to Gloria about something," said Stewart, sitting down on the opposite end of the couch from his sister. "What's on the tube?"

"Queen Latifah, honey. She's got these children on that have that AIDS disease. I was about to turn, because I just can't watch no mess like that. It's something wrong with people that got that AIDS."

"Hey, you know, I think that Gloria's been seeing this guy who's got HIV."

"What?!" exclaimed Jean, turning her full attention to Stewart. "You have got to be kidding."

"Nope. They've been going out for a while now."

"Mm, mm, mm. She's gonna mess around and catch the AIDS from the man. She better watch out."

"Well, I don't know if they are that serious yet."

"So what. . . . I don't even know if I want her hanging around with my baby anymore. Just the fact that she is keeping company with a faggot. Uh-uh . . . I don't think so."

"I don't think that Reginald is gay, but I don't necessarily think I want Mercedes to be hanging out with Gloria much either. At least until I find out more details about the extent of her relationship with this guy."

"What do you mean, he's not gay? Shoot, just 'cause he's with Gloria one night don't mean he ain't with a Gerald the next. You know, he's probably swinging both ways. That's how they get AIDS—from doing it with men. Everybody knows it's a gay people's disease. 'Cause it's wrong. A man should be with a woman and not with a man. He's gotta be doing double duty. Yeah, that's how they get it. I was down at the free clinic the other day and saw all of them sick faggots. I knew they had that mess. I could tell by the way they looked.''

"Well, I don't know or really care about all that. What were you doing at the clinic, anyway?''

"Minding my business and leaving yours alone.''

"Uh-huh. Well, when Gloria gets here, I'm going to have to have a little talk with her. You better tell Mercedes she won't be hanging out with Gloria today.''

"Yeah, you're right. 'Cause my baby ain't catching that mess from your crazy ex-wife.''

"Whatever, Jean. Just tell her.''

The doorbell rang just as Jean got up to go and ruin Mercedes's day.

"I got it,'' she said on her way to the door.

"If it's Gloria, let me talk to her. Don't bring it up, okay?'' called Stewart from the living room.

When she opened the door to see Gloria standing in front of her face, Jean acted like she hadn't heard Stewart's request.

"How could you be getting it on with a faggot?'' Jean asked Gloria.

"What? What the hell are you talking about?'' said Gloria, brushing past Jean.

"You've been going out with somebody who's got AIDS, haven't you?'' Jean accused more than asked.

"Who told you that?'' asked Gloria, suprised, confused, scared, and angry all at once.

"Stew,'' said Jean with a self-righteous smirk. "Do you have it? Do you have the AIDS? How could you? That's just nasty, girl.''

"Now, wait a minute. Not that I have to tell you any of

this, but Reginald and I have never had sex, so I couldn't possibly have the virus. And where is Stewart? How the hell did he know who I was dating?'' said Gloria, forgetting that Reginald had gone to see Stewart at the bank a few weeks before.

''He's in the back. Well, I don't care if you didn't get with that faggot, you ain't taking my child nowhere. I don't want you around Merecedes at all.''

''Will you please stop calling Reggie a faggot? That is a horrible word. He's not gay and anyway, I'm not even seeing him anymore—not that that is any of your business anyway. What do you mean, I can't be around Mercedes? Why not?''

''Well, we just don't think you are the right kind of influence to be around Mercedes right now,'' said Stewart, who had made his way into the room and was glaring at Jean for not leaving this discussion up to him. ''Until I'm sure what is going on between you and Reginald—just how involved you've become—I'd prefer it if you would stay away from Mercedes.''

''I don't care what you find out,'' said Jean with a raised voice. ''That's it. She is never going to be around my baby again.''

''Why not, Mama?'' said Mercedes, who had heard all the commotion from her room and decided to come downstairs to see what the fuss was all about. ''I like Miss Gloria. We're supposed to go to the—''

''Shut up, girl, and go on back upstairs,'' shot Jean to Mercedes. ''What have I told you about getting in grown folks' business?''

''It's okay, Mercedes. I'll see you some other time,'' said Gloria, trying to let the girl know that everything was going to be okay.

''Oh, no, you won't,'' yelled Jean, ''and don't you even talk to her. I don't want you to have any contact with her at all. None, you hear me?''

"But why, Mama? I don't understand," said Mercedes.

"Because I said so. And that is all you need to know," Jean told Mercedes. "Now, the next time I have to tell you to go upstairs, it's going to be with a belt. You are not too old for me to tear your butt up. Go on, now."

"Okay. Okay. Okay, Jean. I'll handle this. You go on upstairs, too," said Stewart as Mercedes stomped up the stairs.

"Don't you tell me what to do, negro. I've handled it. And now I am going out," said Jean, picking up her coat and her cigarettes. "And when I get back, my child better be here and that faggot lover better be gone."

Stewart just shook his head as Jean slammed the front door.

"How could you tell her about Reginald? And how the hell did you know anyway?" asked Gloria, more angry than hurt.

Stewart recounted to Gloria how he had gone for his annual checkup and a new doctor had moved into the same suite of offices as the one that his doctor occupied. The gossipy assistant had told him that most of the patients that the new physician saw were those with HIV or AIDS. He told Gloria that while he was in the waiting area, he'd seen Reginald and the new doctor talking about a prescription. Stewart failed to mention that he'd really found out after he'd happened to see Reginald going into the doctor's office and had then flirted with his own doctor's assistant to find out about the type of patients that the new doctor treated.

"I wasn't really sure he had AIDS until you confirmed it right now," Stewart told Gloria.

"So you told Jean something you didn't even know was true?"

"Well, it is, isnt it? He's HIV positive, right? He didn't look sick, so I guessed that he didn't have AIDS yet."

"Yes, Reginald is HIV positive. No, he does not have

AIDS. But you had no right to tell Reginald's personal business to Jean, or anybody else for that matter.''

"Yes, I did, if it involves my niece. You seem to forget that we are divorced. I don't know why you keep coming around here anyway. You just can't let me go, huh?'' asked Stewart smugly.

"Don't be ridiculous,'' scoffed Gloria. "You know why I come by. To see your mother and to spend time with your niece. I love them both, and just because it didn't work out between you and me doesn't mean that I don't care anymore about Dear and Mercedes.''

"Well, I don't want you to come around anymore.''

"Why? What about what they want? Did you ask them if they wanted me to stop coming around?''

"I don't care what they want, Gloria. I am sick of coming over here and hearing about you and your crap from Mama and Mercedes.''

"Uh-huh. There is the real reason you don't want me around. I knew it didn't have anything to do with Reggie's condition. I knew it,'' said Gloria. "You are a very smart man, Stewart. I know you know that the HIV virus can only be contracted through the contact of bodily fluids—and I don't mean saliva. So you couldn't possibly be afraid that Mercedes is going to become infected by hanging out with me.''

"Well, it's not just that, Gloria. I don't know where you take Mercedes. I don't know who or what you are exposing her to.''

"Oh my God, Stew. You were married to me for seven years. We were together for ten. You know that I would never do anything to hurt anyone in this family. I have been there for every member of this family. And I am not going to stop caring about them because you could give a damn about me.''

"Look, I know you care about them. But that is just not

the most important thing right now. What is important is that I do what is best for me and my family. And I just don't like the fact that you would take up so quickly with someone who has AIDS. I don't want my niece or my mother around those people.''

"Those people! What do you mean, those people? Besides, Reggie doesn't have AIDS. I told you, he is HIV positive. And what makes you think that I'd take my ex-husband's niece around anyone I was dating? That would be a little strange for all three of us—especially for her. You know me better than that. I would never do something like that without discussing it with you first. But it's a moot point anyway because, like I said, I'm not seeing him anymore.''

"Well, have you been tested for AIDS?''

"What?!'' said Gloria, angry that Stewart was confronting her about something she had not yet had the courage to deal with herself. "No, Stewart, I have not been tested yet. Like I told Jean, Reggie and I never had sex. I cannot believe I am sitting up here discussing my sex life with my ex-husband. Jesus,'' she said, exasperated.

"You haven't been tested?'' exclaimed Stewart. "Then you don't know what you have. Until I see some test results, you will not be able to see Mercedes or Mama. And how do I know you weren't with this man while we were married? Shit, do I need to get tested?''

"Oh, you're out of your mind. I'm leaving before we go somewhere we can't get back from. Some things you can never take back, and I think we're headed in that direction,'' said Gloria, nearly hitting herself in the head with the door as she rushed to leave.

Stewart ran out the door, too, calling after her, "Don't you come back over here without those test results, Gloria.''

* * *

As Gloria sped off, her whole body was tingling. She was feeling so many emotions she thought she was going to have a nervous breakdown. How dare he ask her if she had been tested? She didn't need to be tested. She'd never even been with Reginald.

And she'd only been with one other guy since she had been divorced. A few months after she and Stewart had separated, she'd found herself in a really bad place one night and had gotten together with an old high-school boyfriend she'd bumped into on a girls' night out. She'd felt really ashamed of herself as she snuck out of his house the next morning. But she was happy they had used a condom. And as far as she knew the condom had not broken. She basically was using condoms for birth control. She didn't really think about how they also served as STD prevention.

If there was any reason she had to be tested, it would be because of Stewart. Who knew what his ass was doing the last few years they were married? All of those late nights at the office with those young interns and assistants. She never really thought that Stewart would go so low as to cheat on her, but she was never one hundred percent sure, either. She knew she needed to get tested, but she was afraid. She was even afraid to let herself think about why she was afraid. She really needed to talk to somebody.

About the same time Gloria realized she had been stopped at a stop sign for ten minutes, she looked in her rearview mirror to see that she was crying—but not because she was mad as hell with Stewart. She was crying because she realized the only person she could talk to who would understand what she was going through was Reggie.

What must Reggie go through if this was the reaction I got from people who found out that I was dating someone

*who was HIV positive? What must Reggie face every time
someone finds out about his condition?* Had he lost jobs,
friends, family members over this? Had he even told his
family? She realized that she and Reggie had never talked
much about his family besides the perfunctory conversation
about how many brothers and sisters he had, what they did,
where they lived—the basics. But he really never talked
about his family at all. Maybe they had cut him off just like
she was cutting him off.

Gloria felt an immediate pang of guilt. How could she
just end it like that? But how could he keep something so
important from her? She really wanted to see him, to talk
to him, to see how he was doing. But she just couldn't bring
herself to see him, not just yet.

Gloria decided that if she couldn't see Reggie or Mercedes, she could at least sculpt. She hadn't been able to pick
up a piece of clay since they'd broken up, but she needed
something therapeutic to do. She needed to feel that clay in
her hands. She knew it would make her feel better. But
where would she go to sculpt? She had withdrawn from the
Corcoran. Luckily, she remembered passing by an art center
one day that allowed patrons to paint and sculpt if they
brought their own materials. She just needed to stop by the
art store to pick up some supplies before she went.

As she was standing in line to check out, she flipped
through a local arts newsletter. She noticed a want ad for a
few positions to help with a fundraiser to benefit the Imani
Center, an AIDS prevention and awareness center that she
realized was near her house. The announcement said that
local artists were donating their works to be auctioned off
and all of the money collected would be donated to the
center.

Gloria had always wanted to see if she could sell some

of her sculpture. Reggie had always said she was talented, but she really wanted some validation from someone who was not biased. She decided that she would take the few pieces she had to the center. If her pieces sold, she'd know that someone liked her work—someone who didn't know her.

The next day, Gloria packed up four of what she thought were her best works (including a piece that she and Reginald had molded together) and took them to the Imani Center.

Judging from outside appearances, Gloria thought that the center was kind of shabby. But when she went inside, there was beautiful African-inspired art all over the place—paintings and collages on the walls and sculptures placed just so. The place looked like an art gallery, except for the prominently placed pamphlets with such titles as "Protecting Yourself from HIV and AIDS," "Quick Facts about HIV and AIDS," and "Resources for More Information About HIV and AIDS."

"Is this the Imani Center?" Gloria asked the gum-smacking teenage girl sitting behind a high desk. "It looks more like a gallery. There are some beautiful works here."

"Yep. This is Imani. My mother could not decide which idea she loved more, so she's sort of doing both."

"Oh," said Gloria, dumping her box on the desk and walking over to a whole wall covered with information about HIV and AIDS, from statistics from the Centers for Disease Control and Prevention (CDC) to numerous newspaper and magazine articles. "Well, I'd just like to donate some of my work to your upcoming fundraiser."

"Great," said the girl, who yelled for her mother to come up front to take care of Gloria.

"Among African-American men between the ages of twenty-five and forty-four, HIV infection has been the leading cause of death since 1991," Gloria read out loud from a posted *New York Times* article. "In 1998, HIV infection was the third leading cause of death of black women in the same age range. Wow, that can't be true."

"It sure is," said a voice so deep and rich it sounded like thunder rumbling across the sky. Gloria was surprised to turn around and find that the voice was emanating from a woman. "And at least half of all new infections of HIV in the U.S. are among people under twenty-five—our young folk.

"Hello, I'm Sheila and that is my daughter, Shayla," said the tall, colorfully dressed woman, extending her hand. "Welcome to the Imani Center. Shocking stats, aren't they?"

"Well, yes. I had no idea. I mean, it's really bad."

"Yes, that's why we're here—to help keep those numbers from rising. Are you just going to leave me hanging out there?" asked Sheila, her hand still held out.

"Oh, I'm sorry," said a slightly distracted Gloria, shaking Sheila's hand. "Hi. I'm Gloria."

"Well, what can I do for you, Miss Gloria?"

"I'd like to submit a few of my sculpture pieces for the fundraiser."

"Oh, lovely. Our first donation. Come on to the back," said Sheila, her billowing clothing making light swishing noises as she walked down the hallway to a back room. Gloria thought Sheila looked liked an African princess, swathed from head to toe in heaps of blue, green, and gold material wrapped and draped everywhere.

"No other artists have given you any of their work yet?" asked Gloria, somewhat alarmed.

"Nope, just you. You are our first," said Sheila, who proceeded to tell her how she'd had a donation commitment from Mark Lattimore, a well-known local artist, who she thought would be a draw to attract other local artists. Unfortunately, Mr. Lattimore had backed out last week and she'd already put down a nonrefundable deposit on a hotel ballroom to have the event.

"So the show must go on," said Sheila cheerfully.

"You sure are handling this well," said Gloria, marveling at how calm Sheila was about her situation. "Your fundraiser is only a month away."

"Girl, this little setback is nothing," Sheila replied, helping Gloria unpack her sculptures. "All things happen for a reason. I just said a little prayer for guidance and waited for a miracle to come along. And look . . . here you are."

"Oh, I am so far from a miracle it's not even funny."

"Well, your work is beautiful," said Sheila, handling one of Gloria's pieces. "And I have faith that other artists will be walking through that door."

"Thanks for the compliment," said Gloria, wondering where she could get some faith like Sheila's. "I'm just a beginner and I just kind of wanted to see if anyone would actually pay for my little amateur creations."

"They're going to go like hotcakes. Don't you even worry about it."

"Okay, well, good luck with finding some more artists," said Gloria, heading for the door. "Oh, what does Imani mean?"

"It means *faith* in Swahili. We have faith that there is a cure out there for HIV and AIDS. And until it is discovered, we have faith that every time we talk about awareness in a school or hand out a pamphlet or give away a free condom, we are preventing people from contracting HIV," said Sheila. "Faith is a funny thing. You can't see it. You can't touch it. But sometimes it's the only thing that keeps you going."

"I guess so," Gloria said, not exactly sure what Sheila was talking about.

"Don't mind me. Sometimes I get philosophical." Sheila

waved good-bye to Gloria. "Thank you for your contribution and please take some pamphlets with you."

As she sat in her car, Gloria could not shake the feeling that she knew she could help Sheila. She'd hadn't been back to the Corcoran lately, but she decided that she would drop by the director's office and make a few inquiries. She just didn't want to bump into Reginald. She hated feeling like she wanted to see him so badly that she was putting herself in the position where she might run into him. *No,* she tried to reassure herself. *I'm going up to the school for a good reason—to get some contacts for Sheila—a woman I just met—uh-huh.*

On the way to the Corcoran, Gloria almost wrecked her car a number of times, putting on lipstick and shaping her eyebrows in the rearview mirror. She told herself that she was getting all gussied up because it had been awhile since she'd been up to the school, and she wanted to look nice just in case she ran into any of her former classmates.

She ran her hands through her short dreads, which she was glad she'd just gotten tightened up, and walked briskly into the building. She took the long way to the administrative office, avoiding going past the room where Reginald taught most of his classes.

Nearly to the office, Gloria slowed her pace, thinking she was home free. She turned the last corner, and who should be standing in the hallway talking to a few students, but Reginald. *Oh, no,* she thought, *Now what?* She couldn't turn back because she saw that he'd already seen her. So she just kept walking straight past the group and entered the office—almost busting a blood vessel in her eye using every bit of her peripheral vision to see if Reginald was watching her walk by.

"May I help you?" asked the receptionist when Gloria walked in the office.

"Yes, I . . . I . . . um," stammered Gloria, totally blanking on her purpose for coming up to the Corcoran.

"Gloria," said a voice she'd longed to hear for weeks.

She turned around to stand face-to-face with the man she knew she still cared for deeply.

"Hello, Reginald," she said in the most convincing I'm-over-you voice she could muster.

"Boy, it's great to see you," said Reginald.

"It's nice to see you as well," replied Gloria. She could feel him taking her all in, and it was making her a little warm.

"So, what are you doing here? I thought that you withdrew from classes."

"Yeah, I decided to take a little break," she said, searching her mind for the reason she'd come up to the school. Luckily she saw a poster of Mark Lattimore's work over Reginald's shoulder and it reminded her of the Imani Center. "I'm here to talk to Dr. Trevor about getting a list of contacts for local artists who may want to donate some of their work to the Imani Center for a fundraiser they are having."

"Oh, isn't that the new AIDS center over on MLK?"

"Yes."

"And you are helping to organize this fundraiser?"

"Well, sort of. I dropped off some of my work—you know, just to see if anyone would actually pay money for it—and the woman who runs the center told me that Mark Lattimore had pulled out his donations and that they were in need of some artwork. So I just thought I'd see if Dr. Trevor could put her in touch with some artists."

"You know, that is something that I could help you with, if you'd like. I have a list of nearly every visual artist in the area. We could kind of work on it together," offered Reginald as he reached out to touch her arm.

She saw his hand coming toward her and tried not to flinch when he touched her, but was unsuccessful. "I don't think that would be a good idea, Reggie,'' she said, seeing the hurt look on his face at her reaction to his touch.

''Maybe not,'' he agreed, dejected. ''How about I just E-mail you the list?''

''Okay that's fine. I'd really appreciate it.''

After they talked about a couple of the particulars, Reginald excused himself, saying he had some paperwork to get caught up on.

Gloria felt sick to her stomach as she walked to her car. She really cared about this man, but he had kept something very serious from her. And worse, she couldn't even stand to be touched by him. She felt tears well up in her eyes. Why had she come up to the Corcoran? She knew she was going to run into him. And after a couple of weeks of managing to get along okay, now she was all upset again.

All she could think about were those four words he'd said that stuck in her mind. *I'm HIV positive, Glo. I'm HIV positive, Glo.* The words kept ringing in her head. She needed help. She could not go on breaking down every five minutes about him. It had been three weeks since he'd told her about his condition, and she still couldn't keep herself together for more than a few hours.

For some reason, Gloria found herself back at the Imani Center. ''Ma, Gloria is back,'' Shayla announced as she walked into the center.

''I knew you'd be back,'' said Sheila, emerging from the back.

''How?'' wondered Gloria out loud.

''Something in your eyes told me that you would be giving us a lot more than your beautiful sculptures.''

''Well, I was thinking about your situation and I realized that I may be able to help you.''

Sheila was so ecstatic to learn about the list of artists she would be receiving that she gave Gloria a big hug, something Gloria was not expecting, but really needed. Gloria hung on a little longer than Sheila intended, but when she realized that Gloria needed to be held a bit, she gave her an extra squeeze.

"Thank you so much, sweetie. I really appreciate this," said Sheila, stepping back. "This is a serious plague affecting our community, and we've got to get everybody involved in one of the most important aspects—prevention."

"Yes, well, that's why I came back. After reading all of the statistics and literature that you have posted . . . plus I have a friend . . . well, he used to be a friend. Anyway, I wanted to do a little more than just drop off my stuff."

"Well, like I said, we are grateful, and I look forward to receiving that list."

"Okay, so I guess I'll talk with you soon."

"Yes, you can call me or stop by anytime, even if you just want to chat," said Sheila pointedly.

"What time do you open in the morning?" asked Gloria, trying to prolong her visit to the Imani Center, where she was beginning to feel quite comfortable.

"Oh, on Saturdays we try to drag ourselves in around ten or so. Did you want to drop the list off, instead of E-mailing it?"

"Well, since you are so close, it would be no problem. And I could kind of give you a little direction on which artists might be more receptive to donating their work. Maybe I could even call a few for you."

"Gloria, you are a godsend. This is wonderful. Door closes—"

"Window opens," said Shayla, finishing her mother's sentence.

"That's our little saying around here," said Sheila. "We try to keep it as positive as possible."

"I like that . . . door closes, window opens," repeated Gloria. "I'm going to use it. So, I'll see you tomorow?"

"Yep. We'll be here."

Driving home, Gloria realized that she was feeling a little better. Maybe it was because she was helping someone else. She couldn't wait to get home to check her E-mail. She hoped that Reggie had sent the list already. She wondered what he would say in the E-mail. After their meeting today, she didn't expect much.

Gloria,

It was really nice seeing you today. Here's the list. I also wanted to let you know that every Wednesday evening I host Artists Against AIDS at the Renaissance.

Basically, me and a few other people who are HIV positive counsel teenagers and young adults who have just been diagnosed as HIV positive to help them to cope with the initial shock.

The program is three months long. At the beginning of the second month, each of the young people is paired up with a local artist (some of whom are HIV positive), who helps them get started painting—as a creative outlet for their anger, frustration, and sadness at having HIV. All of the artists do this on a volunteer basis. And some of the graduates of the program have even come back to volunteer as counselors or art sponsors.

Anyway, one of our programs is ending next week, and I thought that maybe some of the graduates might want to donate their work to the Imani Center's fundraiser. Maybe their sponsors would want to donate something, too. I could speak to them if you'd like.

As someone who is HIV positive, I think this is a beautiful gesture that you are making to the Imani Center. As someone who loves you, I think—no, I know—that you still have the most beautiful spirit of anyone that I have ever met.

Love, Reggie

Gloria read the E-mail four times before she hit the Reply button. She had no idea what she was going to say. Finally, after half an hour of writing and editing, she came up with a response that she thought was the perfect balance of appreciation and openness.

Reggie,

Thanks for offering to have the works of your young people donated to the Imani Center's fundraiser. I know that Sheila, the director of the center, will really appreciate it. I always wondered why we couldn't go out on Wednesdays, especially since we saw each other nearly every other day of the week. Your program sounds wonderful. I am so proud of the commitment you have made to people with HIV and the way that you are using your business to give back to your community. Not many people would be so generous with their time and money. Anyway, thanks again for the list and the donations from your program. I do miss you. Maybe we can talk one day.

Gloria

Gloria hit the Send button and felt she was opening a can of worms. She didn't know why she'd suggested that they could talk one day. She wasn't ready for that. But the message was gone and there was nothing she could do about it now.

Gloria had been down at the Imani Center nearly every day for two weeks. She'd made at least fifty telephone calls to artists trying to convince them to donate their work. By the time she had explained fifty times what the Imani Center did and why it was important for these artists to contribute in any way they could to the fight against AIDS and HIV, she realized that she liked what she was doing.

Sheila had liked nearly all of the ideas that she had suggested for the fundraiser. Plus, they were getting closer. One night when they were at the center late, Gloria asked Sheila why she'd started the Imani Center, fully expecting Sheila to tell her that she was HIV positive. But that was not the case. Sheila told her that she had married a man named Joseph who was HIV positive. He used to come into a gallery where she was an assistant curator and they would have wonderful conversations about art. He eventually told her about his condition, which he had gotten from sharing needles while shooting heroin.

Sheila said the only reason she believed Joseph's HIV didn't phase her too much was that she'd had a brother die a couple of years earlier from AIDS. Unfortunately, her husband was a heroin addict, and although he'd tried to stop numerous times, he was never able to kick the demon. He developed full-blown AIDS and died from AIDS-related pneumonia. It was his last wish that Sheila locate his daughter and tell her that he was sorry for never being there for her. When Sheila finally found his daughter, Shayla, the girl was living with his extended relatives, basically raising herself. Sheila told Gloria that something inside of her just wouldn't let Shayla stay there unloved and uncared for. Eventually, she ended up adopting Shayla.

Gloria was so moved by Sheila's story and so touched that she would share her story with her that she felt comfortable enough to confide in Sheila about her relationship with Reginald. When she was through, Sheila gave her a big hug and told her that everything was going to be okay.

"You'll be fine, my sister," Sheila told her. "You will make the right decision."

"How do you know that? Do you feel like you made the right decision marrying Joseph?"

"Absolutely. Even though he put me through unimaginable pain because of his addiction to heroin, he was a brilliant man. And he is the reason Shayla and I have each other, and she is the best thing in my life. I wouldn't change a thing."

"I hate to be really nosy, but how did you keep from getting HIV if you were married to him? Did you not have sex?"

"Well, when I met Joseph, he had his HIV in check and he hadn't used herion in three years. Everything was wonderful. We used lots of condoms and lots of spermicide. Sometimes we even used two condoms. And I would test each one before we used it, filling it with water. I know that sounds tedious, especially when you are in the heat of the moment. But we used to play games and make it fun. We loved each other, so we made it work."

"I don't know if I'd be able to do that. I really care about Reggie, but a few weeks ago we bumped into each other and he touched my hand and I flinched. I felt terrible for both him and me."

"Don't you know by now that those things happen? Both you and Reggie have to give yourselves time to adjust to being in a relationship where one person has a serious condition. I can't tell you what to do, because I don't know what you are prepared to deal with. But be open, Gloria. Things have changed so much since Joseph died six years ago. There are all kinds of medical advancements. They even have a female condom. And people have been living for years—I'm talking ten, fifteen years—with HIV. There are people who, except for their HIV, are healthier than your average person. HIV is not a death sentence, Gloria. It could be a long time before Reginald develops AIDS—if he ever does. Who knows?"

"I guess so. It was just such a shock. I guess I had this

preconceived notion of what people with HIV/AIDS were like, and I did not expect for it to be someone like Reggie.''

"I can understand that you were surprised. It's not just a gay white man's disease anymore. Actually, it never was. They just got most of the attention because the white gay male community were more vocal about the way that they were living. They organized, raised awareness, and preached prevention about AIDS and HIV. And now the number of gay white men who are getting infected is dropping.''

"Why aren't the infection rates dropping for black folks?''

"Well, a number of reasons. One is that the prevention messages and educational information that were created in the beginning of the epidemic were all for white gay men. What public health practitioners found years later was that those same messages did not work for heterosexual black women or drug-injecting Latino men, or whoever, because each population needs a strategy that really takes their own situations into account. That is what I am trying to do here at the Imani Center—create a place where young people of color can get information about AIDS and HIV directly targeted at them.

"After my brother and Joseph, I could not just go on living my life day by day seeing how AIDS was affecting our community and not do anything about it,'' Sheila continued. "I started small, volunteering a couple of times a month at an AIDS clinic. After a year or so, I was spending so much time at the clinic that I decided I should take some courses in AIDS education and that turned into a master's degree in public health. It took me another few years to get up enough money to open this place and we've been here for about six months. So now you know all about me.''

"You've had an interesting life. I just hope that I can be as open and accepting as you.''

"Girl, I wasn't accepting of everything. When Joseph started using again, I was heated about it. I could not believe that he would throw away everything he had for a high. It took me a long time to forgive him for that. But I finally realized he was sick. Addiction is a sickness. And by the time he'd quit again, his immune system was so vulnerable that he developed pneumonia. Yeah, it's hard to accept the decisions that some people make about their lives, especially when you love them. But it sounds as if Reginald made the decision to be honest with you and you didn't even give him the opportunity to explain. Do you even know how he became infected?"

"Well, yes. He told me he contracted it from an ex-girlfriend."

"And do you believe him?"

"Yes. But I just don't know if I can be with him. He kept the truth from me for nearly a month and he allowed me to fall for him. I just don't know."

"I think you have an obligation to yourself to at least talk to him again. Make no promises to yourself, except that you will listen to whatever it is that he has to say. You may not end up together, but it is hard to make a decision without all of the information."

"I guess you're right."

"It's not about who's right. It's about doing what's best for you. And obviously not having this resolved is tearing you up inside. In the end you should go with your heart. You can never go wrong if you go with your heart."

"Someone who is very dear to me has said the same thing to me about Reginald."

"Well, not to pat myself on the back or anything, but she must be a very wise woman."

"She is and so are you. Thanks, Sheila."

* * *

"My gift has a gift," Sheila told Gloria one day.

"What do you mean?" Gloria asked.

"Girl, you are great at convincing those artists. Look at all the donations we have received since you started."

Gloria looked around the office at all of the paintings and sculptures lining the walls and covering most of the floor. "I guess I have done some work, huh?" she said, feeling a little proud of her accomplishment.

"Yeah, girl. And we've got another whole week before the fundraiser."

"I'm going to make at least fifty more calls and we should run another advertisement in the paper with the names of some of the most well-known artists who have donated their work. You know, as a draw."

"That is a great idea. I'll handle that end. I actually got a call from your friend, who said he was bringing over about twenty works today."

"Reggie? Reggie is coming here today?" asked Gloria with a little too much excitement in her voice.

"Yep," said Sheila, looking at her watch. "As a matter of fact, he should be here in a few minutes."

"Good gracious, Sheila. Why didn't you tell me?" Gloria ran to the bathroom, nearly tripping over a sculpture.

"You said you guys were just friends," Sheila yelled to the back. "Look at you—about to break your neck to make sure no hair is out of place."

"We are friends," said Gloria, frantically rummaging through her purse for lip gloss and perfume. "I don't like for people to see me looking crazy."

"You didn't seem to mind looking crazy all last week. As a matter of fact, one day you came in in an old T-shirt and some sweatpants full of holes. Remember that day?"

"I was only stopping by for a minute. I just forgot something."

"But there were three or four artists here that day and you proceeded to chat them up for at least thirty minutes—in your holey pants. So what is all this running around for? Y'all a little more than friends, huh?"

"Mind your business, miss thing."

"All right, I'll make sure not to tell him that you nearly took your knee off to slather on some lipstick and bathe in perfume when he gets . . . hello, may I help you?" Sheila suddenly changed her tone.

"These figures don't look right," said Gloria, easing herself into the room, pretending to be consumed in some papers she was reading.

"Here she is now, our beautiful worker bee, or should I say Miss Happy Reason?" said Sheila to Reginald.

"Hi, Reggie," said Gloria, glaring at Sheila. "What's happening?"

"Oh, I just came by to drop off some of the work from the kids in the program. Looks like you guys have gotten a heap of donations."

"Yes, we've been blessed," said Sheila. "I was just telling Gloria that she had the gift of gab—able to get all of these artists to donate their work."

"Yes, I know Gloria is good at what she does," said Reginald, looking at Gloria.

"I'll bet you do," said Sheila.

"Okay, Reggie, let me help you get the stuff out of your car." Gloria glowered at Sheila while ushering Reginald outside.

"Did you tell her about us?" Reginald asked as they walked to his car.

"No. I have no idea why she was acting like that."

"Umhmm. You sure smell good."

"Let's just get this stuff into the office."
"Okay, okay, okay."

Two hours later, Reginald was still at the Imani Center. Sheila had roped him into helping her write the descriptions of the works that she would read at the fundraiser. And for some reason, this annoyed Gloria. This was her project, and here was Reginald in her space. Why couldn't he just go away? He had his group and plenty of other AIDS projects that he could be working on. Why did he have to take over her thing? Gloria wondered.

She had tried to tell Sheila that writing the descriptions was something that she could do. "Why let the student do it, when the teacher is right here?" responded Sheila. "Plus, aren't you really swamped with the phone calls and stuff?"

"Whatever," Gloria sniped.

"You can do it, Glo," Reginald offered. "I don't want to interfere."

"Nonsense. She's got plenty on her plate. Come on, Reginald," said Sheila, motioning him to the back where there were more works that needed descriptions. Reginald threw Gloria a helpless look and followed Sheila to the back.

Gloria sat at the front desk fuming. But she wasn't sure why. She knew she really didn't care if Reginald helped out. She didn't even want to write those descriptions. In fact, she had been dreading doing it. So why was she so upset that Reginald was there? When Sheila sprang it on her that he was coming by the office today, she'd gotten excited. What was wrong with her? *I can't go on on this roller coaster,* she thought. *I gotta do something. But what?*

Gloria had found a great dress to wear to the fundraiser at her favorite boutique—and it was on sale. It was a little red number that wasn't too short or too tight, but accentuated all of her best curves. She'd also gotten her locks twisted and coiled into some small bantu knots that left her dreads curly when they were unfurled. As she stood in front of he mirror, putting on the perfect shade of crimson lipstick, Gloria liked her reflection. She felt beautiful. And she realized it was not because she looked hot (which she did), it was because she was happy with herself.

In the past year, Gloria had realized many of the goals she had put on the back burner when she was married to Stewart. She'd gone natural. She'd taken up an art. And now she was actually helping people. What she was doing was using her talents to help better the lives of others. This type of work was what she had always wanted to do. She just hadn't known how to get into it. Or she had knowingly let other things distract her because she did not have enough confidence to know that this was something she could do.

But all of that was in the past. Helping people was what Gloria was born to do. She wondered if she could get up the courage to help herself. She still had not dealt with Reginald. And she still hadn't gotten tested for HIV. She'd been telling herself for weeks that she could not continue to keep putting off either of those two things. Tonight she was going to enjoy herself at the fundraiser, and tomorrow she was going to make some decisions about her health and her love.

"Hey, hot mama," said Danielle, sneaking up behind Gloria halfway through the fundraiser. "Girl, that dress is on fire. Reginald must be coming tonight."

"Hey, girl. I thought you couldn't make it tonight," said Gloria, ignoring her best friend's mention of Reginald.

"The more I thought about it, the more I realized, sometimes a date is not as important as giving back to your community.''

"He canceled on you, didn't he?"

"No, he's at the bar getting me an apple martini, girl."

"You are a mess. I can't believe you gave up D'Angelo tickets to come to the Imani Center's fundraiser."

"Well, I didn't exactly give them up. We're going to a late show. Plus, you know I've got to support you. I might need you in my old age, if I don't trap a man soon."

"Is that your date over there talking to that young thang in the spandex?"

"And she's drinking my drink!!! I'll be right back, girl. This won't take long," said Danielle as she marched off.

Gloria smiled at her friend as she thought about how well everything was going at the fundraiser. They were getting good prices for all of the work, even the amateur work that Reginald's kids had done. She'd seen a bid of $1,200 for one of the kid's work—more than any other piece that night.

Although Gloria had been happy to see that most of her pieces were getting bids of at least a few hundred dollars, she suddenly felt a sense of regret when she noticed the sculpure that she and Reginald had worked on together up for sale. All night she'd been going back and forth with someone trying to buy the sculpture. The highest she could afford was $400, and that was busting her budget.

"Isn't it a beautiful piece? I promised one of our supply vendors that I'd get it for him if he gave us a discount for the whole year," said Sheila, sidling up to Gloria, who had just put down her highest bid.

"So it's been you? You have been bidding against me?" Gloria asked.

"Well, it's been him via me."

"Well, why does he want my piece so bad?"

"It's not your piece anymore, and the guy just said that

looking at it, he could see the passion put into it," said Sheila.

"I guess I have to let it go," said Gloria. "When I first brought it in, I thought that I would not want it because it reminded me of someone I needed to get past. I kind of want it though, because that person is the reason I am here. But I guess I wasn't meant to have it."

"Why do you keep saying 'that person'? Did you forget that I know all about you and Reginald?"

"Oh, yeah, that's right. I'm just all twisted up in the head. I've decided that I'm going to make a decision about what to do about Reggie by the end of this weekend. I've let it linger on for too long."

"Go with your heart, baby," said Sheila as she walked away to help a bidder.

The rest of the evening went very well—they'd raised over $16,000 for the Imani Center. And they had also raised the level of awareness about AIDS and HIV. Gloria knew that the Imani Center was on the map when she saw reporters from a few local newspapers chatting up bidders.

"It is very important for everyone in the community to get involved, because HIV and AIDS affect all of us," she told the reporter from the local black newspaper. "They are unbelievably pervasive in the black community, affecting one out of every fifty black men and one out of every one hundred sixty black women. And the only way we are going to stop it is by increasing awareness and prevention of risky sexual behavior."

"You sound like you know what you are talking about," said Sheila, coming up to Gloria after the reporter walked away. "I was actually going to talk to you about this next week, but . . . Well, first let me tell you that we have received a grant from the CDC that is going to fully fund us for three years."

"Oh my God, girl, congratulations! That is wonderful," said Gloria, hugging Sheila.

"Yeah, now we'll be able not only to get more materials, but we will be able to do more outreach education, going into schools and Boys and Girls Clubs. And when we start partnering with church-based organizations like Balm in Gilead, we'll be able to bring something to the table."

"Oh, that is so wonderful. I'm so happy for you guys. I'd like to keep coming by and helping out."

"Well, that is kind of what I wanted to talk to you about. We could really use your marketing skills on a full-time basis. This grant will allow me to hire three full-time staffers, and I was hoping you would be one of them."

Gloria didn't even have to think about it. "Yes, I'd love to do it," she replied enthusiastically.

"Now, we can't pay you as much as you've probably been getting at the Department of Health, but I can probably get you about eighty, eighty-five percent of what you're making right now."

"Oh, don't worry about it. We can work out the details later. I know you'll be fair and I've been freelancing anyway. I'll just keep those other side projects going," gushed Gloria. "This is great. I'm going to be working with people I love and at a place I love. And the best part is that I'll be making a living by helping people. I could not have asked for a better night. Thank you so much, Sheila."

"No, thank you, Gloria. I've never seen someone work so hard at something they were not getting paid for. I can tell that you are totally committed to raising awareness about HIV and AIDS. And I want you on my team."

"Well, you've got me. And I am so excited to be here."

Gloria was on cloud nine the rest of the evening. She could not believe her good fortune. She couldn't wait to tell everybody—Danielle, her father, and even Reggie.

*   *   *

The evening was coming to a close and Sheila had announced who'd won all of the works that were up for auction.

"I'd just like to recognize a couple of people before the night is over. Well, first let me tell you about some great news. I found out this afternoon that the Imani Center has received a grant from the CDC that will keep us up and running for three years," said Sheila.

As Sheila was telling the crowd all about what the center would be able to do with the grant, Gloria was glancing around the ballroom and noticed Reginald standing near the back, looking directly at her. She wanted nothing more than to go and talk to him, but she'd have to wait until after Sheila made her remarks.

"Another person I would like to thank is Reginald Waters. Reginald owns the Renaissance, teaches painting at the Corcoran, and is an artist himself. He's very talented, isn't he, Gloria?"

Caught off guard, Gloria smiled and nodded at Sheila, mouthing to her, "I'm going to kill you."

"But the reason I want to recognize him tonight is because of the help that he gave us in putting this night together. Reginald provided us with the contact information for nearly all of the artists whose work was auctioned off tonight. Thank you, Reginald. Please come up to receive a token of our appreciation."

Gloria turned around to watch Reginald walk up to the podium, but it seemed that he was making a beeline straight for her. She was suprised when he grabbed her hand and pulled her up to the podium with him.

Gloria could have been knocked over with a feather when she saw Sheila hand Reginald the sculpture that she and Reginald had made together.

"Thank you for your tremendous contribution to the Imani Center," said Sheila, giving Reginald a hug. "Now there is one more person that I'd like to thank tonight, and wouldn't you know, she is already up here."

It did not immediately register with Gloria that Sheila was talking about her, because she was still reeling from Sheila's gift to Reginald of their art. And she was even more confused when Reginald leaned over and whispered something in Sheila's ear and Sheila smiled and stepped back from the podium.

"Thank you so much for letting me be a part of this wonderful night," said Reginald. "Another one of my contributions that Sheila neglected to mention is the donation of about twenty works of art made by the kids from the Artists Against AIDS program that I run out of my gallery. Basically, the program allows teenagers and young adults who have recently been diagnosed with HIV or AIDS to work out their frustration, anger, and sadness through painting. Tonight I saw that some of those kids' paintings went for upward of a thousand dollars. There's some real talent in these kids, and they will be so excited to know how much their work is appreciated. So thank you again."

As the crowd applauded, Reginald beckoned Gloria to join him at the podium.

"Now, I know that Sheila was going to recognize this lovely lady standing next to me, but I bribed her to let me do the honors."

"We'll be seeing you at the Imani Center all next month, right, Reggie?" reminded Sheila loudly as the audience laughed.

"It will be my pleasure," Reginald replied. "I don't know how many of you know Miss Gloria Rainier, right here. Well, all of the artists in the room should because of her serious skills at convincing you to donate your works—for free."

There were a few "amens," "yeps," and "rights" throughout the crowd to this remark.

"Gloria is a very special person," Reginald continued. "She became involved with the Imani Center only because she wanted to see if some of her beautiful sculptures would sell. And clearly they did. I think this one," he said, pointing to the one that he and Gloria had created together, "went for about six hundred and fifty dollars. But more important, Gloria kept coming back to the center. This is a woman who had never really known anyone with HIV or AIDS before. As someone who is HIV positive, I am really touched by her contributions of just jumping in there with both feet and being instrumental in putting this night together. She makes me a believer in the strength of the human spirit. So, I don't know what Sheila had planned to give her—"

"A full day of pampering at a spa," piped up Sheila.

"Well, she'll definitely need it after all of the hard work she has done," said Reginald. "But I also wanted to give back to her this beautiful work of art that she created. Thank you, Gloria."

Gloria had been trying to keep from crying, but she couldn't help it. Too many amazing things were happening to her in one night. As she hugged Reginald and Sheila, she realized that she was being rewarded for doing something that she loved to do.

"I really can't believe this," said Gloria, looking out on the crowd, many of whom were HIV positive or had AIDS. "I had no idea how serious the AIDS epidemic was until I walked into Imani and Sheila got ahold of me. She talked to me about how important it is for everyone to get involved in fighting this plague on our community—especially the black community. I do not have to tell you that although African-Americans are only twelve percent of the population, we make up nearly thirty-seven percent of all the AIDS cases reported in this country. But I'm going to get off my soapbox, because most of you have heard this speech before.

"You know, I've learned that being diagnosed with HIV or AIDS is not a death sentence. With the advances in medicine and treatment, people like Reginald are living long, productive, and purposeful lives. Shoot, many of the people I've met who have the virus live healthier lives than me. I'd just like to thank you for this recognition. It really means the world to me."

Gloria stepped down from the podium into a crowd of people who wanted to shake her hand, hug her, thank her, and even take her picture. She had such a wonderful night that she didn't even realize the magnitude of what Reginald had said until she got home.

"Reggie, it's Gloria," she said to him as he groggily answered the telephone. "Did I wake you?"

"No, baby," Reginald lied. "What's up?"

"I just realized that you told a room full of people that you were HIV positive tonight."

"I know. I know. I can't believe it myself."

"Had you ever done that before? I mean, do people at the Corcoran know that you have HIV? I mean, you know . . ."

"Well, if you are asking me if it was common knowledge to all of my friends, family, and coworkers that I have HIV, the answer is no. But I guess everybody knows now."

"How do you feel? Are you okay?"

"Yeah, I am. Are you okay is the question. I mean, I saw Danielle's face when I said I was HIV positive and . . ."

"Yeah, she looked like somebody had slapped her. We didn't get a chance to talk before I left, but I see on the caller ID that she's called me four times. I'm sure I'm going to get an earful later. It's funny, I've told her all of my most intimate secrets, but I could not tell her this. I guess I'm okay. It was kind of surprising, though. Did you know you were going to tell everyone?"

"No, not at all. It's strange. I feel a kind of relief. I don't know what came over me. I think it was you, Glo."

"Me? What do you mean?"

"Well, I just was so proud of the way that you stepped in and did all of that great work for the Imani Center. I figured if you could set aside your fears about being associated with AIDS, then so could I."

"Wow, I guess I hadn't looked at it like that."

"One thing still confuses me, though."

"What?"

"If you can work at the Imani Center, why can't you give us a chance? Is it because I wasn't completely honest with you from the start?"

Gloria immediately stiffened up at Reginald's question. She hadn't really called him to talk about them. She just wanted to make sure he was okay.

"Reggie, I don't know what it is. I don't know why I can't let myself get close to you. I guess I'm afraid."

"Afraid of what?"

"Okay, look, I'm afraid I'm going to get AIDS, okay? I don't want to get it. I'm sorry. That is just how I feel."

"It's okay. I can understand that. But baby, there are things that we can do."

"And that's not all, either. I don't want to be involved with someone who is going to die."

"But what about all of those things you said tonight about people with HIV living long, productive lives? Don't you believe what you were saying?"

"Yes, I do. But I am also realistic. Everybody with AIDS is not going to live a long life. And I just don't know if I can watch someone who I care deeply about die from AIDS."

"I know it's hard, but I think we can be together. I'm healthy now. I've been healthy for four years, since I was diagnosed with the virus. As long as I take care of myself, I believe in my heart of hearts that I am going to be fine.''

"I just don't know, Reggie. I can't see myself with anyone else but you. But I just don't know. I'm afraid.''

"Well, would it help if you came with me to my next doctor's appointment? I actually told him all about you and he said he'd answer any questions you had about anything.''

"Maybe. Maybe.''

"Okay, well, just let me know.''

"Reggie, I'm going to sleep now. I'm tired, okay?''

"All right, baby. You looked beautiful tonight—both inside and out. Sweet dreams.''

Gloria lay in bed so exhausted that she was not able to sleep. She'd had the greatest night of her life getting recognized for helping people. She'd gotten a new job. Everything was wonderful, except for her love life. It sucked. She thought about her speech at the fundraiser and wondered if she was a hypocrite for not giving Reginald a chance.

"It's different when it's you,'' she said out loud. "What if I get AIDS? What if he dies?'' Did she care enough about this man to put aside her fears? She'd said that she would make a decision about what to do about Reggie by the end of the weekend. Right before she drifted off to sleep, she decided that she would at least go to the doctor with Reggie. Maybe he could assuage her fears. Maybe he could assure her that she could have a safe relationship with Reggie. Maybe.

"Okay. You did not tell me he had AIDS. How could you keep that from me?'' Danielle demanded of Gloria.

"He doesn't have AIDS. He's HIV positive.''

"Well, I don't care what you call it. Why didn't you tell me?''

"Girl, this was one of the hardest things I've had to deal

with in my entire life," said Gloria, feeling guilty hearing the hurt in Danielle's voice. "It's right up there with my mother dying. I just couldn't tell you."

"You've told me everything else. That's what I'm here for, girl. I'm your best friend. The one you called from jail that time you got arrested for a DUI. The one who lent you a thousand dollars to go see some fool in California who you broke up with the next day. I mean, that really hurt."

"I know, I know, I know. I'm sorry, girl. I wanted to work this out between him and me and, you know, I just . . ."

"Oh, shit, don't even sweat it now. I'm going to try to be understanding. I guess this is what it means to have your best friend be in a 'real' relationship. Well, what are you going to do?"

"I don't know."

"Do you love him?"

"I think so. I sure want to give us a chance."

"Well, aren't you scared?"

"Hell, yeah. But I can't see myself with anyone else."

"I can't lie to you, girl. If you had told me earlier . . . wait, how long have you known?"

"A few weeks."

"You've been keeping this from me that long?"

"I was in a bad place for a minute. I wasn't really talking to anybody about it," Gloria said, deciding not to tell Danielle that she had confided in Sheila about Reginald's HIV.

"Anyway, like I was saying. If you had told me earlier, I'm sure I would have tried to talk you out of being with him. So if you really care about him, maybe it is good you didn't tell me."

"You would have done that?"

"Yes, girl. He has a deadly disease. One that you could get. It could kill you. I don't want to lose you."

"I'm not going to die."

"How do you know that? What, you're going to be with

this man and not have sex? Because that is the only sure way that you are not going to get it.''

"You're right about that. But condoms are between ninety-eight and one hundred percent effective in preventing the transmission of sexually transmitted diseases. So we'll use those.''

"You sound like a doctor. Are you quoting from some of those pamphlets from the Imani Center?''

"Well, actually, I went to one of Reginald's doctor's appointments with him.''

"You what!?''

"Yeah, I went to Reggie's doctor. And he was really nice. He explained all about HIV, AIDS, and prevention and he let me ask all of the questions I wanted to. We were there for nearly an hour and a half. I even got tested.''

"You did? And?''

"And I'll find out the results in a few days. You should get tested.''

"Girl, it's been a few horses in this stable. I don't know if I'm brave enough.''

"I'll go with you.''

"I'll think about it.''

"I'm going to annoy you to death until you do. This doctor was really nice. He told me so much I did not know about AIDS and he helped me understand Reggie's treatment regimen and everything.''

"Well, since you know so much, what is the difference between HIV and AIDS?''

"The doctor said that HIV, or human immunodeficiency virus, kills these cells called T cells, which help your body fight off infection and disease. A healthy T cell count is between five hundred and eighteen hundred. But if it falls below two hundred, you have AIDS. That means that there are not enough T cells to effectively fight infections and diseases. You know, your immune system breaks down.''

"You were really paying attention. How do you know Reggie is not going to get AIDS?"

"I don't. His doctor said he's in great shape, though. His T cell count is around four hundred eighty and he doesn't drink, has never smoked, and is the healthiest eater and exerciser I know. But he could still get sick. Half of the people with HIV develop AIDS within ten years."

"Is he taking that mixed drink thing?"

"The cocktail. Yes, he is. It's not really a liquid drink. It's a combination of medications that keep the viral load— the amount of virus in the body—from increasing. As a matter of fact, it helps to decrease the load."

"So, there is a cure."

"No, there's no cure, but the viral load can be so low that it is undetectable. That's how Reggie has lived with HIV for four years."

"I never would have guessed he had it by looking at him."

"Well, you can't tell a person is diabetic by looking at them, either, can you?"

"Don't be a smart-ass. You are already on shaky ground for taking so long to tell me."

"I know, I know."

"You sure sound like you know your medical stuff."

"I asked the doctor a lot of questions. But he can't answer whether I should stay with Reggie. I just don't think I can lose another person so close to me. I don't think I've ever gotten over my mother dying."

"I can't believe I'm saying this, but you could trip on your shoelace and crack your skull on the ground. You never know who is going to go first. If you really care about this guy, and I can tell that you do, you should really give this one some serious thought. Whatever you decide, you know I got your back, girl."

"Thank you, Danni."

"I did want to ask you one more thing, and I hope that it is not too nosy."

"How did he get it?"

"Yep."

"An ex-girlfriend gave it to him."

"I just had to make sure he wasn't out there turning tricks or something."

"Shut your mouth."

"I'm just saying—"

"And I'm just hanging up."

"Okay, okay. I'm sorry. Really, though. If you need to talk about this, you know I'm here to listen."

"And to give your opinions."

"Which you know you want."

"Bye, girl. I love you."

"I know."

The next morning, when Gloria walked into the Imani Center on her first day as an employee, she was greeted by Sheila and Shayla standing under a makeshift banner that said WELCOME GLORIA and a coffee cake with one big candle on it.

"We're so glad to have you join our small team," said Sheila, giving Gloria a big hug. "This is your desk."

"Thanks so much. This was so thoughtful of you," said Gloria.

"Blow out the candle," said Shayla. "But make a wish first."

Gloria closed her eyes, thanked God for giving her a job that she loved, wished for guidance in her situation with Reginald, and blew out her one candle.

"Great. I'm starving. Can I have a piece?" said Shayla.

"Shayla! That is not your cake," scolded Sheila.

"I know. But you said I could have a piece when Miss Gloria got here."

"I said if you asked her nicely maybe she would give you a piece."

"Go ahead, Shayla, cut yourself a piece and your mama one, too, while you're at it," said Gloria.

"Thanks, girl. 'Cause I'm starving, too," said Sheila. "If you had shown up five minutes later, that cake would have looked like a Pac-Man. Oh, yeah, make sure to save a piece for Reginald, Shayla."

"Reginald. Is he coming by here today?" asked Gloria.

"Yep. I thought that the three of us could have an idea meeting about the types of programs we could start," said Sheila. "You don't mind, do you?"

"Oh, no, not at all," said Gloria, happy she'd decided to dress nice for her first day of work at the Imani Center.

Gloria spent all morning setting up her office, and then she and Sheila went to lunch. They had just returned to the center and were getting out of the car when Shayla burst out the door and rushed up to Sheila.

"There's a girl inside who said she's going to kill herself," said Shayla breathlessly.

"What?" asked Sheila. "Who are you talking about?"

"She just found out that she has HIV and she said she was going to kill herself," said Shayla. "I told her that someone would be back soon and to try to think positive thoughts until you guys got back. I told her to think about her family, her friends. I just let her talk about whatever she wanted to. I didn't know what else to do. She sounds really scary."

"Don't worry, baby. You did the right thing," said Sheila, rushing toward the door. "What is her name, Shayla?"

"Jenine, and she's sitting at Miss Gloria's desk. She's been here about fifteen minutes."

Gloria watched and listened as Sheila talked to the girl, who was so upset she was shaking.

"We're here to help you," said Sheila to Jenine. "Tell me what's going on."

"What's going on?" Jenine said sarcastically. "What's going on is that I've got AIDS and I'm going to die."

"Well, you're not going to die today," said Sheila. "And how do you know that you have AIDS?"

"I got tested at the free clinic and it came up positive."

"What were the exact words that they said to you when they told you?"

"They said that I've got HIV. And that's AIDS, right?"

"Not exactly. HIV is the virus that can lead to AIDS if you don't take care of yourself."

"So I don't have AIDS?"

"No. And you may not develop AIDS."

"Okay, what does that mean? What do I . . ." said Jenine, confused about what she should do next.

"Well, let me tell you a little about HIV, and then we'll talk about what you need to do next. Shayla, get Jenine something to wipe her face with and some water."

Gloria paid attention to Sheila as she explained to Jenine what HIV was and how she needed to be under a doctor's care to get treatment so she could keep from developing AIDS as long as possible.

"Nobody's going to love me with this disease," said Jenine.

"That's not true," said Sheila. "I married a man who had HIV and Gloria, over there, is dating a man who is HIV positive, isn't that true, Gloria?"

"Yes, that's true," said Gloria, putting her hand on Jenine's shoulder.

"So you guys have HIV?" Jenine asked.

"No. Neither one of us is HIV positive, but we have many friends and loved ones who are."

"Aren't you scared that you are going to get it?" asked Jenine.

Just then, Reginald walked in. Shayla motioned him over to the front desk and whispered to him what was going on.

"Well, yes, Jenine, I have to say that I am still a little afraid that I will get infected with HIV," said Gloria. "But there are so many ways to protect yourself when you are having sex these days that I'm probably more likely to get hit by lightning than I am to contract HIV from having sex with my boyfriend. Plus, he's an amazing man and I didn't want to miss out on being with someone that wonderful just because he is HIV positive."

"I don't know. I just don't know. What are my friends going to say? What are my parents going to say?"

"I'm sure your parents love you and your real friends will still be your friends," said Sheila.

"How do you know? You don't have it," said Jenine angrily. "It's different when you have it. I mean, you are making the decision to be involved with someone who has this thing. I didn't. I just got it. You don't know how I feel."

"I do," said Reginald, coming over and kneeling down in front of Jenine. "I know exactly how you feel."

"You've got it? You've got HIV?" asked Jenine.

"Yes, I do, and I've had it for four years."

"Jenine, this is Reginald, my boyfriend," Gloria said, looking at Reginald and realizing that for the first time she was accepting him for who he was. "He's HIV positive, and we are dealing with it."

"I don't believe you," asked Jenine. "Are you serious?"

"Yes, we're very serious," said Reginald, standing up and taking Gloria's hand.

"Don't misunderstand, Jenine. It has been a difficult road for us," said Gloria. "Reginald wasn't completely honest with me when we first started dating. He wouldn't even let me get close to him because he was afraid that I wouldn't want to be with him once I found out he had HIV. And when he finally did tell me, it took me some time to realize that his HIV does not define him. And as a couple dealing with HIV, we won't let the disease define us. We're making a commitment to each other, a commitment to fighting HIV and AIDS and a commitment to living life to the fullest. Isn't that right, Reggie?"

"I couldn't have said it better myself," said Reginald, who stared at Gloria as if he'd just seen her for the first time. "Jenine, do you like to paint?"

"Paint? What are you talking about?" asked Jenine, confused.

"Well, I have this program that I run out of my gallery that I think you might benefit from."

"Well, I don't know. I want to call my mom."

"I think that is a great idea," said Sheila, showing Jenine to a telephone and whispering to Gloria, "I'm so proud of you."

"So am I," said Reginald to Gloria. "You never cease to amaze me, girl. I love you."

"I love you more," said Gloria, squeezing Reginald's hand.

"You couldn't possibly, my Happy Reason," said Reginald.

"Reginald, can you come over here and keep Jenine company a minute, while I talk to her mother?" said Sheila from across the room.

"No problem," said Reginald, sitting down next to Jenine.

Gloria looked around the Imani Center and felt at home. And she looked at her man, who already had a girl who wanted to kill herself half an hour ago, and smiled. She thought back on all of the decisions she'd made about her life in the past year—divorcing Stewart, taking up sculpting, dreading her hair, doing satisfying work, and being with the man she loved. And she felt good about every one of those choices. Reginald was the man she was supposed to be with. He was an asset to her life, no matter what his condition. And even though she was happy that Sheila and Reginald were proud of her, she was happiest that she was proud of herself.

ABOUT THE AUTHOR

Joyce Davis is currently the Entertainment Editor at *Honey* magazine. She was previously a staff reporter at *Fortune* magazine before joining *BET Weekend* magazine. Her work has also been featured in *Vibe, Entertainment Weekly, Essence, Sports Illustrated for Women, Black Enterprise, People Online, Heart & Soul,* and *Am I the Last Virgin?* (an anthology of writings by young women of African descent). A graduate of Howard University, she is a native of Decatur, Georgia, and currently resides in Brooklyn, New York.

ON THE WAY TO THE ALTAR

Mikel Husband

For God, my eternal muse.

I would like to thank K for asking the hard questions and getting me started; my parents for always supporting me in whatever I have attempted to do; Joyce for hooking me up; and Yanick, Ingrid, Frank, Connie, Katie, Abe, and so many other writers and editors, who have inspired me to turn a phrase and release my thoughts to the world.

Chapter One

Intro

Looking into the three-panel mirror, Lydia could see herself as she had always dreamed she would look when the time arrived. She was finally getting married, she thought.

This was the seventh dress of the day, and she thought, *This is the one!*

Hmmm, very princess-y, she thought.

She grabbed both sides of the dress and sort of swished the bell-like skirt from side to side. *I'll have to wear my hair up. . . .*

Although the other dresses she looked at were more of an off-white, this one was pure, snow-white. She didn't know why it appealed to her so much. She started to smile, thinking about how she hadn't been so pure since James Reilly during her freshman year at Howard.

What a waste, she thought. *How did I know he was only interested in his own gratification? But I've moved on to smarter, better, bigger men.* She laughed.

It was as if she were ten years old again, trying on her mother's wedding dress upstairs in the sewing room.

Now, as the skirt of the dress swung from side to side, she moved from mirror to mirror, half looking and half dreaming about the day she thought would never happen.

Lydia had been dating Samuel for nearly six years. She was beginning to believe he was never really going to ask her to marry him. He'd moved to Denver first. He had an incredible opportunity with an Internet start-up. At the time, they had only been dating for about a year and were considering breaking it off. She sure did not want to move back to Colorado, but then a job at the second largest TV station in Denver came up *(Thank you, NABJ,* she thought) and she'd moved as well.

It was almost like a sign, she had always thought.

Like most couples in their late twenties, she and Sam were looking to make serious commitments, but weren't sure either one was *the* one.

But, as they say, if it's meant to be, then it's meant to be. And they were obviously meant to be because, as Toni had told her so many times, they had had their share of drama, and she was standing there with a $2,000 wedding dress in front of her momma and her two best friends.

Sure, he had talked about getting married but—like most men, she thought—he only brought it up when his boys were teasing him about taking "that fine woman" away from him. Or, for instance, in their fourth year into, as she called it, "our little life together," she had broken it off and given him an ultimatum.

"The dress is beautiful, Lydia," her mother said from the chair. "But are you sure about that neckline?" she continued.

Lydia looked into the mirror, tilted her head to the left,

and caught Toni's eye in the first mirror. Toni was her girl and, as long as she could remember, had always been there.

"No, I think it's perfect, Mrs. Peters," Toni said.

"Yeah, I love it," chimed in Dara, Lydia's college roommate, who'd recently moved to the area and rounded out their little circle.

"Well, okay." Mrs. Peters sighed. "I was just thinking you would look so much better with shorter sleeves and a few more beads."

"You want me to get the same dress Aunt Silvia wore when I was her flower girl." Lydia thought, *That was in the early eighties, and she's crazy if she thinks—*

"I always loved that dress," her mother said, obviously not thinking realistically about what her daughter really wanted.

"Well, I won't make a decision yet, okay, Mom?" Lydia huffed like she was sixteen all over again.

Deep down she knew her mother was happy for her, but she also understood from her childhood that her mother always administered a pinch of disapproval with her love, making it nearly impossible to feel truly happy about whatever Lydia was doing.

She thought about this as she slipped off the dress behind the curtain with her little entourage waiting on the other side.

How will I break the news? she thought. *My mother and father are going to die. I can't believe I'm pregnant!*

Last week, she'd felt something was wrong. Her period was like clockwork. She and Samuel could produce and sell a calendar based on her ovulation. But it had been thirty-four days since her last one, and Lydia had begun to worry.

So, on her weekly trip to Wal-Mart, she'd bought a home-pregnancy test. She'd hid it from Samuel and waited until he went back to his place to take the test.

What's he going to say? she thought. *Samuel is such a damn know-it-all.*

"Baby, I know you," she could hear him saying. "We have a few days before the next one drops."

I told him we were out of condoms and he needed to pick some up on the way to the house. If he would just do as I say, she thought. *Oh, well.*

"Lydia," called her mother from the other side of the curtain, snatching her back into the moment. "If this is not the dress you are going to get, we are ready to go for lunch."

Toni and Dara looked at each other and laughed.

"Yes, Your Highness," Dara said. "If you are ready."

"I'm coming," Lydia said, buttoning up her jeans. "I just need to put my shoes on and we can go."

Pushing back the red faded curtain a few minutes later, Lydia found only Toni waiting for her.

"Where'd they go?" she asked.

"Your mother said she was on her way to your car and you know your girl, Dara went running right after her," Toni answered.

"I hate that," Lydia said. "Dara has always been so far up my mother's ass."

"Um-hmmm." Toni smirked.

"At least my mother has finally found a true disciple. I know my mother wishes Dara was her daughter. Only Dara doesn't know she's being led to the dark side," Lydia said, laughing.

"They can't help themselves, girl," Toni said. "Don't even sweat it.

"So, when are you going to tell Samuel?" Toni asked, changing the subject.

"Huh?" said Lydia, still thinking about her mother and Dara.

"Hello, the test? When are you going to break the news to Mr. Thomas?" Toni wanted to know.

"Oh, not until I go to see Dr. Woo," Lydia answered. "I don't want to get him all worked up until I know for sure. I have an appointment with her next week."

Trying to close on a commission, the saleswoman approached Lydia.

"Ma'am, did you want to put down a deposit for any of the dresses?" she said. "We could order any of them and have it here for you in a month."

"Not today. I'm still not sure," Lydia said politely, knowing that, if anything, by the time the wedding came she wouldn't be wearing anything that tight.

As they walked through the door Lydia had a vision of herself walking down the aisle in a green hospital gown with her father holding on to her left arm and her right hand on her hip.

Toni continued her inquisition.

"I don't know why you are tripping," Toni said, flipping her hair and smiling. "I could tell by looking at you from my seat in the store. Your face looks fatter."

"Shut up, Toni," Lydia said. "It does not. I look fine. Even if the test was right, I'm only a little more than a month late.

"It could just be stress," she continued. "I mean, this wedding is driving me crazy, and he just proposed last month. Between my mother and his, I'm going to need a lot of sedatives just to get down the aisle. And work, you know how crazy my boss is."

Toni just smiled. She had known Lydia since the fifth grade, and Lydia knew Toni could tell. For some reason, they were fated to be friends. Toni instinctively knew what was going on with Lydia. Even when Toni went away to Spelman, she would call Lydia in the wee hours of the morning and know something was going on. It was just how the two of them had always been.

"All right," Toni said sarcastically. "Mother knows best." She laughed.

"Girl, be quiet, there they are," Lydia said, closing in on Dara and her mother. "Not a word."

Chapter Two

The Doctor's Office

"Hey, Lydia," said Sara from the nurse's desk.

"How are you?" she replied. "How's your daughter?"

"She's fine. Her field hockey team made the finals," said Dr. Woo's receptionist.

"That's great," said Lydia, smiling. "I'm glad to hear it."

"Didn't you just have an appointment last month, Lydia?" inquired Sara.

"Yeah," Lydia said, trying to come up with a reason, but knowing Sara would ultimately know why she was there to see the doctor.

Sara had been Dr. Julia Woo's receptionist longer than Lydia had been coming to this doctor's office. She could tell each of Dr. Woo's patients all their business almost better than the nurses that worked there could.

"Okay, fill out the form and have a seat. I'll pull your chart," said the heavyset woman behind the counter.

Lydia put down her purse and jacket on the couch, sat

down with the sheet of paper, and began looking for a pen. In the background she could hear the familiar voice of Judge Mablean on *Divorce Court.*

"Sara, can I change the channel?" she asked.

"No." Sara looked up. "Why?"

"Well, I told myself I wasn't going to watch that mess anymore," Lydia said. "It may sound crazy, but ever since getting engaged, I get irritated with people who don't take marriage seriously."

"Girl, you need to cut it out." Sara laughed. "You'll be all right. Dr. Woo will see you sooner than you can get up and change the channel. That's sweet, though."

Lydia had to laugh to herself. Before Sam proposed, she would close her office door at work and turn her TV set on to watch the foolishness. She loathed for it to be found out she was a fan, but she couldn't help it. Like a doe caught in the headlights of an oncoming truck, Lydia was hooked.

How could you not be? It was silliness. Maybe it was her arrogance, but she always got such satisfaction knowing her and Sam's marriage would never fall to the depths of those on the show who shared with the world their marital problems and sued each other over $250 for some raggedy clothes. It was madness, but she had to admit, it was amusing to watch.

"Here you go," Lydia said, handing the form to Sara.

"Have a seat while I give this to Dr. Woo," said Sara, moving through the hallway.

With Mablean questioning why the young couple had gotten married in the first place, Lydia began thinking of how she was going to tell Sam the news.

I know he'll be happy, she thought. *He has been talking a lot about having children lately,* she rationalized. *I mean, we both aren't getting any younger.*

"Lydia," Sara said. "Come on back."

Lydia gathered up her stuff and walked through the door.

Judy, one of the nurses employed in the office, led her down the hall to get all her vital statistics.

"Put your coat and stuff on the chair and change into this gown so I can get your weight," Judy said.

No matter how many times she went to the doctor, Lydia always wished she could skip this part. It wasn't like her weight was a problem. She was actually in very good shape—not overweight but not too skinny. She just felt, like many women, she, too, was caught up in that great American pasttime—preoccupation with one's weight.

"One hundred thirty-five," Judy announced, writing the number on the top of the loose-leaf page in Lydia's folder.

The nurse led Lydia into an examination room halfway to the back of the doctor's office. As soon as Lydia put her jacket and purse on the chair, she jumped up on the examination table so Judy could get her blood pressure.

"One hundred twenty-five over eighty-two," Judy repeated to herself as if Lydia weren't sitting there.

"Have a seat," the nurse said. "Dr. Woo will be right in."

"Lydia," Dr. Julia Woo said, sweeping into the examination room. The middle-aged Chinese woman had been Lydia's OB-GYN since she'd moved to the city five years ago for the job at NABJ. Lydia liked her from the start. Barely five feet two inches, with a sharp salt-and-pepper bob, Dr. Woo was like a trusted aunt, Lydia'd always thought. She was incredibly knowledgeable, with a great bedside manner.

But today, Dr. Woo was a bit puzzled as to the repeat visit by her young patient, whom she'd just seen and given a somewhat clean bill of health just a month or so ago.

"How are you?" Dr. Woo said, opening up Lydia's folder and looking at the form she'd filled out at Sara's request.

"Hello, Dr. Woo. How are you?" Lydia responded

instinctively as one would, having grown up with Southern parents. "I feel fine, but I need for you to confirm something for me. I believe I am pregnant."

"Oh," the motherly doctor let slip. "Really? What makes you think that?"

Lydia relayed the story of missing her period after being like clockwork since she was thirteen years old. She explained that she'd gone back and counted the days and taken a store-bought pregnancy test a few days earlier. She wanted to believe the box test—not to mention Toni—but wanted to be medically sure.

Dr. Woo told her it was not a problem. She had Judy come in and take a blood sample to run the test. While the blood flowed from Lydia's arm through the needle into the capsule, Dr. Woo took the opportunity to run down to the supply closet and prepare a folder full of information regarding healthy pregnancy, which she gave to all of her patients on the road to motherhood. The folder included pamphlets on folic acid, staying active, medicines and foods to stay away from, and even a few *New York Times* articles from its health section about advances and theories about having a healthy pregnancy.

"If you can wait around for a half hour," Dr. Woo said, coming back into the room, "we can confirm your feelings."

Lydia smiled. "Thanks, Dr. Woo. I'll be out front in the lobby."

Judy took the blood specimen down the hall to the women who worked in the laboratory.

Lydia jumped down from the exam table and changed back into her clothes. She walked to the front of the office and made a joke with Sara, who was now thoroughly involved in the misdealing being argued in front of Judge Joe Brown.

"Don't you think he's really handsome, Lydia?" the receptionist asked.

"Actually, I do," Lydia said. "I think he looks like what Samuel will look like in about ten to twelve years."

Lydia chuckled to herself. Sam hated it when she said that. *But for real,* she thought. *Sam's about five quarter-pounders with cheese away from Judge Joe's weight, and he has a round face, dark coarse wavy hair, and light complexion, just like the judge.*

Placing all her stuff on the couch and acknowledging the pregnant Latina sitting on the couch across from her, Lydia pulled out her folder and cell phone.

She was now in work mode. As she looked through the list of story ideas her staff was pursuing for their show in the coming weeks, Lydia dialed her assistant Andrea's number, pulled her hair back, and wrapped a brown scrunchy around the short ponytail.

Andrea answered and put her on hold. Waiting for her young assistant to pick up the line, Lydia heard the Muzak interrupted by the beep of another call coming in.

"Hello," Lydia clicked over.

"Hey, my sister, where are you?" her old college roommate inquired. "I called your office and they said you were out. For someone who's supposedly in charge, you sure don't watch the troops that much."

"And how are you this afternoon, Dara?" Lydia jumped in. "I'm sorry, when did you officially turn into my mother?"

"Well, I think the exact day was August 29th, sophomore year, when you got bumped from the room you thought you had and moved into my room," Dara said matter-of-factly. "But that's not what I called about."

"Speaking of your mom, we were talking, and we decided to make a few more reservations for you to look at dresses this coming weekend," Dara continued.

Damn, Lydia thought. She couldn't even be mad. Toni and Dara were her maids of honor, and she knew Toni had given up the reigns to Dara long ago. Dara was overly organized, which she thought was a good thing—at times.

"That's fine," Lydia said, hiding the reluctance in her voice. "I'll pick up my mom and come to your house first; then we can all drive together."

"Great, I'll call Toni and tell her ol' trifling butt to meet us . . ." Lydia started to tune her out and pulled out another folder. "So it's set," Dara rambled on. "I'll call your mom and set it all up. This is so great, Lydia. I'm so happy for you and Sam. I'm determined, we will find you the perfect dress."

"Yes, we will. Thank you so much, Dara, for taking care of everything. You know you are my girl," Lydia agreed. "Let me go, I have Andrea on the other line."

Dara assured her friend she would indeed make the reservations and make all the calls. Dara was all about business, so it was best to give her a task and let her do her thing. As much as she hated to admit it, Lydia needed Dara. She had been a source of comforting and bona fide friendship for the past thirteen years.

Clicking over, Lydia could hear Andrea having a conversation with David, one of the anchors of the show she produced.

"Hey, Andy," the boss said into the phone. "I read the changes you made in the AOL memo, so you can finally fax it to Malik in New York."

Lydia went on for about seven more minutes firing off instructions to her dutiful assistant. It was a week before November sweeps for the TV station, and she needed to have all the reporters' reels so she could make the final decisions as to whose projects would get top billing and whose segments would get cut down or possibly cut entirely.

"I'll be back in the office in about an hour," Lydia said, looking at her watch. "Please make sure everyone has their tapes ready and is back from lunch so we can start this meeting on time for once.''

''No problem. Consider it done,'' Andrea said.

Lydia pressed the End button, put the phone back in her purse, and went back to reviewing the news segment descriptions in the folder.

''Lydia, Dr. Woo would like to talk with you again,'' Sara said over the front desk. ''C'mon back.''

For the second time, Lydia picked up her stuff and walked back to the exam room she'd sat in nearly an hour ago. Dr. Woo was waiting for her with a large folder sitting on her clipboard.

''Have a seat,'' Dr. Woo instructed.

''Well, you are definitely pregnant,'' the doctor went on. ''Congratulations.''

Wow, was all Lydia could think. She had been thinking she was with child, but actually to hear it from her doctor was another thing entirely. A sense of pride swelled in her. She felt her stomach and just smiled.

''But, Lydia, there were some irregularities with the blood sample,'' the doctor informed her. ''I want you to come in again on Thursday. I need to do some additional tests and should have the results by then.''

Dr. Woo handed Lydia the folder chock full of information regarding what every woman should do from the moment she learns she's pregnant.

''What does that mean?'' Lydia inquired, suddenly feeling a bit nervous. ''Is the baby okay? I thought I checked out fine last month.''

''You did. But there's something else in your blood sample, and I just want to run some more tests to make sure you and the baby have a smooth progression during the nine months,'' the doctor said, calming her sense of anxiety.

Dr. Woo escorted her out of the room and down the hall

and told Sara to make an appointment for Thursday. Lydia could not stop smiling.

I'm pregnant, she thought, laughing to herself. *So much for Dara's outing to look for the perfect dress.*

Lydia felt extremely happy. All she could think about was that she was about to be a mom. She would have to tell Sam immediately. Plans for the wedding would have to be moved up or back or forgotten entirely.

No, she thought. *We have to get married before the baby is born, even if that means going to the justice of the peace.*

Lydia beamed all the way back to the office. The meeting went as all her weekly meetings did: It started late, there was way too much bickering back and forth, but a sequence was hammered out and she put out as many fires as she could.

She seemed to have new energy, some of her staffers remarked to each other after the meeting. Lydia went back to her office and worked through a pile of papers six inches high on her desk. While signing off on David's expense report from his shoot in Seattle of a young entrepreneur, it hit her.

She was going to cook Sam his favorite dinner and announce the coming of the first of what she hoped would be three children.

"That's it," she said under her breath. "I'm going to make it a romantic night we'll both remember forever."

Chapter Three

A Bun in the Oven

Lydia was burning up the kitchen—literally. Smoke was coming from the pot on the back burner of her chrome stove. Rushing to turn on the oven's fan, she nearly ripped her new red silk dress.

I've got to be careful, she thought, looking to see if the fabric tore.

"Oh, well, it was only the veggies," she whispered to no one in particular. She opened the freezer and took out the only vegetables left in the iced-over box.

"I really need a maid to take care of all that built-up ice and frost." She laughed. "My momma would be 'shamed!"

Lydia had decided to tell Samuel the good news over a nice dinner and in one of her sexiest dresses.

Well, she thought, *if I'm going to get big as a house, I might as well put some time in this dress now.*

She shouldn't have bought it, but Toni—talking about how every woman should have a really expensive, sexpot dress—talked her into it. And Lydia convinced herself that one day it would come out of the closet and be put to good use.

Tonight it would be, she thought: *It's the dress in which I'm going to tell the man I love he's going to be the father of our first child.*

That is, if she didn't tear it to pieces or spill grease on it trying to cook him one of his favorite meals.

Consumed by the steam coming off the broccoli and swaying in a trance to the Jill Scott album she'd taken from Sam's apartment, Lydia didn't hear him come in the door and put his keys on the table.

Up against the sultry strings and hypnotic drumbeat, Jill was analyzing the method in which she loved her man. Lydia had been feelin' this album ever since it dropped, but this song in particular made her swoon.

"Is it the waaayyy you love me, baybay?" the singer released. "Is it the waaayyy you love me, baybay?"

Sam could tell something was up. He saw the candles burning on the fully detailed dinner table. Table linen, full place settings of silverware, Lydia's grandmother's salt-and-pepper shakers, and the crystal wine glasses. *What is up?* he thought.

She looked amazing to him. Her hair was up and he could see her neck gently covered by individual strands of curled hair.

He knew she obviously wanted to surprise him, but he would turn the tables. He walked softly through the living room into the kitchen.

When he reached the kitchen, before she could turn around, Sam put his hands on her swaying hips and pressed his lips to her neck.

"Ahhhh," Lydia cooed. I didn't hear you come in," she continued as she turned around to face her man.

Sam didn't let her say anything ease, kissing her lips.

Lydia felt excited and felt heat. *Was that the stove or him?* she asked herself.

It doesn't matter; I knew there was a reason I stayed with him this long, she thought to herself.

"So," Sam said, coming up for air. "What's going on?"

"Oh, nothing," Lydia said coyly. "Just do me a favor. Go take a shower and get dressed in one of your suits. The food will be ready when you finish."

"For real, what's the deal? Can't we just eat?" Sam replied.

Actually, Lydia was looking sexy as hell in that dress, and he would have preferred to skip dinner altogether and go right to the dessert.

"Is this a hint about how we don't go out that much?" Sam asked.

"No," Lydia said. "Just do as I ask."

Twenty minutes later, Sam came out of the bedroom, smelling sweet but spicy. Lydia could tell he was wearing the Angel cologne she had bought last week (she knew it would smell good on him when she tested it in the store). She felt a bit turned on looking at him all dressed up and smelling good but she was on a mission.

Sam looked at the table. Roasted pork chops, mashed potatoes, bread and . . .

"Corn?" he blurted out.

"Yeah, well, I kinda burnt the green beans while I was taking a shower and it was the only other thing I had in the fridge."

"It doesn't matter," he said. "It all looks good, baby, thank you."

"Nothing's too good for my man," she joked.

As Lydia started to dish out the food, the two talked about the minutiae of their day. Sam's workday was always filled with something crazy. Being a marketing manager for a small company, he always had a tale of something going wrong to tell Lydia.

Lydia talked about her boss, whom she thought was crazy and felt was about to be fired. Sam had heard the complaints before, but he always obliged her the opportunity to vent.

Sam reached across the table for the potatoes, spilling his glass of wine on the place mats.

Lydia jumped up to wipe up the merlot. "Now, is that how you are going to teach our children how to get what they want?" she asked.

"No, I'm going to tell them to ask the person to pass them what they need," Sam said. "But, since it's just us . . ." he trailed off, flashing her a mouth full of teeth.

"I see," Lydia said, sitting back in her chair.

"So, you never answered my question from way earlier," Sam continued. "Why the clothes and dinner?"

"Well, you know how I've been feeling kinda sick, right?" Lydia started, feeling a bit sheepish.

Sam looked at her and leaned in from his chair.

"I went to the doctor and we're pregnant."

Sam chuckled and jumped up from the table. He knocked the chair over, running to her side of the table.

"Us, what, I don't know what to say," he mumbled.

"Yes, I do!" he said.

"Lyd, really? I'm stunned," he said. "I can't believe it. I'm going to be a daddy. You're going to be a mom. You just found out today?"

"Well, I took a pregnancy test last week, but I wanted to get a professional opinion before I told you."

Sam pulled Lydia up from her chair and hugged her. He kept his grip around her tight for several minutes.

Lydia felt comfortable and happy. She could not move in the embrace. It was a perfect moment, she thought.

To be honest, she replayed all the times in their relationship the subject of children had come up. He had said he wanted children, but she wasn't sure what his reaction would be.

"This is fantastic," Sam said, releasing her from his arms. "Have you told your parents or mine yet?"

"No, I wanted you to be the second person to know."

Sam put his hand on her stomach. "I'm going to be a father," he said aloud to himself.

"1 wanted to tell you so we could tell them together," Lydia continued. "Especially with my mother. You know how she can be."

"Not with this, Lydia—this will soften her up," he reasoned.

I hope so, the pregnant and beaming Lydia thought.

Sam sat down in the chair next to Lydia's. Holding her hand, he inquired how many weeks along she was and when she thought it had happened. She reminded him of their interlude over a month ago sans the protection.

"Sam," Lydia started.

"Yes." He looked in her eyes.

"I do have to go back to Dr. Woo. She said she wanted to run some additional tests."

"Why, you're only thirty-two," Sam said, feeling the concern grow in his mind. "And you're healthy; what's the problem?"

"She didn't say," Lydia said, trying to calm any fears he might have. "She just said she wanted to see me again to make sure everything was fine."

A flag popped up in Sam's mind, but he was busy thinking about his newly planted offspring, and he felt happy.

"It's cool, right? Just go see her and everything will be cool," he said.

"Yeah," Lydia said, trying to hide the concern in her own voice.

"Well, I guess this means you now have kitchen duties, so get to bustin' those suds, my brother," she said, laughing.

"Oh, you think you're slick," Sam replied, smiling at Lydia. "Don't get too comfortable."

As Sam started to clear the table and clean up the kitchen, Lydia began thinking about the other day in the bridal-gown store.

"You know, we are going to postpone the wedding," she said, trying to see what he was thinking.

"Naw, we can move it up," Sam responded. "We haven't put down any deposits yet, right?"

"Yeah, but what are we going to tell our parents?" Lydia said softly.

"Your mom's the only one that's going to trip," Sam said. "My parents and your dad will be cool. Your mom will be all about the hysterics."

"Ohhhh, Laaawd, what about the wedding?" Sam said, doing his best impression of Mrs. Peters. They both laughed.

Lydia moved into the kitchen and pressed her body into Sam's, put her arms around him, and crossed her wrists on his chest. Laying her head on his back, she could hear his heartbeat. The two of them stayed like that as Sam finished up the last pot.

Sam, too, felt the emotions warming his body. He was finally going to be someone's daddy. It was a huge responsibility. He had always figured he and Lydia would have kids. He was happy about it, but felt that he'd just asked Lydia to marry him. Everything was happening so fast. His knees were a little weak, but with the pressure from Lydia gone, he felt reassured.

Yeah, this whole scene is a bit corny, he thought. But then again, he did love her and knew she would have his back no matter what.

As he scraped the last of the plates, Sam thought about the big breakup he and Lydia had had right before she moved to Denver from Washington, D.C. It was ugly, and he'd figured it was over for sure. Sam had been getting cold feet about committing to Lydia. He hadn't been sure she was the one. He was handsome and well educated. There were many ladies who warranted his attention.

He smiled, thinking about how foolish he'd been, getting so caught up in that whole stereotype about women having to fight over the "good" men. He chuckled.

I was tripping, he thought. *Straight tripping.*

"What are you laughing about, honey?" Lydia said, pulling herself away from him.

"Oh, nothing," he said, turning away from the sink and wiping the suds from his hands on the dishtowel on the stove.

"I was just thinking about how happy you make me," Sam cooed, sliding his hands around her neck and bringing her head forward in order for him to kiss her.

"Sam," Lydia started. "I love you for loving me so much—"

"Are you kidding, baby?" Sam interrupted. "I'm indebted to you."

Turning off the light in the kitchen, Sam walked Lydia into the living room and they both sat down on the couch. Sam got up and ran over to the CD rack.

"I know exactly what will put us in the mood," he said slyly.

"Be careful," Lydia broke in. "That's the reason we had this dinner tonight."

They both snickered and Sam returned his attention to the stacks of CDs. Guiding his finger up and down the plastic covers, looking at each name as his finger passed, one caught his eye.

It was an album he had burned for Lydia for Valentine's Day two years ago.

"Ahhhh," Sam said with a smile on his face. "This one is the bomb."

Sam took the CD from its case. It contained twenty of

his favorite love songs. It was an eclectic mix that spanned "If I Were a Bell" by Teena Marie and "Big Brown Eyes" by the Isley Brothers to "Zoom" by the Commodores and "The Lady in My Life" by Michael Jackson.

Sam put the CD in the player, turned up the volume, and walked over to the bar in the corner to pour himself a glass of wine.

As the familiar drumbeat and whine of Maurice White signaled the beginning of Earth, Wind & Fire's "Reasons," Sam stopped just short of the coffee table in front of the couch and pretended to be singing the words to Lydia.

"The reasons, the reasons that we are here," he sang, way off-key.

Lydia just laughed. In that moment she knew she loved him and that he loved her. He was a fool, but he was her fool, and that was enough. She felt in her heart—with Earth, Wind & Fire playing in the background and the father of her child in front of her—they had what it would take to make it, no matter what the situation.

"You're a mess. You know you can't sing," Lydia joked as Sam joined her on the couch. The two spent the night discussing baby names and deciding just how they would break the news to Lydia's parents, who lived in town, and Sam's parents, who lived in Los Angeles. A plan that still would have to be finished in the next week as Lydia fell comfortably asleep on Sam's chest.

For nearly an hour, as Lydia slept easily, Sam's mind went to work on the logistics. He would move into Lydia's apartment. His was small, and he wondered why the two of them wasted so much money on rent when he spent the majority of his time at her place anyway. It was time.

Time to admit he was getting married and ready to make the larger commitment. He was thirty-four years old with a fiancée whom he had been dating for nearly six years. It *was* time for him to get out of what Cameo made so famous—the single life.

Finishing his glass of wine, Sam, too, nodded off.

Together, as one little family, the three of them slept on the couch in one of the best slumbers either Sam or Lydia had had in a long, long time.

Chapter Four

On the Job

"Lydia," Andrea said, poking her head in the door. "John called and said he was coming down to your office to talk with you about Jeff's segment."

"He knows I'm here?" Lydia said quietly.

I just walked in ten minutes ago. I swear he has a camera in one of these potted plants, she thought.

John was Lydia's hard-nosed boss. He was one of the last curmudgeons left at KTRW from the seventies when journalism was still a men's club. The twenty-four-hour news cycle of the nineties left John reeling. Unfortunately for him, he didn't see the train coming, and got off the track a little too late. Thus the world and the TV station passed him by.

Since he was executive producer of Lydia's show, *Urban Express,* she had to fight lots of battles with him—too many, if you asked her. Her show was news and features for a younger audience, and Lydia felt John just wasn't in touch. He was divorced, with no kids even to know or be around the culture. They had a fight at least once every two weeks and usually had to go to the editorial director, Taylor Hicks, as a tiebreaker.

"Damn, what does he want now?" Lydia said, putting on her left shoe and turning on the TV set on the corner of the credenza behind her desk.

Not two seconds later, John, looking gruff as usual, swung open her office door.

"Lydia, how are you this morning?" the balding man asked. "Glad to see you make it in this early."

It took everything Lydia had not to say something rude, although she did imagine that scene from the beginning of *The Matrix* when Trinity kicked the crap out of the cop.

If only fantasy could be for real, she thought.

"Hi, John. How are you? Is that a new tie?" she said, disarming her crabby boss.

"Uh, yes, actually," John said, looking a bit lost.

Smoothing his tie with a slight smile on his face, John moved farther into the office and sat down in one of the chairs opposite Lydia's desk. He had a manila folder in his hand.

"Andrea said you wanted to talk to me," Lydia said, sitting back in her chair. "What can I help you with?"

"I was going over these expense reports from your staff," John said, getting a little red in the cheeks.

He opened the folder and began to flip through the reports, dropping some of the receipts on the floor.

"Compared with the other staffs," he continued, "your people seem to be a bit extravagant."

Lydia had fought this battle before. Her staff's budget was fine. She always made her numbers. The entertainment expenses could be a little high, but she generally cut costs in other areas.

"John, we've done this dance before," she said matter-of-factly. "My show is not over budget. I'm sorry if you don't understand some of the expenses, but running an entertainment and news show is not easy when you want to be objective."

John interrupted by quoting a $200 invoice with no receipts.

"As we've gone over before, Jeff and his crew cover the streets. He's working on a piece about underground parties. He just can't ask for receipts at these functions," she continued.

"I trust Jeff, and his work always speaks for him. He always brings back the story and it's always good." She defended her top reporter, knowing this was more about her promotion last month than anything else.

"I'll talk with him, to tell him to try and keep things in line, but when he's out there working, I'm more worried about him gaining entry than receipts."

"Okay, Lydia," John mumbled. "It's just my job to scrutinize a department's overall budget. It all comes back on me when we have financial issues. You know I hate having to go into Taylor's office and explain why we are spending more money than the station has."

"No problem. I'll talk with Jeff about it," Lydia said—anything to end this conversation.

John left her office. Both John and Lydia had received promotions last month. Only John was resentful of his promotion. Taylor had promoted John to an advisory position that had little effect on the day-to-day operations of the news staff that kept many of the younger members.

Lydia was talented and worked like a dog championing the ideas of those under her. Taylor saw great potential in her and moved her up for it.

Andrea poked her head in and smiled. She looked down the hall, came into Lydia's domain, and shut the door.

"So . . . ," Andrea inquired.

"You know how he is," Lydia said. "Anything to let me know he's still around."

They both laughed.

"Toni called twice," Andrea announced. "What's up? She was all urgent-sounding, like you need to tell her something."

"It's official, I'm pregnant," Lydia nearly squealed.

Andrea jumped up from the chair, clapping and running around the desk to give Lydia a hug.

"I'm so happy for you," Andrea said. "Wow, I knew it. I knew. I could tell something was different about you."

"No, you didn't," Lydia said, smiling at her assistant. "I'm only a little over a month."

"Wow," said Andrea. "What did Sam say? Is he excited or what?"

Lydia moved to the cabinets in the back of the office and riffled through some papers on the top shelf.

"He is," Lydia said, hiding her blushing face. "I cooked dinner for him last night and told him. I couldn't believe how excited he was."

"When are you going to tell your mother?" Andrea said, half laughing.

"I don't know. I think Sam wanted to invite them all over this weekend for brunch and tell them," Lydia said, turning and facing Andrea.

Andrea turned in her seat halfway toward Lydia and the cabinet and listened.

"I can't believe I'm thirty-two years old and I feel like the time I was sixteen and got caught with a boy in the house." Lydia laughed as she cupped her mouth thinking about that event so long ago.

"My mother's going to die, and *his* mother. Lord, be with me." Lydia burst out in laughter.

The green light blinked on Lydia's second line on the phone. The ringing came instantly.

"That's your second line," Andrea pointed out. "Must be Toni again. I'll go get you some coffee," she said, walking to the door.

"Girl, what?!" Lydia screamed into the speakerphone, laughing.

"How you know it's me?" her friend said. Lydia could see Toni's smile through the receiver.

"Who else is calling me at 9:30 A.M. on a number I rarely give out?" responded Lydia.

Lydia could only hear laughter on the other end of the line.

"Well, you know why I'm calling," Toni said. "Is it yes or no?"

"Yes," Lydia screamed playfully into the phone.

"Ha, I knew it last week when we talked. You should have just listened to me and saved your insurance company the trip to Dr. Woo," Toni said, laughing. "Great, I can go collect my lunch money for this week," she continued slyly.

"What?" Lydia said, bewildered.

"Oh, I just put a little pool together here in my office. Girl, them heifers down the hall owe me eighty-five dollars." Toni laughed.

"Okay, Toni, hold up," Lydia snapped. "Why is it that everybody in your office knows all my business? Don't you have clients or something to keep y'all busy over there?" she said, getting annoyed.

More laughter came through the phone.

"Girl, are you kidding? You and Sam are as good as it gets. You two are better than *The Bold and the Beautiful.* Plus, momma needs a new pair of shoes—want to go to Aldo's at lunch?"

Holding the receiver six inches from her ear to keep from

going deaf from Toni's chuckles, Lydia knew she could not be mad. That was her girl, no matter how trifling she was.

"Yeah, girl," Lydia said. "Meet me at the Starbucks at one-thirty and we'll walk over from there. Bye."

Chapter Five

A Second Visit

Lydia had heard what Dr. Woo had said, but she wasn't sure. It was as if she were dreaming, floating along. Eavesdropping on the conversation of someone else, but definitely not her.

"I'm sorry," Lydia mumbled to the doctor, not understanding. "What did you just tell me?"

"Lydia, you have tested positive for HIV," Dr. Woo said sympathetically.

Lydia felt numb. It was as if she had left her own body. She was floating in the room, watching what she thought was the end of her life unfold. The clock continued to tick. The bird in the tree outside the window continued to build its nest. She could hear people talking in the hallway. She could even see Dr. Woo put her hand on her shoulder and mouth something to her, but she heard nothing. *Was she in a coma?* she thought. The world had continued to move and grow, yet she felt she was being passed by.

"Lydia, do you need a cup of water?" the Asian woman offered. "I need for you to respond to me."

"I'm—I'm sorry, Dr. Woo," Lydia answered with tears forming in her eyes. "What does this mean? Am I going to die?"

Taking some tissues from the box across the room, Dr. Woo walked back over to Lydia and offered them to her to dry her eyes.

The news was unfortunate, the doctor thought, but she had seen it before: young women in the prime of their lives who were contracting the disease. *It's not because of ignorance,* the doctor thought to herself, *it's sheer laziness and self-deception disguised as manners. No one wants to be the one to bring up the question. Everyone's so busy being polite. People need to ask the questions before the clothes start coming off.*

Yes, it may seem a bit rude, but it's an appropriate question to ask. It's your life you are putting into that person's hands. The risk is far too great.

It was the year 2001, nearly twenty years after the first HIV and AIDS cases began. It was amazing to Dr. Woo that young people continued to have unprotected sex, and what was worse, they didn't even inquire about the sexual habits of the people they were most intimate with. It just made no sense.

She let Lydia cry a bit more before placing her hand on Lydia's left shoulder to let her know she was still there.

Raising her head out of her lap, Lydia took more tissues from the box and began wiping her face. The tears had smeared her makeup, and she could only imagine how crazy she looked. But it wasn't nearly as crazy as she felt.

Lydia had butterflies in her stomach. She felt she was losing everything. What would she tell Sam and their parents? Could she just go away and not say anything? *How cowardly,* she thought.

Would she tell Toni and Dara? She just didn't know the answer to anything. What about the people at work? *Who has to know? Does anyone outside of my doctor have to or need to know?* What was she going to do?

"What does this mean for the baby? What's going to happen to it?" Lydia asked as more tears ran down her face.

"I want you to know that HIV is no longer a death sentence, Lydia," Dr. Woo started to tell her.

Dr. Woo pulled out a thick folder from her clipboard. It was the packet she gave to all of her patients if diagnosed with HIV. It contained many brochures about the disease, the current drug treatments, and information regarding how to go about adjusting their lives.

"Lydia, I want you to take this home and read every bit of it, okay?" the doctor urged.

"It's all about the disease and the many ways people today are living with it," she continued. "It outlines the different drugs that are available. I would also encourage you to speak with Dr. Henderson. She runs a group for women with HIV. Her card is also in the folder."

Lydia was still sobbing. She was hearing Dr. Woo, but still a bit shaken up. How had she gotten the disease? How could this have happened to her? She had always been careful, but given the news she just received, she wasn't as careful as she had thought. Then it hit her.

Oh my God, Sam needs to get tested, she thought, horrified. Again, the tears began to flow.

Lydia looked down at her watch. *Two-thirty P.M.,* she thought. *I've been gone for more than two hours. I need to call Andrea and let her know I'm not coming back to work.*

Standing up from the chair, Lydia walked to the mirror and began to wipe her face clean. Using the soap, she gently washed her face as Dr. Woo watched from her desk.

"So, Lydia, I'm going to write you a prescription," Dr. Woo said. "You will need to see another doctor who specializes in the disease, but I can still be your OB-GYN in regards to dealing with the pregnancy. I want you to make an appointment with Sara to come back in two weeks. Okay?''

Lydia listened to her doctor intensely and agreed to come back in.

As she began to open the door, Dr. Woo touched her hand. ''We will get you through this, Lydia. Really, nowadays it really is a case of a long-term chronic disease,'' she told her patient empathically. ''Please call Dr. Henderson.''

Pushing her way through the heavy revolving door in the lobby of the building, Lydia took out her phone and proceeded to call Andrea. She wasn't paying attention to what she was doing as she walked right into the street.

A loud horn blew as Lydia stood there like a doe caught in the headlights of a truck in a dark forest. All she heard was the screeching of tires skidding to avoid hitting her. Luckily, a large man was watching the event unfold and pulled Lydia back onto the sidewalk.

''You should pay more attention there, honey,'' said the man nearly twice her size.

''I'm sorry. Thank you . . . thank you very much,'' Lydia mumbled. Again, her tears began to well up. ''I'm having such a bad day.''

''Well,'' continued the man, ''no matter how bad it is, there's no reason to step out in noonday traffic. I hope you have a better day.''

Lydia put her hand on her chest. She could feel her heart racing. She was a wreck. She waved to the man as he stepped away.

''Thank you so much,'' she said as the man walked into the building she had just left.

I need to get it together. I'm tripping, she thought. *I need to go home.*

After waiting for her light to turn green and the Walk sign to turn white, Lydia rushed to her car. She unlocked the door, put her purse in the passenger sweat, got in, and just sat there. She put her gloved hands on the steering wheel and placed her head on her hands.

I have HIV, she thought. A cold streak went through her spine. She'd just gotten her promotion, she was pregnant and about to get married. So much, it seemed, was going perfectly in her life. Now this. The world could be so cruel, she thought.

"Lord, what did I do?" she asked.

At the sudden blast of noise from a car horn, Lydia was jolted from her self-pity. Again, a horn blew. She turned to see another woman in a green Saab blowing her horn, as if that was the polite way to get her parking space.

Lydia felt like rolling down her window and cursing the woman out, but it wasn't her fault things had gotten so out of control today. She simply put the key in the ignition and started up her midnight blue BMW.

I'm going to be nice, Lydia's thoughts continued. *But she'd better stop blowing that horn.*

Driving down the street in the direction to get to her apartment, Lydia took out her phone and hit the memory number for Andrea's desk.

"Lydia Peters's office," her dutiful assistant answered on the other end of the line.

"Hey, Andy," Lydia said, her lip quivering. "I'm going home, okay? If anyone needs me, they can call me on my cell phone."

"Are you okay?" Andrea asked instinctively.

"Yeah, I'm fine. I just need some rest," Lydia continued.

"Okay, call me if you need me to do anything," Andrea offered.

* * *

Parking her car in the space she used but for some reason never got billed for, she sat for more than two minutes in the driver's-side seat and just stared at the brick wall in front of her.

"Hey, Lydia," Alex said, startling her. "I haven't seen you or Sam—isn't that his name?—in a while. How's it going?"

Alex lived down the hall from her in 4R. He was cool. When she'd first moved into the apartment, he'd seen her moving in and helped. He was cool, but nosy. And she wasn't in the mood.

"Hey, Alex," Lydia said, opening her door.

"I'm on my way to the gym and then the grocery store. What are you doing home this early?" Alex inquired.

"I'm not feeling well; no biggy," Lydia said, locking her doors. "See ya."

Lydia walked quickly toward the elevator to avoid any more conversation with Alex. She just couldn't take it. Plus she didn't want to start crying in front of him—she'd never get rid of him then.

She pushed the Up button and held on tight to her workbag and purse. *What is it about bad news that just paralyzes you?* she thought.

Just then the familiar ding, the one elevators use to let you know they have arrived, made Lydia smile. *I'm home,* she thought. *Maybe I can sleep and I'll awake from this nightmare.*

Looking for the keys in her purse, Lydia rushed down the hall and found them just as she arrived at her door. She quickly unlocked the door and pushed it open.

"Damn him," Lydia said aloud. She began to cry. She

was looking at a dozen white-and-blush roses in the most beautiful vase.

Lydia shut the door, walked across the room to the dinner table, and took the card from the little plastic fork

I hope you and our child had a good day today.
Stevie Wonder said it so perfectly:
You are the sunshine of my life.

Love,
Sam

Still holding onto the card, Lydia went into the kitchen and got herself a bottle of water. *I need to call him. I have to tell him what Dr. Woo said,* she thought.

She moved down the hall to her bedroom as she had so many times before. She decided on a long, hot shower, and then she would call Sam at his job to make sure he came directly over after work.

The shower did feel good. She wondered if she could just stay in the shower for the rest of her life. As the steam rose up and the hot spray of water relaxed her muscles, she thought about how her tears blended so well with the shower water and no one had to see her in pain. What was it about hot water that made everything else secondary? *Maybe it's our suppressed memories of the safety of our mothers' wombs,* she thought, closing her eyes and letting the water wash over the top of her head.

Speaking of wombs, what was she going to do to keep her child from being born with the virus? She had to look over the materials Dr. Woo had given her and make an appointment with the specialist she'd recommended.

"I'm sorry, baby," Lydia said, rubbing her stomach.

Chapter Six

Honey, I Have Something to Tell You

After getting out of the shower, Lydia put on her bathrobe and went into the kitchen to make some tea. She put some water in the kettle and put it on the burner. Looking in the upper shelves for the tea, it suddenly struck Lydia that she needed to find out from whom she'd contracted the virus.

This thought sent a bit of terror through her whole body. Again, she thought, *How am I going to tell Sam that he needs to get tested?* She could not believe this was happening to her.

How could she have gotten the virus? It wasn't by intravenous drug taking. It couldn't have been. Yeah, she'd smoked pot a bit in undergrad, but had shut it down with the mention of anything that had to be injected. That was crazy, she had always thought. Plus, she wasn't too excited by needles, especially just to have five minutes of pseudo-elation.

It had to be someone she'd slept with. *But, who—?* she wondered.

The steam whistle on the kettle blew and Lydia moved

to turn the stove off. Looking for the sugar container, she put the tea bag in her favorite mug and shuffled over to the dinner table, where the sugar sat.

"It's not like I was a 'ho," she said to herself, thinking of the guys she had slept with. "Three in college, none the first two years after I graduated, then one each the next two years," she said to herself, picturing each guy in her mind.

I don't even speak with more than half of them, she thought, stirring her tea. *This is going to be hard.*

Moving to the couch, she curled herself up and then thought about Simon Hall. It was the first time she'd thought of his old crazy behind since leaving Washington, D.C. He'd been her rebound when Sam decided to move to Denver and she broke up with him.

Simon had come on the scene just in the nick of time; at least that's what she'd believed during that moment. *Why, oh why did I go to that club that night?* she thought.

He had a honey-brown complexion with beeee-autiful locks. He was straight out of the Alayé calendar. He'd been so much fun in the first couple of months of their relationship, which was exactly what she'd needed after ending her and Sam's year-old relationship.

Sam was so selfish, she remembered. *He could only see what was good for him. Now look at him.*

Look at them: They were about to get married and things had suddenly changed so drastically. Lydia's thoughts went back to those summer days in 1996 when she and Simon had just hung out. He'd been a struggling musician, heavy on the struggling. But Lydia had had faith in him. Plus, he'd been so very different from the other guys she had dated up to that point in her life.

Lydia dropped her cup. What tea she had left in the cup was now all over the floor, coffee table, couch, and her robe. *It was him,* she was convinced. She got up, went to get

a small towel from the hall closet, and began to wipe up
what liquid she could.

Simon did do a lot of drugs, she finished.

Shaking her head, she also thought about all the times
they had had sex without a condom.

"What the hell was I thinking about?" She sighed.

In fact, his drug usage was one of the main reasons she
had had to end that relationship. Simon had been out of
control. She'd wanted to hang out with him and enjoy life,
but wanted to do so without having him impaired by drugs.

Lydia knew finding the source of the HIV was not going
to be as easy as that, but at least she knew he was definitely
a point in her past where she could start the investigation.

If only I had kept my legs closed like my parents told me,
she thought. *But it's even too late to go there.*

Lydia was working on her second cup of Earl Grey when
she heard keys rattle in the door lock. Panic hit her. She
wasn't ready to talk with Sam. She needed to relax more
so she would be calm while explaining the morning's events.

"Oh, hey, baby," Sam said, startled. He wasn't expecting
Lydia to be home. He had taken a half day so he could start
moving his stuff into Lydia's place.

He already had a great deal of his wardrobe in her closets
and drawers. But he had given notice to his apartment building's management that he was moving out and packed a
few boxes of his stuff. He'd wanted to bring some of it over
and put it out around the apartment to see if Lydia would
have noticed.

Sam knew she would. She knew when he moved something. It didn't help that he was pretty messy.

Putting the box on the dark walnut dinner table, Sam
asked her how her day was.

"Why are you home in the middle of the day in a bathrobe?'' Sam asked. ''What happened at work? Did Whatshis-face say something to you?''

Sam knew all about problems she was having at work with John.

''Baby, you can quit that job after you have the baby,'' he said sympathetically. ''I'm up for a promotion anyway; we'll have more than enough money—''

''No, no, it's not that,'' Lydia cut him off. ''Plus, I love my job. You don't want me to work?''

''Hey, if you think you will be up to it . . . but I'm thinking this baby won't be the only one we have,'' Sam continued, moving toward Lydia in the kitchen. He gently kissed her on the forehead.

''What are you doing here with that box?'' she said, holding her cup in one hand and pointing to the box with the other.

''Oh, that.'' Sam walked to the box and began to open it up. ''Well, I've been thinking ever since you told me about the baby.''

''Thinking's good,'' Lydia joked.

''Anyway,'' he responded to her little gibe. ''I was think-ing we should move in together, and I was going to start putting stuff around the house and see how long it would take you to realize I moved in.''

Lydia laughed. ''That's cute, but I would have found you out after a day or two. If you moved in, I'm sure there would be an even bigger mess here than usual.''

She walked through the kitchen and sat back on the couch. ''I would have known.''

''Well, I'm going to go down to the car and bring in the rest of the stuff,'' Sam said, picking up the box and putting it on the top shelf of the hall closet.

''Honey,'' Lydia started. There was a long pause as Sam came from the hall and moved closer to where she was seated. "I need to talk with you about what happened at Dr. Woo's."

"Whaa . . . what's wrong?" Sam asked, holding back a growing sense of dread. He sat on the couch next to her feet, which were partly curled under her, and put his hand on her thigh.

He did not know what to think. A million terrible things went racing through his mind. What was he supposed to believe? Lydia was home in the middle of the afternoon and she looked depressed. All he could think was that something was wrong with their child.

Lydia moved so that she was facing Sam directly. She put her hands in his lap and looked him in the eyes. Tears began to fall. The image of Lydia crying mixed with the heavy silence in the apartment scared Sam. Lydia could feel the nervousness in his hands as they slightly quivered.

Lydia wiped her face with the sleeve of her robe. She started the conversation that, for good or bad, would change both of their lives forever.

"Sam," Lydia said, barely opening up her lips. "When I went to the doctor to get the pregnancy test, Dr. Woo found something else in my blood—"

"Cancer," Sam interrupted loudly. "Oh my God. We are just getting started, Lydia. We both have really good insurance, we can get through—"

Lydia put her index finger on Sam's mouth, quieting him.

"No, I can't say it's cancer, Sam," she told him. "It's not that easy."

She paused, took a breath, and said, "Sam, I tested positive for HIV and I need for you to get tested."

Sam was stunned. He could not move, nor did he know what to say. He knew every couple had their problems, but why this and why now? Things were going so well, he thought. He hung his head.

An uncomfortable silence filled the air for nearly five

minutes before Sam made a move or said a thing. Lydia, not knowing what else to say, just sat there, still and quiet, with tears steadily flowing down her cheeks.

"Lydia," Sam started. "What the hell are you telling me?"

He took his hands away from hers, got up from the couch, and began to pace back and forth in front of the coffee table. Lydia was not sure what he was going to do or say, but she knew it was not going to be pleasant.

"I mean, what the fuck does this mean? Do I have HIV, too, now? How the hell did you get it? What am I supposed to say or do here?" Sam continued, his voice getting louder with each word.

"Sam," Lydia tried to say.

"What else are you going to tell me?" He yelled. "Will the baby be born with the virus, too?"

"Not necessarily," she said sheepishly.

Sam collapsed into the chair near the entertainment center. Holding his head in his hands, he began to cry. Lydia, still unsure of what to say to Sam, stayed in the couch on the other side of the room. She positioned herself sitting forward with her feet on the floor.

"How could you do this to me?" Sam angrily shouted. "This is going to ruin us." Sam was beyond upset. All he could see was that the plans he had were all being shattered. Just five minutes ago, he was happily moving his stuff into his future wife's apartment, and now she was sitting across from him, telling him she had HIV and he might as well.

"I can't believe this," Sam said while getting up and storming across the room. "I just do not believe this."

On his way to the kitchen, Sam hit one of Lydia's twenty-four-inch speakers and knocked over her aunt's crystal vase. The crash of the glass on the floor scared Lydia, who jumped up at the action. Water was everywhere.

"Watch out, Sam, don't cut yourself," she warned.

"Oh, so now you're worried about my health and well-being," Sam said spitefully.

"That's not fair and you know it," Lydia said, walking past Sam on her way to the hall closet to get a towel to clean up the stale water.

"If it's not, then tell me what is fair, Lydia," Sam said, pulling a bottle of water out of the refrigerator. "What is fair, that the woman I love has HIV and passed it on to me? Oh, yeah, that's really fair."

"You're such a selfish bastard!" Lydia shouted at him while sopping up the water with the towel. "The truth is that you've always been selfish—so unable to think about anyone but your damn self.

"The truth is that it's pretty unlikely that you even have the virus," she continued. "What about me? What about the baby?"

Lydia went to the kitchen to get the broom to sweep up the glass she could not get up with the towel. Sam walked over to the couch and sat down.

"Honestly, what am I supposed to do, Lyd? Honestly?" he said between sips. "It's a little too Disney to think I would just be all, 'it's okay, honey, we'll get through this,' you know?"

Sam began rubbing his head. He could feel heat coming from his forehead.

"Of course you are wondering about yourself, it was the first reaction I had when Dr. Woo told me," Lydia tried to explain. "But, as my future husband, I expected a bit more concern for all of us, including the baby, not just you."

"So what, you want me to apologize? 'Cause I'm not going to," Sam said.

"You know what, go to hell," Lydia barked. "You know this is *our* problem. Is this how you are going to act every time problems come up in the marriage? Trying to take sides and assign blame? That's not the way to deal. It's just not."

"Well, what, Lydia? How would I have reacted if I were you?" Sam said sarcastically.

"If you are through yelling at me," Lydia said, "you need to go get tested. Dr. Woo gave me a folder full of information that has the phone numbers of a few places you can go get tested anonymously, or you can just call your doctor and get tested by him."

"This is so easy for you, huh?" Sam said. "I'm just supposed to call my doctor and say I need an HIV test. What's he going to think?"

"That's your problem, Samuel. You are too worried about what others think of you," Lydia began lecturing. "He's not going to think you are gay. That's what you really are worried about, right? Well, don't sweat it. He should be more worried about making sure you are fine than your sexual orientation.

"Your ignorance never ceases to amaze me," Lydia said, almost dismissing him.

"You know what, Ms. Know-it-all? Screw you," Sam said, getting up and moving toward the dinner table. "If you hadn't contracted the virus, we wouldn't be having this conversation and our lives would be fine."

"You know," Lydia said sadly, "I'll take that, Sam. But I'm just wondering what would have happened in the future when we ran into problems. Marriage is not just about the good times."

"Well, hold up, who says there still is going to be a marriage?" Sam said matter-of-factly.

Lydia was stunned. She had no words. Had she just heard what Sam said? *Is he threatening to call off the wedding?* she thought.

"I gotta think, I'm out!" Sam shouted, grabbing his keys and opening up the door.

"Sam, don't leave, we have to talk," she yelled after him.

Sam shut the door behind him and walked briskly to the elevator. He pressed the Down button more times than needed. He couldn't wait for the door to open and take him away from this building and this conversation; although, he would later realize, the conversation was over, but the problem would persist, and he could not walk away from it— no matter how much he tried.

When the elevator got to the lobby, Sam ran to the doors and burst through them. Standing in front of the building, he suddenly could not remember where he'd parked. "Man," he whispered to himself. "Where is my car?"

Scanning the parking lot, he saw the forest green Jeep Wrangler. It was cold out. Walking through the rows of cars, he wondered why it seemed so much colder than when he'd gone upstairs not a half hour ago. In the course of feeling claustrophobic and needing to leave Lydia's place, he'd walked out without his jacket.

It didn't matter; he was inches away from the car's door, and he would soon be inside. Once in the car, he turned on the ignition, put the car in reverse, and hit the gas. The car backed up wildly. Sam slammed on the brakes just inches from the bumper of a pricey Lexus. Sam didn't care. His life had just been thrown a loop, and he had no idea how to deal with it. He wanted to call Issac, his best friend, but was unsure if he could share the contents of this afternoon's events with anyone. He put the car in drive and took off. First, he tore out of the parking lot, then down the small street. The entrance to the highway was on the right.

Why not? he thought. He got on the on-ramp and merged into traffic. He had no idea where he was going, but at this point, he felt, it did not matter. He wasn't even sure if he'd ever be back.

*   *   *

"I can't believe he left," Lydia said, standing over the sink and sweeping hair from her face. She microwaved a cup of water to make some tea and walked back to her bedroom. She didn't bother turning on the light. It was sunset, and she could see the muted orange-and-purple sky the sun made when it started to go down behind the Rocky Mountains.

She pushed all the pillows off the bed except the two she slept with. For the first time she realized what Sam always complained about. Why did she have so many damn pillows?

I guess I can't really blame him, she thought. *I did just give him some of the worst news you can give a person.*

Lydia stirred her tea and eased farther under the covers. Thinking about the conversation, she began to cry. "Lord, be with me," she prayed, "I know we can get through this. Just hold us together, Lord. I need you."

Lydia smiled. *Why am I always doing what I want to do until I get in trouble, and then running back to God?* She hated being reduced to a Biblical cliché, but that was exactly the place in which she was standing. She needed His forgiveness and His strength. And, in the typical manner of most of us sinners, she promised God she would be in church the following Sunday.

The clock read 4:47. *I need to call that doctor and make an appointment,* she thought. She got up and walked back into the living room to retrieve the folder Dr. Woo had given her. She found the card, went back into the room, and lay in the bed with the portable phone.

"Balm in Gilead," the woman on the other end of the phone said cheerfully. Lydia wanted to slap the woman, but she was just being mean.

"Hi, my name is Lydia Peters and I need to make an

appointment to see Dr. Henderson. Dr. Julia Woo suggested that I see her immediately.''

"No problem," the receptionist said. "She's had a few cancellations on Monday. Can you come in then, say one P.M.?"

Lydia agreed, gave the woman her insurance information, and hung up the phone.

She wanted to sleep but she couldn't. She just lay there staring at the ceiling. The world was going on. It was rush hour and people were trying to get home to pick up their kids and make dinner. Everyone's lives were continuing, it seemed, but hers. But it was—just in another direction than the one in which she'd believed it was going when she'd woken up that morning. She wanted to call her mother, but decided to wait. She felt she didn't have the strength for another showdown. Not today.

It was Thursday. She decided she would call in sick tomorrow and deal with her parents that weekend.

Several hours had passed, and the room had gone from slightly lit to pitch black. Still she could not sleep. Her eyes hurt and her body felt numb, but sleep would not come.

Suddenly the silence was broken. The phone rang. Lydia let it ring. She couldn't possibly talk with anyone, she thought. It rang again.

On the fourth ring she thought it might be Sam. She limply reached for the receiver, but by the time she picked it up, all she heard was the dial tone.

She had barely put the receiver back on the base when the phone rang again.

"Hee . . . hello," she eked out.

"Hey, girl, it's Dara and me on the other line." Toni's voice was cheerful. "We got plans for this weekend and we wanted to run them by you."

Dara and Toni had called on three-way to discuss the plan Dara had put together regarding the coming weekend's trip to yet another bridal shop and lunch. Lydia had totally forgotten she had put Dara on the case.

"Hey, y'all," Lydia said weakly with the phone barely to her mouth. "I totally forgot."

"How could you forget? I just talked to you this morning, Lyd," Dara started in. "I thought my efforts were appreciated. I know you are not trying to weasel out of this weekend."

"No, no, that's not it at all, I'm just not feeling up to it," Lydia told her friends.

"What's wrong with you, Lydia?" Toni said, picking up on the low energy of Lydia's voice. "Are you sick, or did you and Sam have a fight?"

"Well, I kind of got some bad news from the doctor," Lydia said.

"That's it," Toni said. "I'm on my way over."

"No, no. You don't have to come over. I just feel like being by myself," Lydia pleaded. "Please don't—"

"Oh, no, I'm coming over there. I knew you didn't sound right," Toni said.

"Toni, she said she didn't want us to interfere," Dara said weakly, bracing for Toni's response.

The conversation suddenly turned into a two-way call without either side realizing the third person was still on the line.

"Okay, do what you want," Toni told Dara. "I'm glad you aren't the first person I would call if I needed help. What kind of friend are you?"

Lydia listened as the remnant of an old argument reared its ugly head. Although they were definitely better about it, it took Dara and Toni a while to stop trying to prove who was the better friend.

"That's my friend," Toni continued, "and she obviously needs our care. Again, what is your definition of friendship?"

"You know what, Toni, you call yourself a friend, but most of the time your care and compassion are nothing but you being intrusive," Dara read her back. "I *am* Lydia's true friend, but sometimes when people ask to be by themselves, they really need to be."

"Okay, ladies," Lydia butted in. "I'm going to go, okay? I just need to get some rest."

Lydia hung up the phone, but knew the abrupt ending of the call meant both Toni and Dara would be at her front door in about half an hour. She wasn't sure what she was going to tell them. She really didn't want to tell them anything, at least not yet. But they were coming, and she needed to come up with something.

Toni was the first to pull into the apartment complex's parking lot. Locking her yellow Saab, she saw Dara pull in and park. She waited for Dara to catch up in the lobby. They rode the elevator up to Lydia's floor together. By the time they reached the fourth floor, the two no longer harbored any ill intentions toward each other. Their friendship had grown beyond just being friends through Lydia. They all had their own relationships independent of the others. Toni liked Dara, and as much as Dara thought Toni was ghetto, she really did like her.

The two women stood in front of Lydia's door and looked at each other. Toni grabbed Dara's hand and rang the bell.

"I hope she's all right," Dara whispered. Toni gave her hand a reassuring squeeze and rang the bell again.

A few moments later, Lydia unlocked the door and opened it. She was still in her bathrobe. All her girlfriends could think was how disheveled she looked.

"Why is it so dark in here?" Toni said before saying hello. Lydia gave them a weak smile and began walking over to the couch.

Dara starting turning on the lights in the living room and closing the blinds. "Dara, you can turn the kitchen lights on, but turn off that lamp," Lydia said, pointing to the light fixture next to the entertainment center.

Toni put her stuff on the table, followed her friend to the couch, and sat next to her. After closing the blinds, Dara walked to the kitchen. Eyeing the teakettle, she added more water and turned on the burner. "We might as well have some tea," she said, smiling.

Dara, too, went to the couch and sat on the other side of Lydia. She had no idea what to say. The coffee table was covered with used tissues, and the dustpan by the speaker was full of glass.

"What happened here?" Dara wanted to know. "Did you and Sam have a fight or something? I'm sorry to say, but you look crazy."

Dara got some more tissues and began to wipe Lydia's face. Toni got up, moved the broom, and put the glass in the trash. She took out three cups, put tea bags in all of them, and brought them over to where they were sitting.

"Lydia, honey," Toni said, sitting back down next to her. "What's wrong? Why was it so dark in here? Why was your aunt's vase in pieces? Why are you crying?"

Lydia lifted the tissue to her nose and blew hard. "Uhhhhhh," Dara complained. "That's so nasty." All three ladies gave a short laugh.

"Thank you for coming, you guys, but really . . ." Lydia tried to get out.

"No, don't even try to act like everything is all peachy," Toni said. "Girl, you and your apartment look a hot mess." Hearing the kettle whistle, she got up and went to get the water for the tea.

"Really, Lydia, what's going on?" Dara added.

Lydia knew she would have to eventually tell her two best friends in the whole world what Dr. Woo had explained to her. *How would they take it?* she thought. *Will I lose my friends? Do they really have to know?* All these thoughts swirled around in her head.

Toni filled all their cups to the brim and asked where the sugar was. "Oh," she said, seeing the container on the dinner table across the room. "I see it."

"Y'all my girls, right?" Lydia said, reaching for their hands.

"Of course," Toni said.

"Yeah, why?" Dara inquired.

Lydia hesitated but continued. "I got some news today that made my world come crashing down."

"Not the baby," Dara said, agasp.

"Well, in a way," Lydia said. "Before I tell you guys this, you must swear to me that it will not leave this room. Promise me."

Both women pledged to keep the secret. They had no idea what Lydia was going to let them in on, but it worried them both. Dara started to bite her bottom lip while Toni felt something tighten in the pit of her stomach. They both wanted to cry, only they didn't know why. Emotions were running high with the three of them sitting in the near dark on the verge of hearing something that was obviously changing Lydia's life and could possibly affect the other two.

"Today I found out that I am HIV positive," Lydia confided.

The silence in the room was deafening. Both Dara and Toni could not move or say anything. All they could do was look at one another—Toni to Dara, Dara to Lydia, and Lydia to Toni. A circle that had been through a lot together through the years, but this was something more. It had the potential to break down what had once been so strong, or it could strengthen the bonds that were already there.

Tears formed in the corners of Toni's eyes and they began to make their way down her cheeks to the corners of her mouth. She reached for the tissue box and grabbed a few to wipe her face. She moved closer to Lydia and put her arm around her shoulders.

Dara was unsure what to do, but she knew she felt completely uncomfortable. She stood up, walked over to the large panel windows, and looked out on the world through the blinds. *What does this mean?* she thought to herself. She, too, started to cry.

Lydia buried her head into Toni's neck. She didn't know what to say to Dara. *Will she totally reject me now?* she thought. She had no idea how to feel about Dara's move away from her.

Dara turned around, bringing the other two women back into focus. *Lydia is my girl,* she thought. *It's weird, but I know I have to support her through this.*

The silence was broken: "How could you let this happen, Lyd?" Dara said with indignation. Lydia heard Dara. Once again Dara had taken the motherly role and was going to start lecturing. Only this time, Lydia didn't mind it. She knew she was in the wrong. But what could she do but sit and listen?

Toni looked at Lydia. Toni's eyes said it all. Although she didn't say anything, she was wondering the same thing. Lydia was unable to respond. She just felt embarrassed having to tell her friends about her indiscretion. All she could think about was how ridiculous it was that teens were still getting pregnant by not using condoms and here she was pregnant and HIV positive. She was no better than many of those ill-informed kids.

Dara moved back over to the couch and joined them. Together the three of them cried and sat there until Toni broke up the moment.

"All right, you had your time to feel sorry for yourself," Toni said, walking over to the wall and turning on the lights.

"So, what happened? Do you know how you got it? What kind of treatment are you going to have to go into?"

"Well, tomorrow I need to go put in the prescriptions Dr. Woo gave me," Lydia said, wiping her face. "I made an appointment to go see another doctor. They say if I start taking certain medication and have a C-section, it won't be passed on to the baby."

"Lydia, how could this happen?" Dara asked. "Did you get it from Sam?"

"I'm pretty certain I didn't get it from him," she said. "But I'm scared to death that I could have given it to him. That's why the vase is broken. He broke it while I was telling him the news."

"He didn't threaten you, did he?" Toni asked.

"No, he got up, stomped past it, and bumped into the speaker," Lydia said, playing back the scene in her head. "He was pretty upset when he left."

"Well, you can't blame him," Dara let slip.

Toni and Lydia both turned and just looked at Dara, who realized her foot was in her mouth.

"Thanks," Lydia said, getting up. "As if I could not possibly make myself feel any worse."

"I'm sorry, Lydia, but Sam's not exactly a bad guy here," Dara continued.

"I know."

Lydia picked up her mug and moved to the dinner table. The others followed. Around the table, the three of them began asking questions Lydia was not sure she was able to answer. As at so many other times—through the death of Dara's mother, tens of Toni's men, and other general problems that arose to cause drama in their lives—they began to break down the issue and work on a plan of action.

"It's going to be all right," Toni reassured her friends. "We're going to get you through this."

Chapter Seven

Dealing With the Disease

The Balm in Gilead seemed all abuzz. Lydia wondered what was going on. It just seemed to her that there were too many people to be in a doctor's office at the beginning of the day. Something had to be happening, she thought.

She was early for her appointment with Dr. Gwen Henderson. She was the HIV specialist whom Dr. Woo had recommended to her. Apparently, she and Dr. Woo were medical-school classmates and worked together on cases such as Lydia's. Dr. Henderson took on the virus and the diseases it caused after one of her nieces died from AIDS-related causes in the late 80s.

Lydia filled out her paperwork and sat in the waiting room reading through a script submitted by a young woman she was considering hiring as a reporter. Time seemed to pass slowly. Each minute seemed to take an hour. She read through the script and decided that she liked it. She had watched the woman's tapes last week, and decided to call

Andrea to make an appointment with the fresh-from-undergrad reporter for a second interview.

"Ms. Peters," the receptionist called out. "Can you come back, please?"

Lydia closed her phone, grabbed her stuff, and walked through the door. Just as at Dr. Woo's, she was taken to get her weight, height, and blood pressure and told to sit in another room to wait for Dr. Henderson to see her.

"Lydia Peters," said the voice from behind the door. "Hello, how are you? I'm Dr. Henderson." The doctor came in and sat down facing Lydia. "I see Dr. Woo sent you to me," she continued. "I need to give her a call. So, how are you feeling?"

"Other than the nausea from the baby, I feel fine," Lydia explained.

"That's good. I'm going to take some blood so we can run some tests," Dr. Henderson said, putting on her latex gloves. "That way we can get an accurate count of your T cells and find out anything else we need to know about what's going on in your body. I'm sure you have a bunch of questions. What can I try and clear up for you?"

Lydia winced a bit as Dr. Henderson injected the needle into the vein in her left arm.

"Well, although I'm not sure what I should be feeling, I'm mostly concerned about my unborn child," Lydia let out. "What is the probability I'll pass on the virus to the baby?"

"Well, it really depends on you, Ms. Peters," the doctor said. "There are a number of medications that I can put you on in addition to your own prescription drugs that will help the baby fight off the virus. It also depends on how committed you are to your body and the health of you and your baby."

"I'm very committed," Lydia said. "I want to learn everything I can possibly know."

"Great, that's good to know," Dr. Henderson acknowledged. "The medication schedule along with the general rigors of pregnancy is not going to be the easiest thing, but, Lydia, you can do it. To help you along the way, I would like to see you join our support group for HIV-infected mothers."

Lydia was amazed. How could there be enough women in her situation to have a support group?

Dr. Henderson pulled out a flyer touting the meeting schedule for the group. "It's run by a wonderful therapist, Kay Brown. There are about eight women who come on a regular basis. They are a great resource. I urge you to join them."

Although it was a good idea, Lydia felt a bit overwhelmed. She was still getting used to the fact that she was pregnant and had the HIV virus in her blood. She didn't want anyone to know it. When she'd told Sam, he'd completely freaked out, and she had yet to hear from him. She'd told Toni and Dara, but still wondered what the fallout would be from that.

Things were so crazy. She guessed she would probably need to speak with these women and hear their advice about medicinal cocktails, and just hear from women who were in her situation. She agreed to meet the therapist.

"Good, she's actually in her office this morning," Dr. Henderson said. "As soon as I finish up writing these prescriptions for you, I'll walk you down there. Now, please get these prescriptions filled today. I want to start you on a group of medicines that will boost your immune system and help the development of the baby."

Lydia was not prepared for all of this, but figured it was too late for preparation; she was going to have to go with the flow. It was now time for improvisation in her life.

Dr. Henderson gave her four prescriptions and walked her out of the office, down the hall and into the other side of the clinic. There were several large rooms sectioned off by those plastic accordion walls and a bank of small offices along the back wall.

They walked up to a door that was shut and Dr. Henderson knocked on the glass. A pretty brown-skinned woman with twists opened the door but signaled for the two women to wait as she finished up a phone call.

"Hey, Gwen, I've been trying to get in touch with my roofer for two weeks, so I had to take that call," she explained. "How are you?"

"I'm fine," Dr. Henderson responded. "I'd like you to meet Lydia Peters. She's a new patient and I would like to get her into your Tuesday group."

"Hi," Kay said, reaching her hand to shake Lydia's. "Well, welcome."

"I have to go, but, Lydia, please feel free to call me anytime," Dr. Henderson said. "If I'm not in, my staff knows how to contact me, so please, if anything comes up or you have any questions, call."

With that she was out the door, and Lydia was left standing in Kay's office, feeling a bit awkward.

"Have a seat and tell me a bit about yourself," Kay invited. "And I'll tell you about the group."

Lydia explained her new situation. She left out the part about Sam storming out and not calling her. *No need to give these people* all *my information,* she thought.

Kay proceeded to explain to Lydia the boundaries of the women's group. Everyone was free to discuss whatever they were dealing with, and none of the information left the group. Kay had been running groups like the current one for nearly six years and had a reputation for conducting safe havens for women with HIV. She told Lydia that she should think of the group as a group of friends that all shared a secret. Many of the women involved were in different trimesters, and Kay encouraged her to ask as many questions as she could think of. Several of the women had been coming for months and could provide her with firsthand knowledge of dealing with the issues that would come up.

Lydia thanked Kay and told her she would make the next meeting.

Lydia turned down the radio in her car. She was on her way to her parents' house. She didn't want them to be too freaked out. It was the second time in nearly two weeks that she'd "just stopped by." Her mother had nearly passed out when she and Sam had showed up at their house to tell them she was pregnant and they wanted to push up the wedding.

Her mother was always such a drama queen. Lydia had always believed she took things to the dramatic end of the spectrum of life to keep her father's attention. Her father had cheated on her mother in the late seventies, and from that time on, everything was always a production when Mrs. Peters was involved.

I guess I can't really blame her, Lydia thought. *He did step out on her.*

But the one thing Lydia had the biggest problem with was the way her mother made every woman, including Lydia, a rival. It was the reason she believed her mother always had something negative to go with whatever positive she did.

Lydia had to roll down the window and let the car fill with crisp, fresh air. Her heart rate increased as she thought about what she was about to share with her parents. Her father, a retired army officer, had always supported her— even to her mother's displeasure—but this was something entirely different.

How do you tell your parents you contracted a life-threatening virus that you could have avoided completely? she thought. The twenty-five-minute drive into the 'burbs seemed like it was taking twice as long as usual. It did give her an opportunity to think about how she would bring it up. Would she sit them down, or just mention it casually in the midst of conversation? She didn't know what to think. She just knew she would have to tell them. It was going to be hard, but she figured this was cake compared to Sam and whatever might come up in the future. *Time to pay the piper,* she thought. *I'm sure there will be more things to come.*

Pulling up to her parents' brown, two-story stucco rambler, Lydia noticed how much nicer the yard looked. Her father had just shelled out a great deal of money to landscape the front yard. And it looked to her like it was worth every penny.

She wasn't expecting her father to be outside.

"Hey, baby. How's my grandchild?" Mr. Peters said, waving to her. She hadn't even opened the car door before he descended on the car. "Your mother's been trying to call you. Do you have your cell phone turned on?"

"Hey, Daddy," Lydia said, getting out of the car. "Actually, I've been out running some errands. I thought I turned it on before I left the house, but I guess not." She reached into her purse and looked at the phone. She was wrong; it wasn't turned on.

"Do you like my new yard?" he asked, showing his daughter the expanse of the yard. "Those guys cost me too much money, but everyone in the neighborhood is now trying to get the same thing. So, in the end, I guess it's all right."

Lydia grabbed his arm and walked with him to the back of the house, where her mother was digging up some plants.

"Dot, look who's here," Mr. Peters said to his wife.

"Hi, Mom." Lydia smiled. Mrs. Peters turned around and pushed herself off the ground. She was dressed for gardening with a sun hat, gloves, and some old, beat-up tennis shoes. All Lydia could think was that her parents had really taken to retirement life.

"Lydia, we have a lot to do if you are going to push up

this wedding. I've been trying to get in touch with Dara for three days.'' Her mother wasted no time in getting started in on Lydia. ''Is she out of town or something? Come on in the house. We have a lot to do.'' Mrs. Peters moved toward the back door as Mr. Peters started walking in the other direction, toward the shed in the far back corner of the yard.

Lydia followed her mother into the house. She noticed her father was walking to his shed, but she figured she would get an opportunity to talk with them together without causing them to think something was up before it was time.

It was getting to be lunchtime. *He'll come in to fix something to eat. Then I'll break their hearts, while they are in the same room,* she thought. *I just don't think that I can do it twice, so they have to be in the same room.*

Walking into the kitchen from the back, Lydia noticed a few changes around the house. ''You have to take off your shoes if you go into the living room,'' her mother called back from the pantry. ''I decided we needed new carpet on Wednesday,'' she continued. ''You know, that home-shopping network is the devil. They make you think you need stuff you don't need.''

Lydia just laughed. Her mother knew she didn't need any spirits telling her to buy something. It was at her mother's side that Lydia's need to shop was cultivated. ''Mama, you know you didn't need new carpet, and light beige at that?''

''Well, I had some stains in the other one that I couldn't get out,'' she said, bringing out some pasta noodles and sauce to warm up for lunch. ''Are you hungry? You know, you have to eat for two now.'' Under her breath, just loud enough for Lydia to hear her as she put her purse down, she said, ''I just hope you don't get too big.''

Lydia perked up. She continued to go about what she was doing—looking through her parents' mail as if she still got letters delivered there. *It's not even worth it,* she thought.

"Daddy said you had been calling me this morning," she told her mother. "I forgot to turn on the phone."

"Well, it wasn't too much," Mrs. Peters said, emptying the red sauce into a pot and putting it on the range. "I'm just concerned that if you are going to have a ceremony before you are too big to wear a nice dress, we need to get started immediately. Before all this, you hadn't even chosen a church. You know, Pastor Jacobs was hurt when I told him you weren't planning on having the wedding at Third Baptist."

Lydia cut her mother off. "Mom, you didn't have to tell him that."

"What, you were going to lie to the pastor?" she shot back.

"No, but the inside of that church is just ugly." Lydia turned up her nose. "I don't see how Jennifer did it. I know the only reason she agreed to have her ceremony there was because her dad was the head trustee. I'm sorry, if we have a full ceremony, I'm not having it there."

"What? So you and Sam aren't planning on having a ceremony now?" Her mother wanted to know. She turned from the stove and turned up her lip at her daughter. "You two are so difficult. What am I supposed to do now?"

Lydia just smiled. There was no real reason to go on and explain to her mother that if they were going to get married it would be something small and intimate. And, in the wake of the past week, there would possibly never be a marriage between Sam and her.

"Mom, it's okay, we'll get everything taken care of," she reassured her mother, who went back to cooking.

"So, you've accepted that I'm pregnant, have you?" Lydia asked.

"Lydia Michele," her mother started. Lydia knew she'd struck a nerve. She sat deeper in her chair and braced herself for what was going to follow. "You and Sam are grown.

You guys are damn near middle-aged. I can't direct what you do in your lives. Your father just told me to let it alone. So that's what I'm going to do.''

Wow, that was pretty mild, Lydia thought. She got up and kissed her slightly disapproving mother. She knew her mother was trying her hardest to make nice and not be judgmental. *I'll give her credit for this as I don't know what's going to come out of her mouth when I tell them about the virus.*

"That's great, Mom. I really appreciate that," she said. Lydia got out the garlic spread from the refrigerator and began to butter some French bread. At that moment, Mr. Peters came into the kitchen from the backyard.

"Honey, honey, take off your shoes," Mrs. Peters instructed. "You'll forget and tramp dirt all on my new carpet." He stopped, took off his work boots, and walked through the kitchen on his way to the staircase.

"That's what I like to see, my two favorite ladies," he said. He paused to give his wife a peck on the cheek. "When's the food going to be ready?"

"Change out of those clothes," Lydia said. "It will be ready by the time you come back down."

When Mr. Peters did come back down dressed in an Adidas running suit, his wife was putting the garden salad on the table and engaged in conversation with Lydia. "Come on, Daddy," Lydia said. "Come sit next to me."

"I don't know why she loves you so much," Mrs. Peters added.

He sat down at the head of the table. Mrs. Peters brought over some Parmesan cheese and sat down on the other side with Lydia between them. After a short prayer, they began to pass around the plates of food and dish out their servings.

The conversation around the table remained pleasant.

Lydia reported to her parents about what was going on at work. Her father was concerned about her relationship with John Rosen ("Don't let him bully you," he said) and her mother wanted to make sure Lydia wasn't overworking Andrea ("She's such a nice girl, you should pay her more," she admonished).

After finishing the last of the garlic bread, Mr. Peters inquired about Sam. "Where's my boy?" he asked Lydia. She was quiet, but Mrs. Peters took up the slack. "Didn't he just get a promotion, too?" she inquired. "How's he feel about being a father?"

"Well," Lydia started. "That's kind of what I came over here to talk with you guys about."

Mr. Peters put down his glass and gave his daughter his attention. Her mother put her left hand on her chest and reached out toward Lydia. "I knew something was wrong. I felt it earlier," she said.

"Mom, you did not. I have something very serious to tell both of you."

Lydia swallowed hard. "I went to the doctor," she got out. "I hate to have to tell you this, but I've tested positive for HIV."

"Oh, Lord," Mrs. Peters screamed. She immediately began to cry. She scooted closer to her daughter and hugged her as if she weren't going to see her again.

Lydia's father got up from the table and walked over to the sink. He put both his hands on the edge and leaned all his weight on his arms. He looked defeated.

"Does this mean you are going to die, baby?" her father asked. Lydia felt terrible. In all her days, she never wanted to hurt her parents. Today, she felt she finally had.

"Dad, we are all going to die one day," she said solemnly.

"Don't play, Lydia. Don't play," he answered her back. He turned around and faced his weeping wife and daughter. "You're a smart girl. How could you let this happen?"

Mr. Peters kicked the cabinet under the sink. All he could think was that his daughter was in a lot of trouble, and this time, he was powerless to help her.

"Mom, Dad, I'm sorry. I never meant for this to happen," Lydia continued. "But for me to get through this, I'm going to need your love and support all the more. It's going to be hard, but I need you to be supportive of me."

Mr. Peters just looked at her and he, too, began to cry. Lydia felt crushed. In her thirty-two years, she had never seen her father seem so broken. This was the first time in her life she had seen her father cry. Her heart sank.

It had been nearly two weeks since she'd told her parents the news. Sitting at her desk, Lydia was distracted. Ever since this all had started, she had been just a bit off. She even got called out in the senior management meeting with her boss. The virus was changing the way she lived her life, but she was determined not to allow its grip to affect her career. She'd worked too hard to get what she had. But she had to get it together; all this staring blankly at the walls had to stop. There was a knock at her door. It was Andrea.

"Hey, boss," she said, peeking in. "Your mother's on the phone again. She's asking me why you haven't returned any of her calls, and I'm running out of excuses. Are you okay?"

"Yeah, I'm fine," Lydia smiled. "Transfer her to me. Thanks for asking. I'll be okay." Andy closed the door and sent the call to Lydia's phone.

"Hi, Mom," she said weakly. She half expected to get yelled at. She knew she was wrong not to return her mother's calls. She had called both Lydia's home and office daily for the past two weeks and was very worried about her daughter. *I guess I would be upset, too,* she thought.

"Lydia, your father and I are so worried about you. Why haven't you answered any of our messages?"

"Well, Mom, I saw how much I hurt you guys when I told you what was happening," she started to explain. "I guess I was ashamed and was unsure of how or what you were going to say to me."

"Lydia, you should never be unsure of our love for you," Mrs. Peters said. "You are our only daughter, and we would do whatever was needed when it comes to you. I know I can be a little critical at times, but we love you and we'll help you through this."

Lydia could feel the smile on her mother's face on the other end of the phone. She felt reassured from what her mother said. She felt a bit foolish as well. She knew her parents would be there, but this news was a very touchy subject, and she never quite knew on which side of the coin people were going to fall, even family.

"Thank you, Mom. It's just been a very trying time, you know," Lydia said. "It's a whole lot, plus I think all these medicines I'm taking are making me crazy."

"Well, come by for dinner sometime this week, okay?" her mother said. "We want to see you. You may have done something wrong, but it's something we can't change now. You know you will always be our daughter. Don't forget, come by sometime this week. Bye." Her mother hung up the phone. Lydia sat with the receiver in her hand for a minute before hanging it up. She called Andrea into her office.

"Hey, Andy, I have some stuff I need you to do for me," she said as Andrea sat down.

"Is everything cool?" her assistant asked. "You've kinda been in a funk for the last month. I thought you were happy about being pregnant."

"Well, honestly, I am," Lydia said, knowing her relationship with her staff was entirely too personal. "It's just, it's taking me a bit to get adjusted to all these prenatal pills I have to take. And, girl, my body is totally out of whack. You wait until you have a baby. You'll see.''

Lydia and Andrea ended up wasting thirty minutes talking about baby names and planning a shopping trip to Pea Pod and Nordstrom to get Lydia some nice maternity clothes. She was now nearly two months along, and wanted to start buying clothes, because she knew one day soon she would look around and no longer have the same waist size. But deep down inside, Lydia knew she was only planning on spending money because she wasn't feeling too good about herself and wanted comfort. Sam had completely stopped coming by. For the last prenatal visit to Dr. Woo, he'd met her at the doctor's office. Something had to give her some pleasure, and she thought it might as well be her Visa card.

Finally, they got back on track. ''Andy, I have to call an Urban Express staff meeting. Please talk with everyone and see when everyone is in town so we can meet,'' she instructed. ''It needs to be no later than the end of next month. In the senior staff meeting, George called for all the shows to put together a large, weeklong package that the station can pub the hell out of for ratings.''

Andrea got up to go back to her desk. ''Oh,'' Lydia said, stopping her in her tracks. ''Everyone needs to come with two well-defined ideas. Tell Jonathan I said *everybody*.

Andrea laughed, because she knew Jonathan was never prepared for meetings. She closed the door behind her and left Lydia alone to do some work.

Walking through the front doors of Balm in Gilead, Lydia felt like a high-school student who had to explain to a teacher why she hadn't been in class. She'd missed the first session Kay had invited her to. It wasn't that she'd been sick, Lydia just hadn't wanted to go. She thought she would be depressed sitting in a room full of women with the disease. It had to be four times as dreadful as Toni's little powwows after she dumped yet another brother over something senseless. *There's nothing more pathetic than a bunch of women sitting around, stuffing their faces with Ben & Jerry's and complaining about how men are all whack,* she thought. And she saw this group session as an amplified version.

She saw Kay talking with a colleague. She tried to be inconspicuous, but the group leader spotted her. "Hi, Lydia, we missed you last week," Kay said. "Come with me, I'll show you the room. It's not our usual one."

Lydia was shamed. "Yeah, I couldn't get away from work," she lied. "How are you?"

The two walked down one corridor and then another. At the end of that hallway, they came to the door. "I would have never found this room," Lydia said. Kay agreed. "I know, I just hope this is the right room." She giggled.

Opening the door, the pair saw several other women sitting around drinking coffee and chatting. "Great," Kay said. "It looks like everyone's here."

She put a stack of papers she was carrying on the desk and pointed out a chair to Lydia. "Ladies, this is Lydia Peters. She'll be joining our little group."

Hellos were spoken from each side of the room. Lydia graciously nodded and greeted all six of the women: Anne, Maria, CeCe, Kim, Janice, and Veronica. *They all seem nice,* she thought, going around the room and shaking their hands.

"Okay, let's get started," Kay said. "How was everyone's week?"

"I'll start," said Veronica, who looked oddly like a younger Star Jones. "Kay, I know what you said about keeping a journal to write down how I'm feeling, but I just can't get into that. I don't think I really want to relive some of the stuff I'm going through."

A low murmur could be heard from the others. Anne

jumped in before Kay could say anything. "I understand," she said. "I didn't want to do it, either, when I first started. It's annoying to make it a part of your daily schedule. But, honestly, I have found that going back and reading what I've written makes me stronger."

"Yeah," CeCe chimed in. "I know what you mean. It's great to go back and read what I was dealing with and see how far I've come emotionally."

Kay quieted down the group. "Veronica, if you aren't comfortable writing every day, try once a week until you feel up to it," she said. "It's not mandatory. I'm not grading it. I've just found it to be helpful to write down your feelings and have them there. Sometimes you need to get things out and you may or may not have someone as a soundboard."

Veronica nodded in affirmation. "I'll try some more."

"What else is going on?" Kay asked, looking around the room. "Lydia, why don't you tell us a little about yourself and how you came to our group."

Lydia felt put on the spot. She didn't know these women. Although she was getting a better response from those she'd told about her condition than she had ever anticipated, she didn't know these women. *I can't believe she did that,* she thought with seven pairs of eyes now focused on her.

"Well, as I said earlier, I'm Lydia Peters. I found out I have HIV around the same time I realized I was pregnant." Lydia went on for about five minutes. She explained how dumb she felt for contracting the virus and putting her child into danger. She told the women about how her friends and parents reacted, but stopped short of talking about Sam and his distance since finding out.

Just as she thought her moment was over, Kay said, "How does the father feel, or does he know? How is your relationship with him?"

Damn her was all Lydia could think. She paused.

"I'm sorry to put you on the spot, Lydia, but you'll learn

this is a very intimate group," Kay said. "We talk candidly and honestly. We are there for each other in ways others can't be. We would like for you to feel comfortable, but if you're not yet, we understand."

"No, no," she said. Lydia uncrossed her legs. *Oh, trying to let me off the hook after she already hung me out there,* she thought.

"Well, he's around, but I think we are officially over," she tried to explain.

"How do you know?" Anne asked.

"Are you sure? He might just be trying to figure it all out," Janice chimed in.

"No, I think it's over," Lydia continued. "He meets me at the OB-GYN when it involves the baby, but that's about it. When I told him about me being positive, he all but said the wedding was off. He's even taken most of his stuff from my apartment."

"Oh, you guys were getting married," Maria said. "That was my situation. My Hector left me when he found out. Men can be really selfish, you know. They are a lot more fragile than we are."

A few of the women got up to get more coffee. CeCe took some tissues out of her purse and handed them to Lydia.

"We have to remember that this is a difficult situation for everyone involved," Kay told them. "It is very hard for us, but we have to give those around us space to deal as well. No, it's not always fair, but it's a reality."

The meeting continued pretty much the same way for the next hour. Although Lydia found the group annoying at first, she saw how she could really get into it after a while. She left the clinic with a remarkably different view of the group than when she'd first arrived. She appreciated the other women. She thought it was a good thing to have others in her life who could truly empathize because they were going through the same things she was. And she really liked Kay.

Although she did not have the virus, she was a great group leader, always bringing the conversation back around and leaving every woman with a positive view of whatever particular problem she was facing.

More than a month had passed since Lydia'd asked Andrea to schedule a planning meeting for her fourteen staffers. It was pandemonium when Lydia, three-and-a-half months pregnant, walked into the main conference room.

She was finally getting used to her medicine schedule. It turned out getting comfortable with the drugs wasn't that bad. It took her a while to work it into her schedule, but she was healthy, and decided if she wanted to stay that way—especially for the baby—she needed to be serious about it.

Finally, her staff members, many of whom she hadn't seen in weeks, surrounded her. Her show was a jewel in the crown of KTRW. Lydia had proven to the station's owners that she could produce a top-rated news show that drew in young viewers, and the people sitting around the long table were the reason. She wasn't afraid to make risky or unproven hiring decisions, and she had the respect of the staff.

"Hey, everybody," she announced, smiling. "I hope everything is going well. Andrea is passing out the ideas that you all turned in. I have to say, overall, the stories were good jumping-off points."

Her trusty assistant gave the last set of copies to Marvin, took her seat next to Lydia, and turned on her laptop. Andrea was always about business.

"And some of you," Lydia said, looking directly at Byron, "need to come talk with me about why the ideas you turned in were incomplete or just not in. You know who you are. I'm free right after the meeting." Eyes began to search the room for the guilty parties. A few smirked while others let out a bit of nervous laughter.

"Okay, let me explain what's going on. Then we will discuss the ideas and break, 'cause we all have work to get back to."

Lydia told the group how all the show staffs were under pressure to come up with a weeklong series that they could include in their lineup and the station could publicize greatly. Together for the next hour they walked through the ideas laid in front of them. Some were better than others. Marvin wanted to do an in-depth look at the new White House and political lobbies. Carrie wanted to do something completely opposite and do a business feature on the fashion industry. Andrea even had an idea: retention rates of minorities at colleges and what universities were doing to make them better.

Lydia thought the meeting was going very well, but she needed some air and a break, so she called the meeting and scheduled a follow-up for the next day. This would give her an opportunity to think about the discussion and weed the list down to the best three or four concepts.

"Okay, everyone, tomorrow, ten-thirty A.M.," she announced. Lydia got up, only to be surrounded by her staffers. Some were inquiring about the baby, others wanted validation that their ideas were heard, and, in true journalistic narcissism, others were just jockeying for their ideas to make the cut.

The barrage of conversation followed her all the way down the hall and into her office. Lydia loved her staff's energy, but she was through. It was late in the afternoon, and she needed to take some of her prenatal pills. "Okay, everyone, give me five minutes," she finally said.

"Can I get you anything, Lyd?" Andrea said, pushing folks out of Lydia's office.

"Yeah, could you just get me some water so I can take my calcium pills? That would be great," she answered.

Lydia put her notebook and papers on the corner of her desk and sat down. "Hey, Margo," she said to the woman at her door. Margo was the director of the evening news department. She had always been extremely supportive of Lydia and her rise through the company. Lydia looked up to her because she was the first woman (and the only one for years) to make it to executive level within the station.

"How's that baby of yours?" she inquired. "How are you doing in general?"

"We are doing fine," Lydia said. "What are you doing on this side of the building? I don't think I've seen you in a while."

"I know." Margo laughed. "I took a vacation. That's why you haven't seen me. I got a call from John this morning about the price of some equipment I ordered before my vacation, so now I have to go face the bulldog."

Lydia chuckled. "You look different, more refreshed," she said. The red-haired woman laughed. "That vacation must have been great."

"It was. If you promise not to spread the word, I'll tell you about it," Margo said, closing Lydia's door. She moved closer to the desk and whispered so low, Lydia could barely hear her.

"I had my eyes and neck done." She just glowed. "I knew it was going to take some time to heal, so I did it and went to Belize with Adam. It was two weeks of heaven. You have to go down there. You'd love it."

"Wow, you look great," Lydia said. "Did it hurt a lot?"

"Well, yeah, at first, but I feel fine now," Margo admitted. "Well, call me so we can have lunch really soon and I'll tell you all about it. I'm about forty minutes late for this meeting. I'll see you. Don't forget to call me."

With that, Margo opened the door and went down the

hallway. Lydia was surprised that Margo would get cosmetic surgery. She'd always seemed very empowered. *But,* she thought, *if taking time and age into your own hands isn't power, what is?*

Just then, the phone rang. It was her second line, so she knew it had to be Toni.

"Hey, girl," Toni said on the other end of the phone. "What's up?"

"Nothing, what's going on with you?" Lydia replied. "I've been trying to get in touch with you for days."

All she heard was giggles. "Well, you know, I've been a bit busy," Toni surrendered. "You know that guy who I thought was married or something?"

"The guy two suites from your offices?" Lydia asked. She knew whatever it was Toni was going to say, it was going to be scandalous. She started to laugh. She needed a comical break, and this call from Toni was what she needed.

Andrea brought in a water bottle and put it on the desk.

"Well, he's not," Toni screamed. "Girl, turns out, he's very single and doesn't have no kids. I bumped into him getting coffee on Monday and I think I'm in love."

"Toni," Lydia said, momma-like. "You don't know enough about that man to know you are in love with him. And you are too grown to be having these crushes. Please don't have me bring up Malik and James and Phillip and—"

"Okay, I got your point, but he's fine, girl, and paid." Toni laughed through the phone lines. "I told Dara all about him. She's mad, but he's got a friend and I'm setting her up with him this weekend."

Lydia just laughed. *Toni is so crazy,* she thought. Plus, she knew that foursome would be nothing but jokes on Monday.

"Don't set up Dara with nobody crazy, you know how she is," Lydia warned. "Anyway, what did you really call for?"

"Nothing, I'm just checking up on you, *mamacita,*" Toni said. "Have you heard from Sam?"

"Not really," Lydia said sadly. "He E-mailed me to say he would meet me for the baby's exam on next Tuesday. And that he set up a checking account that he can put money in for the baby's expenses. He's going to give me the ATM card when he sees me next week."

"Are you cool with that?" Toni inquired. "He's still tripping, huh? It's not like he tested positive or anything. He should want to step up and truly be the father of this child."

"You know, if that's the way he wants it," Lydia said, "that's fine. I'd rather keep the space between us the way it is now, than to have him around treating me like a leper and resenting me. So, I'm leaving things the way they are for now."

"But don't you miss him, girl?" Toni asked. "He was almost living with you, and I know you was giving it up to him several times a week." She chuckled.

"Well, yeah, I'm lonely. I really do miss his touch. I mean, I'm still in love with him, you know," she responded. "I wish things were different, but they aren't, and there's nothing I can do about it. I'm doing what I think I need to do to get through this, and I guess he is, too."

Lydia began to feel a bit down. "Okay, girl, I have to go. Call me tonight if you're not out with Mr. Love."

Toni laughed. "Okay, bye."

Chapter Eight

Hope Sophia's Arrival

The nine months of Lydia's pregnancy seemed to go faster than she thought they would. She had the support of her parents and her girls. And although it wasn't one hundred percent of the backing she wanted from Sam, she had his support. He went with her to all of the prenatal visits.

They only had a few conversations that could be construed as talks about their relationship. Nothing was ever verbalized regarding it being over. They both kind of felt it but avoided saying it. Lydia had even gotten wind of him going out on a couple of dates, but apparently she could never confirm the information.

Sitting in her overcrowded living room, surrounded by her friends and family, she felt blessed.

She was even feeling a lot better about the virus and her life with it. She ended up supporting all the stories her staff discussed for a five-night package about women living with HIV and AIDS. It was a newsworthy peg, and she enlisted the help of her support group. All but one agreed to tell their stories under a cloak of anonymity. It was great. She spoke with a lot of doctors about what was happening and what could be done. The project empowered her. She even got out from behind her desk and did most of the reporting herself. She felt so much better about her life. And it made all the difference.

It was a wonderful afternoon for the baby shower. Her dad was the only man in the room of twenty or so women. But he was fine. Lydia enlisted him to videotape the party. Two of her aunts and her grandmother flew in from Louisiana. It was great. Sam even stopped by to drop off a bunch of presents before everyone showed up.

She asked Sam to stay, but he declined. He gave some random reason; Lydia didn't even remember what it was. Toni told her a while back that she needed to cut the emotional strings to Mr. Thomas, but she couldn't. Deep down, she still loved him. He was the father of her child, and before the events of the past year had begun, she'd been planning on spending the rest of her life with him.

And, she felt, even though he had kept her at arms' length, he was still in love with her. He wasn't looking that great. He always looked tired and unhappy.

Andrea was passing Lydia presents to open when she felt a pain in her abdomen. Lydia stopped unwrapping the gift and placed her hands on her stomach. Again, the pain came. *This cannot be happening,* she thought.

"Lydia," her mother called out from the kitchen. "Are you okay?" The anxious guests began to look at one another, trying to understand what was happening.

"I . . . I think I need to go to the hospital," Lydia said, trying to stand up. "I think the baby is coming."

Her father put the digital recorder around his neck and helped his daughter get to her feet. "Uhhh, there it is again," she said, half bent over.

"Oh my Lord," her grandmother said. Suddenly the apartment was abuzz with everyone trying to help at once.

"Okay, party's over," Toni said, trying to direct traffic. "Everyone cannot go to the hospital, okay? We could use a few folks to stay here and help us clean up."

"Dara," Lydia called. "Can you get my suitcase? It's on the right side of my closet."

Her father started to lead her out of the apartment and down to the car. Dara went to get the suitcase. Lydia's mother, aunts, and grandmother followed them into the elevator. *This is definitely one for the history books,* Lydia thought. Andrea and some of the women from the station stayed with Toni to help clean up so things wouldn't be such a mess when she returned.

"I'll call Sam, Lydia," Toni yelled so she could hear her as the elevator doors closed.

As her father went to go get his car, she stood in front of the building with her maternal relatives. "I always thought this moment wouldn't be so drama-filled," she said.

"Lyd, it's okay, the baby never comes when it's supposed to come," her aunt, Suzie, said. "It's just the Lord's way of letting us know He's in charge."

Mr. Peters pulled up and they got into the Lincoln, Lydia in the front and the other four women squeezed in the back. Mr. Peters drove faster than Lydia had ever seen him drive. He was nervous. But she was kind of glad he was driving so fast—the labor pains were growing frequent. "Slow down, Daddy," she said, touching his arm. "I would think you've been through this before."

He smiled and lessened his pressure on the gas pedal. "I have, baby girl." He smiled. "But this is just different. I'll get you to the hospital safely."

*   *   *

By the time Sam showed up at St. Vincent's, Lydia was being prepped for the operating room. At the reception desk, they told him the maternity floor was on level four. He took the elevator up and saw the Peters clan as he rounded the corner of the waiting room.

"Sam," Mrs. Peters said, happy to see him. "They are getting her ready."

"How . . . when did she go into labor?" Sam stammered out. He was a little nervous. "She was fine when I saw her this morning."

"It's okay, son, we were in the middle of the baby shower and the pains hit her," Mr. Peters detailed. "We got her here in no time."

Sam was actually glad to see the Peters family. He knew with them around Lydia must be fine. He actually had been avoiding them. He and Lydia had never officially broken up, but he still felt awkward about seeing her family and friends.

"Sam, did you ever meet my sisters and my mother?" Mrs. Peters asked.

"No, I don't think I have," he said. He walked over to where they were sitting and shook their hands. Sam was full of nervous energy. He started to pace. "When was the last time the doctor came in here?" he asked.

"The nurse came in to tell us what was going on about twenty minutes ago," Mr. Peters said. "She'll be okay, Sam. Have a seat. All we can do now is pray, sit here, and wait."

Sam hadn't really thought about this moment before. It wasn't like he hadn't had plenty of time to think about it, it just had never occurred to him that the baby was really going to come. Within weeks of Lydia telling him she was HIV positive and him testing negative, Sam began having insomnia. He would only sleep about two or three hours a night. He found himself sitting in his favorite recliner every night until the early hours of the morning, just staring out the sliding glass doors of his patio, unable to sleep.

He thought about a lot. Work, Lydia, the baby, but for some reason he never once thought about how it would be to be sitting in the waiting room waiting for his child to be born.

Mostly, he wanted things to return to the way they were last October. He wanted his woman back, and life to return to what he thought was normal. But how could it? he often thought. How could they live knowing she had this disease? He had so many questions, and felt he had no one with whom to discuss them. He wanted to know if they could ever have sex again, and if there was any way their baby could be born without the virus, but it could just be dormant and show up later. There was so much he was unsure of, but he was there.

Two hours later, Toni and Dara showed up. Toni was carrying cans of soda and a large plate of food.

"Anyone thirsty or want something to eat?" Toni said. She put the food on the corner table and took a seat next to Mr. Peters. Dara followed and sat in the chair next to Sam. She put her hand on his knee and smiled.

"You okay?" she asked.

"Yeah, I'm cool," Sam answered. He leaned back in the chair and picked up a magazine.

"You're about to be a daddy, Sam," Toni said from across the room. "How do you feel?"

"I'm excited, but a bit scared," he said to her. Mrs. Peters and her sisters just smiled.

"That's the way I was," Mr. Peters spoke up. "There's nothing you really can do to prepare for fatherhood. You read all kinds of books, but you just have to be inducted in by fire." He laughed.

Sam was scratching his head. "Yeah, I guess so. It's a new thing for me. I'm going to take it one step at a time."

Dr. Henderson appeared in the doorway. Everyone but Mrs. Chester, Lydia's grandmother, stood up.

"Lydia had a healthy baby girl," she announced to the room. Everyone smiled and started hugging one another. When Dara let him go, Sam pulled out his cell phone and dialed his parents in California. The room was buzzing.

"Lydia will be waking up from the anesthesia soon. As you know, we decided to have a C-section operation to avoid any unnecessary risk to the baby. You'll be able to see them in about thirty minutes."

"Congratulations, Sam," everyone said. Sam felt very proud, but a little confused. He and Lydia had never discussed what the situation would be regarding him, her, and the baby.

Well, I guess we can worry about that later, he thought. *Now is time to celebrate.* "Hey, Mom, it's Sam," he said when the line picked up. "Lydia had the baby, she's healthy, and I'll get to see her in a little bit."

When Lydia finally came out of her sleep, she saw the usual suspects. "Don't move, honey," her mother warned. "The doctor said you are going to be very sore for a while."

Lydia moved anyway, scooting up higher in the bed and sitting up a little. Sam was at her left side; Toni, Dara, and her father were on the right.

"Your aunt and grandma saw the baby from the nursery window," her mom continued. "Mom was getting tired, so they took her back to the house. They will be up here tomorrow to see you."

"Thanks," she said. "Sam, have you seen her?"

"I saw her in the nursery," he answered. "She's beautiful. The nurse is supposed to be bringing her in soon."

"Girl, she's so precious," Toni said.

"Yeah, girl, she's perfect," Dara chimed in.

"Congratulations, baby," Mr. Peters said as he leaned in to kiss Lydia on the forehead. "We are so happy she's here."

"Lydia," her mother said. "Have you and Sam decided on a name?"

"Um, well, we really haven't discussed it too much, Mrs. Peters," Sam answered. "But as long as it's not a name brand like Lexus or Mercedes, I'm fine with whatever Lydia decides."

Toni and Dara laughed.

"Well, I was thinking about naming her after Daddy's mother, but I've changed my mind," Lydia said. "While I was in the operating room, I was thinking about my life and how things are right now, and I want to name her Hope."

Smiles crossed all of their faces. "I like that," Mr. Peters said. "I think that says it all."

"Is that okay, Sam?" Lydia wanted to know. "You can choose the middle name."

"No, no, that's fine," he said. "I actually like that a lot. What about Sophia for her middle name?"

"Ah, after your aunt," Lydia said.

"Oww, I like that," Toni cooed. "That really goes together. Hope Sophia, that's really pretty."

"I do like that," her mother said. "I think that will work. Now where is that nurse with little Hope? I want to hold my grandchild."

Sam caught Lydia's eyes and smiled at her. He brushed her hair with his hand. She was thankful for his touch. It had been nearly eight months since the last time she'd felt it.

The door opened and all five of them turned and saw the nurse carrying the newly crowned Hope into the room.

"She's so beautiful," Sam said.

The nurse put Hope into Lydia's arms and the group crowded in. "Congratulations, you guys," Dara purred.

Lydia smiled up at everyone around her. Sam touched the tiny arm of his daughter. He said nothing, but everyone knew exactly how he was feeling, as tears of happiness began to run down his face.

"We know, son," Mr. Peters said, smiling. He reached over and squeezed Sam's shoulder. "We know."

A month after Hope's birth, Issac invited Sam out for one of their usual Saturday morning breakfasts. Sam hadn't seen his friend since before the baby was born. He'd seen the huge teddy bear and Pampers he had delivered to Lydia's apartment.

It will be good to see and talk with Issac, Sam thought, driving to Cookie's. He could already taste the grease the bacon would be fried in on that ol' dirty stove. Calories and cholesterol be damned, that was their spot. Together, he, Issac, Jim, and Greg used to go to Cookie's at least one Saturday every month to catch up on one another's lives. Jim had moved to L.A. to pursue the acting bug ("When was the last time you saw a movie being filmed in Denver?" Jim had explained before breaking out). Greg had fallen in love with a med-school student at the university where he taught economy classes and had moved with her when she got accepted to Meharry Medical College.

So that left him and Issac. And they had been unfaithful to their ritual. Pulling into the parking lot, Sam felt his grin grow into a smile thinking about the familiarity of Saturday morning breakfast with his friend.

Issac was already there, waiting for a table.

"Yo, that X-5 is hot. When did you get it?" Issac said, pulling Sam in for a "brotherman" shake and hug. "What's up?"

"I'm cool. I got it right before Hope's birth," Sam replied.

"I should be asking you what's up. Love done got you wrapped up, no one has seen you anywhere."

"True that, true that," Issac said, happy to see his friend.

The two were seated at a window booth and the waitress took their orders for coffee and promised to come back in a few minutes for their meal orders.

"Thanks for all the stuff you sent over to Lydia's," Sam said, checking out the menu as if he hadn't already decided what he wanted to eat on the way to the restaurant. "It's great, I really appreciated it."

"No prob," Issac said. "I didn't know if I should have sent it to your crib or hers. I figured the baby was with her. I really wasn't all that sure you still go over there."

"Naw, I try to get over there a couple times a week," Sam answered.

Sam ordered exactly what he had been thinking about in the truck. Issac settled on the French toast, bacon, and grits.

"You know, Stacy doesn't let me eat any of this at the crib," Issac said, laughing after finishing his order. "You know, you turn thirty-five, folks want to start acting like you're a slice of bacon away from a heart attack. I think I'm pretty healthy."

They laughed.

"So, how are things, Sam?" Issac inquired. "Really, what's up with you and Lydia? I heard the baby hasn't tested positive. That's a good sign, right?"

"Who told you?" Sam wanted to know.

"I ran into Toni the other day. Her company is working on this event the partners are throwing for the mayor. I took her to lunch and we talked," Issac detailed.

"That Toni, always running her mouth," Sam said as the plates of hot food were put on the table.

"Hey, it wasn't even like that." Issac calmed Sam. "She wouldn't even tell me anything. I begged her. I told her I hadn't been able to get in touch with you. It was cool. She's not going around telling all y'all's business.''

"Well, to tell the truth, it's been mostly Mrs. Peters, Toni, and Dara who have been taking care of Lydia and Hope,'' Sam confessed.

"Hold up,'' Issac said. He prayed over the meal for both of them and started to dig into the grits. "These need some salt and pepper. I probably should have ordered the eggs to mix them up with.''

"Yeah, brutha, you know, nothing beats mixing your grits with the eggs,'' Sam said, cheesing over his plate full of mixed eggs and grits.

"So what's up?'' Issac asked of his friend. "Are you going to be an absentee father? What's the deal? How are you and Lydia going to work things out?''

"Whoa, that's a whole lot of questions over breakfast. Slow down, partner,'' Sam said, trying to stuff his face with a piece of bacon. Sam knew he would have to break down what had been going on with Lydia and him. Issac was not the type of cat to just let folks be slack. He had always been the serious one in the group—he was always checking up on everyone to make sure things didn't get too out of control.

Sam took another bite out of his toast, slid to the back corner of the booth, and looked out the window. He was halfway interested in the people he could see walking by, but in reality he was avoiding Issac's questions.

"Sam.'' Issac continued his interrogation. "You don't have to tell me anything if you don't want to. I'm just concerned about you and this situation with Lydia and your daughter.''

Sam pulled his plate over to where he was now sitting in the booth. He looked up at Issac and said, "Why you have to always guilt brothers into giving you the dirt? You're always trying to be everyone's daddy.''

Issac just laughed, eating the last of his French toast.

"Naw, bro, that's not it at all," he said. "If you feel guilty about something and, knowing our group, most of y'all had something to feel guilty about, then it was going to come out eventually. I figure, it just might as well be someone with a sympathetic ear."

"Man, shut up and pass me the jelly," Sam responded.

Sam continued to eat. Issac dropped the subject for a new chapter on an old discussion: music. Issac had decided in 1995 that he no longer would listen to contemporary music. He said it all was irrelevant. He went into this buying frenzy. Anything before 1989 that he didn't already own became a must-buy for him. Santana, Cameo, even Miles Davis. Now, he thought he was the unequivocal historian on jazz and R&B.

Sam wasn't hearing it. Today's installment was Sam trying to convince Issac he should be listening to Erykah Badu's *Mama's Gun* and Outkast's *Stankonia*.

"See, that's why you sound like you just stepped out of an episode of *Good Times*," Sam said to Issac.

"Whatever, man, with what I listen to, lyrics and the actual musicality count," Issac boasted.

They had finished their breakfast a while ago and had been talking, bringing up the memories that were once shared in this restaurant with their other friends.

Finally Sam came out with it. "Dude," he said. "The whole thing just really scares me." Sam started to rub his temples. Issac sat quietly, looking directly at him. He didn't say a thing, hoping the silence would coax Sam into saying what he needed to say.

"All I'm feeling is pressure, you know," Sam continued. "I was crushed after she told me about the virus. I couldn't believe it. First, she tells me we are going to have a baby. I was really excited. I was planning on moving in with her—we were going to be a little family, you know?"

Sam alternated looking at Issac and peering out the plate-glass window. To his knowledge, this was the first time he'd even thought about articulating what he was feeling with anyone.

"Then she drops this bomb on me. What was I supposed to do? She put my life in danger. I just keep waking up in the middle of the night and thinking about all the good times we've had. Then other nights I wake up and I can't believe I was going to get married to her."

Issac sat back in the booth and listened intently.

"You know, I don't think I've slept through the night since that night in October. I've become an insomniac. And I hate it."

"Well, I'm not going to be preachy, man," Issac said. "I just want you to know that I'm always here for you. You have to talk about what you are doing there. The past nine months have not been a picnic for you or Lydia. It's not what you guys had been planning. So I understand."

Issac continued as the waitress placed the check on the table.

"But you have to make some decisions. It's not just about you and Lydia anymore. You're someone's father," Issac made clear. "It's just not about you anymore. I don't want to tell you how or who to love, but you had made the decision to marry this woman and take care of her the rest of your life. Do you really want to start over? Plus, don't be like Greg with his girl *and* his baby's momma."

They both laughed. "C'mon, let's get out of here," Issac said, picking up the check and motioning to the door. He paid the cashier at the counter and put on his jacket.

Sam let Issac's words hit the back of his brain. He did need to make some big decisions—soon.

"Yo, how does the truck drive? I want to take it for a test drive," Issac said as they walked through the parking lot.

"If you think I'm letting you drive my new car, you're tripping," Sam shot back.

"C'mon, yo, I need to go to the hardware store. Let me drive it over there, it's just a couple of blocks," Issac asked. "Then you can swing me back over here to pick up my car."

Sam threw Issac the key and walked around to the passenger side. "Just be careful, man," Sam said, buckling himself in.

As soon as Issac turned on the ignition, the two were blasted by music coming out of the speakers. "Man, what's wrong with you?" Issac turned down the volume and changed the channel. He changed it to 92.1 AM. Moremi Hawkins, the usual Saturday morning host, was in the middle of playing a block of ConFunkShun songs.

"Now, that's music," he said, bobbing his head. "You don't know nothing about that, son."

Moving out into traffic, Issac continued what he'd started in the restaurant. "So, you're not getting much sleep. What are you thinking about?"

Sam slumped toward his window, put his elbow on the door handle, and held up his head with his fist. "I guess I've really been avoiding any real, deep thinking," he said. "I just get up and jump on the computer. Do you know how liberating it is to do the majority of your shopping at your own crib in your drawers? The Internet is great. It's going to be the downfall of the malls."

"So, when are you going to start thinking seriously?" Issac inquired. "Do you think you need to see a doctor?"

"Naw, I'm not going to take sleeping pills," Sam responded.

"No, fool." Issac laughed. "Not a regular doctor, a therapist or psychologist. Someone who you can let it all out to and get feedback from."

"I thought that's why I'm letting you wheel my new ride to the store," Sam joked.

They laughed.

"Well, yeah, but my expertise is contract law. You have real problems, and you might want to think about seeing a professional who can really put things in perspective for you," Isaac suggested.

"Yeah," Sam said. "Maybe I do."

Issac pulled into the parking lot of the hardware store. It was packed with weekend do-it-yourselfers. They went in for the wall hangers Issac needed to pick up for Stacy. They talked a bit more while walking through the aisles and testing all the Black & Decker drills they wished they could justify purchasing.

On the way back to Cookie's, Sam promised he would call Issac if he needed anything and he would, indeed, consider making an appointment to see a counselor.

"The ride was smooth," Issac said, pulling up next to his own car. "Good buy, although I would have gotten leather everything." He started laughing.

"Thanks for everything," Sam said, walking to the driver's side. "I needed this. I'll be in touch. Peace."

"No problem, man. Call me." Issac waved him off.

Sam got in his SUV and drove off. *He's right, I probably do need to talk with someone. I need to stop avoiding what's bothering me.*

In his apartment, Sam searched through his CD collection. *Hmm, what do I want to listen to?* he thought. He needed to wash his clothes and clean up a bit. No matter what he did, Sam always thought he needed some music playing in the background. His world was one little music video.

He also needed to pack his suitcase. He was flying out in the morning to attend a trade show in Los Angeles for the company. The show was only two days, but he was extending his trip to spend some time with his parents, who lived just outside the L.A. city limits. *I need to go pick up my suits from the cleaners before they close,* he thought. *Oh, I guess I should call and let Lydia know I'm leaving town.*

Los Angeles was great. As with most of the times he visited his hometown, Sam thought the city looked more and more like the postcard they sold at LAX. His hotel was in Santa Monica. He didn't mind the drive in traffic to get to the convention center near downtown. He just liked being near the water. It was one of the things he truly missed living in a landlocked city like Denver.

The trade show was successful. *My bosses will be happy with the buzz the company's products received,* he thought on his way to his parents' house for lunch. Sam drove the freeways with ease: the 10 to the 405 to the 91. It was as if he'd never left. *Yeah, new developments go up,* he thought, *but the freeways pretty much always stay the same.*

Sam saw his father in the garage when he drove up. Sam was glad to be home. He always felt safe when at his parents' house. It was as if he were a teenager again. Their presence made him feel like no problems were too big.

Turning off the engine, he could see his father yell through the garage door, most likely to Sam's mother, letting her know he had arrived.

She opened the front door and met her husband near the garage entrance. They stood there, waiting for Sam to walk up the driveway.

"I'm so happy to see you," Mrs. Thomas said. She hugged her son and gave him a kiss on the cheek. "Glad to see you home, son," his father chimed in.

"C'mon in. I didn't cook, but I figured we could go eat

at Red Robin or something,'' his mom said, walking him inside the house.

"Not Red Robin.'' Sam turned up his nose.

"I thought you liked their burgers,'' she said. "Well, we haven't been to Marie Callender's in a while.''

"That's fine, I actually could go for one of their Frisco burgers,'' Sam said.

"Have a seat,'' Mr. Thomas said, motioning to the couch. Sam sat down next to his mother. His father went into the kitchen to pour a cup of coffee and came back into the family room to talk with his son.

"I thought you were going to bring the baby with you,'' his mother said. "I guess I'm going to have to come to Denver to see my only grandchild. I downloaded the pictures you E-mailed us. See, I printed them out on the new color printer your father bought me. I put them in a frame.''

She got up, took down two frames from the mantel over the fireplace, and showed them to Sam. Hope was really cute. He still could not believe he had a daughter.

"How's Lydia doing?'' his father wanted to know.

"She's fine,'' Sam stuttered. "Mrs. Peters told me to tell you guys hi for her. Mom, she said she's sorry she hasn't E-mailed you in a while.''

"Oh, that's fine, I'll call her next week,'' she said. "Well, let me get my purse and we can go.''

Lunch went well. Sam talked about his job and the new responsibilities received with his promotion in May. His parents inquired more about the baby and talked about how much they wanted to visit. Mrs. Thomas tried to catch Sam up on the lives of all his cousins and old friends who still lived in the area. After lunch, they bought a strawberry pie to take with them and went back to the house to devour the tasty dessert.

Later in the evening, Sam followed his father out to the garage, where his father had converted half the space into a workshop. Mr. Thomas used to work for Amtrak, and his hobby was collecting toy trains. As a child, Sam used to help his father build the little landscapes the trains chugged around.

"Got any new engines, Pop?" Sam asked.

"No, I'm just trying to repair Big Red," he answered, pointing to a large engine with most of its pieces lying near it on a table. "She broke down about a month ago, but I've had her since before you were born. I guess I should just let her go and buy a new one."

Sam went over to the table and thought about all the times he'd played with the train engine.

"I didn't want to mention it at lunch, but your mom's real worried about you and Lydia, son," Mr. Thomas said. "And I am, too."

Sam knew he didn't want to have this conversation with his father. But he knew it was coming.

"She wants to see her grandchild, and is worried that if you and Lydia don't work things out, she's going to miss out on Hope's life," the senior Thomas continued. "We know what happened was hard on you, but you haven't let us know what your plans are."

Sam leaned back on the hood of his mother's car. "I hear you, Pop," was all Sam was ready to say.

The funny thing, he thought, was this conversation was starting to sound just like the one he'd had with Issac on Saturday. Maybe it was a sign: He needed to get it together.

"Well, I've been going to her place a couple of times a week to take groceries and baby stuff," Sam explained. "Mrs. Peters has been staying there with her and, of course, I can't go over there without running into Toni and Dara."

"How are Toni and Dara?" Mr. Thomas asked. "We haven't heard from them in a while. You know, Toni used to send your mom products from the events her company was involved in. She really liked that girl."

"Yeah, they are fine. They seem to be doing the job I guess I am supposed to be doing," Sam said, feeling a bit defeated. "I just don't know what to do, Pop, I don't know how to approach it. It's weird."

The elder Thomas sat at his workbench. "Son, life throws us curveballs," he said. "Sometimes I think we did you an injustice. You were an only child who was completely spoiled. We gave you the best we could and tried to protect you from everything. But the problem with that was you were never able to cope when things didn't go your way."

Sam stood up and moved closer to his father. He found a seat on the step stool and listened to his father's wisdom. *Forget the shrink,* he thought, *my father's breaking it down.*

"You know, Sam, I have to tell you how proud your mother and I am of you. You went to school and even got a master's degree. We were so proud of you when you moved to Denver to be a junior partner at Phelp's," he said. "You know, Mr. Anderson asks about you every time I go into his shop to get my hair cut."

Sam smiled. He hadn't seen Mr. Anderson in a while. *Maybe I'll stop by there since I'm here,* he thought.

"Son, I love you . . . your momma loves you," Mr. Thomas said. "But it's time for you to stop running and do right by Lydia. I understand about the disease. That's some heavy stuff to deal with, but you have to be strong."

Wow, was all Sam could think. What was he going to say in response to his father?

"Yeah, I know," Sam said, scratching the back of his neck. "Actually, I've been thinking a lot about that lately. It's just a lot, Pops. It's a lot to take on—"

His father interrupted him. "Didn't you ask her to marry you?" he asked.

Sam nodded his head in affirmation. "I did."

"In thirty-six years of marriage to your momma, I've learned the true meaning of 'in good times and bad,' " he said. "Things haven't always been great with me and your momma. Did you know she almost left me?"

Sam had never heard about this near breakup. He was a little shocked to hear it. He had always thought of his parents as happy and problem-free. *As you get older, your parents see you in a totally different light and tell you all kinds of stuff,* he thought.

"I didn't know that, Pops," Sam said. "What happened?"

"I'll tell you another time," his father said. "I'm trying to relate this to you and Lydia. You see, marriage is more about the rough spots than the easy road. When you called and told me last year you were going to ask Lydia to be your wife, I thought that was great. I thought you had finally put someone else's well-being in front of yours. I thought you had finally realized that if you could make it through the bad times with someone, it would make the good times even better."

The elder put down the tools he was cleaning. "It's terrible what happened to Lydia, and we are so glad the baby is fine," he continued, "but, son, you were about to marry this woman and say in front of everyone you knew you would be with her 'in good times and bad, in sickness and health.' Not enough people understand the meaning of those words anymore. When you popped the question to her, that was when you were married. The wedding is just for show."

Sam sat there for a minute. "You've given me a lot to think about, Pop. Thanks," he said.

"We want the best for you, son, and we want you to be happy," his father said, patting him on the shoulder.

Sam got up from the stool and moved toward the door into the house.

"No matter what you decide, I want you to know your mother and I will respect and support your decision," his father continued. "Oh, and when you go into the house, tell your momma to bring another piece of that pie."

Sam walked into the kitchen and gave his mother the message. He then went upstairs to his old room, which had been turned into a sitting room. He fell into the plush chaise opposite the TV. His father had given him an earful to think about. He had some huge decisions to make, and the world wasn't slowing down. He needed to pick up the pace and figure out what he wanted in his life and how Lydia would fit into that, or even if she would be a part of the plan.

Chapter Nine

Samuel Wants Back In

Sam enjoyed the few days he spent with his parents, but the last day or so began to be a little awkward as the three tried to avoid the conversation they all seemed to want to have. The distance his parents placed between themselves and Sam gave him a lot of time to think things through on his own terms.

At first Sam thought he was caving from the pressure everyone seemed to be putting on him to get back with Lydia. Or maybe he felt sorry for her and, after all, she was the mother of his child.

But on the plane ride from L.A., it all came together for Sam. He hated to admit it, but Issac and his father were right to say there was more at stake in his relationship with Lydia than he had given thought to. Trying to maneuver his knees for just a little bit more space, he replayed the conversations over and over again. By the time the plane landed, he decided Lydia was the woman with whom he wanted to spend the rest of his life. He asked her to marry him once and knew that he still loved her.

Somewhere in the midst of everything, things had just gotten out of control. She had said things, he had said things, and the awkwardness had grown to a point where Sam did not know what to do. Little did he understand that he'd never bothered to say those two important words—I'm sorry—that would have put them back on the same path so long ago. Sam always had a hard time with those words. He preferred to let time pass and move on as if whatever problem he had had never happened. He finally admitted that, as his father had said, he was not one who dealt with stress well. But he was determined to start anew with everything, and that included asking Lydia to marry him again.

Driving home, Sam continued thinking things through. Marriage was taken all too lightly, he thought. It was an ancient blood covenant that meant more than just standing in front of people and lighting candles. It was the commitment of two people coming together and building a life as one—no matter what. He definitely would have stood in front of everyone who attended the wedding and said those words: *in sickness and in health*. Why was it so different before the ceremony?

It was eating at him the entire time it took him to get to his apartment. *I do love Lydia,* he thought. *She is the love of my life*. It was the reason he was having problems sleeping since that night he'd walked out of Lydia's apartment. He had to tell her. He wanted to do whatever it took to repair their relationship and get back on that road-for-two he'd put on hold nearly a year ago. It seemed as if a giant load was released from Sam's brow.

Sam reached for the phone and hit the memory button programmed with Lydia's phone number. Waiting for her to pick up the line, he went over and put in a CD. Sam felt jazzed about his new commitment to work on his issues and a bit of Lenny Kravitz was just what he wanted to listen to. Sam considered Lenny a master of love, loss, and celebration. He found "Let Love Rule." Still waiting for the other end to pick up, he pressed Play and went to the fridge to see what he had to eat.

"Hello, Peters's residence," Toni answered on the other end.

"I figured you would pick up," Sam said.

"It's nice to hear from you, too, Mr. Thomas," she snapped.

"Naw, it's not like that." Sam backed out of a confrontation. "I know you guys are doing a lot for Lydia and Hope. I really appreciate all you and Dara are doing."

"Mmm-hmm," Toni said. "Hold on, I'll get Lyd."

"Hello." Sam heard Lydia's voice and for the first time in months, he felt excited—not confused, sad, or hurt—just generally happy to hear her voice.

"Hey, Lydia," he said.

"Oh, hey, Samuel," she responded.

"I just got back from L.A.," he stammered out. "My parents told me to tell you hi and that they'll be making a trip out here soon to see Hope."

"That's fine," she said. "It will be good for them to see her."

"I wanted to know if I can take you to dinner sometime soon," he blurted out as if he were in high school again, begging Yolanda Brown to the junior homecoming dance.

Lydia was somewhat taken aback. Sam had been so distant in the past few months that an invitation to dinner was the last thing she expected from him.

"Um, yeah," she said, surprising herself. "Let me know when."

Sam did not hesitate. "What about Monday night?" he said.

"No problem. I'll drive since I already have the baby seat in my car," she responded.

"Cool. I'll come over around six," Sam said. "Do you or Hope need anything? I'll bring some more formula and diapers by tomorrow."

"Okay, see you then." Lydia hung up the phone and took Hope from Dara. "What did he want?" her friends inquired.

"He wants to take me to dinner," she said. "What do you think he wants?"

"Who knows?" said Toni, washing out baby bottles in the sink. "Just be cool, whatever he says."

"Well, I'm done and I'm out," Toni yelled, walking toward the couch to pick up her purse. "I'll call you tomorrow. I'm going out with Steve tonight. He's taking me to the Four Seasons."

"Girl, don't do anything I wouldn't," Dara said in jest.

"Then I guess I won't be going out tonight, huh?" Toni shot back as she closed the door.

"You are so wrong." Lydia laughed. "Don't mind her, Dara."

"I'm not studying her," she said.

Dara put another load of Hope's bibs and stuff in the washing machine and told Lydia good-bye.

Scanning her apartment and holding Hope in her arms, all Lydia could think was how blessed she was to have such good friends.

Sam was actually early for his outing with Lydia and Hope. He rang the doorbell, which annoyed Lydia, because he still had his key and she was busy trying to get their fussy baby into her clothes. He rang the bell again, and Lydia yelled for him to use his key.

"Hey, you need any help?" Sam said, shutting the door.

Lydia finishing putting on Hope's clothes and packed her into the car seat that doubled as a holder, a gift from Andrea.

"We're almost ready," she said. "Let me get my purse."

Sam took Hope from Lydia and headed out the door. Everything seemed fine until he attempted to fit Hope's seat into its base in the back of Lydia's car. After a few failed attempts, a frustrated Lydia told him to get out of the way so she could do it. *I can't believe he doesn't know how to do this,* she thought, locking in her child. *It just goes to show just how much he isn't around.*

The ride to Red Lobster was pleasant enough. Sam told her all about his trip to L.A. and his visit with his parents. Lydia got along well with the Thomases. His mother had been nothing but sweet to her, even when they broke up. And Lydia thought Sam's father was fine (for an older man). She always prayed Sam would look the same way as he matured.

It being Monday night, the wait was only five minutes. The wait staff didn't take long to find a table that would accommodate the three of them.

Dinner was good. Lydia hadn't been out in public much lately. Hope was only a little more than a month old, so she didn't have time or the strength to be lugging the baby all over the place.

Sam told Lydia he'd had breakfast with Issac before he left and used that as a segue to discuss their reconciliation.

"Lyd," Sam said, feeling nervous about the conversation they were about to have. "I just haven't been the same since things got bad between us. I haven't been able to sleep. I've been tripping at work and unable just to focus on anything for too long."

Lydia rolled her eyes and turned to make sure Hope was still asleep.

"My Visa bill is out of control. You'd be amazed how much stuff you can buy on the Internet at three o'clock in the morning,'' he continued, trying to inject a bit of levity. Lydia picked up her fork and took a bite of her snapper.

"Well, I've figured out the cause of all my problems,'' Sam said.

"Really?'' Lydia said. She put down the fork, clasped her hands, and brought Sam into focus. She knew he was doing his best to wiggle his way back. But as much as she wished they were back together, she wasn't going to make it easy for him. Lydia'd felt let down and abandoned during the pregnancy. Yes, he was good enough to accompany her to her prenatal doctor appointments and brought over more than enough stuff once Hope was born, but the time was completely devoid of any type of emotional support.

And if this fool thinks he can just take me to Red Lobster and apologize and everything is going to be okay, he's got another thing coming, she thought, looking at him across the table.

"I guess''—Sam paused, not quite sure how this was about to go down—"what I'm trying to say is that I'm sorry. I was a jerk, I know now. I apologize for how I've treated you in the last ten months. I've been incredibly whack.''

Tears were starting to well up in Sam's eyes. He did love Lydia, and although this was a breakthrough moment for him, he was unsure how she would take all of this.

"My life has been shit since I walked out of your apartment last October,'' he pleaded. "And I've figured out why; it's because we haven't been together. You were my world, and with you out of my orbit, things were just crazy.''

Lydia saw Sam pouring his heart out. One side of her wanted to run to the other side of the table and hug his old pitiful ass, but she was standing firm. It was going to take more than just tonight for him to prove himself worthy of being back in her emotional life. She took a sip of her juice and started to address Mr. Thomas.

"I hear what you are saying, Sam," she began. "And I can appreciate the self-actualization you've gone through. But it's just crazy for you to think that just because you've finally chosen to get over yourself, I'm supposed to melt into your arms and we'll be cool again." Lydia paused to drink some more juice.

"Naw, I don't think that," Sam attempted to get in edge-wise.

Lydia was quick to shut him down and continue her point. "Sam, I loved you more than I ever loved anyone. I thought we were invincible and that no matter what our problems were, our love was strong enough to weather the storm. And the way you acted during my pregnancy completely shattered my belief that we had what it took to make a marriage work."

She put her hand on the sleeping baby and tried to keep her voice down. *There is no reason to make a scene in this restaurant. That was clearly a Toni move,* she thought.

"So many times I needed you," she explained. "And not just to bring over diapers. We were blessed. I had an extremely uncomplicated pregnancy with Hope—and praise God she wasn't born with the virus—but I had a really hard time emotionally. I needed you and you weren't there for me."

Lydia felt herself starting to cry and she didn't want to—not here, not now, not in front of this fool and all these random people.

She was hot. She was letting him have it, but her temper was getting the best of her. She knew she needed to shut it down and not speak for a minute. She picked up her fork again to finish her meal.

Sam, looking like a dog that had just gotten beaten by its master, was on the retreat. *What did I say?* he thought, finishing his red potatoes. *Should I continue?*

Sam let the sound of their forks against the plates fill

their booth for a few minutes before he said anything more. "Look, Lydia," he said. "I understand I hurt you and I wasn't there emotionally. I do. I was miserable, too. The discovery of the virus in your body was a disaster for me. I shut down to everyone. I'm really sorry that it took me this long, but I'm here. I just ask that you think about it, okay?"

The rest of the meal was eaten in near silence, and the ride back to Lydia's apartment was the same. Sam believed he'd made his point and had a valid request. Lydia was still mad, but she didn't want to come off as bitter and mean. She had listened to what he'd said, but was not entirely sure Sam was worthy of her trust. So together, all the way home, the silence was their pool, and they swam in the possibilities of their futures.

Once at the apartment building, Sam helped Lydia with Hope, who was surprisingly quiet all night. Sam took her sleeping as a good sign. Hope had not woken up, and he'd gotten two uninterrupted hours with Lydia.

Lydia, on the other hand, felt her maternal instincts kicking, and she became a bit worried. She figured once Sam was out the door, she would wake Hope just to make sure everything with her daughter was fine.

Their silence was broken in the elevator. Young Hope had awoken, and Lydia could tell it was the cry of hunger. She rushed to her door and put her stuff and the baby holder on the table once she was inside the apartment.

"Can I do anything?" Sam asked, feeling out of the loop.

"Yeah, can you look in the refrigerator and pull out one of those bottles, then use that pot on the stove to warm it up? Just fill the pot to about half full and heat the bottle," she said, pulling the baby from the seat and placing her on her shoulder.

Hope was comforted a little, but she wanted to eat—right

then, right now. Her cries continued. Sam did as Lydia asked. "Is there anything else you need me to do?"

Lydia was pacing the living room with Hope to quiet her. The milk would not be ready for a few minutes. She knew she would be hungry. Hope had eaten well before they'd left for dinner. Lydia was surprised Hope had waited this long to wake up demanding food.

"If you want, you can put the clothes in the washer into the dryer," Lydia requested. "And, if you are still interested in helping, you can hold your daughter while I go change into something else."

She handed Sam Hope and went into the bedroom. She changed out of her shoes and jeans into a pair of old sweatpants and put on some socks. Looking into the mirror, she thought to herself, *How long is he going to stay? I have to cut this short.*

Lydia moved back into the front of the apartment. She went into the kitchen to check on the milk.

"So, what else do you have planned for tonight?" she asked. Sam had already made himself comfortable with Hope. He was sitting on the couch and had turned on the TV.

"Oh, nothing," he replied. "I can stay and help out with the baby for a while."

Damn him, she thought, testing the milk from the bottle on her wrist. *That's all I need. Be strong, Lydia. Be strong.*

She walked over to the couch and gave Sam the bottle. She watched him as he gently rolled Hope off of his shoulder and cradled her in his arm. He tested the milk's temperature and put the nipple in her toothless mouth. The cries were gone. "See, that's all she wanted," he said, looking down at Hope. "That's all you wanted, huh, Hope? Just want something to eat."

Lydia was resigned that Sam would be in the apartment longer than she'd anticipated. She started to straighten up a bit. There was baby stuff everywhere. Her mother had been there earlier in the day. Mrs. Peters had spent most of her time playing with her granddaughter while Lydia had gotten out to run some errands. And from the looks of the apartment, they'd gone from the crib to the playmat with the toys that hang from above to the couch. There were baby blankets, towels, and toys everywhere.

"I'm going to fix myself some tea. Would you like a cup?" she asked him.

"Yeah, that would be great," he replied.

Lydia put some water in the kettle and found some tea. She was drinking decaffeinated Earl Grey and, just for good measure, she put a bag of chamomile in Sam's cup. She figured it would make him sleepy and he'd leave on his own accord.

By the time Lydia brought over the tea, Hope had finished her bottle and Sam had put her over his shoulder to burp her.

"Here you go," she said, putting the tea on the coffee table and curling up in the armchair. "You could get real good at that."

"Yeah, I guess I could use some more practice." Sam smiled. "You think I can take her for a weekend?"

Lydia smiled, taking the teacup from her mouth. "Let's not get crazy, okay?" she joked. "I'm not really ready for her to be away from me for that long. Maybe we could work something out where you could come and stay here some weekends."

Sam got excited but tried not to let Lydia know just how excited he was. *I got to her,* he thought, moving Hope to the other side. *Maybe she really was listening to what I had to say.*

"We can move some of Hope's stuff and pull out the couch bed for you," she continued, making sure he understood the ground rules from jump.

"Yeah, that would be cool," Sam said. "That would be cool."

The two talked for another two hours before Sam got up to go to his place.

"Okay, so I'll be over again on Wednesday," Sam said. He grabbed his key and headed for the door. "Call me and let me know what you're running out of and I'll bring it with me. Thanks, Lydia, for hearing me, you know."

"No problem, Sam," she said. "I'm open to talk, but we have to take it slow, okay?"

"Okay," Sam said, hopeful. Lydia held the baby in her arms as he shut the door behind him.

Hope was asleep, but she was scared to put her down and wake her up. *He was kind of cute tonight trying to apologize,* she thought to herself. She had seen Sam through his best and worst in the five years they'd dated, and she recognized a new man tonight. *He just might be ready,* she thought, locking the door. *He just might be ready.*

During the next few weeks, Sam had stepped up his game. Instead of coming over to Lydia's apartment twice a week, he stopped by every day after work. He even spent the majority of his weekends at the house running errands, going grocery shopping, washing clothes, and generally trying to impress upon Lydia that he was a changed man and was ready to take on his responsibilities.

On this Saturday, Sam had come over early. He was going to watch Hope all weekend. As a gift, Sam had bought Lydia a two-day package at the Oasis Day Spa. It was approximately an hour and a half outside of the city. When he presented it to her, Lydia broke down and cried.

"This is for being such a great mother to my child," he told her. She couldn't believe it. She was starting to really open up to him, and this was unexpected. She agreed to let him watch Hope for the weekend she used the certificate. Sam was psyched. He was finally going to prove he could take care of Hope just as well as she could, and he was racking up brownie points with Lydia.

Of course, Lydia was excited about the trip. She secretly looked forward to an entire weekend away from Hope. Motherhood was great, but a few days away from the smell of formula and the thought of not having to wash any dishes or change any diapers made her praise the Lord. A few days after Sam had given her the certificate, she called Dara and Toni. She had made reservations for all three of them. Taking her cue from Mr. Thomas, she paid for her friends to come along with her. They had been so wonderful to her and Hope. They'd unselfishly offered themselves up throughout the pregnancy and even once Hope was born, they'd continued to pitch in. They deserved it, she thought. Plus, how much fun would they have getting pampered all weekend?

Toni decided she wanted to drive. Although it was clearly in the middle of the fall season, she insisted on driving her Saab with the top down.

"Y'all need to learn how to live," she told her passengers. "I drive like this until it gets below forty degrees. How do you think I get such wonderful skin? The cool air keeps the muscles in my face tight."

Dara laughed. "You have got to be kidding. It's cold, Toni, you should want to put the top up on this thing. Plus, I just got my hair done two days ago."

"Oh, you did?" Toni asked playfully.

"Naw, girl, I kind of like it," Lydia chimed in from the backseat. "The air feels good. This is going to be a good weekend."

Not a minute had passed before Lydia began to take out her cell phone. Toni saw her in the rearview mirror. "Girl, who are you calling at eight-thirty in the morning on a Saturday?" she inquired.

"Oh, I'm just going to call Sam and make sure everything is fine," she said innocently. "I can't remember if I told him where everything is at."

"You need to cut it out," Toni said, flipping her hair out of her face.

"Yeah, that doesn't make any sense," Dara joined in. "We just left him twenty minutes ago."

"Y'all will understand when you have your babies," Lydia said in her defense.

To which Toni replied, "Yeah, whateva. You need to quit tripping. That's what this whole weekend is about. Relax, enjoy yourself. He's Hope's father, not some random teenage baby-sitter. They will be fine. You can call when we get to the resort."

Toni laughed and stepped hard on the gas. Dara and Lydia sat back in their seats and enjoyed the ride. Smiles of contentment flashed across all of their faces. This was going to be a good respite from their daily lives in Denver.

"Time for our five P.M. mud baths," Dara reminded her friends. Lydia couldn't afford single rooms for all of them, so she'd reserved a villa and had the front office bring another bed. It didn't matter to any of them; the villa was great, and it had two bathrooms and a huge living room with overstuffed cushion chairs. "It's better for us all to be together," Dara had said upon arrival. It gave them all face time so they could talk.

"Okay, who died and gave you the schedule?" Toni said, coming out of the bathroom. "I thought we weren't on a schedule, that we could just go and do whatever, whenever."

"Well, when we were checking in, I was talking with one of the bellhops, and she said a lot of the amenities get crowded quickly, but you can make reservations to bypass all that," she recounted.

"Girl, you got played," Toni started in. To Toni, there was nothing worse than somebody trying to be her momma. And to her, Dara was always trying to be Lydia's and Toni's mother. "That woman just wanted some tip money."

The three put on their bathing suits and wrapped themselves up with the extra long, incredibly plush towels they found in the closet.

Down in the mudrooms, at least fifteen women had formed a line. They were sitting and talking. It was very much like the waiting area of any hair salon on a Saturday morning.

"Oh, no. I can't be waiting all day for this. I'm going to the pool," Toni said, looking at the backup.

"Hold on, Fasty," Dara said, looking at the sign. "It says if you have an appointment, to go through the door and check in at the desk. See, I told you we would need an appointment." Dara felt triumphant and led her girlfriends through the crowd and into the next room.

"All right, all right," Toni joked. "I'll give you your props."

They were shown into a room with four larger-than-standard-sized bathtubs. They were full of warm mud. Showers were on the other side of the shaded room. The mineral water showers, the woman with the salt-and-pepper short 'fro explained, were for when they were done.

The three stripped down and got into their individual tubs. As they slid down to their necks, a chorus of appreciating "mmmms" and "awwws" were all that could be heard.

"Okay, I could live the rest of my life like this," Toni said. "I'm going to have to get me a man that can install one of these in my house." Dara laughed.

"I don't know," Dara said. "If I had this much mud in my house, I think I would be mad. But here, oh, yeah, I'm all about it."

"They could have made the tubs a little bigger, you know," Toni observed. "Did you see those two big women out there in the line? They are going to squish all the mud up out of the tub."

"You know, you are wrong for that, girl," Lydia said, laughing. "Leave them people alone."

"That wasn't right," Dara said. "But it's kinda true."

"See, I knew you had a mean streak somewhere, Dara," Toni said. They all laughed and enjoyed the warmth of the mud. The steam nearly made Lydia fall asleep. She kept thinking about Sam and Hope. *How can I call without the M.P. down my throat?* she thought, swirling her arms around in the mud. *I'll call him later when I get a moment alone.*

After their forty-five minutes were up, the three washed off and went back to their villa to dress for dinner. The Oasis had a five-star restaurant on the premises, and they couldn't wait to order up something fabulous.

Lydia was the first to be ready. Dara was curling her hair and Toni was still in the shower. Alone in the living room, Lydia decided to call Sam. She took her cell phone, went out onto the balcony, and shut the door so they couldn't hear her.

"Hello," Sam answered. "Oh, hey, Lyd, how's it going?"

"We're fine," she said. "It's really nice. Much nicer than I expected. How's Hope?"

"Oh, she's fine. She's asleep right now." He calmed her nerves.

Lydia could hear the TV blasting, and she thought she heard someone else in the background.

"Who's over there, Sam?" she asked. She felt herself getting hot.

"Oh, it's just Issac," Sam said. "We are watching the game. He had a fight with Stacy and she kicked him out the house, so I invited him over here. It's cool. We are just watching the game."

"Well, tell him I said hi," she said, bringing her temper

back down. "Sam, I wasn't expecting company. I hope you straightened up the place."

"Yeah, yeah . . ." Sam interrupted his thought by screaming about the bad call the ref had just made. He must have startled Hope, because she woke up crying.

"Sam, is Hope crying?" Lydia asked.

"She's okay," he assured her. "Issac and I got a little loud; it's a very intense game. I've got her. She'll be asleep again soon. Is there anything in particular you wanted?"

"No, I'm just checking up on you," she said, missing her child. "I gotta go anyway. We are going to dinner."

"Don't worry about us," Sam said. "I've got it under control."

"Okay, bye," she said. Lydia opened the door only to see Dara and Toni staring at her, looking disappointed.

"Okay, leave that man alone," Dara said angrily.

"You guys don't understand. I can't believe I left Hope all weekend," Lydia said, feeling sorry for her.

Toni went over to her, put her arms around her shoulders, ushered her into the bedroom, and sat her on the bed.

"Girl, Hope is going to be okay," she started while looking for her chocolate brown dress. "The whole point of him giving you this freebie was for you to give him some space. He wants to be in both of your lives, and you're giving him five minutes here and five minutes there. Can't you tell he wants more than that?"

"I guess you are right," Lydia said sheepishly. "I don't know; I just worry."

"Toni's right," Dara said. The other two looked shocked, Toni so much so, she turned from the closet and stood there slackjawed. They looked at each other and laughed.

"Well, whatever," Dara continued. "Sam is a good man. He's got his issues—all men do—but he's a decent guy and he wants to make things right, right?"

They all laughed and Toni found her dress. They walked

all the way down to the restaurant with their arms locked. They were seated near a large window in the back of the restaurant.

"The men of Denver must be partying tonight," Toni said, giggling.

"Why?" the other two asked.

"Have you seen so many women in one place?" Toni continued. "The estrogen level is so high up in here, I feel like I'm going to have a heat flash."

Laughter burst from the table.

"So," Dara said, turning to Lydia after ordering her filet mignon. "What are you going to do with Sam? Are you guys definitely going to get back together?"

Toni put down her wine and moved her chair a little closer to the table to get a good position so she could hear.

"Well, as much as I was fighting it at first, I think I want to." Lydia blushed. "I love him. I never stopped loving him. But I felt he really let me down, you know?"

"Yeah, but he's starting to make up for it, girl," Toni said. She took another sip of her wine. "Sam's cool. I like y'all together a lot. I always thought you guys made sense."

"Yeah, well, Lyd, I think you should have cut him more slack," Dara dug in. "I mean, he is Hope's father, and it wasn't like what happened happened only to you."

Lydia just let it marinate for a bit. The waitress brought over some warm bread and butter. Dara ordered a wine spritzer. Toni held her tongue and ordered another glass of merlot.

"I understand that, Dara," Lydia said. "I don't discount what we both have been through, but the fact is he chose to be emotionally unavailable to me, and now that he's seen the light, I'm just supposed to fall to my knees and be like, 'oh, thank you for coming back'? That just sounds crazy to me."

"Well, I'm just saying that you both have to take steps

toward each other in order to make it work. It's not like he has to do all the giving," Dara explained. "You both have to make the effort, and it seems he is doing that."

"You're right. I am recognizing," Lydia confessed. "I do need to give him his props a little more. But, my whole thing was that I wasn't going to drop the panties just because he walked in the door, you know?"

"Speaking of which, how is that going to work?" Toni asked. "I mean, your doctor said you were very healthy and your T cells were high, but how are you guys going to handle sex?"

"I don't know," Lydia replied. "Condoms, I guess. I really need to ask Dr. Henderson what is the best way to deal with it."

"Great," Dara butted in. "Now that we've gotten that out of the way, can we get into Toni's business?"

"What business? I don't have any business," Toni tried to say.

"Whatever." Lydia laughed. "You always got business."

"Yeah, and Tim, the ad sales guy whose office is next to mine, said he saw Fred trying to give you a golf lesson at the club. I thought you said you cut him off."

"Busted." Lydia laughed more. Two waitresses brought their food to the table. As one of them lifted the silver-domed cover from the cart, steam rose from the plates. "Mmmmm," all three said in a chorus of culinary delight.

The plates were in front of them and the food smelled just as good as it looked. Lydia grabbed Dara's and Toni's hands and started to pray.

"Lord, you are so great and mighty. Thank you for this time together with my girls. Thank you for letting this opportunity come together. I pray that you bless the food we are about to eat, bless the hands that prepared it, and allow us to continue this fellowship through the rest of the weekend. Thank you for giving us so much. Amen."

"Let's dig in," Toni said.

"You don't have to even say it," Dara said, picking up her knife and fork.

"Can I taste that?" Lydia said. Looking at her friends, she saw how blessed she was. They had stuck by her in her darkest hour, and although they were prone to lecture time and time again, she was glad she had them, and would trade them for nothing.

At halftime, Issac went into the kitchen to warm up some of Hope's milk in a pot at Sam's request.

"Man, I still can't believe that you are somebody's daddy," he said to Sam, who was tucking more blankets around Hope. "It's just wild, you know." He retrieved another beer for himself and got Sam a Pepsi.

"So, I take it things are going smooth with you and Lydia, huh?" he inquired.

"Yeah, so far," Sam responded. "But it seems there's one last wall that we can't seem to get over. I don't know how to get past it."

"Well, you know, Stacy's got us going to this relationship counselor because she thinks I have commitment phobia," Issac informed his friend.

"Man, she's really trying to marry you, huh?" Sam said, laughing.

"Man, she don't know," Issac hissed. "It's about to be over, for real. She's just too young, you know. I need a mature woman who knows what she wants out of life."

"Seems to me she knows what she wants," Sam joked. "She wants the two-carat rock and you at home every night." They laughed.

"Naw, but for real, she's not the one," Issac said sadly. "You and Lydia are meant for each other. Me and Stacy—

it's just jokes at this point. She's holding on, but we both know it's over.''

Hope was waking up, and Sam could see her little lips starting to quiver. "Right on schedule. Man, babies have the life," Sam declared.

"Okay, eat, sleep, poop, and everybody's changing up their schedule on your behalf. Too bad you can't ever go back to that," Issac said. Sam motioned for him to go get the bottle.

"Back to what I was saying," Issac said from the kitchen. "Maybe you guys could go for a session or two and see what you can work out. You never know."

"True that," Sam said. He picked up Hope and felt her diaper. His baby skills were getting good, but the weekend without Lydia around to interfere bestowed on him pro status.

"Give me the number before you break out," he said to Issac, returning from the kitchen with bottle, bowl of chips, and sandwich in hand.

"No problem, at least one of us should end up with a relationship that works and is worth fighting for." He sat on the couch and focused again on the game, which was going into its third quarter.

Chapter Ten

The Nuptials

Less than a week later, Sam asked Lydia if she would be open to going to the counselor Issac had suggested. Surprisingly, she agreed without so much as a conversation about it. He took it as an open declaration that she was truly interested in healing their relationship.

Sam was happy. His plans were coming together. From the beginning of his quest to win Lydia's love and trust back, he'd kept a positive outlook, and it seemed the Lord was answering his prayers. If they could just get through Lydia's security issues, he would soon propose to her again. He made the appointment for the following Thursday and called Mrs. Peters to see if she could watch Hope while they worked out their problems.

Mrs. Peters was more than happy to watch her granddaughter. She was very interested in doing whatever it took to get Sam and Lydia back together. Lydia'd been so unhappy with Sam gone, so she was glad to hear of Lydia's weekly efforts toward reconciliation. She was happy because, for a long time, she'd worried that Lydia's positive status would send Sam away from her and Hope forever. The past three months were a blessing she was happy to hear about.

This was Sam and Lydia's second session with Lindsey Monroe, Ph.D. He was an older brother with graying hair at the temples and a fully gray beard. Lydia thought he was sexy. She told Toni and Dara about his looks after the first session. Unfortunately for Toni, he wore a wedding band and had pictures of his family on the desk. Supposedly, she'd sworn off married men after breaking it off with Fred yet again. Still, Toni wanted to arrange a meeting. Lydia just laughed. "You'd think you would learn something from all your mistakes," she told Toni.

"Go back to Whitney Houston's first album," Dara chimed in. "She's got all the jilted lover songs for you to marinate in." They all laughed.

The first session had consisted mainly of setting the ground rules for their conversations with the psychologist. "The truth is of the utmost importance," Dr. Monroe had repeated over and over. He'd told the couple they had to be completely honest with each other, no matter the cost. That was the only way to get over this hurdle in their relationship and go on to the next level.

They'd recounted for the counselor their plans to get married and their eventual breakup a month later. Lydia'd expressed her hurt during her pregnancy and Sam had talked about his insomnia and change of heart. Tears had come to both of them at different parts of the first session, but in the end, they'd both agreed this was a good thing and something that they needed to do.

This week, Dr. Monroe wanted to explore Lydia's trust

issue. To him, it seemed it was the heart of their issues, and once it was corrected, everything else could fall into place.

"How are you two this week?" Dr. Monroe inquired, ushering them into the decent-sized office with two distressed-leather couches set on the opposite side of the office from his desk and file cabinets.

"Fine," Sam and Lydia replied in unison. They hung their jackets on the hooks on the back of the door and took seats on the couch facing the window.

The older gentleman went to his desk, picked up a folder and a notebook, and sat on the couch facing Sam and Lydia. "So," he started in, "where did we leave off last week? Sam, I think you were discussing the realization of your need for Lydia back in your life."

Sam scooted up on the couch a bit. It was deep, and the tendency for anyone sitting there was to lounge back in its pillows.

"Yeah, well, it really happened in a short period of time," Sam said. "It just hit me one day. I was miserable and it was because I'd let Lydia down and pushed her away. It was like I woke up, you know?"

"I see," the psychologist mumbled. He wrote some notes and asked Lydia to comment on what Sam had said.

"Like I've said, I can appreciate Sam's realization, but how am I supposed to just believe that he's not going to abandon me again?" she repeated. "There's nothing else that I would love than for the two of us to be married, but I told myself, I wasn't going to let anyone destroy my self-esteem again like that. And what's to keep him from doing it again?"

Lydia was comfortable challenging Sam about his metamorphosis. She thought it was a great help to have a third party there to officiate.

"I have a long-term chronic disease and a child to raise,"

she continued. "Honestly, I would rather not go through this if I knew Sam might turn cold again."

"I'm right here," Sam said defensively. "You can direct your conversation to me. I'm grown; I can take it."

"Hold on, I don't think she's disrespecting you, Sam," Dr. Monroe jumped in.

"Lydia," Sam pleaded. "I'm here to stay. I really believe it. I can be trusted. But you are never going to be sure unless you jump this ridge with me. You have to let me in and hold on for the ride."

"That's easy for you to say, Samuel," Lydia said, turning to face him. "I was dealing with making sure the baby was fine, my own crazy medicine schedule, and, after five years, life without you. To say it was very hard is an understatement."

"So, Lydia, is it fair to say you are still harboring resentment toward Sam?" Dr. Monroe said. "I think the question that needs to be asked here is, are you willing to let it go?"

The room went silent for a moment. Lydia looked at the doctor, who had put her on the spot, then turned to Sam, who was looking like a puppy that had done something he shouldn't have.

"To be honest, I want to, I really do," she said. "I just don't know if I can. I feel like it is all I have left, and if he is to take what little I have and stomp on it again, I don't know what I would do."

Sam reached over to her hand and looked Lydia in her eyes. "I am in love with you," he started. "I know I can't take back what I've done. Lord knows I wish I could. If I could, I would take it all back and things would have been entirely different. But what's done is done."

Sam took a breath. Dr. Monroe leaned forward as if to say something, but Sam continued. "I can only ask you to take my hand and walk forward with me. There's going to be ups and downs. We don't know how we are going to handle the sex thing or even if we can have more kids. But I'm here to tell you I want to weather the storm with you."

Sam looked more serious than Lydia had ever seen him. He continued to pour out the longings of his heart.

"How could I not be there? You gave me my beautiful daughter and you've supported me, even though I didn't always deserve it. I want to do for you and be there for you for the rest of our days. A life without you is not worth living. I'm just sorry it took me so long to realize it."

Lydia put her left hand to her mouth. She had started to cry halfway through Sam's soliloquy. *How can I resist him? I love him,* she thought.

Dr. Monroe went to his desk to get some tissues. He didn't want to say anything, but in fifteen years of counseling couples, this was one of the more sincere admissions of love he had heard. He knew it wouldn't take long for this couple to meet each other halfway. They just needed a little coaxing.

"You'd better be good to me." Lydia laughed between her tears. "Or the next time, I'm not going to stop my father from going after you with his pistol."

Sam put his arm around Lydia and held on to her tightly. "He was going to shoot me, for real?" Sam asked. Lydia just looked up at him and smiled.

"This has been a good session," Dr. Monroe announced. "I would like to see you guys a couple more times. You can make an appointment with Brenda on your way out. Be good to each other."

Putting on their jackets, again they answered in unison. "We will."

In addition to the counseling Sam and Lydia had begun, Sam also talked with his doctor regarding life with an infected partner. Condoms were definitely a must, and they had to be thoughtful and careful about Lydia's blood and other bodily fluids, but Sam felt deep down he was up to the challenge. He understood the boundaries their life would have, but the alternative was not worth it. Life without Lydia drove him nuts. She was the joy in his life, and that's all there was to it. Yes, the virus made things complicated, but he was willing to do what it took to build a life together.

To Lydia's surprise, Sam was in her kitchen cooking something that smelled fantastic. "Ummm," she said, placing Hope gently on the table and taking off their jackets. "Hey, I didn't know you were going to be here tonight," she said. She placed Hope in the playpen and walked into the kitchen. "I thought you were playing ball with Issac tonight."

"Ah, yeah, I was, but something came up and we had to cancel," he answered. Sam had a definite plan. Tonight he was going to propose to Lydia for the second time.

She hugged Sam and kissed his lips. "You taste good," she said. "What kind of sauce is on your lips?"

"Oh, I just made a cream sauce for the pasta," he said proudly.

She looked for a free burner on the stove to put the teakettle on, but all four were cooking something. "What's all this?" she asked. She glanced around the kitchen and saw the mess. She thought he must have been in there most of the day.

"Nothing. I figured I would make dinner for my two favorite girls," a smiling Sam replied. "Go set the table for me."

"I will in a minute," she said, hearing Hope starting to cry. "I'm going to see about Hope. She probably needs to eat."

Lydia went and picked up the hungry baby and began to feed her with one of the bottles that was in the bag she carried with her everywhere.

Sam continued to steam his vegetables and took out some

plates while he waited. He set the table and let Lydia feed and burp Hope before he brought out their food.

"You know, babies have the life." Sam laughed. "Feed me, clean me, love me, and let me sleep. It's a shame you don't remember how good you had it when you grow up."

They sat down at the table and Sam dished out the food. He'd made sautéed chicken and white sauce over angel-hair pasta with asparagus. *It tastes delicious,* Lydia thought, putting a forkful in her mouth.

"Your skills have truly improved," she told him.

"Huh, what?" he said. "I've always been a good cook. If it's one thing I learned from my mom, it was how to cook."

"I don't know about that," she continued to dig. "When I first met you, you were a big ol' Burger King-eating fool." She laughed and got some sauce on her cheek.

"Whatever, I like a Whopper every now and then," he tried to explain. "Plus, back then I didn't have anyone to cook for, so you just didn't know the extent of my skills."

They laughed and finished their meal. As Sam started to put the dishes in the sink, Lydia went over to the playpen to check on their daughter, who was sleeping soundly.

She chose her Will Downing CD and put it in the player. Walking across the room, she picked up her chardonnay and sat on the couch.

Sam came over, too. Lydia wondered what he was up to. She could always tell when he was up to something. Sam was a corny romantic at heart, and his Cheshire-cat smile always betrayed him.

On the coffee table there was a medium-sized box. Lydia hadn't spotted it. She thought it was funny that anytime someone came in and moved the littlest item, she noticed. But tonight, for some reason, she had walked past it several times and hadn't paid it any attention.

"What's that?" she asked, pointing to the box.

"Oh, I got you something," Sam said nonchalantly. "Why don't you open it?"

Lydia looked at Sam. He was still dressed up from work. She thought he looked so sexy all dressed in slacks, a nice shirt, and his bow tie. He looked like a professor, but she thought his style was cute.

Lydia reached for the package and put it on her lap. It was a brown cardboard box wrapped in clear moving tape. She used her nail to break the tape and opened up its flaps. Within the box she found another that was nicely wrapped in iridescent white paper with a hand-tied bow of natural-colored raffia.

She pulled the smaller box out and put the other one on the floor next to the couch. She did not know what to think. It was strange to her. Sam was a card giver, but rarely went out and bought gifts unless it was someone's birthday or it was Christmas or something.

She was smiling, unable to figure it out. She tugged at the string and started to open the gift at the sides. Lydia never ripped at wrapping paper the way lots of people do. She was always very meticulous about it.

She was so busy unwrapping the box that she did not notice that Sam had moved from the couch and was kneeling in front of her.

Once the paper was off the box, she realized what it was. She was not expecting another engagement ring. Sam took the ring box from her hands and opened it.

"Lydia, it's been a long year and a half," he started. "We've definitely been through some good times and bad."

Lydia put her hand to her mouth in amazement.

"But I want you to know you are the love of my life, and I can't live without you." Sam took the ring from its nesting place and put it on her left ring finger. The diamond was bigger than the first one he'd given her. Sam had never asked for it back, but she'd taken it off two months after

Sam had walked out on her. She'd kept it in one of the little drawers in her jewelry box. She actually hadn't looked at it since.

"Would you do me the favor of spending the rest of your life with me?"

"Oh, Sam," she crooned. "Of course, I will. I guess I should ask if you will be with me the rest of your life?"

"I love you, baby," he said. Lydia nearly knocked him down as she put her arms around his neck, slid down the side of the couch, and met him on the floor. She kissed him and he kissed her.

This is so perfect, she thought. Since the counseling sessions, they had been seriously discussing being back together, but she'd just thought they would move in together, and hadn't really thought about getting married. But she was happy he'd thought of it first.

Sam got up and helped her back onto the couch. She stuck her hand out and looked at the ring. He just sat there and watched her. *She is beautiful,* he thought.

"Are you sure, Sam?" she turned to him and said. "I mean, are you really sure?"

He cupped his hands around hers and stared into her eyes. He leaned forward and kissed her cheek.

"Lydia, I love you and I'm in love with you," he said. "I tried to live without you, you know. We are soul mates, and no disease is going to keep us apart. I want to be here as your man and as Hope's father. I want to be with you for as long as the Lord grants us. I'm very serious about this step. Please follow me down this path."

Lydia began to cry and laid her head on his chest. "Sam," she said, letting the tears run down her cheeks into his tie. "I love you as well. I'll try to make you happy and I will follow you anywhere."

The familiar piano beginning of Will Downing's duet with Rachelle Ferrell on "No One But You" filled the room.

They both just sat on the couch, all hugged up. *There aren't many moments like this one,* Sam thought. *But tonight is perfect.*

Four months after that night, on a bright sunny afternoon, nearly eighty people were assembled in the backyard of Mr. and Mrs. Peters. The yard was beautifully decorated with blush and white roses everywhere. Mr. Peters had built a small trestle for Sam, Lydia, and the minister to stand in front of. Dara and Mrs. Peters had done a wonderful job decorating it with draping ivy vines and had stuck more roses in the lattice on both sides. Mrs. Peters had ordered a huge arrangement to sit on the top.

As Lydia peeked out the window of her old bedroom, where Toni was trying to get her to sit down so she could finish doing Lydia's hair, she could only smile. This wedding was nothing like what her mother had been planning before. It was going to be small and intimate. She'd even chosen a simpler dress than what she had looked at in the bridal shop so long ago. It was brilliant. And instead of a veil, she'd chosen a wickedly sly white sun hat. So she didn't know why Toni was making such a fuss—her head would be covered anyway.

"Girl, I don't care if you are wearing that big ol' hat," Toni said. "Your head still needs to be done. Hello. I don't know why you want to be Scarlett O'Hara with that big thing."

"It's nontraditional, and I thought it was great," she explained to her friend for yet another time. "It's just different and goes with the whole informal thing."

"Whatever, girl, just let me finish bumping these curls," Toni said, holding a hot curling iron.

Dara came into the room and asked if they were ready. "It's ten minutes to two P.M.," she told them.

"Come in and close the door," Lydia said. Toni took Lydia's dress from the back of the door and removed it from the garment bag. Dara grabbed some tissues and dabbed her eyes.

"You are so beautiful," she told Lydia. "I'm so happy for you and Sam."

"Thank you," Lydia said, slipping on the dress. "Now stop crying, you're going to make me cry and mess up my eyes."

"I wish y'all two biddies would cut it out." Toni laughed. She zipped up Lydia's dress in the back as Dara fixed her lipstick.

Mr. Peters knocked on the door. "Lydia, baby girl, are you ready?"

"Just a minute, Daddy," she answered. An electric shock ran the length of her body. She just looked at herself in the mirror. *I'm finally getting married to Sam in the backyard of my parents,* she thought. She felt extreme bliss. This was going to be the beginning of yet another chapter in her life. *So much has happened in the past eighteen months,* she thought. Yet she'd been able to get through it. It had been a trying time, but she was loved and those around her supported her.

I have to be the luckiest woman in the world, she thought, seeing her friends fussing over the back of her dress in the mirror. *HIV is a stumbling block, but I'm dealing with it. I may be positive, but it doesn't mean I can't have a happy, productive life.*

Tears were coming to her eyes, but she fought them back. "I'm ready, Daddy," she said through the door. "I'm ready."

As Lydia, her father, and her bridesmaids got to the back door of the house, the flutist and harpist began playing "The Wedding March." Dara and Toni walked down the aisle first. Sam was standing at the end, flanked by Issac and Greg, who'd flown in from Atlanta with his girlfriend.

Lydia and her father began their walk down the aisle. Everyone was standing and watching her. So many of their friends had come into town for the wedding. It was good to see them—for them to be there for Sam and her on this day. And people from both of their jobs. She almost dropped when she saw John there. She hadn't thought he would come. He was sitting between Margo and Andrea.

Suddenly Sam came into full view. She was so happy to see him standing there waiting for her. *He looks so handsome,* she thought. *He and the guys look so great in their navy sports coats, white slacks and shirts with yellow ties. I knew it would look good.* Sam had to be talked into the ensemble, but to her, he never looked more handsome.

She began to cry walking through the crowd of her family and friends. It was good to see her in-laws sitting in front and smiling at her in approval. Hope was sitting on her grandmother's lap and cooing. It was good to see she was with them, since she hadn't been able to spend that much time with them. But mostly she thought about how Sam and her life were back on track and everyone was here to witness it.

To Mr. Peters, it seemed to take an eternity to get down the aisle. He was handing his only daughter over to Sam. He'd thought no other man could be as good to her as he could, but believed she had finally found someone whose love for her surpassed his own. He was proud. *They will have problems,* he thought, placing her hand in Sam's. *But they'll be fine.* He smiled and told the minister that he and his wife were giving Lydia away. He walked to his wife, who was crying.

Through the twenty-five-minute ceremony, Sam and Lydia felt their bond growing. They were inextricably tied to each other. The words they repeated before the crowd made all the more sense.

"Through good and bad, sickness and health . . ." It all meant so much more than they had ever felt. It was a powerful line. And because of Lydia's virus, the line was a real factor in their relationship, and meant more to them than most people in the chairs realized.

"I present to you Mr. and Mrs. Samuel Thomas," Pastor Jacobs announced. Neither one of them could stop smiling. As they looked out on the crowd, they saw so many accepting faces.

They began walking down the aisle to a loud chorus of handclaps. They were the first steps down the path of their marriage, and it felt good for both of them.

"I love you," Lydia said, nearing the last row of seats. Sam squeezed her hand and said, "I love you."

ABOUT THE AUTHOR

Mikel Husband was born and raised in Southern California. He attended Howard University in Washington, D.C., where he received a B.A. degree in English. Most recently, he has received an M.S.J. from the Medill School of Journalism at Northwestern University. He is currently living on the East Coast, where he continues to pursue his passion for the written word.

SECOND TIME AROUND

Kendra Lee

ACKNOWLEDGMENTS

Thanks to the Lees, Stephen, the Darryls, John, Matt, and Mike for letting me borrow their lives.

Chapter 1

It was rainy, chilly, and gray the day Emmanuel Johnson brought sunshine into our lives. Joseph and I had been taking in foster kids for just a short while then, and only as respite parents. As such, we provided temporary care for the children of other foster parents while those parents were on vacation or had family emergencies to tend to without foster children in tow. Most of the children we provided respite for stayed with us only briefly. Sometimes barely overnight. It was difficult to get the feel of a child's true personality in those spurts.

Emmanuel, though, was different. He came giving the impression that he was setting down roots, establishing a permanence. You know the kind of child—with a smile as wide as the Mississippi, a heart as big as the Kansas prairie. Emmanuel hugged us when he arrived and immediately started calling us ''Mommy'' and ''Daddy.''

We weren't used to this behavior, not even from our own three children. Tristan, thirty, had gone through the typical teenage rebellious years, refusing to be hugged or kissed and calling us by our given names. Duncan was the extremely withdrawn middle child who, now twenty-seven, hadn't blossomed until she'd moved away to New York City, landed a job on Wall Street, and married Greg. And Madison, our twenty-three-year-old baby, though affectionate enough, still kept a large part of herself, her life, a secret from us. We usually found out about her major life decisions—like her current one of putting law school on hold and joining the Peace Corps—after the fact.

Still, Joe and I felt we'd done a pretty good job with our kids. And it was that knowledge that led to our decision to become foster parents. I'd run my own interior-design consulting business from our home since shortly after Duncan's birth, and Joe was two years shy of retiring from his job with the National Security Agency. We were empty nesters, and the adjustment had been somewhat difficult. We had no grandchildren, but lots of love to give to young people in need.

I don't think we were quite prepared for how in need some of these kids were going to be—or for how hard their lives were. At six, LaShaun had seen more of the drug culture than I had in my entire fifty-six years. Terry woke screaming each of the five nights we kept him. Twins Tya and Tara had never seen a blanket, and spent a weekend at our house sleeping tucked inside their pillowcases. Kevin had been abandoned on the street at eighteen months, and at five was a battle-scarred testament to the human will to survive. Dwight burned his arms with cigarettes and set the bathroom trash can on fire. Mark, Stevie, and Jason, brothers, had been fending for themselves while their drug-addicted mother paraded a train of equally impaired men to her bedroom to finance her habit. All under the age of ten, the boys had been removed from her home when they were found digging for food in the garbage can of a bad-neighborhood

7-Eleven at midnight. Regina went back to live with her biological parents after a two-day stay with us; police found her five-year-old lifeless, bruised, and broken body in a garbage can three days after that.

Abused and largely abandoned, most of them arrived on our doorstep sullen veterans of the system, distrustful of all adults, old before their time. They had the thirty-yard stare of combat soldiers. Sometimes they hoarded food, afraid Monday morning's breakfast might be their only meal that week. On the rare ocassions that one of them opened up, he or she told us horror stories about crazy and abusive biological parents, as well as noncaring foster parents. Their broken spirits tore at my heart. Yet our training manual told us not to hug them or show them too much love for fear we'd become attached. We were to perform only the basic caretaking duties: providing food, clothing, shelter. Joe and I, never ones to follow ridiculous rules (the reason he'd never joined the military and I'd never pledged a sorority), ignored the manual.

"We signed up to be foster parents," said Joe the night we came home from our fourth foster parenting class. "Not caretakers. These are kids, not summer homes."

So we doled out clean socks and cereal, jackets and soap— all wrapped up in nice packages of love and discipline. I was convinced that though their stay in our house might be brief, they'd learn—maybe through osmosis—that some adults could be trusted. I packed positive affirmations in their lunch bags; Joe taught them how to play solitaire. We learned the language of Pokémon, Digimon, Sisqo, Lil' Kim, and DMX. We went to more movies than Joe and I had been to in the past decade. Friday nights were filled with high-school football or basketball outings. There were picnics in the local park and church on Sundays. Our intent was to provide as normal a life as possible while they stayed with us. Each smile, no maker how tiny and tentative, elicited joy from my husband and me.

"Do you think it's possible," I asked Joe one night, "that these children can learn to be productive members of society? After all the things they've suffered?"

"We have them for such a short time." He sighed, understanding that my questions had been mainly rhetorical.

Chapter 2

The blinking message light on our answering machine turned out to be Patrice, the social worker assigned to a thirteen-year-old boy named Emmanuel. His father, she said, was in jail, his mother in a drug rehab; both of their parental rights had been taken. His last foster family had decided, rather abruptly, that they no longer wanted to provide foster care. But he was in the process of being adopted. Could we, she asked, keep him for a couple of weeks, just until his adoption was finalized?

"Mommy!" cried the waif standing in the foyer two days later. He looked more like seven than thirteen. Tristan at thirteen had been nearly six feet tall; Emmanuel stood closer to four-foot-eleven. He was thin, except for the distended belly that poked out like that of a famine victim. He had the nearly blue lips of a heavy smoker (I was willing to bet money he'd never touched a cigarette in his life), and his skin looked somewhat ashen. But Emmanuel's coffee-colored eyes flashed brilliantly. And he immediately threw open his thread-thin arms to give me a hug. Then he repeated the process with Joe.

"Thank you, Patrice, for bringing me to my new home." There was a hug for his social worker, too. "You have a nice home, Mom," he said. "Where's my room?" While I showed him to Tristan's old room, Patrice sat down with Joe.

"Whose room is this? It's awfully big!"

"It used to belong to my son, Tristan. It's yours now."

"Cool. Cool beans." He fished out another hug for me. Emmanuel tried out the bed, then the chaise longue. Then he bounced over to the desk, ran his fingers over the cherry wood, and returned to the chaise. "I like my room, Mommy."

"I'm glad," I said absentmindedly, as I unpacked his clothes. Two pairs of pants, a shirt, one thick white athletic sock, one dressy black sock, no underclothing. His belongings would get lost in the walk-in closet, so I folded them and put them in the chest of drawers. Though few, his clothes were at least clean. Sometimes I spent the first two days of a child's stay with us washing clothing so filthy it felt hard. Sometimes I threw the stuff away, finding it easier just to buy new things. Most of the time the children had outgrown what they had anyway.

"Are you hungry?" I asked. He nodded, kicked off his scuffed Keds, and padded down the hall to the kitchen after me. I noticed he didn't have on any socks. When he and Patrice arrived, he'd worn no coat. "Where's your coat, sweetheart?"

"Don't have one. Can I have that apple?"

"You don't want anything else? Something more substantial?"

He shook his head and bit into the apple. "Thanks for letting me stay here. I don't think my last mommy was too happy with me," he said. "They're not even doing the foster thing anymore."

Chapter 3

That night in bed, Joe gave me the war story: Emmanuel was HIV positive. We had a slew of medications to feed him on a schedule. So far, according to Patrice, his T cell count was pretty high, his viral load low, and he'd suffered none of the opportunistic infections that signaled the cross-over to full-blown AIDS. Fortunately for him—if there can be such a thing when a child is HIV positive—he'd entered the foster care system at a young age and started receiving his drug cocktail almost immediately. That was something that more than likely would never have happened had he remained with his biological parents.

His mother, now thirty-six, had been strung out on meth-amphetamines, heroin, crack, you name it, since she was twelve. She'd been in and out of a series of rehabs, doing just enough of the required programs to get released back to her life on the streets. Somewhere along the line, she'd acquired the virus that causes AIDS and passed it on to her son. Though current medical treatments could prevent the disease transmission from mother to child, Emmanuel's mother hadn't been receiving medical care herself when they were kicked out of the shelter they'd been living in because of her drug use. She'd had no prenatal care during her pregnancy, and had delivered her only child on the kitchen floor of a makeshift methamphetamine lab. He'd been removed from her care by Children's Protective Services and placed in the foster care system when he was four; her parental rights had been taken eighteen months later. His father had been sentenced to life in prison without the possibility of parole for a murder he'd committed before Emmanuel was born.

From what Patrice had explained to Joe, most of the parents Emmanuel had been placed with freaked when they found out about his HIV status. Some of them had small children of their own and were concerned about transmission. Others didn't have any idea about what precautions to take, and were leery of trying to stick to his strict medicine regimen. And Children's Protective Services didn't provide any kind of training for parents taking care of HIV-infected children.

Being shuttled from foster home to foster home didn't appear to have dampened his spirits any, however. About two hours after Emmanuel's arrival, Tristan came by—he tried to meet all the kids who came through our doors—and he, Emmanuel, and I played a rousing game of Monopoly. Emmanuel, after some crafty cheating, got his hands on all the high-rent districts and won by a not-close-at-all margin. He whooped with delight each time one of us landed on one of his properties and had to fork over a handful of Monopoly cash. Then he doled out more of his great big little-armed hugs, as if he intended to heal the pain he was inflicting by winning. All the while, he humored us with awful corny jokes.

"Why did the monkey fall out of the tree?" He was giggling so hard he could barely ask the question.

Tristan and I looked at each other, clueless about why the monkey fell out of the tree.

"Why?" Tristan asked.

"Because," Emmanuel managed to stutter between great gulping giggles, "because he was dead!" Soon all three of us dissolved into fits of laughter. His laugh was infectious.

It was the same during dinner. Emmanuel told jokes, laughed openly, rolled his shiny dark eyes, amazed us with his grasp of current events and politics. And—as if in answer to my prayers—he ate heartily, asking for seconds of everything.

"Mashed potatoes," he said with a dreamy sigh, "my favorite." I made a mental note to fix them more often during his stay with us.

Joe and I were sharing dishwashing duties when Duncan made her weekly phone call. Emmanuel insisted on talking to her, then spent the next half hour regaling her with funny stories. It was as if he was truly part of our family—and in such a short time frame.

I pulled up mental snapshots of our happy, laughter-filled day as Joe recounted for me Emmanuel's short, sad history. But the memories of his loud laughter and quick ease on his first night with our family did nothing to stanch the flow of tears. Joe and I have been married long enough for him to know that I'm a big crybaby (I've been known to bawl during Hallmark commercials, particularly touching episodes of *ER* and each of the nearly two hundred times I've seen *Terms of Endearment*), so he'd brought a box of tissues to bed with him. He held me, whispering softly in my ear, gently stroking my back as I cried myself to sleep.

Chapter 4

We spent a couple of days buying Emmanuel the basics. His dirty Keds were two sizes too small, and the missing underwear in his suitcase extended to his person. Two of his three pairs of pants were high-waters, even after I let the hems out. The only shirt he owned was the one he'd been wearing when he arrived. And though it was still October, the temperatures felt more like late December. I was amazed Emmanuel didn't have the sniffles since he not only had no coat, but also no gloves, no hat, and no scarf.

"Mommy," he said as I was putting away his new belongings, "I think you spent too much money. Are you sure it's okay?"

Joe, standing in the doorway watching us, got a little emotional and had to step away for a moment.

"Oh, sweetie, of course, it's okay. We didn't do anything extravagant, but you needed a few things," I said.

"Well, I sure do appreciate all this. It's like Christmas," he said. "Or, at least, what I imagine Christmas to be like."

It was the first time since his arrival that I had seen any semblance of sadness in Emmanuel.

"What have your Christmases been like?" I asked, almost afraid to hear his response.

"When I was with Sandra—that's my real mom—the only reason I knew it was Christmas was because of the decorations at other people's houses. And for the past few years, I haven't really been with a family that kept me around for the holiday."

I pulled him into a hug so he couldn't see that I was crying. Intuitive beyond his years, he knew anyway. "Don't cry, Mommy. I'm okay. Besides, I'm about to have a permanent family for the first time ever. And in the meantime, I've got you and Daddy."

And we've got you, I thought to myself. I realized I'd miss him once he moved on to his adoptive parents.

Emmanuel's two weeks with us passed too quickly. They were busy, but fun-filled, with school and activities. He and Joe couldn't be in the car together without playing Punch Buggy Madness—seeing who could spot a Volkswagen Beetle fastest, then punch the other first. It was a game Emmanuel introduced to us. He played basketball, badly, at the hoop in our backyard, pretended he was swimming each night when he took his bath. We managed to squeeze in a trip to Busch Gardens in Williamsburg, Virginia, on the last weekend the amusement park was open for the year; Emmanuel was fearless, sitting in the front row of every roller coaster and throwing his small arms into the air with abandon as we swooped down every hill.

He was Dracula for Halloween, and we learned it was his first time trick-or-treating. He was giddy with joy as he plowed through the bag of goodies, insisting that we let him sleep in his mini black tuxedo and red-lined cape. In spite of his serious illness and the variety of medicines he had to take each day, he was a happy, pleasant child, very unlike the other preteens and teens we had kept during the ten months we'd been foster parents. If he understood that his time on earth was limited, he certainly lived his life to the fullest every day, something most people only dream of doing.

Chapter 5

Patrice took Emmanuel to his adoptive parents' home the day after Halloween. As usual, I fought back tears as I packed his new luggage with his recently acquired outfits. Sending the children back to their lives was the only time I wondered if our training manual was right about getting too attached, but it was always only a fleeting thought. Emmanuel was his usual cheerful self as he ate his breakfast. And as he hugged Joe, Tristan, and me good-bye, he promised to write.

Though the sun was high in the sky when Emmanuel—still smiling, dark eyes full of good-natured mischief—waved good-bye from Patrice's car, it was cloudier at our house than the rainy day he'd arrived. But we consoled ourselves with the knowledge that Emmanuel was going to a stable and loving family and that we had done a wonderful job of taking care of him—and he of us—while he'd been part of our family.

For a week Joe and I rattled around, acting as if our

favorite pet had died and our dream house had burned to the ground. We played our own games of Punch Buggy Madness, games that made us giggle like teenage girls at the mall on Friday night. We missed Emmanuel's silly stories, his spontaneous hugs, and his boisterous laugh.

"If we're like this after only having him two weeks, maybe we shouldn't seek out long-term placement," Joe said. "Maybe we should just continue providing respite care."

"I'm not sure I can do even respite care anymore," I said. Joe looked surprised; foster parenting originally had been my idea. "I mean, I just don't understand how people can treat children this way."

"Baby, Emmanuel is going to a wonderful family, and he's going permanently. It's not going to be a repeat of Regina or back into the system, which we all know doesn't work," Joe said.

"I know, but—"

"No buts. Emmanuel's out of this crappy system. And we provided a wonderful pit stop for him on his way out. We should be happy for him."

"I am happy for him. But I miss him. The house feels like it's missing something without him here," I said.

"I know. That's why I'm wondering if we can do long-term foster parenting. Imagine how empty a house must feel after you've kept a child for the eighteen-month limit," Joe said.

"Maybe we should join an AIDS activist organization." My heart started beating faster. I knew my eyes probably had that startled look they sometimes got when I had one of my bright ideas. "We could maybe help Emmanuel, maybe help find—"

Joe put his fingers to my lips. "Shhh," he said. "One project at a time, baby. One project at a time."

For the next three weeks, I buried myself in my work. I

looked at so many fabric swatches I saw plaid when I closed my eyes. I met with several new clients, sometimes having more than one meeting a day—something I hadn't done for more than a decade. I'm sure I neglected Joe, but he didn't complain. He knew I had to say good-bye to Emmanuel in my heart in my own way and in my own time. Emmanuel had promised to write, but I didn't know if his adoptive parents would allow that. I wasn't even sure where his new family lived or even if their home was local.

Children's Protective Services preached continued contact so children wouldn't feel abandoned by yet another adult, but in reality, hardly anyone practiced it, including the agency that advocated it. Biological parents typically didn't want reminders of how they had screwed up their children's lives (or else they were still too messed up to keep up contact), and other foster parents had their plates full with psychiatrist and psychologist visits, social worker checklists, court dates, and foster parent association meetings. They were loath to add more time-consuming activities to their schedules, and that included letters or phone calls to former foster parents. Most of our updates came in the form of missives from social workers, and many of those were outdated by the time we heard them.

We did hear, during our training classes, about former foster children—all grown up, some with children of their own—returning to say thank you to particularly attentive foster parents they'd had along the way. It was still too soon to tell if we were helping any of the young people who came through our house in that manner.

Chapter 6

Thanksgiving came and went. Duncan and Greg blew into town from New York, but Duncan was battling severe indigestion, so she didn't eat much and they only stayed for the day. Tristan brought his latest fling— a pleasant-enough woman named Charlyne, about whom I knew he wasn't serious. Madison managed a four-minute call from Mozambique. I was preoccupied designing a playroom for a major client, so Joe did the cooking. We hoped to hear from Emmanuel. We didn't.

We did hear from Patrice the Monday after the holiday. Emmanuel's adoptive family had been kept in the dark about his HIV status during the months-long adoption process. Now they knew and, angry, were withdrawing their application. He was still staying with them for the moment, but they wanted him gone by week's end. Patrice wasn't sure if they'd told Emmanuel of their decision, and if they had, how he was reacting to it. She wanted to come by that afternoon to meet with us.

"I'll get straight to the point," she said, as soon as I'd made her a cup of tea. "I want you and Joe to consider adopting Emmanuel. He got along famously with the two of you while he stayed here."

"Adopt?" I hadn't expected this. "Joe and I have already raised our children. Yes, we're doing foster parenting, but adoption? I don't know about that. Aren't we too old?"

"Exceptions have been known to be made. Perhaps you should speak to Joe first, before you make your decision."

"Be clear I will, just as soon as he gets home from work. But we'll need time to digest this. To consider this."

"You have until the end of the week."

"What will happen if we can't take him?"

"He'll be placed back in foster care. Possibly a group home if I can't find an available family right away."

"Why were his adoptive parents kept in the dark in the first place? This is just going to break his heart."

"It was an oversight. A mistake on our part. One hand didn't know what the other was doing. This has been a complicated case with more than one social worker. There was just some confusion. Each division thought the other had already informed the parents. They found out the day I dropped him off, along with his own personal pharmacy," Patrice said.

"How can that kind of mistake happen?" I was flabbergasted. Patrice told Joe about Emmanuel's HIV status on day one. Adoption took several months and many visits, yet no one had realized the potential parents were clueless about Emmanuel's health. I was horrified at how lousy the system was, though I shouldn't have been. We'd seen firsthand how things really worked in foster care.

More than one social worker told us the burnout rate in their field was so high because the system flat-out didn't work. The very children they were supposed to be helping often got short shrift, being returned to biological parents still crippled with the bad habits that got their children taken from them in the first place. Budget cuts took precedence over appropriate care. Social workers left in frustration and weren't replaced; those left behind were forced to double, sometimes triple and quadruple their caseloads. Foster parents were in short supply, so the powers that be eliminated some of the checks and balances in the system. Bad apples slipped through the cracks and abused or neglected the children worse than their real parents.

"And there's no way Emmanuel's new parents will change their minds?"

"None. They're furious because they believe they were duped. That we lied to them on purpose."

"So he'll still be up for adoption?"

"Mrs. Parker." She took my hands. "Riley, you know that's a long shot. He's thirteen; most people want infants. He's black. Most people want white children. Asian babies have come into vogue, foreign adoptions are in right now. But black and Hispanic children are still at the bottom of the list. Add to that his HIV status . . ."

Patrice finished her tea and got up to leave. "Please let me know your decision soon, Riley. I know this is difficult. Talk to Joe."

We didn't sleep at all that night.

"Riley, I'm sixty-two. I'll be nearly seventy when he's twenty," Joe said.

"I know, Joe. I know all the arguments."

"I won't be able to throw a football or shoot hoops with him for much longer. We're both about to retire. What will happen to him if something happens to us before he's an adult? Will the kids be expected to take him in?"

"Joe, he might not live to see twenty."

"That's another thing: I don't know if I'm strong enough

to bury one of my children." I didn't know how to respond
to that comment, so I said nothing. But Joe is one of the
strongest people I know.

"His medical bills will be astronomical. Will our insurance cover him?" I asked by way of refocusing the discussion.

"We'll have to look into that."

"So are we saying yes?"

"No. I don't know," Joe said, pacing furiously around
the living room. "I don't know what we're saying. We need
more time."

"That's the one thing we don't have. He'll be shuffled
somewhere by the end of the week," I reminded him.

"I don't want to talk about this anymore tonight, Riley."
He went down to the basement and began working on his
latest woodwork project. I could hear the sander through
the floor of my office, where I'd retreated to go over design
plans. The only thing I was certain of was that we were
both too old to be pulling all-nighters.

We weren't any closer to a decision the next morning
when Joe left for work. I tried to get him to take the day
off—if ever there was a need for a mental-health day, this
was it—but he preferred busying himself with work to baring
his emotions.

I didn't fare so well with keeping myself preoccupied.
Instead of nailing down color schemes, I stared out the
window. I drank more cups of coffee than I cared to remember, thinking of the two happy weeks Emmanuel had spent
with us. I worried about his emotional state once he found
out his new family didn't want him. How do you tell a
child—again—that the life-threatening legacy his mother
left him was preventing his happiness? And if we didn't
take him, wouldn't that just be another rejection to add to

a long list of rejections in his life? Would he think we were turning away from him because of the HIV? Or would he understand that a lot of factors came into play when making a decision as serious as adopting a child?

Yet saying yes presented its own set of problems. Joe was right about our ages; keeping foster children for short periods was one thing, making a lifetime commitment quite another. Would Joe or I be able to handle single parenting if one or the other of us died before Emmanuel grew up? Could we expect our children to finish raising Emmanuel, an HIV-positive teen, if something happened to both of us? And though they might willingly do it, what kind of responsibility was that to place on them? Duncan was the only one married, and I wasn't even sure if she and Greg wanted children. And if they did, they might not want an extra mouth to feed.

I also had to face Emmanuel's mortality. Though he was generally in good health right now, and though the media talked less about AIDS now that drug cocktails had increased the lifespan of those infected, there was still no cure. It was still killing people. The side effects from those drugs were sometimes horrific, and if our insurance didn't cover Emmanuel's treatments, we might not be able to pay for the extended life those treatments afforded him.

Or ours. Joe and I had grandiose plans for our retirement: travel, buying a yacht, getting that summer home for which we'd longed. I quickly put those thoughts out of my head, because thinking about ourselves, our dreams, seemed particularly selfish when a child's life hung in the balance.

Then there was the question of adopting him at our ages. Patrice said special circumstances warranted special actions, but I knew if we'd wanted to adopt a child not part of the foster care system, we'd be considered too old. I was thinking in circles, and my head started spinnning. I knew if I wasn't careful, I'd stress myself into a migraine. Then I'd be out of commission for a few days, and we just didn't have that luxury.

I also knew we couldn't make this decision without talking to our children. Tristan was the only one who'd spent any time with the children who had lived with us. Duncan seemed somewhat bothered by the whole idea of our foster parenting, as if somehow we were sinking beneath her expectations of us. This was just a feeling I had, as she and I had never discussed it. Madison was busy with her peace corps work.

That evening I made meatloaf, Joe's favorite meal. I hoped a good meal would put him in a better frame of mind. Good mood or not, we had to settle this. I wanted to call Patrice with our answer the next day.

To my surprise, Joe had contacted our health insurance carrier that afternoon. If we adopted Emmanuel, we would be able to make major health decisions for him: whether or not to insert a central line should he need repeat IV treatments, the right to consent to surgery or medication adjustments. These decisions would be up to his guardian if he remained a foster child, and that meant someone else would have to be contacted in the event of an emergency. That someone oftentimes had not even met the child over whom he or she held guardianship. If we adopted him, we would become Emmanuel's legal guardians, and the need for outside approval could be circumvented.

That was the good news. The bad news was that unfortunately, our insurance would not cover Emmanuel's HIV treatment. As a ward of the state, he was eligible for Medicaid; as our child, he was not. A catastrophic illness was going to cost us a not-so-small fortune. And that was without taking into consideration that Joe and I weren't getting any younger and might soon be facing our own health issues. If we decided to do this, retirement would have to take a backseat for a while.

"You know we need to talk to Tristan, Duncan, and Madison, too," I said.

"If we do this, yes. I've already asked Tristan to come over tonight. We can call Duncan and Greg. Madison will have to wait, but I don't think she'll mind."

"I'm concerned Duncan won't approve. I don't think she approves of this whole foster care business."

"I don't care about her displeasure with our foster parenting," Joe said. "Adoption, though, is a whole 'nother jar of chicken soup."

"But have you sensed that she doesn't like us being foster parents?"

"Like I said, I wasn't seeking her approval," Joe said. Then he sensed I was going to keep asking until he answered my question (he frequently called me his own private pit bull). Big sigh. "Yes, she has mentioned a few times that she thinks someone else, not her parents, should be applying for jobs in the sainthood."

"She mentioned this to you?" I could feel a mad coming on. "Why didn't you tell me?"

"Why? So it could hurt your feelings? I didn't see the need to tell you she disapproved. I also asked her not to say anything to you. I guess she kept her promise to me, technically. Guess your mother's intuition picked up on it, though."

I was putting plates on the table when we heard Tristan's key in the front door.

"I smell meatloaf!" he yelled from downstairs. He bounded up the steps and kissed me, shook his father's hand. "Just in time for din-din." Though long past the eat-us-out-of-house-and-home teen years, Tristan still had the appetite of a football player—a sport he'd been much too thin to play during high school.

* * *

"So what's the big news?" Tristan asked between bites.

"Emmanuel's adoptive parents have halted the adoption," I said. "They didn't know he was HIV positive until he landed on their front porch."

"Wow," Tristan said. "Talk about mind-blowing. So what happens to the little fella now?"

"Social services wants us to adopt him," Joe said. Tristan whistled.

"The adoptive parents want him gone by week's end. We have to let them know something before then or he goes back into the system," I said.

"And no chance for adoption because of the HIV, not to mention that he's a minority," Tristan said. "Maybe the system's the best place for him. I mean, he'll have the medical care he needs."

"And no parents to keep him on his meds schedule. And another year without Christmas, without clothing that fits, without love," I said.

"Sounds to me like you've already decided."

"We haven't," Joe said. "But we have been considering all the players in this. You, your sisters. What will happen to Emmanuel once we're gone—if he isn't gone himself by then."

"We already know our insurance won't cover his medical expenses."

"And Dad's about to retire. So you can't cover his expenses, either. I don't understand why they're asking you two to take on this burden," Tristan said, then saw my expression and held out his hands. "Mom, I know you're a bleeding heart for this kind of thing. You make great foster parents, and I applaud what you're doing for needy kids. But starting over at your age? God willing, Emmanuel will live a long life. And if that happens, I can't promise that I'll be able to take on helping to raise someone else's problem.''

"You think of Emmanuel as a problem?" I was horrified.

"Yes, Mom, I do. He's ill. Barring health problems— which we know he'll have—he's certain to have emotional issues. He's been abandoned, abused, neglected, mistreated, more than once, his entire life. I don't know about Dunc and Maddy, but I know I haven't asked for a little brother since I was about eight or so. I don't mean to sound cruel, but . . ." Tristan threw his hands up in the air, out of words. "You two are about to enter your golden years. You don't need this right now, no matter how much this child is in need. Let someone else take this on.''

There was silence around the table.

"I've lost my appetite," Tristan said finally, pushing away his plate.

The phone rang.

Chapter 7

It's funny how you think of the oddest things at the strangest moments. While Joe spoke on the phone, I realized I hadn't started decorating for Christmas. It was too early for the tree, mind you, but by now I normally had the wreath on the front door, and the mantel above the fireplace covered with an extensive manger scene. Missing Emmanuel and Patrice's stunning announcement, however, had completely thrown me for a loop. Suddenly Joe was handing me the phone.

"It's Duncan," he said.

"Hello?"

"Mom! I have the most amazing news! We're pregnant!" my daughter said. She was gushing, something she rarely did.

"Oh, congratulations, sweetheart! I didn't even know you were trying."

"We weren't, exactly. But I suspected I might be when I was sick last week on Thanksgiving. I've been feeling kind of blah for the past few days. Saturday I did a home test, and it was positive, but I waited until today and got confirmation from my doctor," she said excitedly. "Now it's official, and if all goes well, you'll have your first grandchild late next June."

Though I was happy for Duncan, my mind was elsewhere. I also knew we would have to talk to her about Emmanuel, but I didn't want to do it in the same conversation as her news.

"Mom? Is something wrong? You sound distracted."

"No. I'm just tired, I guess. Your father and I didn't really sleep last night."

"I think that's too much information," she said with a wicked giggle.

"Behave!" I said. "Joe, she and Greg are going to have a baby!"

Tristan grabbed the phone out of my hand and started jabbering with his sister. Joe and I began cleaning the table; it didn't appear we'd be finishing dinner. "I didn't want to mention it when she sounded so excited," Joe whispered.

"Me, either. She deserves to have this time."

"Sounds like Tristan's right; we have decided to adopt Emmanuel," Joe said.

"I didn't expect Tristan to react so vehemently against the idea," I said. "He's been the most supportive of our foster parenting efforts."

"I'm a little surprised, too," Joe said. "Maybe once we've nailed down all the loose ends he'll come around."

"I hope so. Emmanuel is going to need love and support from our entire family."

"The biggest issue is finances. Other than that, I see no reason why we can't adopt him," Joe said. "I think adopting him means I'll have to put off retirement for at least another five years, possibly longer."

I put down the platter I was carrying and hugged my

husband. After a long career, one in which classified missions had often taken him far away from his family, sometimes for extended periods, he was looking forward to sleeping late and traveling only for pleasure. We had a pretty well-lined nest egg and a hefty stock portfolio, but we had done our financial planning based on an entirely different set of circumstances.

"There are a few projects I turned down because they were long-term. I'm almost certain it's not too late to change my mind and take them," I said. Joe kissed me tenderly on the forehead.

"All things through prayer," he said quietly as Tristan hung up the phone.

"Great news about Dunc. I didn't mention this whole adoption craziness. I figured you two would want to talk to her about this some other time."

"You figured right," Joe said. "Now, son, your opinion is important to your mother and me—"

"If that was true, you'd forget about this whole silly plan," Tristan interrupted. "But as you two have said to me on more than one occasion, you're grown, you'll do what you want to do. I have to go." He grabbed his jacket and stormed out before Joe or I could say anything more.

"I don't believe he'll take his difference of opinion with us out on Emmanuel," Joe said. I agreed. Tristan had spent quite a bit of time with the boy during his two-week stay with us back in October. Still, it hurt that the one child I thought we'd be able to count on to be allied with us was so opposed to the idea of us adopting Emmanuel. A sudden wave of guilt washed over me; my oldest daughter had just told us we were going to have our first grandchild, and Joe and I were thinking about nothing but adopting an HIV-positive little boy.

"Maybe we should go to New York Saturday and take Duncan and Greg shopping for baby furniture," I said. "I feel like we've swept her good news under the rug because of Emmanuel.''

"If we decide to adopt Emmanuel, we'll have him with us.''

"I know. But I'm sure he's never been to New York. We can make a weekend of it, take in a Broadway show. Maybe *The Lion King*. I think he'll really enjoy that.''

"And we'd get to spend some time with our unborn first grandchild.''

"And our daughter,'' I added.

"And spring the adoption on her then?'' Joe asked. "I still think we need to tell her before we talk to Patrice. And I don't know that she's going to take it very well.''

"I thought we'd give Patrice our decision tomorrow.''

"We can tell her the day after. We have to tell our children before we do this. Given Tristan's reaction, I think it's only fair to give them all a heads up.''

"Joe, let's go to the church and pray about this,'' I said suddenly. Our faith was an important part of our lives, and it seemed like the right thing to do: Let God guide our hearts and our decision.

We drove to Trinity Baptist Church, where we'd been members for the past twenty-six years. It was late, after ten P.M., but the church's doors were always open. There was something about the rose-colored interior of the sanctuary, with its multihued stained-glass windows, that had always had a calming effect on me. Our pastor and his staff kept candles burning twenty-four hours a day, and the soft flickering somehow added to the wonder and mystery of the Lord. I grabbed Joe's hand, a feeling of warmth and peace settling over me, and I knew before we knelt at the altar and prayed that adopting Emmanuel was right. And I could tell in the way Joe's large hand squeezed mine that he felt it, too.

Still, we knelt in prayer, asking for God's guidance.

"Father," Joe began, "you know our hearts. We ask that you bless us with your infinite love and grace as we seek the path of righteousness. Guide us, Lord, in our decision about Emmanuel. Give us patience and courage to deal with his illness."

"And we ask a special blessing upon Emmanuel's mother, Lord," I added. Together, Joe and I said, "Amen."

We continued kneeling silently, our faces bathed in the muted candlelight. Then, slowly rising, we headed down the aisle and out of the sanctuary. Neither of us spoke until we were back in the car.

"We're doing the right thing," I said quietly.

"We'll tell the kids tomorrow," Joe agreed.

Chapter 8

"Tell me my mother didn't just say they were going to adopt that little street urchin," Duncan said. A vein throbbing at her temple told Greg she was furious, and he knew it was going to be a long night.

"Honey, I don't think you should be getting all upset right now. It can't be good for the baby," Greg said, touching her arm to placate her.

"Upset?" She jerked her arm from Greg's grasp. "If you think I'm just upset . . ." Duncan sputtered to a stop, so angry she couldn't continue her thought. "I'm pregnant and they're adopting this, this, this sick child." She emphasized the word *child* as if she thought of Emmanuel as anything but.

"I gather they've grown rather attached to him. And you spoke to him a couple of times when he stayed with them the other month. You said he was charming."

"I said he sounded cute. I did not say my parents should

bring an AIDS baby into the family. What could they be thinking? What if he spreads this disease to one of them?''

''Duncan . . .'' Greg interrupted.

A look of horror crossed her face. ''What if he spreads this to me? Or the baby? I've never understood their desire to take in the dirty, drug-addicted offspring of all manner of . . . Greg, I grew up in that house. I'll bet half of my childhood treasures are gone now, taken by these thieving, bad-apple kids they insist on keeping.''

''Honey, I think you're . . .''

''I'm what? Greg, we're better than them. Growing up, I had the best. I went to the best schools. Tristan and Madison, too. Why would they befoul the house, our memories, with this obsession to do good? Yes, these kids' parents screwed up their lives. That's too bad. Why does that mean my parents now have to screw up my life and the life of my child?''

''Duncan, you're upset.'' He winced; she'd already taken offense to that word, and he didn't want to rile her any more than she already was. ''I think we should talk about this more when you've had a chance to calm down.''

''I'm not going to calm down. Don't you understand? They're going to make this wretched boy a part of my family.''

''And that's bothering you so much because . . .''

''Because I can't believe they would do this to me. People who can't take care of their own children shouldn't have them. His mother should've aborted him when she found out she was pregnant. Then this wouldn't be happening!''

''Sweetie, you don't mean that! I can't talk to you when you're like this.'' Greg looked at his wife's tear-streaked face. ''Maybe a cup of tea would make you feel better,'' he said as he walked toward the kitchen.

Chapter 9

Duncan hung up on me, so I let Joe call her back.

"Dad, she's too upset to talk right now," said Greg. "And since she's pregnant, I'd like to keep her as calm as possible. You should want that, too, seeing as she is carrying your first grandchild."

"Perhaps you can talk some sense into her, son," Joe said. His voice was tight, so I knew he was fighting to restrain his temper. "This little guy needs a loving home; we can provide that. Check that. We're going to provide that. But we do have some concern about his well-being should something happen to us. We need to know that our children—"

"Is that fair to ask, Dad?" Greg asked. "We're about to have a child of our own. We've given a lot of thought to family size. We don't want two children."

"And if Duncan is pregnant with twins? They run in the family, you know."

"Duncan's really upset. I have to go and calm her down. Maybe we should try discussing this sometime next week."

Joe was visibly shaken when he hung up. "Duncan was screaming in the background: 'We'll put the little freak back into the system when you two die!' I think it's fair to say she's even less in favor of this than Tristan."

"I E-mailed Madison earlier today. I would have rather done it by phone, but under the circumstances, this was the next best thing. There's been no response yet, but you know her."

"We raised our kids better than this," Joe said, shaking his head. "I knew Duncan was against the foster parenting, but to behave like this . . ."

"In time they'll come around."

"Will they?"

Maybe Joe was right, and they wouldn't come around. When I'd called Duncan and explained what her father and I planned to do, she'd asked how we could do this to her. I think she felt we were trying to steal her thunder with an announcement of our own. I couldn't make her listen to reason, and, furious, she'd hung up the phone. She hadn't even talked to Joe, sending her husband to chastise him instead. Perhaps they wouldn't come around. But I was determined not to let that affect our decision to do the right thing. Just as soon as the adoption could be finalized, Emmanuel was going to be our son. Maybe he didn't have a long life ahead of him, maybe someone would develop a cure and he'd live to be a gray-haired old man. It didn't matter. God had placed this mountain in our path for us to climb, and we were strapping on our hiking boots.

Chapter 10

A week and two days after Thanksgiving, Emmanuel returned to us. "Hey, Mommy," he said. He hugged Joe and me and went up to his room to deposit his stuff. We were a little concerned about his mental state, but his smile hadn't lost any of its luster. He asked for Tristan, but he was away on a business trip. I believed he'd volunteered for the trip, but I'd probably never be able to prove it. Madison hadn't responded to my E-mail, but she was notoriously bad about checking hers, so that might not mean anything sinister. Though Joe and I had discussed a trip to New York to see Duncan, she still wasn't speaking to us, so we shelved that idea.

Instead, we spent his first day back decorating the house. Joe and Emmanuel went tree shopping and brought back two huge Frazier firs for the living room and the kitchen, while I put smaller, artificial ones in Emmanuel's room and the library. Joe always accused me of going overboard with the holiday cheer—truth was he was right; I like a blinking and flashing house—but this year he kept quiet while I hung ornaments and homemade paper snowflakes from the ceiling and made sure there was something red and green in every room of the house, including the bathrooms. He even helped, stringing lights down the staircase railings, something he usually never did until it was time to take all the decorations down each January.

"This has been the best day ever," Emmanuel cried in a way that made him seem much younger than his thirteen years. Joe played the soundtrack to "A Charlie Brown Christmas," and Emmanuel danced the way white people do—all offbeat but oblivious. He doled out so many hugs I was surprised his arms weren't stuck in a permanent outstretched semicircle.

Late that night, after Emmanual was asleep and we sipped sparkling apple cider in front of the fireplace, Joe and I knew we'd made the right decision.

"Baby, I believe he's going to keep us young," Joe said, nuzzling my hair. All the indecision and tension of the week melted away. Adopting Emmanuel felt right.

"The kids will accept this," I said, and somehow I knew, in time, they would.

The next few days passed uneventfully, with me enrolling Emmanuel in the same middle school my three kids had attended and him getting settled into his new routine. Each day he asked if Tristan's trip was done, and each day I had to say no. It wasn't until almost a week later that he finally opened up to me about the aborted adoption.

"They were nice enough, I guess," he said, out of the blue.

"They? Who are you talking about, honey?"

"My new parents. Guess they're not my new parents anymore."

"Do you understand what happened? Why you're no longer staying with them, and why you'll be living here now?"

"They didn't want me, I guess." He shrugged. "It's okay. I've moved a lot."

"I don't believe they didn't want you because of you," I said, hugging him. "A lot of people are afraid of how to handle your illness. God willing, Joe and I are going to adopt you, and you won't have to move anymore."

"I hope you don't think I'm a bad person for saying I'm a lot happier here than I was there." He smiled shyly. "Are you going to make Christmas cookies?"

"You bet I am, when it gets closer to the day. And of course I don't think you're a bad person. We're a lot happier with you here, too. We missed you something terrible when you left."

Madison still hadn't responded to my E-mail, and Duncan hadn't returned any of my phone calls. I wasn't sure what to expect from her come Christmas Day. Ordinarily, she and Greg rotated Christmases between Greg's family—they lived in Nashville—and us. This was supposed to be an "us" year. It was doubtful they'd spend two years in a row with Greg's parents and brothers; Duncan had never been entirely comfortable going there on the "them" years. She said they did Christmas "weird," with everyone kind of getting out of bed whenever and opening their gifts separately. Tradition at the Parker household found us all enjoying a family breakfast, then gathering around the tree together and oohing and aahing over each other's presents. But tradition, apparently, be damned this year; for the first time since she'd left to go to college, Duncan had missed her weekly phone calls. What was turning out to be Emmanuel's best Christmas was shaping up to be this family's worst.

Chapter 11

Christmas was bittersweet. Emmanuel had the time of his life, squealing with delight as he attacked his presents. His greatest joy, however, came from watching us. Somehow he had managed to buy Joe, Tristan, and me gifts, and he could barely contain himself as we opened the badly wrapped packages. There were also odd-shaped packages under the tree for Duncan, Madison, and a squishy something that looked suspiciously like a stuffed teddy bear for Duncan's unborn baby.

"When did you find time to buy gifts?" I asked, wrapping myself in the Pashmina he gave me. For a first-timer, he'd done well, learning our likes and dislikes in a relatively short time period.

"Tristan took me. Do you like it?" he asked me. Then, before I could answer, "Daddy, open your gift! Open your gift!"

After his nine-day business trip, Tristan had popped by and taken Emmanuel out to the movies and dinner. Though he'd expressed something akin to anger at his father and me for wanting to adopt Emmanuel, Tristan stepped right in and started playing big brother. It was clear the younger boy idolized our oldest child, and Tristan did nothing to jeopardize the developing relationship. Joe was right, we had raised our children better—and Tristan was proving that something we taught him had sunk in.

The same couldn't be said of his sisters. We still hadn't heard from Duncan, though she did ship boxes full of gifts for us. There was nothing for Emmanuel, but I bought him a Minnesota Vikings (his favorite pro football team) stadium jacket, wrapped it, and wrote DUNCAN AND GREG on the gift tag. I was certain she'd bought the gifts prior to the announcement of the addition to our family, and she was not the type to return them to the store.

Among the score of holiday greeting cards we'd received was one from Madison. But she'd never responded to my E-mail, or the subsequent ones Joe sent to her. The period between Halloween and Christmas was my favorite time of year—with the exception of the year, just after Joe and I got married, that both my grandmothers died within days of each other—but this holiday season had been filled with more misery than mirth.

As I checked on the progress of the turkey, Tristan followed me into the kitchen.

"It'll be okay, Mom," he said quietly.

"What's that, sweetie?"

"Dunc. I think she'll come around eventually. She's just concerned about having an HIV-positive person around her while she's pregnant."

"You've talked to her? She won't return any of our calls."

"I have. I don't agree with your decision to adopt Emmanuel, and not for the same reasons as Duncan, but I know you and Dad feel you're doing the right thing, helping someone less fortunate. And just because we have a difference of opinion doesn't mean I'm going to treat Emmanuel any differently than I did when he stayed with you before.

"But Duncan, she's . . . well, Mom, it is a deadly disease."

"That she knows she can't catch just by being in the same room with Emmanuel. Come on, Tristan. Your sister isn't an idiot, and we know a lot about HIV, starting with the fact that it isn't an airborne disease. In addition, it's not as if she's around Emmanuel all that often—Christmas between now and the baby's due date."

"She's not thinking logically right now, Mom. She's, well, you know how pregnant women are. They're afraid of everything. Are they eating enough of the right things? Is anyone around them smoking? Did they start getting prenatal care soon enough? Did they have that last glass of champagne before or after conception?"

I smiled, remembering my first pregnancy. "When I was first pregnant with you, I was afraid to take a shower without your father in the house. It was completely out of character and irrational, I know, but I had a fear that I'd slip and fall and hurt you, possibly miscarry. And if I was home alone at the time, who'd know?"

"So you understand Duncan's point."

I sat down beside Tristan at the counter and patted his hand. "Joe couldn't be here with me all the time. He had one three-week trip right at the end of my first trimester. I remember I was still suffering serious morning sickness— though I've never been quite sure why they call it morning sickness because I was sick all day long with all three of you—and I got really hysterical," I said. The memory was rather funny now, but at the time I had acted like a woman crazed, lying on the floor, clinging to his legs, begging him not to go. Joe had been beside himself, trying to deal with me. "Your father, out of desperation, called your grandmother, and she had to come stay with me. And believe me, she badgered some sense into me."

"So all pregnant women get a little irrational," Tristan started.

"I don't know that it happens to all of us, sweetie. Where'd you get to be such a chauvinist?"

"Whatever. You got irrational. Duncan's being irrational now. Maybe it runs in the family. Just give her some time."

"So irrational that she can't act like a decent human being? She didn't even buy him a Christmas gift, for crying out loud," I hissed. "Buying him a gift is somehow going to endanger her baby? You know what? Never mind. I'm trying not to ruin this holiday for Emmanuel. It's his first Christmas, and I want it to be memorable."

Joe's brother, Frank, his wife, Arnelle, my sister, Solange, and Tim, her no-account latest boyfriend, came for Christmas dinner.

"Isn't this an 'us' year? Where's Duncan?" Solange asked after Frank said grace so long my hand holding the wineglass started to go numb.

"She's pregnant and having a rough go of it," Joe said.

"I can't believe you didn't tell me, Riley," Solange said, throwing a roll at me.

"We've been a little crazed getting settled in around here. Plus, I think she wanted to get safely through the first trimester before she started telling the world at large," I said, giving Joe a look that asked what on earth he was doing.

The rest of the evening passed quickly, as only Christmas can, with good cheer and lots of laughter and holiday giddiness. My parents called from Phoenix, where they had moved six years before to help my mother's emphysema. Joe's mother called from St. Thomas to make sure we'd received the coconut tart she'd sent via Fed Ex (we had, and by the time she called it was but a delicious memory). Emmanuel delighted everyone with more of his silly stories and contagious laughter. But I felt Duncan's absence acutely, even more than I felt Madison's, though I missed both my girls.

I prayed Duncan and I could settle this before too much longer. I couldn't imagine going through my pregnancies without the guidance and wisdom of my mother. Plus, the stress of not communicating would not be good for Duncan or the baby. And I didn't know how long Greg would be able to act as a buffer; I liked my son-in-law well enough, but he was a bit of a spoiled brat. When things got too difficult for him, he rolled up, pouted, and started whining, "Why me?"

Solange and I had kitchen duty. Arnelle had had hip-replacement surgery two weeks before Christmas, so we shooed her into the living room with the men. When the kitchen was clear of everything but the two of us and a mound of dishes and leftover food, Solange swooped in for the attack.

"So what's going on, Ri? Duncan's pregnant and you don't mention it? And she's too sick to come home for the holiday? So, what, they stayed in New York? They've never done that."

"There's been a little drama with Emmanuel's adoption. But, honestly, I hadn't mentioned the pregnancy because she just told us three weeks ago. She's not that far along and I'm not sure how many people they've told. And she hasn't been feeling well. Remember, I told you she was sick on Thanksgiving."

"What kind of drama?"

"She hasn't really talked to us since we told her we were going to adopt Emmanuel. Suffice it to say she's not happy with the plan. I guess she's told Tristan that she's concerned about his HIV status around her child."

"And he hasn't talked some sense into her thick head?"

"Truth be told, he's not too keen on this adoption, either."

"What? He seems to get along so well with Emmanuel."

"He does. His concerns are different. He's worried that we're getting older, facing retirement, and that this isn't the best action at this time in our lives."

"So he's packed you both up and buried you already."

"He's concerned. And, of course, if something happens to Joe and me, the kids would be responsible for their little brother."

"Bump that," Solange said. I smiled at her benign word choice. My younger sister is family famous for her colorful language. "If something, God forbid, happens to you and Joe, I'll take Emmanuel. He's a wonderful child. Kids! Honest to God, I could strangle the both of them. Maybe it's a good thing I never married and had any of my own. The last thing I thought about when you told me about this was the strain it would put on my life when you and Joe croak."

"It is an issue, Solange."

"Sure, sure, in the big picture, I guess you have to consider that. It's the reason people choose godparents for their offspring. But I'm sure Duncan isn't considering what will happen to her child should she and Greg drop dead."

"Oh, Solange." I swiped at her with a dishtowel. "You've never had children. . . ."

"Okay, maybe somewhere deep down she's thinking about godparents. But right now, her death isn't foremost in her mind. They're thinking about decorating the nursery, learning how to change a diaper, things like that. What's Madison's take?"

"We haven't heard from her since Thanksgiving, except for a card. We've both E-mailed her, but there's been no response."

"You really raised a bunch," she said, shaking her head. We finished the cleanup job in silence.

Chapter 12

Madison called early the morning after Christmas. Unable to reach the capital city of Maputo from her base at a small northern village near Mocimboa da Praia because major flooding had blocked even the best of roads (and most of the best amounted to little more than dirt-packed trails), she hadn't been able to get to a phone since the Thanksgiving call she'd made to us. When it was dry and sunny, it was a dangerous and arduous multiday trip between the northern part of the country and the south, where Maputo was located. Now flooding from an active cyclone season forced buses to stray off the main roads and take paths that passed dangerously close to unexploded minefields left over from the country's civil war. Madison had been traveling for nearly a month; she sounded exhausted, but happy when she heard my voice.

"Merry Christmas! I know I'm late, but . . . it's ever so good to hear people from home!"

"We've been trying to reach you through E-mail for weeks now!" I said.

"Haven't seen E-mail. Haven't even touched my laptop. I've been sleeping on a beat-up old bus for most of the last few weeks. Did you get my card? I mailed it before Thanksgiving."

"We got it. Your sister is pregnant," I began, feeling some relief at learning she hadn't been ignoring our messages, while also experiencing trepidation about her living conditions.

"It's about time. Haven't they been married for four years? Is she there? Let me talk to her. Or did they go back last night?"

"They're not here. She's due in June. You'll be coming home around that time, right?"

"End of May. My two-year stint will be up then."

"There have been other developments here, too."

Her breath caught. "Is Dad okay?"

"Oh, he's fine. We're adopting a little boy, Emmanuel."

"That's so cool! Is this the same kid you guys spoke of at Thanksgiving?" She didn't wait for an answer. "Listen, Mom, I don't have a lot of time on this call. Put Dad on the phone, okay?" I handed the receiver to Joe, who held my hand tightly during his brief exchange with our youngest child. *Next to youngest now,* I quickly reminded myself.

"Well," Joe said as he hung up the phone, "at least one of our children has some sense."

"She doesn't know about Emmanuel's HIV status. She might feel the same way as Duncan when we tell her."

"I don't think so. She seems genuinely happy with our decision to adopt."

"I'm just glad she wasn't ignoring us. But I'm not so happy about her being in a mine-infested country, no matter that she's doing something good," I said.

"Baby, I'm sure they're taking every precaution. Besides, she's just following in her mother's footsteps in the do-gooder department."

Chapter 13

The next couple of months were quiet and blissfully normal. Emmanuel made new friends at school, which wasn't surprising given his spirited personality. Our days were full of work, homework, birthday parties, sleepovers, movies, running here and there. I had forgotten how tiring having a popular and active youngster in the house could be. Joe and I, both night owls, suddenly found ourselves struggling to see the eleven o'clock news each evening.

I was a little worried that all the activities might tire Emmanuel out, especially with his medicine already having a weakening side effect. But he seemed to take everything in stride. Some nights he got so many phone calls that Joe and I considered getting a separate line installed for him.

It was a happy time for us, though things were far from perfect. Emmanuel had a stubborn streak a mile wide, and getting him up in the mornings to go to school was tougher than the back wall of a shooting gallery. At school, though he was a fairly good student, his teachers complained that he wanted to be the class clown rather than a serious scholar. He was such an active child that we wondered if he might have an attention disorder, but his psychiatrist said he was a normal thirteen-year-old boy. Normal, that is, except for the HIV.

Shortly after his fourteenth birthday in March, Patrice called to say his mother, whose HIV-positive status had been upgraded to full-blown AIDS just days before Christmas, had lapsed into a coma. I thought we should take Emmanuel to see her before she died, but Joe disagreed.

"If she was conscious, maybe. But what good does it do for him to see her in that state? I think it will only serve to scare him," he said. "Get him to thinking about his own fate."

"People should make peace with their parents before a parent dies." I knew I was treading a slippery slope; Joe's relationship with his father had been contentious at best. And when his dad had a massive heart attack fifteen years ago, he'd lingered in the hospital for seven days, begging to see Joe, the youngest of his three sons. Joe, still bitter, never went to see him. His mother told me the last word to pass his lips was his son's name: Joe. It had caused a major rift in his family, and Joe's oldest brother, John, stopped speaking to him, an issue they never resolved before John died in a car accident three years later. Frank had spent the years between his father's and brother's deaths playing neutral go-between. John's death freed up his time, and he met and married Arnelle.

His mother finally called a truce, then moved to St. Thomas, where she and Joe's dad had owned property. We usually saw her for two weeks each July, before she went on her annual cruise with one of her sisters.

Joe harrumphed at my suggestion that we take Emmanuel to see his mother. It didn't matter whether or not we agreed anyway. His mother's rights had been taken, and the county forbade us from letting him see her until he was eighteen, when he could decide for himself if he wanted to visit her. Problem was, it was clear she wasn't going to make it another four years. Short of sneaking him into her hospital room— which was next to impossible because we had no idea where she was—there was nothing we could do. Emmanuel's mother was going to die without him having an opportunity to say good-bye. That weighed heavily on my mind.

I was also bothered mightily by the continuing standoff with Duncan. I sent gifts for the baby, which she apparently accepted because none were returned; still, we didn't communicate verbally. Greg wasn't even ferrying messages anymore, which was actually fine by me. The news from Mozambique was equally disturbing: A cholera outbreak was sweeping the country. Joe was sure the Peace Corps would bring Madison home if it got too bad; I wasn't as certain. She was scheduled to come home in two months. I prayed night and day she'd be okay until then.

Chapter 14

Emmanuel wasn't in his bed the morning after my row with Joe about taking him to see his mother. Thinking perhaps he'd turned over a new leaf and gotten himself up for school, I went to the bathroom. He wasn't there. I headed for the kitchen, ready to scold him for stealing food—a bad habit of his I was still having a hard time breaking. At least once a week he'd steal cookies, apples, bananas, and juice boxes and hide them in his closet. I knew his behavior stemmed from the years of neglect and hunger, but it was behavior I was determined to get under control. I'd explained to him several times that he didn't have to hoard food. He didn't have to steal it. All he had to do was ask if he could have something. Clearly, it hadn't sunk in yet.

But he wasn't in the kitchen, either.

"Emmanuel!" I called. "Emmanuel, where are you? It's time to start getting ready for school."

He wasn't upstairs. He wasn't anywhere else in the whole

house. And Joe had already left for work about an hour earlier. I pressed the speed-dial button to his office.

"Joseph Parker."

"Emmanuel's not here."

"What do you mean, he's not there?"

"He's not here. I've looked everywhere."

"Ri, he's got to be there somewhere."

"But he's not." I could hear panic creeping into my voice. "I've looked all over the entire house. Can you come home?"

"Honey, I think you're overreacting. Where else could he be?"

"Joe." I swallowed a sob. "Emmanuel is not in this house. Where else could he be—how about dead on the street somewhere? Or hurt and helpless . . ."

"Okay, now you're jumping to conclusions. He didn't say anything about having to go to school early today? A field trip or something?"

"You think he would've left without saying good-bye to go on a school trip? Besides, the school would've sent home permission papers weeks ago if there was a planned trip. Joe, what's the matter with you?"

"Listen, honey, calm down. I'm sure he'll turn up and it'll be some kind of odd misunderstanding. I'll come home for lunch. I have to go to a meeting now."

"Okay, fine." I hung up and called the school. There was no seventh-grade field trip. Then I began calling Emmanuel's friends. No one had seen him. As I was hanging up the phone from the last phone call, my eyes wandered over to the pill case that held Emmanuel's myriad medications. It was still there, and it was full of today's dosages. He was out there somewhere without his meds. I felt faint and had to sit down, head between my legs, for a few moments or I would've blacked out.

Once I recovered, I called the police to report Emmanuel

missing. Then I called Tristan at work and left a message with Joe's assistant.

Tristan and Detective Stephen Grayson arrived at the same time.

Grayson took my statement, then searched Emmanuel's room for any kind of clue.

"Ma'am, I'm sure this is a simple runaway situation," he said. "There's no sign of forced entry, and your security system is very advanced. You know how teenagers are— one small argument over curfew, and they're off to stay with a friend for a few days."

"I've already called all of his friends. No one has seen him. And we didn't argue about anything. When he went to bed last night after completing his homework, everything was fine. And even if he has run away, he left here without his medication. Detective, Emmanuel is HIV positive. He has to take his medicine every day at prescribed times. Without it, he could get very ill."

"Should we call his school?" Tristan asked. "Maybe he's there. And if he's not, don't we have to let them know he won't be in today?"

"I've already called them earlier," I informed Tristan.

"There's really nothing we can do until he's been missing for at least twenty-four hours. And if it turns out he's run away from home, then our hands are really tied," the detective said.

"Missing for twenty-four hours? But he's ill. And how can your hands be tied when a minor disappears, even if he ran away on his own? That's the dumbest thing I've ever heard," I said. I was close to yelling at the detective, though I knew he was only doing his job. That he was only doing his job was small comfort when I knew twenty-four hours without Emmanuel's drug cocktail could be a life-and-death matter. Plus, I couldn't imagine a reason why Emmanuel would leave of his own free will. He was happy here. And he had a real family for the first time in his life.

Grayson handed me his card, then took his leave. Tristan called the school again and then Patrice. I was too shaken up to speak coherently.

"Patrice said they have an investigator for situations like this. He'll start to work immediately, whether or not this is a runaway situation," Tristan said. "She also said she'll be over here tonight."

Feeling helpless, I searched the house again. Tristan fielded a few phone calls, then got in touch with Solange. "Auntie, Emmanuel's missing. The police think he's run away. Mom's beside herself. I think you should come."

"Joe?" she asked.

"Dad's in a meeting. Said he'd be home as soon as it was over. Emmanuel left his meds."

"Get her to lie down. I'll be over soon, and we'll make flyers," she said.

By the time Joe rushed in, I was lying in our darkened bedroom, a migraine raging. I could hear Tristan's hushed voice bringing him up to speed; then the two of them went through the Christmas photos to find a good picture of Emmanuel for the flyers.

Before Solange left her office, she called in a favor from a friend who worked the assignment desk of the ABC affiliate. The friend promised to get our story on the six o'clock news that evening, provided Solange could get a photo to them in time.

Chapter 15

Duncan raced to the bathroom as soon as she got home. She'd barely made it home without stopping to vomit on the side of the road. This morning sickness thing was no joke. Someone suggested crackers, but so far, that hadn't helped. The smell of perfume, car exhaust, scrambled eggs cooking—she never knew what would set it off. One thing was certain: Her mother had once said morning sickness was an all-day affair; that was definitely turning out to be the case with this pregnancy.

By the time she got herself together and changed clothes, Greg was coming in the door. He found her in the kitchen, head resting on the kitchen table. He kissed the back of her neck, then gave her a brief massage.

"Morning sickness?" he asked.

"Um-hmm."

"Shouldn't this be over by now? I mean, you're six months along now. You're showing," he said. "I don't recall my sister-in-law Rashika having this trouble."

"Um-hmm," Duncan said again.

"Listen, you put your feet up. I'll handle dinner."

"Oh, baby, the mention of food is making my stomach do flip-flops," she said. "But I appreciate the gesture."

"You have to eat, Duncan."

The phone interrupted what was becoming a daily dialogue in the Williams household.

"Hello?" Greg answered.

Duncan sensed her husband getting tense.

"Um, no, we just got home," he said into the receiver. "Duncan's in the bathroom. . . . What? I'm sorry. . . . I'm sure he'll turn up. The police are right; it's probably a misunderstanding. . . . I'll, I'll tell Duncan. . . . I don't know, but I'll let her know. . . . Yes, okay. Good-bye."

"What was that about?" Duncan asked.

"That was your dad. Emmanuel's missing. The police think he might've run away."

"Good riddance," Duncan said.

"Oh, Dunc," he said, shaking his head. "Anyway, your mom is apparently taking this quite hard. Apparently, Emmanuel didn't take his medicine with him." He sat down beside his wife, trying to think of a neutral way to couch his next words. "Maybe you should call her."

"I will not."

"But, sweetie. . . ."

"Don't 'but sweetie' me. I thought this adoption was a bad idea from the start. No one in that house cares about anything except their precious Emmanuel. I'm pregnant. This is her first grandchild."

"But Duncan, you haven't talked to your mother—or your father, for that matter—since the night they told you about adopting Emmanuel. I'm sure they're excited about the baby. It is, as you pointed out, their first grandbaby. And they have sent us stuff. But you won't even let me tell them how sick you've been. You talk to Tristan every week, and you still haven't told him. You haven't given anyone a chance to coo over you.''

"That shouldn't matter, Greg. They should do it just because. But everything is about him now.''

"I hate to say this, honey, but you sound like a ten-year-old.''

"They ignored me when I was growing up, and they're ignoring me now,'' she said, eyes flashing. Greg wondered what had become of the sweet, shy woman he'd married. "It's like I'm invisible again,'' she said.

"They didn't ignore you—not then and not now, Duncan. Your parents love you. That house is full of love, which is why they're able to open their hearts again and love someone else,'' he said, knowing he was stepping out on a treacherous limb by taking the unpopular foster-parenting-is-a-good-thing stance with his wife. "Someone less fortunate.''

"You weren't there,'' she protested. "Tristan was the hellion, cutting classes and drinking. And Maddy was the do-no-wrong baby. She never finished anything she started—piano lessons, ukelele lessons, baton classes, law school. Hell, she's still not finishing anything. And she's always been such a loner. Mom and Dad spent my teenage years trying to rein Tristan in and draw Madison out. I got lost in the shuffle. The good kid, the quiet kid. The ignored kid.''

"Are you trying to tell me you think your parents don't care about you? About our baby? Duncan, I don't buy it. Sure, they're a little preoccupied right now . . .''

"And they shouldn't be. This is my time. I'm the one who's pregnant. They should be paying attention to me now.''

Greg gave up and started fixing a stir-fry dish for dinner.

Chapter 16

Two days after Emmanuel disappeared and his story ran on the local news, we got word of a possible sighting. Patrice's investigator, Bob Richards, took off for the boarded-up fun house of an abandoned amusement park where someone said they'd seen a young boy hanging out. But when Bob got there, the boy was gone. He found signs that someone had been staying there—discarded soda cans and McDonald's wrappers—but nothing said that someone had been Emmanuel. He watched the place for a while, but it appeared whoever was using it as a temporary shelter had moved on already.

When Bob gave us the news, he knew we were disappointed, but I was happy he was on the case. The police, as Detective Grayson had said they would, did nothing. But Bob kept us informed as he worked—and he made Emmanuel's disappearance his top priority. He spent hours sifting through the leads the news story had generated. Joe, Tristan, and Solange plastered Emmanuel's flyers all over town, while I, migraine finally under control, contacted AIDS specialists at the National Institutes of Health to see how much missing his meds might affect Emmanuel.

"Studies show adherence to treatment at a level of ninety-five percent or better is associated with a failure rate of nineteen percent. With adherence of ninety to ninety-five percent, the failure rate increases to thirty-six percent. Skip meds eighty-six to ninety percent of the time, and the failure rate rises to fifty percent," Dr. Bruce Dannenberg told me. "And I'm sure I don't have to tell you that the less medicine in his system, the higher his viral load gets. The higher the viral load, the quicker he progresses to full-blown AIDS. You also know HIV develops resistance to the combination therapies very quickly if medication doses are missed or delayed."

"Gobbledygook, doctor. What I want to know is how bad is it that Emmanuel has missed his meds for the past three days? And what happens if he misses them for a week?"

"Let's just say it's not good."

"Thank you." It was the news I had been both expecting and dreading. I tried hard not to let panic overwhelm me.

That evening, the phone calls started.

"You need to move," said a muffed, disguised voice, probably male.

"Move?" Joe asked. "Who is this? What are you talking about?"

"You've got a diseased boy living in our neighborhood, and I don't like it. Many of your neighbors don't like it." Joe hung up on the voice.

"We've lived here for decades," he said to me after the call. "What neighbor of ours is acting crazy?"

"I'm sure it's some kid pulling a prank," I said, after he explained what the caller had said.

Then one of Emmanuel's friends, a boy named Josh,

called. "My mom says I can't play with Emmanuel anymore," he told me.

"May I speak to your mother, Josh?"

"Um, yeah. Hold on. Mom!" I heard footsteps in the
background, but it took Josh's mother about five minutes to
get to the phone.

"Mrs. Parker."

"Mrs. Barrett, what's this about Josh not playing with
Emmanuel anymore?"

"I know we're a lot of years into this AIDS epidemic
and we should be a lot more understanding and informed,
but I just can't chance it. What if years from now someone
discovers this disease is airborne? Then what? I can't believe
you didn't tell us he was HIV positive before this," she
said.

"You're being. . . This is just wrong, Mrs. Barrett. The
boys have played together for months now. . . . Josh is
Emmanuel's best friend."

"Josh doesn't want to be around Emmanuel anymore.
He's scared of him. We don't want them spending time
together. You understand." She hung up before I could say
anything.

When Joe opened the front door to leave for work the
next morning, he saw that someone had egged the house.

Solange called around lunchtime. "Any news?"

"Nothing substantial since the possible sighting at the
old amusement park," I said. "We're starting to get calls."

"What kind of calls?"

"Someone, a kid I think, said we should move. The Barretts are refusing to let Josh and Emmanuel hang together.
The house had egg on it this morning. I'm wondering how
much worse it's going to get."

"Riley, we had to get word out," she said.

"I know, I know. But at what cost to Emmanuel? The school's administration and his teacher know about his HIV status, but we purposely kept it from his classmates. Now everybody knows."

"The most important thing is we find Emmanuel."

Chapter 17

"Mrs. Parker, we've found him," said Bob Richards. Emmanuel had been missing for six days.

"Where? How is he?"

"He's fine. A little dirty, scraped, and bruised. Hungry. Afraid you and Mr. Parker are mad at him. We're headed to the Memorial Hospital Center now to make certain he's okay. He's been staying several different places, including the fun house. We just missed him the day we got the hit at the fun house. For the past thirty hours he's been in an empty store near the hospice where his mother's living out her last days."

"I'll meet you at Memorial," I said, then hung up the phone. While Bob was explaining where Emmanuel had been during his absence, I'd slipped on my Keds and grabbed my wallet and keys. I picked up Emmanuel's pillbox almost as an afterthought just before going out the door.

I sped through the early hours of evening rush-hour traffic, trying to keep my considerable road rage in check each time I got behind slow-moving cars in the fast lane. Memorial Hospital Center was about fifteen miles from our house; during rush hour it could take as long as an hour to get there. I wondered how Emmanuel had made it across town to his mother's hospice. Had he been hitchhiking? Had anyone taken advantage of him? How much had missing his daily medication taken a toll on his frail body? How had he known where his mother was staying? Or was his final location just a coincidence? I wouldn't know the answers to these and the other questions swirling around inside my head until I saw Emmanuel, but they swirled nevertheless.

Forty-five minutes later—the last ten in a bumper-to-bumper, barely moving sea of vehicles—I parked in the visitor's parking lot at Memorial. It took another six minutes to get to Emmanuel. I had called Joe during the trip to the hospital, and he was on his way.

Bob was right; he looked a bit worse for wear. His little body shivered in the hospital gown, and his skinny arms and legs were filthy. Big, dark circles lay under his eyes like huge, dirty fingerprints. He looked small and lost.

"Emmanuel!" I cried. My life, which felt as if it had been passing in slow motion since the morning Emmanuel went missing, came flooding back at full speed. I held out my arms to hug him. He hesitated, something he'd never done with me before. "It's okay, I'm not mad. I'm just so glad to see you."

Slowly, he climbed down from the gurney and walked over to me, head hung low. I put my fingers under his chin and lifted his face to look into his eyes. "We have lots of questions about where you've been, why you went, but no one is mad at you, Emmanuel."

He smiled shyly, then gave me one of his trademark hugs. "Where's Dad?"

"He's on his way. He was still at work and he was going to swing by and pick up Tristan. We've all been so worried about you."

"The doctor will be back, but he seems to think Emmanuel is in good condition," Bob said. "He'll be fine, Mrs. Parker, really."

Just then, Joe and Tristan rushed into the curtained-off area. "Hey, squirt," Tristan said.

Joe looked tired. I wondered if I had identical worry lines etched across my forehead. "I haven't seen the doctor yet," I told them, "but Bob has, and says he said Emmanuel's going to be just fine."

"You had us worried, son," Joe said, anger creeping into his voice. "Really worried. Why did you run off like that? Your mother . . ."

I caught Joe's eye and shook my head. "Come, give Dad a hug," I said. He hugged Joe, then Tristan, but his normal enthusiasm was missing.

"Hi, I'm Dr. Garabedian," said a young man coming around the curtain and shaking our hands. "You must be the Parkers. Emmanuel is fine. A little dehydrated, but other than that, he's in good condition. We'll get him cleaned up, put a little ointment on his scratches; then he should be good to go."

"Doctor, he's HIV positive and hasn't had his meds in six days," I offered.

"Mr. Richards mentioned that. Exactly what cocktail is he taking?"

"ZDV and lamivudine."

"We'll check his viral load to see if there has been any change," said Dr. Garabedian. "But I suspect he's fine. And you know those test results won't come in right away. Meantime, just get him back on his regimen right away."

"I brought his meds with me," I said, handing the pillbox to the doctor.

"Good. We'll draw blood and give him the appropriate dosage. A nurse will be right in to clean those scratches."

Chapter 18

With Emmanuel cleaned and bandaged (a cut on his hand required four stitches), we headed home. He rode up front with me and was unusually quiet, breaking his silence only to ask for a McDonald's Happy Meal.

"Oh, sweetie, you haven't had a decent meal in a week. I think we should skip McDonald's today and get a good, home-cooked dinner, okay? How's that sound?"

He nodded and squirmed further back into the seat. I resisted the urge to come at him with a barrage of questions. I was also concerned about how to broach the subject of Josh Barrett. Should I tell him Josh was no longer allowed to be his friend or should I let him figure it out on his own when Josh began avoiding him?

Five miles before we reached the house, Emmanuel put his small hand on top of mine on the gearshift. I looked over at him and he favored me with a smile.

"Tristan, help Emmanuel get settled. I need to call

Solange and Duncan to let them know he's home safe and sound," I said. I really wanted to pull Joe aside and tell him to let Emmanuel be for the night.

"I don't think we should give him the third degree tonight, Joe," I said. "Let's let him have a night to get comfortable again."

"I'd like to know why he ran away," Joe said.

"I'd like to know that, too. Plus a whole series of other questions, but I think he'll be overwhelmed if we start in on him right now. He needs a good night's sleep. And he's got school in the morning."

"All right. If you think that's best . . ." he began.

"I do." We heard childish laughter from upstairs. "It's so good to hear that laugh again," I said. "Tristan is good with him."

"Did he say anything on the drive home?" Joe asked.

"Nothing. He asked about McDonald's, to which I said no, but other than that, nothing. Not a word."

"Is Bob going to alert Patrice?"

"I'm sure he will, but I'll give her a call myself in the morning."

"You said you wanted to call Duncan and your sister," my husband reminded me.

"I'll call Solange. You call Duncan; I'm not in the mood to talk to Greg this evening," I said. Joe smiled, kissed me tenderly on the forehead, and picked up the phone.

"Greg, hi. It's Dad. We just wanted to let you and Duncan know that Emmanuel's home . . . a little banged up is all. Four stitches . . . No, we haven't discussed anything yet. He seems a bit ashamed. . . . How's Duncan? I'd like to speak to her . . . ," Joe said, then looked in my direction and blew a kiss. "Oh? No, no don't wake her. Let her know we called. . . . Yes, our love to her, too. Good-bye, son." He placed the receiver back in its cradle. "Your daughter was 'sleeping.' "

"Figures. It seems to be all she does lately. I'll have Tristan call her later. I'm sure she'll be awake when he calls."

Solange and Tristan stayed for dinner, which was a relatively normal affair considering the events of the past week. Our prodigal son told jokes, kicked Tristan under the table, and blew bubbles in his milk. He giggled when Solange forgot her manners and uttered a curse word.

"Okay, time for some little boys to hit the hay," I said, knowing once Solange got started, it was hard for her to stop. "You've got a big day back at school tomorrow. And I'm sure you're going to have a lot of makeup work with you when you come home."

Sloppy kisses and hugs all around; then Emmanuel disappeared down the hall to his room.

"I feel like I need to check on him through the night to make sure he doesn't leave again," I said.

"Did he say why he left?" Solange asked.

"No," Joe said. "Riley and I think we should let him tell us in his own time."

"Bob Richards said he was in an empty store near where his mom is staying," Tristan said. "Did he know where his mom was staying? Maybe he just wanted to see her and thought we wouldn't let him."

"I've thought about that. But we didn't tell him about his mother. We're not allowed to tell him, actually, which I think is just wrong," I said.

"And we just found out ourselves that she was near death," Joe added. "The night before he ran away. Even then, we didn't know where she was staying. Patrice called—"

"And we fought about letting him see her," I interrupted, a lightbulb suddenly flashing on in my head. "What if he heard us, Joe? That could be the reason he ran away. He overheard us talking about his mother's imminent death and thought he wouldn't get to see her before she died.''

"Let's not jump to conclusions," he said. "He's home and he's safe. We'll find out why he left and make sure he knows we're not angry with him.''

"I'm angry with him," Solange said. "He had us worried sick. Not to mention he missed his medication for days. What did the doctor say about that?''

"The same thing they've all said: Missing his daily cocktail could make him resistant to the medication. If that happens, they'll have to find something else that works for him. *If* they can find something else that works. The emergency room doctor didn't seem to think he was in any trouble, though. But they did test his viral load," I said.

"Isn't it about time they change his meds anyway?" Joe asked. "I thought once he hit puberty they'd switch him from the pediatric cocktail to the adolescent one.''

"Ordinarily that's the plan. But Emmanuel hasn't started his growth spurt yet," I said.

"I don't know how y'all keep up with all of this," Solange said. "But I'm so proud of both of you.''

"I don't know why they want to," Tristan interjected.

"I don't want to have this discussion," I said, a note of finality in my voice that they all recognized.

"Have you talked to Duncan lately?" Solange said by way of changing the subject. It was my other least favorite subject.

"No," said Joe.

"Yes," said Tristan, simultaneously.

Our faces turned toward our oldest son. "When did you speak to her? Your father tried calling her today. Greg said she was sleeping.''

"Two days ago?" He appeared to be thinking. "She's fine. Getting bigger. Thinking she might not go back to work after the baby is born. I tried to convince her to call you, but she won't even discuss it. She's just being stubborn. Clearly, she inherited that streak from you, Mom."

Tears sprang into my eyes. This was a special time in my daughter's life; we shouldn't have been estranged from each other. "But you say she's doing fine?" I asked.

"Fine." He nodded. "She sounds good, too. She said they've got the baby's room half ready."

"Half ready?" Joe asked. "What does that mean?"

"I didn't get all those details, Dad. But she seems to be doing okay. Greg, too."

"Yeah, we've talked to him," Joe said. "He's been running interference for your sister. And I'm getting plenty tired of it, let me tell you."

"I need to go check on Emmanuel," I said, slipping out of my chair and padding down the hall. His room was dark, and for a second my breath caught in my throat. Then I saw a small moving lump under the covers. "I just wanted to make sure you were okay," I said softly. "I'm so glad you're home."

When he didn't respond, I rubbed my hand over his head, straightened his covers, and turned to leave the room. Small fingers gripped my wrist, and I turned.

"Mom?" he said.

"Yes, Emmanuel?"

"I'm sorry."

I sat on the side of the bed, waiting for more; he didn't oblige. "You know we were beside ourselves with worry, don't you?"

No sound except breathing. Fearing I'd pushed too soon, I started to leave once again.

"Can we talk about this tomorrow? I just want to sleep right now," he said, so softly I barely heard him.

"Certainly," I said, leaning down to kiss him on the cheek. "I love you, Emmanuel. Get some sleep, son."

Chapter 19

For about three months when Madison was ten, she'd been bothered by a bully. Her breasts had started developing six months before her tenth birthday, and one of the girls in her class—Cynthia Gleason; it was funny how I remembered her name after all these years—had teased her about it relentlessly. Cynthia and a group of her cronies left training bras on Madison's desk and paid a few boys in the class to chase her down and snap the back of her bra against her back each day during recess. For the final two weeks of the torture, Madison had come home crying every day.

My normally wonderful and understanding husband had been completely useless handling the situation. Had it been Tristan, I was certain he would've pulled him aside and taught him a few boxing moves. But it wasn't his son, it was one of his daughters, and the problem had to do with her developing body. He put on blinders, convinced it would go away. After all, he'd said, he'd snapped a few bras in his day, too. This advice only made Madison cry harder.

I hadn't been completely sure what to say to her to make her feel better; there's no class on how to deal with your child's bullies squeezed in between how to change diapers and infant CPR. I'd told her she was becoming a woman and that Cynthia Gleason was probably just jealous of her new womanly figure. Madison had gone to school and told everyone Cynthia was jealous and the bullying had stopped.

If only dealing with the aftereffects of Emmanuel's HIV-positive status being made public were that simple.

His first day back at school, there were parents picketing in the building's courtyard. The nicest of their homemade cardboard signs advocated home schooling for HIV-positive children. I prayed he hadn't seen some of the harsher signs, the ones calling him a faggot and a child of Satan. I'd thought we'd come so far since the days when Ryan White had been ostracized. I was wrong. Several students, including his former best friend Josh, refused to sit anywhere near him, leaving at least a row of empty seats all around him in every class. Another group of kids called him names and threw unwrapped condoms at him in the hallway. By noon, I'd received a call from the school's principal, asking me to bring Emmanuel home until things quieted down a bit.

"Bring him home? That's preposterous!" I said. "You're kicking him out of school? What about these other kids? The troublemakers throwing condoms? What are you doing about them? Their behavior?"

"Mrs. Parker, we're dealing with them, believe me. In fact, the condom throwers have been expelled. I just think it best if you pick Emmanuel up a little early today—for his own safety."

"And what happens tomorrow? Or the next day? Will you be better prepared to watch out for my son's safety then? Or are you ordering me to keep him home until you get things under control?" I asked. To say I was hot under the collar was more than a major understatement. "How many days will that be?"

"Mrs. Parker, please calm down," Dr. Klein-D'elia said patiently. "When you first enrolled Emmanuel in this school and told us of his special health needs, I told you we were prepared to handle the situation. And I believe we've done a very good job—both in making sure he gets his medication on time and in keeping his HIV status quiet. Unfortunately, the word is out now. But, Mrs. Parker, we didn't alert the public to his HIV status." She paused long enough to let it sink in that we were the ones responsible for people knowing about Emmanuel's condition.

"Until we can get things back under control—that includes the students here as well as the parents picketing in front of the school—I believe it best if Emmanuel stays at home. I'll make sure he gets his assignments, and his teacher, Mrs. Taylor, has offered to communicate with him through E-mail in case he needs help with his schoolwork," she said.

"I'm sorry," I said, humbled. The school had bent over backward for us. "How's he taking this?"

"He seems to be handling it very well, actually. Better, I must say, than I would. We'll have his assignments—those he missed during the past week and those scheduled for the rest of this week—ready when you get here, Mrs. Parker," she said and signed off.

I practiced what I'd say to Emmanuel during the short drive to his school to get him. The picketing, stay-at-home moms, complete with babies in strollers, parted to make way for my car as I drove up the circular drive. I guessed that none of them knew I was Emmanuel's mother, and I was right. They were fairly quiet when I walked into the building. When I came out, Emmanuel in tow, they started shouting, "Take him home! Take him home!" and "No AIDS in our schools!" We loaded into the car, and they began pounding on the doors. Afraid they'd break a window, I gunned it and we lurched forward, almost running over a protester. As I rounded the curve, I saw the TV cameras. "Great," I said. "That's all we need. More publicity. I can hear the news briefs now: Crazed mother of HIV-positive child tries to kill picketing parents."

"Don't worry, Mom. You didn't actually hit anybody," Emmanuel said with a small giggle.

Oh, to have the simple logic of a child again, I thought. Aloud I said, "Are you okay? Did anybody hurt you?"

"I can't say I'm happy about this," he began. "But I've been teased my whole life 'cause I'm a foster kid."

I was struck again by the pain foster children had endured in their short lives. The words I'd practiced on the trip over died on my lips, and we drove the rest of the way home in silence.

"Mrs. Taylor said she was gonna call you tonight," he said after changing out of his school clothes. He munched on an apple, his favorite snack.

"Your principal said Mrs. Taylor was sending home all your assignments for the rest of the week."

"And all the stuff I missed last week. It's a lot. I'll barely have time to eat," he said.

Children have such a flair for hyperbole, I thought, though we had carted a stack of books and papers home.

"Do you want to talk now about why you ran away?" I asked him after a beat.

"You and Dad were arguing about keeping me. I thought I was becoming a burden."

"Arguing about keeping . . . When did you hear us arguing about keeping you? Emmanuel, we told you we're going to adopt you," I said, dismayed. The only argument he could've overheard had not been about canceling his adoption.

"The night I left. You said take me; Dad said no."

"And just where did you think we were talking about taking you?"

"Away. As much as I like it here—and Mom, I do like it—I don't want to make your life more difficult. I know my illness, my being HIV, is a problem," he said. He hadn't made eye contact once during his short speech.

"Emmanuel, look at me," I said. He struggled to lift his eyes to mine, afraid, perhaps, of what he might see. "Dad and I knew what we were getting into when we decided to make you a part of this family. We love you. You are not a burden, do you hear me? And you are not HIV; you are HIV positive."

He nodded solemnly.

"We were having a heated discussion the night before you ran away," I said. Then I took a deep breath, knowing I was about to break a foster parent rule. "Patrice called me earlier that day to tell me that your mother had taken a turn for the worse around Christmastime. Since her rights to be your mom have been taken, we're not supposed to tell you this information. And we're not allowed to take you to see her. Two rules that I think are completely stupid and wrong."

"Is she going to die?" he asked, eyes suddenly filling with tears.

"I don't know, honey. She's not doing well, but she's been holding her own for the past three months."

"Why were you arguing?"

"I wanted to take you to see her, rules be damned, pardon my French. Your dad thought seeing her that way might make you sad."

"It would make me sad, but I'd still want to see her. I don't want her to die alone." His eyes still glistened, but he didn't let any tears roll down his face.

"Mr. Richards, the investigator Patrice hired to help find

you, said you were staying in an empty store near the place your mom is staying. Did you know she was there?''

''No, I was just looking for a place to lay my head. I didn't want to stay on park benches. I tried to pick places with a roof in case it rained at night. And I kept moving, so no one would prey on me, a kid alone,'' he said, seemingly wise beyond his years.

''You shouldn't have been eavesdropping on your father and me, but since you did, you should've asked about what you heard,'' I said. ''Promise me you'll ask questions in the future. I don't want any more misunderstandings like this one.''

''I promise,'' he said.

''We also need to talk about what happened at school today.''

''People can be mean. They don't understand about my illness.''

''Yes, this is true. But your dad and I and your Aunt Solange, Tristan, too . . . well, when you ran away, we were desperate to find you. We were especially frantic because you left without taking your medicine. Solange got a friend at the TV station to run a story about you, and we put up flyers with your picture on them all over town. We let the cat out of the bag about your HIV status in the hope that it would help us find you faster,'' I said. ''We didn't realize that two decades into this disease, people still don't understand it, how it's spread. I didn't know there would be this backlash. For that, I am sorry.''

''Do I have to go back there, Mom? I don't want people throwing any more of those funny-looking rubber bands at me.''

I stifled a laugh; it wasn't a laughing matter. ''Sweetie, those 'funny-looking rubber bands,' as you call them, are condoms. They are devices people use to keep from having babies. And I don't want anyone else throwing them at you, either. I don't want adults picketing your presence in front of the building. But at some point you're going to have to go back to school."

"Why can't I keep going to school at home? Like I am this week?"

"Because you can't, honey. I know that's not a satisfactory answer; when I was your age I always hated it when adults responded to perfectly logical questions with unsatisfactory answers. But you'll understand better one day. Trust me."

Joe, unable to break away from work earlier, chose that moment to come home. I thanked him silently, because I was out of explanations.

"Daddy," Emmanuel cried, racing down the steps to meet Joe.

We're going to be all right, I thought. Emmanuel's running away had all been just a big misunderstanding. Now that it was cleared up, we were going to be okay. We just had to get through the drama at the school, but I was convinced we would manage just fine—as a family.

Later, I made dinner while Joe and Emmanuel waded through his stack of homework. From the sounds of laughter coming from Emmanuel's bedroom, I doubted much homework was getting done. It was more likely they were playing one of those computer games. Tristan had loaded a bunch of them onto Emmanuel's computer, and the two of them often spent hours playing against each other.

The sound of the phone ringing interrupted my happy musings. I hesitated before answering, worrying it might be another "well-intentioned" neighbor with unsolicited advice about what we should do with Emmanuel. The calls usually came around dinnertime.

"Hello?"

"Mrs. Parker? This is Mrs. Taylor, Emmanuel's teacher."

"Oh, hi. Emmanuel said you'd be calling, and I spoke to Dr. Klein-D'elia earlier today."

"Yes, I mentioned to Dr. Klein-D'elia that I'd be available by E-mail if Emmanuel runs into any trouble or doesn't understand something in the work I've given him," she said. "But I'm calling about something else tonight."

"Oh?"

"I'm worried about what's going on now that everyone knows about Emmanuel's HIV status."

"It was pretty intense today," I agreed. "As we drove away, there were people pounding on my car. I almost ran over one of them. And Emmanuel has already asked if he can be homeschooled for the rest of the year."

"I was afraid of that. It was pretty ugly, both inside the school and out. I can't do much about the picketing parents— that's Dr. Klein-D'elia's responsibility. But I've been thinking the school should sponsor an AIDS awareness day, culminating in a concert featuring one of those rappers the kids are so crazy about," she said. "Emmanuel could help pull the event together since he already knows so much about the disease. It could serve two purposes."

"Educate the students and get them off Emmanuel's back by helping them understand what he's going through," I said, catching her enthusiasm. "I think it's an excellent idea! I'll mention it to Emmanuel tonight."

"I haven't talked to Dr. Klein-D'elia about it yet, so I'd prefer if you'd hold off on speaking to him. I doubt she'll be opposed to the idea, but let me bring it up to her first."

"Of course. I understand. I'll await word from you," I told her, then hung up the phone.

Chapter 20

Duncan wasn't sure she was going to return to work after the baby was born, but the way things were going, she might have to quit before the baby got there. It was getting more and more difficult to work the phones and keep up with the ticker tape from a bathroom stall. Greg joked that she should carry an airplane barf bag everywhere with her. His words, meant to be funny, had stung. But he was right; she spent at least a third of each day leaning over a toilet.

She splashed water on her face, then looked at herself in the mirror. She looked haggard. Where was the glow pregnant women were supposed to have? It was difficult enough being a woman in an all-boys club without having to excuse herself every few minutes to deal with the demands of her growing body.

"Hey, you okay?" asked Alicia Hayes, one of the other five women in the firm. Duncan hadn't heard her come into the bathroom.

"Oh, yes, I'm, well, as well as can be expected, I guess," Duncan managed with a weak smile.

"Don't let it get to you," Alicia said, then ducked into a stall.

After rinsing out her mouth, Duncan went back to her office. Leaving her career was going to be hard, she thought. She worked hard to get to where she was. And her talents were appreciated. It was the first place she'd felt like part of a family, albeit a competitive one. Now her haven was being threatened by the life growing inside her.

As soon as the thought crossed her mind, she felt guilty. Duncan wanted this baby. She just didn't realize how difficult being pregnant could be. She needed her mom. Thinking about her mother brought tears to her eyes. She wished they were on better terms, but her parents were too wrapped up in their latest project to do more than buy the baby a few trinkets and hope that placated her.

Her stomach lurched. Duncan pawed through her desk drawer, looking for crackers. "Sylvia," she called to her assistant when she came up empty, "are there any crackers in the breakroom?"

"You polished off the last ones last week," Sylvia said. "I don't know why you keep eating them; they don't seem to be working. I've heard mustard helps."

Duncan smiled, rubbed her stomach, then swallowed hard. "Can you get Greg on the phone? Tell him to pick me up. I don't think I'm going to be able to drive home," she said, then dashed toward the bathroom again.

Greg was quiet on the drive home, which was fine with Duncan. She didn't want another lecture about how little she was eating.

"I'm going to make you some soup," he said when they got into the house.

"Greg . . ."

"No arguments. And I really think you need to talk to someone. This is getting worse instead of better. You're six months pregnant, and you've gained only seven pounds,' " Greg said. "Doc Mosley agrees with me."

"I just need to get some rest," Duncan said.

"After you eat your soup," Greg said, putting his foot down. He wanted her to call her parents, but he didn't dare broach the subject with her. It would just start another argument, and he didn't want that. But Duncan hadn't even called while her little brother had been missing. And when her father had called to say Emmanuel was home, she'd refused to take the phone. Greg knew her family; he was certain this was tearing them up inside.

He poured a jar of Campbell's Hearty Chicken Noodle into a microwave-safe bowl, punched in the code for soup, and went into the living room to comfort his wife. That quickly, she'd fallen asleep. He removed her shoes, put her legs up on the sofa and covered her with a blanket. By the time the microwave beeped, signaling Duncan's soup was ready, Greg had dozed off, too.

Bile in her throat woke Duncan. She looked around, dazed, trying to get her bearings, then had to rush to the bathroom. A groggy Greg was a few steps behind her. Duncan hadn't eaten anything since breakfast, so she had more dry heaves than anything else. Still, it was painful.

"You okay?" Greg asked. "Do you need me to do anything?"

Duncan shook her head. "What time is it?" she asked. It had still been light when they'd come home; now it was pitch black.

"I don't know. You fell asleep before I could get your soup ready, and I guess I joined you. Guess we're both tired," he said with a small chuckle. "I'll go reheat the soup."

"Okay." They both went back into the kitchen. "Sylvia said something about mustard helping with morning sickness," she said, while Greg restarted the microwave.

"On what? Bread? Or just plain?"

"I don't know. I guess I'd have to eat it on bread. I don't think I could stomach a spoonful of mustard," she said.

Greg sat down and took her hands in his. "Baby, I know you don't agree with me, but maybe you should call your mother."

"Greg, I don't—"

"Just listen to me, Duncan. Maybe your mom knows something that can help with how you've been feeling. You don't have to talk about your little brother."

"That boy is not my brother," she spat.

"You know what I mean. Just talk to her about the pregnancy."

"I'll think about it," she said. It was the best he'd gotten out of her.

The microwave beeped. Duncan sipped the broth, leaving the noodles, chicken, and vegetables in a pile on one side of the bowl.

"Here," Greg said, handing her a slice of mustard-covered bread he'd just prepared. "Anything's worth a try."

"Especially if it works," she said with a smile.

Chapter 21

The AIDS awareness project was coming together quickly. After Dr. Klein-D'elia's approval, which she'd readily given, Mrs. Taylor pulled together a unit for her class on AIDS. Three weeks had passed since Emmanuel had returned home after running away. He was back in school, having spent a week at home studying and catching up with the rest of the class. His classmates weren't acting any friendlier, but the picketing had stopped. His teacher was sure the AIDS awareness activities would bring the kids around, too. I hoped so.

For the first time in his life, Emmanuel felt important. He came home each day, full of exciting news about the planning he was doing. "Mom," he said one day early in April, "we might get Will Smith to perform for awareness day! Can you believe that?"

"That's good, honey," I said, having no idea who Will Smith was. I made a mental note to ask Tristan. It was wonderful to see him so happy, though I knew I'd feel better if Josh's parents stopped behaving like children and let the boys play together again.

Emmanuel made posters, displaying a previously undiscovered artistic flair. He called doctors at the NIH, inviting them to speak during the day's activities. And with the help of his assigned partner, a nervous girl named Lauren Day whose parents were both doctors, he made buttons for the students to wear. I was amazed at his emerging leadership abilities.

"Mom," Tristan said one night after he'd joined us for dinner, "I may have been mistaken about you and Dad adopting the squirt. He's been good for you guys, runaway episode notwithstanding. He's keeping you young."

"This project is really bringing out the best in him," I said. "By the way, who is Will Smith? Emmanuel said something a couple of days ago about him performing at the concert."

"Okay, maybe I was wrong about him keeping you guys young," Tristan said with a laugh. "Remember the show *Fresh Prince of Bel-Air?* He was the kid from Philly sent to live with his well-to-do aunt and uncle. I can tell from the blank look that you never saw that show. It comes on every afternoon on the WB."

"And he's a rapper?" I asked. "Mrs. Taylor wanted a rapper for that evening's performance."

"Yes, Mom, he's a rapper. In fact, he was doing hip-hop before the TV show." His face suddenly lit up. "*Independence Day.* I know you've seen that. You and Dad love sci-fi."

"That's the one where aliens swoop in and fry New York City?"

"Yes, and Will Smith and Jeff Goldblum fly an alien spacecraft into the mothership and save the day."

"We did see that. That's Will Smith?"

"That's Will Smith," he said.

"You're going to have to take him to the concert, Tristan. I don't think my old ears can take it."

"That's fine," he said. "I need more bonding time with my little brother."

"The adoption will be final three days after the awareness day," I said, changing the subject. "Then everything will be complete. Except for Duncan." I sighed.

"She still hasn't talked to you or Dad?"

"Nope."

"For what it's worth, I've tried to get her to change her mind. And I know Greg has, too."

"She's stubborn. And you're right, she got that from me," I said before he could throw it up in my face again. "I just wish she'd give a little. We should be celebrating the arrival of two new family members right now."

"Squirt's not suffering any ill effects from missing his medication, is he?"

"Thank God, no," I said. "The tests say his viral load hasn't changed. But have you noticed his voice seems a little deeper? They may have to change his cocktail anyway, if he hits puberty and starts growing."

Two days later, Mrs. Taylor called. The concert lineup was set: Will Smith, Lil' Bow Wow, and Common. I didn't even pretend to know who the two additions were, but I trusted Mrs. Taylor would choose only positive rappers. One of the teachers had called in a few favors, and Dr. Helene Gayle, director of the National Center for HIV, STD and TB Prevention at the CDC, was coming to speak. Metro TeenAIDS, a local AIDS organization staffed by teenagers, had been tapped to perform a few skits.

"They'll also lead a roundtable discussion," Mrs. Taylor told me. "These Metro TeenAIDS counselors are really good. And they're good about getting other kids involved, opening up. Something about being in the same age group, I think.''

"Emmanuel has been so excited about this," I said. "Thank you, Mrs. Taylor, for doing this."

"No need to thank me. We think everyone knows about this disease because we've been living with the reality of it for so long. But statistics show young people are still getting it at alarming rates, testing positive in their early twenties, which means many of them contracted it during their teen years. Clearly, an AIDS awareness day is long overdue," she said. "I'm glad it's bringing out some of Emmanuel's strengths. He's really quite a little leader."

"I've noticed. I'm very proud."

"You and your husband will be able to attend some of the day's activities, right?"

"I will attend some of the daytime events. I'm not sure if Joe will be able to get off work. My oldest son is taking Emmanuel to the concert," I said.

"Good. I look forward to seeing you," she said.

Chapter 22

A week before the AIDS awareness day, Patrice took Emmanuel out for dinner. It was the last of their social worker foster child dinners. The dinners, usually at an Olive Garden or Applebee's, were a time for the social worker to see what was going on in the child's life, to find out if there were any major issues the social worker would need to handle. Though Patrice and her office had been wonderful when Emmanuel ran away, they had offered absolutely no help with the backlash to his HIV-positive status being made public.

No one from Children's Protective Services had commented on the upcoming AIDS awareness event, but I got the feeling they didn't exactly approve. There had been some mild animosity over our public search for Emmanuel the month before; an unwritten rule for the department advocated keeping the lives of the children in the system secret. But since Emmanuel was so close to belonging to us, no one came down on us very hard. That is, until the night of the Patrice-Emmanuel dinner.

They surprised me when they came back to the house in about twenty-five minutes; usually their dinners lasted slightly longer than an hour. Emmanuel tossed his light-weight jacket on the sofa and stomped up the stairs without saying a word. I looked at Patrice, puzzled. My normally happy-go-lucky child had a storm cloud over his head.

"We didn't even make it to Ruby Tuesdays," she said, sitting down in Joe's recliner.

"You were going someplace new this time. What happened?"

"Why did you tell Emmanuel about his mother?" she demanded.

"He overheard Joe and me discussing it the night you told us. It's the reason he ran away, or part of the reason, anyway. He thought he was a burden to us," I explained.

"He's rather angry with me," Patrice said. "There are reasons we keep this kind of information from the children."

"I understand those reasons, though I don't necessarily agree with them. But when I found out he'd heard Joe and me, well, I thought he deserved to know exactly what we were talking about. I didn't want him thinking he was making our lives difficult, which is what he took away from that conversation. You'll get over him being mad at you; he may never get over his mother dying without being able to say good-bye," I said.

"Once the adoption is final, you can take him to see his mother. We won't have any say about it then," she said. "But until then . . ."

"His mother may not be alive by that time. This is a dumb rule, and you know it."

She sighed heavily. "We weren't even to the end of the street when he asked why I hadn't told him. And why you were prevented from telling him."

"What did you tell him?"

"I tried to explain the rules and the reasons for those rules. He wasn't having it. Told me to bring him home."

"Patrice, he's been so happy these past few weeks, working on this AIDS awareness project. I don't want anything to bring him down," I said.

"And you don't think telling him about his mother is a downer?"

"He needed to know. I'd do it again. CPS might not like it, but it's the truth. And as you said, the adoption will be happening soon and Emmanuel will be our son."

"Well, I'll try to get back out to see him before then. I don't want to leave things like this between the two of us," Patrice said. We exchanged a few pleasantries; then she left.

"Emmanuel," I called up the stairs.

"Yes, ma'am?"

"Get down here now." I'd been the disciplinarian with our first three children; Joe felt his temper might get the best of him and he'd say things to them, in anger, that he'd regret later.

Emmanuel came down with a sheepish look on his face, so I knew he knew he'd been rude to Patrice. "What happened at your dinner with Patrice?" I asked.

"Um, well, um," he began, scuffing at the floor with his athletic shoe. "Um . . ."

"You asked her about your mom, right?"

"Patrice said she was my friend. But if she had really been my friend, she would've told me my mom was sick," he said angrily.

"Honey, Patrice does care about you. She has to follow the rules of her job, though."

"She still should've told me," he said, more like a stubborn child than an angry one.

"You shouldn't have been rude to her. There was no

reason for that behavior, no matter how mad you are at her. You know that, right?"

"Yes, ma'am."

"We'll call her tomorrow to apologize, okay?"

"Yes, ma'am."

"Now, go back up to your room and think about what you're going to say in your apology. Since you'll be eating dinner here now, you can come out in time to eat."

"Yes, ma'am." He hung back, still scuffing the floor.

"Scoot, young man."

"Did Patrice say how she's doing? My mom, I mean?"

"No, honey, she didn't. But she did say she'd be back out here to see you in the next week. We can ask her then," I said. "Now go."

Chapter 23

The next week passed fairly quickly, though it didn't seem that way to Emmanuel.

"Friday's never gonna get here," he whined each morning at breakfast.

"Whining about it isn't going to make the day come any faster," I said on Wednesday. "Now eat your cereal. And hurry up; I have to meet with a client this morning."

"So that's why you're wearing lipstick," he giggled.

"Eat!" I commanded.

As usual, getting Emmanuel to move his slowpoke self was next to impossible, and we went scurrying pell-mell out of the house to get him to school on time. "Have a good day, son," I called to him as he climbed out of the car.

"Hey, Mom," he started, turning back toward me, "did you hear the one about the grape?"

"No, and it'll keep until you get home from school this afternoon. Go to class."

I met with my client, the owners of a new dot.com, went

over the designs for the lobby to their building, then headed home. Joe had left a message during my absence.

"Sweetness, I can get Friday off. We'll go to Emmanuel's event during the day, then have a romantic dinner somewhere, just the two of us, that night while Tristan takes him to the concert. Call me."

"A romantic dinner sounds wonderful," I purred when he answered the phone. "We haven't had a moment to ourselves in the past few weeks."

"Don't I know it. I thought these were supposed to be the beginning of our golden years," he joked. "I figured we could go to Cyclic. They've got live jazz on Friday nights."

"Mmm. I can't wait. Like Emmanuel's been saying all week, Friday's never gonna get here," I said. "I'll see you tonight around five-thirty?"

"Probably closer to six-thirty. Got some stuff I need to clean up here."

"Okay, baby, I'll see you then."

Tristan came by after dinner, and he and Emmanuel spent an hour getting Emmanuel's concert outfit together.

"I've never seen boys spend so much time on clothing." Joe sighed. "Don't they just wear some baggy jeans and a T-shirt?"

I hunched my shoulders and went back to the pants on which I was letting out the hem. Still small for his age, Emmanuel was growing. This was the third night this week I'd spent taking the hem out of a pair of his pants. "This is important to Emmanuel, Joe, you know that. It's a big night for him."

"I know, baby, I know. But those two are cackling like a bunch of teenage girls up there," Joe said. "Has he done his homework?"

"Done and checked," I said. "And I, for one, am enjoying the relationship he's developing with Tristan."

"Well, I am glad Tristan has come around about the adoption. When is Patrice supposed to come for their dinner do-over?"

"That's tomorrow," I said.

"We've got a lot to do in the next few days," he said, sounding tired.

"And Tristan thinks this is keeping us young," I said with a smile. "Come, let me give you a massage."

Friday dawned clear, but windy, more like a day in March than late April. When I went to wake Emmanuel for school, I found him already up, showered, dressed, and in the kitchen attempting to make his breakfast.

"Today's the day, huh?" I said. I gave him a quick hug.

"I didn't sleep very well," he said. "I hope I don't have bags under my eyes."

I smiled. The vanity of youth. "Let me have a look at you." I spun him around and made a big show of inspecting his face. "Hmm. Um-hmm. Umm. Hmm."

"Mom." He giggled.

"Well, I don't see any bags or dark circles. But we're gonna have to do something about that growling stomach," I said, tickling him. He laughed more, then spilled Rice Krispies all over the floor.

"Oops!" he said. "It was an accident!"

"I know. Sit. I'll get your breakfast."

"Guess I'm a little nervous about today," he admitted.

"You've worked so hard," I said. "I'm sure everything will be fine." I sat down across the table from him. "I'm very proud of you, Emmanuel. No matter how today goes— and I believe it will go very well—I just want you to know how proud I am of the work you've put into this project."

"At dinner last night, I asked Patrice about my mom. She said as far as she knows there's been no change." The laughter of a few moments ago had all but disappeared.

"Oh, sweetie, I'm sorry. Monday you'll be our son, though, and we'll be able to take you to see her. Now, finish your breakfast so we can get going, okay?" I left the kitchen so he wouldn't see the tears in my eyes. Unlike Emmanuel's, if tears filled my eyes, they spilled down my cheeks, as they were doing now. No change was good, I told myself, then ducked into the bathroom to splash cold water on my face.

Joe, Emmanuel, and I rode to the school together. Emmanuel chattered nervously the whole way. We planned on staying until lunchtime, so we'd miss the skits and panel discussion with Metro TeenAIDS. We would, however, get to hear Dr. Gayle speak, and that's the part I really wanted to see anyway.

Handmade posters hung everywhere, announcing the school's first annual AIDS awareness day. We were ushered into the auditorium, which filled quickly with noisy middle schoolers. The lights dimmed, the students calmed, and Dr. Klein-D'elia took the podium.

"Welcome to Hancock Middle School's first annual AIDS awareness day," she began. "You students see and hear from me all the time, so I won't take up much of your time." She introduced Dr. Gayle, who stepped to the podium. I was surprised to see the director in jeans and a light blue sweater twin set, but assumed she had dressed in a way that would relate to the kids. I looked around the room and saw at least half the girls in the audience were dressed identically to the doctor. I was amazed that with her busy schedule she found time to keep up with youth trends.

"Research indicates that every hour of every day, two young Americans aged thirteen to twenty-five are becoming infected with HIV," she began. "Of the estimated forty thousand Americans who will become infected this year, half will be young people under age twenty-five. If the threat of HIV is to be reduced, young people must receive messages about prevention and testing and have easy access to health-care services. We must end the silence and secrecy that prevent us from talking openly about HIV and AIDS in our families, our communities, and physicians' offices.''

She spoke passionately, but in language the kids could understand. The audience was mesmerized for her twenty-minute speech. Then the lights came back on and she took questions from the students. Joe and I sat, fingers linked, both hoping this day would bring an end to the torment Emmanuel had been suffering at the hands of his peers. I scanned the audience, looking for our youngest son, but I couldn't see him.

We slipped out at the end of Dr. Gayle's segment. Mrs. Taylor, Emmanuel's teacher, was in the hall.

"I'm so glad you could come," she said.

"She was good," I said, speaking about Dr. Gayle.

"Very. And did you notice how attentive the students were? I think the day's going to be a huge success!" she said, then headed back toward the auditorium.

Joe and I walked slowly back to the car.

"I hope she's right," he said.

"You saw how interested the students were in what Dr. Gayle had to say. I think they've just never had anyone provide them with information about HIV and AIDS. The sex education curriculum is abstinence-based, so I don't think they even mention AIDS," I said. "Emmanuel didn't even know what condoms were, even when he had them thrown at him."

"Hopefully, today's activities will put an end to that kind of behavior," Joe said.

"Yes. And get his friends to stop avoiding him. I didn't notice too many other parents there, though. Did you?"

"I saw Lauren Day's parents," he said. "But they aren't the parents who need the education."

"Well, parents had to give consent for their children to participate, so the fact that the auditorium was packed is a good sign."

We'd been home about an hour when Patrice called with bad news.

"Emmanuel's mom's condition has worsened," she told me.

"Oh, no. He just mentioned this morning that you told him last night there'd been no change in her status."

"It happened sometime during the wee hours of the morning. I know you wanted him to see her before she passes. The hospice workers don't think she's going to come out of this," Patrice said. "I don't know if this is the best way for him to see her."

"Are you saying you'll bend the rules?" I asked.

"Can you get him to the hospice in the next couple of hours?"

"He's in the middle of his AIDS awareness day activities," I said, my heart dropping.

"I'd forgotten about that. I thought you and Joe were going to go."

"We went to the morning portion. Dr. Helene Gayle gave a really good speech. And I think it was well received by the kids."

"What time will he be done?"

"Not until tonight. The day ends with a concert."

"Okay, call me at home in the morning," she said. "We'll make arrangements for him to see her tomorrow."

"I will. Thanks, Patrice." I hung up the phone. "Emmanuel's mom is in a coma," I said to Joe. Then I burst into tears.

"Oh, honey," Joe said, taking me into his arms and pulling me down on the sofa with him.

"I knew I should've pushed harder to get him in to see her," I sobbed. "He's going to be so angry and upset."

"Baby, you did all you could," Joe said soothingly.

"But . . . but . . . they don't think she's going to come out of the coma." I was blubbering by this time.

"Shh," Joe whispered.

I wasn't sure how long we stayed like that, but the phone made us stir.

"Please get that, honey," I said. "I don't want to talk to anybody." It wasn't quite two in the afternoon, by the clock above the mantel, but it had grown dark outside. Was it supposed to rain? I wondered. I hadn't seen a weather report in a couple of days.

I couldn't tell who Joe was talking to on the phone, but suddenly, he thrust the phone in my hand. Shaking my head, I had no choice but to answer or drop the receiver.

"Hello?" I said a little shakily.

"Mom, it's me. I had a few minutes, so I decided to call home and see how things are going with you guys. And my new little brother," said Madison's voice over a static-filled line.

"Madison!" I cried. "Oh, sweetie, how are you? I've been worried; we keep hearing reports about the cholera outbreak."

"It's pretty bad, Mom. I'll be coming home a little early because of it," she said.

"Thank God. When?"

"In two weeks. How's Emmanuel doing? And Duncan? How's her pregnancy going? I've tried calling her once or twice, but you know the life of a stockbroker. She's never home."

"Emmanuel has settled in nicely. He's at school right now. We haven't had any more luck than you in catching up with your sister. Tristan has talked to her a few times, though," I said. I didn't want Madison to catch wind of any weirdness in the family, not while she was still so far away.

"What's old Tristan been up to? I haven't even tried to call him. I don't want to get his latest fling on the phone," she said with a laugh.

"Actually, your brother's been spending a lot of time with Emmanuel. In fact, they're going to a hip-hop concert together tonight."

"Figures," she said. "Listen, Mom, I've gotta go. But I'll be in contact soon to let you guys know the flight information and all of that. Love you." Then she was gone.

"Joe, our baby's coming home," I said. Talking to Madison lifted my spirits a little.

"I told you they'd bring her out of there if the cholera epidemic got too bad," Joe said. "Everything is coming together at once. Emmanuel's going to be officially ours in three days, Maddy's coming home, and Duncan will be giving birth in another couple of months."

His mentioning Duncan and our grandchild darkened my brightening mood. I felt like it was beginning to look outside. He picked up on the change and took my hand. "I'm sure things with Duncan will get better. She's going to need us once the baby gets here," he said.

"I hope she doesn't wait that long to make contact with us. I'm just heartbroken that she hasn't allowed us to be a part of her pregnancy. My relationship with my mother got so much stronger during my pregnancies," I said.

"I know, baby. We just have to hope she comes around. Tristan did."

"But he never objected to Emmanuel. His concerns were totally different," I said.

"Nevertheless, he's changed his mind. He's seen that Emmanuel is a wonderful addition to the family," he said, kissing my forehead. "Once Duncan has spent some time with Emmanuel, I'm sure she'll feel the same way."

"I'm not so sure. But I've been praying."

A loud thunderclap made both of us jump. Then Joe smiled the mischievous smile that had made me fall in love with him. "Our reservation isn't until six-thirty," he said. "We've got all afternoon to—"

I cut off his words with a passionate kiss and we moved into the bedroom. By the time we came out, we had to rush to make our dinner reservation on time.

Chapter 24

"Slow down, squirt," I heard Tristan say.

"But I have to tell Mom and Dad," Emmanuel's excited voice replied.

"And you will. Don't kill yourself getting to the door, though."

I opened the front door before Tristan could slide his key into the lock. "Heard your voices," I said in response to his puzzled look.

"Mom, Dad! Guess what? I got to go up on stage! Lil' Bow Wow performed, then Common, then Will Smith, and he called me up on the stage and I got to perform with him and at the end everyone was cheering and chanting my name and—"

"Whoa," I said. "Slow down, take a breath, and start from the beginning."

"What's this about my son the hip-hop star?" Joe asked, coming out of the bedroom in his robe. We'd been home from dinner about an hour and had picked up where we'd left off before dinner.

"It's true," Tristan said. "During the middle of his performance, Will Smith called Emmanuel up on stage, saying he'd heard about the brave teenager who pulled the day's activities together."

"Yeah, and I got to perform with him!" Emmanuel said, his eyes shining. "And then everybody was clapping and cheering and saying my name. It was wild."

"Then Will hugged the squirt and the lights went down. But they kept clapping and calling Emmanuel's name, so he came back for an encore bow."

"And I got his autograph," Emmanuel chimed in. "And Lil' Bow Wow's and Common's."

"It sounds like the concert was a success," I said.

"But I'm pretty tired," our youngest son announced, which was a surprise, because getting him to go to bed was as hard most nights as waking him for school in the mornings.

"It has been a long day for you," I said. "Go on up. I'll be up soon to say good night."

"Okay," he said, then high-fived Tristan. "G'night, Dad." He gave Joe a hug, then headed up the stairs.

"It's good he had a nice time," Joe said.

"That's not all," Tristan said. "Josh came up to him on our way to the car and invited him to his house for Sunday dinner."

"I'm sure the Barretts won't be too pleased to see him," I said.

"Apparently, the invitation was extended from Josh's mom," Tristan said. "I guess the parents were at the school for the events this afternoon. When I picked the squirt up, Mrs. Taylor said Emmanuel spoke a lot during the roundtable discussion. And Will Smith's hug at the end of the concert went a long way toward proving to the kids that Emmanuel's not contagious. I don't think Josh ever really wanted to stop hanging with Emmanuel anyway. I think that was a parent thing.''

My lazy, relaxed mood began to fade. "I have to go tell him about his mother," I said.

"What's happened?" Tristan asked.

"Her condition took a turn for the worst sometime late last night or early this morning," Joe said. "And it looks like she's not going to make it."

"Damn," Tristan said. "How do you think he's going to take it?"

"I imagine not well. He just asked Patrice about her last night, and at that point, there'd been no change."

"Are those fools going to let him see her now?" Tristan asked.

"Yes. She told me to call her in the morning, and she'll arrange a visit."

"A day late," Tristan began.

"And a dollar short," Joe finished.

I smiled at my two men, then went to tell Emmanuel the news about his mother.

Surprisingly, he didn't cry. He hugged me tightly and his thin body shook. His voice quivered a little when he said, "So, Patrice is going to let me see her tomorrow?"

"Yes, baby. Dad and I will go with you, if you like."

"No, Mom. This is something I have to do alone," he said. Then he snuggled back under the bedclothes. I was almost across the door's threshold when he said softly, "Mom?"

"Yes, Emmanuel?"

"I love you."

"I love you, too, son."

Chapter 25

Three days later, we became parents for the fourth time. During a quick ceremony with the three of us and Tristan present, a judge declared Emmanuel our son, and we formally added Parker to his name. The newest Parker wanted to celebrate at Chuck E. Cheese, so pizza and games it was. And though it was a joyous occasion, it was tinged with a little bit of sadness. Emmanuel was a shade less bright than he normally was, which was to be expected with his mother in a coma. He played with the younger children in the plastic ball pit, but spent much of the time near Joe and me, as if being close to us would keep us safe and alive.

Patrice had picked him up early two days earlier to take him to the hospice to see his mother. He hadn't talked about his visit or mentioned his mother since, and I was worried that he was keeping too much inside. But Joe and I were very happy the adoption had finally taken place.

When we came home from the celebration, a frantic message from Greg said Duncan had gone into labor.

"It's too early," I said worriedly to Joe. "She's not due for another two months."

"Go. I'll make sure the squirt gets to school on time in the morning," Tristan said. Joe and I stayed at the house only long enough to throw a few things in a bag. Then we kissed Emmanuel, hugged Tristan, and hit the road for New York. Traffic was light until we hit the northern part of the New Jersey Turnpike, where everything slowed to a crawl. I squirmed in my seat like a first grader denied a bathroom break. Finally, however, we reached the city and pulled into a garage near the hospital.

We found Greg pacing in the hall.

"It's way too early," he said. "Way too early."

"Greg, calm down," I said, pulling him into an awkward hug. "What happened?"

"She wasn't feeling well today, all this past week, really. Morning sickness, but really bad. I thought that was just a first trimester thing, but she's had it almost all along. We thought today was just going to be one of the really bad days, you know."

He looked ragged, like it had been at least a couple of days since he'd last shaved. And he kept running his hands over his scruffy chin.

"I didn't know what to do. We tried everything—crackers, ginger ale, someone even suggested mustard. Nothing was working. And she wasn't able to keep anything down. I was worried about the baby, you know? Like, was it getting enough to eat?"

Joe pulled him down into one of the hard plastic chairs across from the nurses' station. "You've got to get ahold of yourself, son. You'll be no good to her in this condition. What are the doctors saying?"

"About two this afternoon she doubled over in pain. We raced here. She's having contractions, but her water hasn't broken. They've given her something to try to stop the contractions. It's just too early for this child to be born.''

"Why didn't you let us know what was going on with this pregnancy?'' I asked.

"She didn't want me to tell you. But once all this started today, well, I didn't have a choice.''

A nurse rushed out of Duncan's room, followed by a much calmer woman in surgeon's scrubs.

"Mr. Williams, we've managed to stop the contractions,'' she said.

"Dr. Lucas, these are Duncan's parents, Joe and Riley Parker.''

"I assumed as much,'' she said.

"What happens next?'' I asked. "And can we see her?''

"We'll keep her overnight. Keep an eye on her, make sure the contractions don't start again. I'd like to keep the baby inside just a little while longer. Its lungs aren't fully developed yet. But yes, you can go in now.''

Seeing your child hooked to IVs, looking small and frightened despite being seven months pregnant, is a terrifying thing. I well understood Greg's feelings of helplessness.

"Duncan, honey, your father and I are here.''

"The medicine is making her a little groggy,'' a nurse said. "Hopefully, she'll sleep through the rest of the night.''

Though visiting hours had long been over, no one asked us to leave. Joe and I sat on one side of the bed, Greg on the other, holding her hand. She opened her eyes long enough to know we were there, then drifted back to sleep.

By morning, the contractions were still being held at bay, so we went to Duncan's condo to shower and change. I called Tristan at work to let him know what was happening, and to make sure he and Emmanuel had fared okay getting him ready for school.

"I didn't have any trouble getting him to wake up, Mom.

I think he only gives you a hard time because you let him,"
he said.

"Ha, ha, funny. Your sister started contracting, but they
gave her medication to stop it. Apparently, she's been having
a really rough pregnancy, but didn't want Greg to tell us.
Has she talked to you about this?"

"We've talked a few times, as you well know, but she
never mentioned that she wasn't doing well. In fact, she
always told me the exact opposite, that things were fine,
that she felt fine. I'm not Greg; I would've told you if I
knew something was wrong."

"We spent the night at the hospital with her. Just came
back here to get cleaned up before going back."

"Don't overdo it, Mom. We don't need both of you laid
up in the hospital."

"Your father has to call work. I'll touch base with you
later today. Hopefully, Duncan will be able to come home
by then."

I took a quick shower while Joe called his boss. While
he showered, I sank down into the overstuffed sectional sofa
and started dozing. Joe didn't even get that much of a nap
because we returned to the hospital after his shower. Duncan's status hadn't changed, so we made plans to bring her
home.

She was released later that evening, but she was going to
be restricted to complete bed rest for the remainder of the
pregnancy. Greg was still a nervous wreck, so Joe and I
made sure she settled in comfortably, and I got her on a
schedule. One trip to the bathroom in the mornings before
Greg left for work, then back in the bed for 24 hours. Repeat
the cycle every day until the baby was born.

"Did you see the nursery?" she asked me groggily that
first night, still a bit drowsy from the medicine. "It's all
sky and clouds."

"I'll go look at it now, sweetie. When we were here

earlier, we didn't do anything except a quick turnaround back to the hospital.''

"Mom?'' she said, as I neared the door.

"Yes?''

"Thanks for coming.''

"No thanks necessary.''

"I don't know how I'm going to stand this bed rest thing,'' she said. "I'm already missing the hustle and bustle of work.''

"You'll do it because you have no choice,'' I said. "Remember Elizabeth? Your second cousin? She did bed rest with both her pregnancies. The entire nine months.''

Duncan rolled her eyes. "You've got to really want to have a baby bad to do that!'' she said. "Makes my two little months seem like a song.''

We stayed two more days, but the full-size bed in the guest room was too small for Joe and me. He'd always been a bad sleeper, his nearly six-foot-two-inch frame spread-eagled across the bed. I folded my much shorter five-foot-five-inch body into whatever nooks and crannies I could find. There was also no normal food in the house—carrot juice, powdered carob, and a freezer full of broccoli, spinach, and lima beans. When did Duncan start eating lima beans, I wondered. Greg certainly wasn't a health food nut.

"We haven't had time to do much grocery shopping,'' he said, spying me in the near-empty kitchen pantry. "And there's been so little that Duncan could keep down. I think we have some soup somewhere.''

"Don't worry, Greg. I think Joe and I are going to leave in the morning,'' I said.

Her contractions were under control, so we headed home, hoping we wouldn't have to return for another two months. As we were leaving, a big bouquet of flowers from Tristan and Emmanuel arrived.

Chapter 26

Joe and I waited impatiently in the international arrivals area of the airport. Madison's flight was already three hours late, and the arrivals screen only said DELAYED. Joe tried to get information out of the ticket agent, but she knew little more than we did. I found a soda machine and bought us both a Sprite. I was craving a Coke, but the caffeine would only make me jumpy, and I was already an anxious ball of nerves.

"If we could find out a real time of arrival, we might be able to go home, then come back," Joe said.

"Maybe I should leave Tristan a message," I said. "He and Emmanuel will be back from the movies before long, and they'll wonder where we are."

Joe nodded, and I dialed from my cell phone. Service from the airport was patchy at best, and I couldn't get a signal. "I'm going to find a pay phone," I told Joe. He nodded again, distracted, and headed back toward the ticket agent.

A bank of pay phones stood across the hall from the hard, uncomfortable airport chairs in which we'd been sitting. Two were out of order, businessman-types were occupying three others, and a frazzled woman with five small children all under the age of six was using the remaining phone. I waited, trying not to hover, but still drew dirty looks from one of the men. It didn't appear any of these people would be ending their calls anytime soon, which annoyed me. Airport pay phones weren't designed for long conversations; they were for emergency calls.

I began a search for other pay phones, knowing that if I stood there and waited any longer, I'd begin to get rude. It was one of my least pleasant traits, and had almost kept Joe from marrying me. I hit pay dirt two long corridors and a people mover later, placed a call to Tristan's apartment, and left a message for the boys.

Things were humming when I got back to Joe.

"They said the flight should be here within fifteen minutes," he said.

"Oh, thank God." My back was beginning to ache. "You'd think airports would have more comfortable chairs since people spend so much time waiting in them," I said.

"There's probably some economic reason, like, the more uncomfortable the chair the more likely you are to spend money in one of the fast food joints," Joe offered

"Um," I said. "You could be right. I am getting hungry."

Joe sighed, then headed off to find a Burger King for me.

Twenty minutes later a nearby baggage carousel began turning, the luggage chute gaping open like an empty mouth. Someone sitting near us started clapping; then several others joined in.

"Is that the claim area for Flight 483?" I heard a woman ask the door agent.

"It's the baggage claim for all international flights," came the answer. How many other international flights were landing right this minute? I wondered. Then passengers from Madison's flight started coming through the gate. If I knew my daughter, she'd come straggling off the plane at the tail end of the line. Everyone except Joe and me crowded around the gate, awaiting loved ones; we stayed seated.

"She's gonna be last," Joe whispered in my ear.

"Yep."

"And her luggage is gonna be last, too," he added.

"I know."

Then Madison surprised us by coming through the door.

"Mom! Dad!" she called, spotting us right away. She looked so thin, my baby girl. Thin, but happy. Joe reached her first and scooped her up in a big bear hug.

"Where's Emmanuel?" she asked. "I thought he'd be with you."

"He went to the movies with Tristan," Joe told her.

We may have missed it about our daughter, but her luggage didn't disappoint. Tattered, dirty, and looking worse for wear, all seven pieces spilled down the chute dead last.

"You don't know how good it feels to be home," she sang as we walked to the car. "I haven't had a Big Mac or seen a TV show in two years."

We made small talk on the drive home, until Madison fell asleep. Tristan's car was in the driveway when we pulled up to the house.

"Did you leave the message here or at his house?" Joe asked.

"His house. I didn't think he'd come here. He'll have checked his messages anyway."

Madison stirred in the backseat; then the front door opened and our sons spilled out.

"Maddy!" Tristan called, waking her. Joe began emptying the trunk. Madison got out, stretched her legs, then walked over to Emmanuel.

"You must be Emmanuel," she said. He looked down

shyly, then nodded. If his skin were a lighter color, we would have seen him blushing. "Well, it's nice to meet you finally," she said, holding out her hand to shake. The two shook hands.

"It's about time you got home, little sis," Tristan said, then hugged her.

"I was just telling the parents how good it feels to be here," she said. "You look good, Tris."

"You, too. A little on the skinny side. What have they been feeding you in Africa?"

"These last few weeks I've been almost too busy to eat," she said as we carted her belongings into the house.

"I thought y'all would never get home," Emmanuel said.

"Madison's flight was more than three hours late," I said. "I left a message at your apartment, Tristan."

"I haven't even checked. I figured the flight was delayed. No worries. We've already eaten."

"Yeah, we ate at the mall after the movie," Emmanuel said.

"How was the movie?" Joe asked.

"Surprisingly good," Tristan answered.

"Madison, are you hungry?"

"No, Mom. I ate some brown mystery meat on the plane. I just want to take a shower in a real bathroom," she said and disappeared up the stairs.

"She's pretty," Emmanuel said after Madison left the room.

That night Madison cornered me in the kitchen. "Okay, Mom, what gives?"

"What do you mean?" I asked.

"I mean, what's going on here? Each time you mentioned Duncan's name on the phone the last couple of times we talked, there was something funny in your voice. And why isn't she here to welcome me home? Is something going on with the baby?''

''Duncan's on complete bed rest. She started having contractions in April. The doctors were able to stop them, but she had to go on bed rest. Apparently, this whole pregnancy has been pretty rough on her.''

''Apparently?''

''She didn't tell us. We didn't find out how sick she'd been until she started the contractions. Your dad and I went to New York to help out Greg.''

''That sounds like Duncan,'' Madison said with a bitter laugh. ''Suffer in silence, then blame us for ignoring her.''

''She hasn't been too pleased with our adopting Emmanuel.''

''Why? He seems like a delightful little boy,'' she said.

''He's actually a little bit subdued, believe it or not,'' I said. ''Madison, Emmanuel is HIV positive. Duncan, never really all that happy with our decision to become foster parents, began boycotting us when she found out we wanted to adopt an HIV-positive child—''

''That's just stupid,'' Madison interrupted.

''We hadn't even talked to her for months until April. Since then, she's talked to me a few times on the phone, but she still doesn't talk about Emmanuel, only the baby.''

''I hope he wasn't subdued at dinner on my account,'' Madison said thoughtfully.

''No, he's been like this since his biological mother went into a coma right before we adopted him.''

''The HIV?''

I nodded. ''She developed full-blown AIDS around Christmas,'' I began. Then Madison and I stayed up all night, talking and catching up.

Chapter 27

A week after arriving home from Mozambique, Madison landed on her sister's doorstep.

"I figured you'd need some help around here. And that you'd be bored out of your mind with this bed rest thing," Madison told Duncan after Greg let her in the apartment.

"You're right on both accounts. Madison, it's good to see you," Duncan said, stretching her arms for a hug. The sisters hugged. "Greg, love him to death, is absolutely worthless in situations like this. He's like a nervous Nellie."

"And you're having a child with this man?" Madison joked.

"Believe it or not," Duncan said with a laugh. "So, tell me, how was Africa?"

"It was wonderful. I'm glad I did it. And I'm equally glad my peace corps contract is complete," she said. "I learned a lot, grew a lot. I don't think Americans ever fully appreciate what we have in this country until we spend some time in another country. It's the little things you take for granted: paved roads, running water.''

"Sounds so exciting, adventurous. Especially being trapped in this bed," Duncan said. "And poor Greg . . .''

"I doubt Dad would be any better under these circumstances, and he's been through this three times," Madison said with a laugh. "Speaking of our parents, sis, what's going on with you and them?''

"What do you mean?''

"God, you sound just like Mom. You know what I mean. Where do you get off not talking to them and not telling them you'd been sick? And what's wrong with Emmanuel that you protested the adoption?''

"You mean what's wrong with him besides that he's got AIDS?" Duncan said angrily.

"Dunc, he doesn't have AIDS; he's HIV positive, and you know there's a difference. He's a good kid. It's not his fault that his mother wasn't able to take care of him.''

"I'm not saying it is his fault. But why does he have to become our problem?''

"Since when is Mom and Dad adopting him our problem?''

"What happens to our dear little brother if something happens to our parents?''

"I can't believe how shallow you are! I think it's wonderful what Mom and Dad are doing. And I think he's a wonderful kid. You'd think so, too, if you spent the time getting to know him," Madison said.

"Well, Mom and I have talked a few times lately.''

"Yeah, she mentioned that. But you still don't even mention Emmanuel's name. How could you go through an entire pregnancy without Mom? I can't imagine that.''

"I don't want to argue about this, Madison. I'm just happy you're back home.''

"This isn't going to go away. Like it or not, we have a little brother. He's officially a Parker, Dunc."

"Why is everybody on my case about this? Tristan didn't want them to adopt him, either."

"For different reasons, Duncan, and he's come around since then. He and Emmanuel are actually really tight."

"Oh, he didn't mention that to me," Duncan said quietly.

"Probably because everybody's been afraid to bring his name up for fear you'd bite their heads off," Madison said. "You've always been selfish, Duncan. I can't believe you'd begrudge a child the wonderful upbringing you and Tris and I had."

"All right, already. I'm a horrible person. Can we talk about something else?"

"For now. But this conversation isn't over."

"What are your plans now that you're back from Africa?" Duncan asked, changing the subject. "Are you going to go back to law school?"

"I don't know. You'd think since I had two years to think about this, I'd have some clue. But I don't. I'm not really sure I want to do the law school thing now. I'm sure I'll get a job, just don't know where," Madison said.

She left Duncan in the bedroom and went to the living room to see if Greg needed help with anything.

"Just keep her company while I'm at work," he said, adjusting his tie. "I think that's the most difficult part of this whole bed rest for her, the loneliness. And keep working on her with, you know, the Emmanuel issue. You're the only one who seems to be able to penetrate her thick skull about this."

"I don't know if I've penetrated it," Madison responded.

"You've done better than any of the rest of us. She won't talk to your parents and each time I bring it up, we have an argument. I've gotta jet." He hugged Madison and left for work.

* * *

"Time for breakfast," Madison called cheerily to Duncan fifteen minutes later.

"Maddy, Greg put you up to this, didn't he?"

"You need to eat. It's only cereal and a small bowl of fruit."

"I don't need a nursemaid," Duncan said, pouting.

"Apparently, you do. Now eat. And stop turning me into our mother, badgering you into cleaning your plate."

That got a smile out of Duncan, and she started spooning the cereal into her mouth. "Only six more weeks," she sighed between mouthfuls. "Are you going to stay here until the baby comes?"

"Are you out of your mind? I love you, but not that much," Madison joked. "I just came up for a few days to see if there was anything I can do to help. But I'm not staying cramped up in this tiny apartment for six weeks."

"You said this little boy is a good kid?" Duncan asked a few minutes later.

"Emmanuel? Very good. He's going through a bit of a rough time right now; his mother—the biological one, I mean—is in a coma and it doesn't look like she's going to come out of it."

"When did this happen?"

"A few months ago, I think. The day of his school's AIDS awareness event."

"What AIDS awareness event?" Duncan asked, feeling left out.

"If you had been communicating with anybody . . . Sorry. I'm not going to beat you up about this anymore. One of his teachers organized—with Emmanuel's help—an AIDS awareness day. I guess there was some major backlash when the kids at school found out Emmanuel was HIV positive; this was an attempt to bring about a little understanding."

"I didn't know about any of this."

"Yeah, well, I guess it was pretty ugly. Mom said parents were protesting at the school and everything. But the AIDS awareness day helped. It did with his classmates, anyway. I'm not sure about the parents. No one's protesting anymore," Madison explained.

"Mom and Dad have been having a time of it," Duncan said. "I guess I haven't helped matters any."

"I think Mom has been pretty depressed about what's been going on between you two. You know how easily her feelings get hurt," Madison said. "That you two are talking a little bit now, even if it's only about the baby, has made things a little better."

"I didn't want to make anybody's life more difficult."

"Yeah, well, you have."

"I thought you said you weren't going to beat me up about this anymore."

"I'm not beating you up, just being honest with you. You've been giving everybody a hard time. Mom and Dad. Greg."

"I guess I just thought the only kinds of kids in foster care are the bad ones. You know, violent tendencies, mental instability. The stereotypes."

"I'm sure there are some like that in the system. Mom has told some horror stories. Did you know one kid set the bathroom on fire?"

"What? We haven't really discussed the kids. I mean, I usually know when a new kid has come to the house, but . . ."

"I know, you weren't really happy with the whole foster parent thing. I don't know if they're going to continue doing that now that they've adopted one. And they have a grand-baby on the way," Madison said.

"So you think I should talk to Mom about Emmanuel?"

"I shouldn't have to tell you how important family is,

Duncan. Mom and Dad have supported us no matter what we wanted to do."

"And you've wanted to do some doozies," Duncan said, laughing.

"I have not."

"Have too. Remember bartending school your junior year in college?"

"Don't remind me!" Madison said, trying not to remember that horrible semester.

"I might need you to run to the drugstore for me, pick up a few things," Duncan said. "We're almost out of toilet paper. Greg will let us run out before he remembers to get more. And I need more Nivea. And can you see if they've restocked Max Factor Lipfinity in Wicked?"

"That's why I'm here, sis."

"Think I'll call Mom while you're gone," she said softly, reaching for the phone.

Madison headed for the front door, smiling.

Epilogue

The newest Parker family addition—Stephanie Parker Williams—came screaming into the world on schedule in late June. The six-pound baby was greeted by her grandparents, Joe and Riley Parker and Steve and Sue Williams, her Aunt Madison, and her uncles, Tristan and Emmanuel.

"Aren't families wonderful?" Emmanuel beamed as Duncan placed his squirming baby niece in his arms.

"Indeed," Duncan said. "Indeed."

ABOUT THE AUTHOR

Kendra Lee has been a professional editor and writer for the past decade. She holds a bachelor of arts degree in mass communication from Emerson College. An award-winning writer, she has been both a contributor and a staff member for *Heart & Soul, Upscale, YSB,* and *Essence* magazines, and for Web sites such as NiaOnline.com and Kidshealth.-org. She resides in Alexandria, Virginia.